The Medic

Miracle on Hacksaw Ridge

Adam Palmer

Cover photo and graphic design by Caleb Palmer.

Printed in the United States of America

First Printing, 2014

DJ PRESS

DJPRESS81@YAHOO.COM

ISBN-13: 978-1492898566
ISBN-10: 1492898562
BISAC: Fiction / Biographical

15 14 13 12 11 10 9

AUTHOR'S NOTE

The first time I remember reading the story of Desmond Doss was in the mid 1970's. Like many teenagers, I liked to read comic books, and in my hometown of Vincennes, Indiana was a small store across the street from Gregg Park that sold them. One day while perusing the selection, I came across a series titled *True Comics*, with a subtitle of "Truth is Stranger and a Thousand Times More Thrilling Than Fiction." The cover promised 13 exciting features including "Pirate Patriot," "Human Howitzer" and "Hero Without a Gun." The comic was published in 1948, so the cover price was only ten cents, but that was the 70's and inflation was working its magic; I probably paid closer to seventy-five cents for it. (*True Comics* #48 in mint condition, if you can find one, now sells for around fifty dollars.)

I didn't retain any details of the comic book story except the dialogue in "Hero Without a Gun" where Desmond's arm was shattered by a tank shell and he calmly says, "This rifle stock should do for a splint." At the time, I thought it was one of the hokiest things I had ever read, and several times over the next 30 years that phrase would pop into my mind.

Later in my life, after I became a Seventh-day Adventist, I sometimes heard other Adventists talking about Desmond Doss. I became curious and decided to learn more about him, so I read the two books written about his life: *Desmond Doss: Conscientious Objector* by Francis M. Doss, his second wife and *The Unlikeliest Hero: The Story Of Desmond T. Doss, Conscientious Objector Who Won His Nation's Highest Military Honor* by Booton Herndon.

In 2004, *The Conscientious Objector,* a documentary about Doss, directed by Terry Benedict was released and received multiple awards at film festivals around the world. A few years later, I began hearing rumors that a feature film, along the lines of *Band of Brothers*, based on Desmond's war experiences was in the works. Several announcements were made in the Hollywood trade journals, but the movie never got off the ground. In one article, I learned that the screenplay had finally been written by Robert Schenkkan. Schenkkan is also an actor. His most famous character was that of Lieutenant Commander Dexter Remmick in *Star Trek: The Next Generation*. As I was growing up, *Star Trek* was, by far, my favorite TV show. I loved *Star Trek* so much, it greatly influenced me in my career choice of Laser Electro-Optic Technician.

One day, on a lark, I decided to e-mail Schenkkan and ask him what was holding up the Desmond Doss movie. I was surprised when I received a personal response from him later that day. About every six months thereafter, I would send him another e-mail and he would politely reply that the movie was in pre-production, or that they had signed a director, or that they had a certain (unnamed) famous actor in mind to play the part of Desmond Doss. I was starting to get frustrated at the lack of real progress, so in one of my e-mails I made the suggestion that Mr. Schenkkan should write a novel about Doss.

Over the next few months, I kept having the impression that maybe I should write the novel. This was very weird, because I had no experience at writing. I started wondering if the impression was coming from God. One day I prayed. If God wanted me to write a novel about Desmond Doss, I would be willing to try, but first I wanted some sort of sign that this was God's idea, not my own.

My son and I had a routine of reading a page from a worship book each night before he went to bed. A worship book contains 365 pages, one to read each day of the year. The book we were reading that year was titled, *Peer to Peer* by Stella Duncan-Bradley. It contained stories and thoughts written by teenage students at the Mount Pisgah Adventist Academy. On the very day after I had asked God for a sign, I opened the book, turned to the page for November 15th and read the short story written about Desmond Doss by Andy Rodriguez titled "The Conscientious Objector." I started working on *The Medic* the next day.

My idea was to write an entertaining, biographical historic fiction novel, which would incorporate the character of Doss into a story that included typical experiences of WWII soldiers from the time they were drafted until they were discharged from military service. Because *The Medic* includes incidents and dialogue, which Doss may or may not have experienced, the "Doss" in my book must be considered a fictional character. If you want to discover the true story of the "real" Desmond Doss, I recommend the documentary and two biographies that I mentioned above.

Faith is the invisible hand
that we hold,
while waiting for God's plan
to unfold.

- Donice Jewell

The Medic

OCTOBER 1940
WAITING TO BE DRAFTED

No matter what the outcome, Desmond Doss knew that this meeting would change the course of his life.

In October of 1940, Desmond had filled out his draft card in accordance with the new Selective Service Law. A short while later, he received a questionnaire in the mail asking him to provide some basic facts about his marital status, physical condition, work history, etc. The form included a box to check if he had a conflict that might prevent him from performing military service because of his religious belief. Desmond acknowledged that the law required him to register for the draft, but he also felt strongly that the Bible forbade him from taking another man's life, so he decided to check the box. A few months later, he received another letter from the Selective Service. This time the government was demanding a written response to ten questions inquiring about his religious background and the reasons for his objection to war. The instructions directed him to "immediately fill out and return enclosed form DSS 47."

After Desmond returned the paperwork, months passed without hearing anything back. In the meantime, he moved to Newport News to take a well-paying job as a carpenter at the local shipyard. He also was dating an attractive young woman named Dorothy, who he had met at church, and their relationship was starting to get serious. Desmond's life seemed to be going along pretty well when out of the blue he received a letter ordering him to appear, along with his pastor, in his hometown of Lynchburg, Virginia, at a hearing to determine his draft status. The inquiry was scheduled to take place on October 15th 1941, almost a year to the day from when he had first filled out his draft card.

Desmond arrived at the post office building at 8:00 pm and had been testifying for almost an hour, when the chairman of the draft board posed his last question. "Mr. Doss, if a man was raping your sister, and you had a gun, are you telling me you wouldn't use it?"

"Wouldn't have a gun," Desmond replied.

"Let's just assume for the sake of argument, that you do have a gun. Are you telling this board that you would just stand there and do nothing?"

"Who said anything about just standing there? That's a different proposition altogether. I never said I'd just stand there, and boy, when I got through with him, he might wish he was dead, but to kill a man? No, I couldn't kill him."

"Mr. Doss, even if this board grants you conscientious objector status, I believe the time you might spend in the Army would be extremely difficult. Are you sure you don't want to pursue a deferment? One most likely would be available to you because of your work at the shipyard. Or perhaps 4-E status?" asked the chairman. "Then you would be allowed to work with other conscientious objectors in a civilian labor camp on some work of national importance instead of serving in the military."

"But, you see, I'm not a conscientious objector. I'm a conscientious cooperator. I just want to be classified as a non-combatant."

"I'm sorry Mr. Doss," replied the chairman. "There is no such legal classification as a non-combatant in the U.S. Army."

"I'm willing to serve in the Army," Desmond countered, "but I won't kill anybody."

"Thank you Mr. Doss. Would you and Pastor Howard be kind enough to step out of the room for a moment?"

Desmond Doss and his pastor waited nervously in the hallway outside of the hearing room, knowing that the board members on the other side of the door were taking a vote to decide the young man's future. Desmond was familiar with the board members, because they were prominent businessmen in Lynchburg. They each had a reputation of being fair, and Desmond could only hope they lived up to that reputation.

After a few minutes, one of the men came to the door and asked Desmond to step back in.

"Mr. Doss, if this board grants you conscientious objector status, the law says that you cannot then be forced to bear arms; however, we feel that your insistence on being allowed to keep the Sabbath will be a problem in your military service. Nevertheless, after reviewing your written answers and considering the testimony you have given at this hearing, the Selective Service Board has voted to approve your application for 1-A-O conscientious objector status. I must remind you that with a classification of 1-A-O, you are still obligated to serve in the Army if drafted."

Desmond shook hands with and thanked each member of the draft board. As he left the building, he thought, *I'll never be drafted anyway on account of my high lottery number.* Desmond couldn't help but believe the meeting had been nothing more than pointless government red tape, which needed to be put behind him.

Two months later, Desmond agreed to drive his friend Caleb to Fairhaven, Massachusetts in exchange for gas money and five dollars, so he could visit his family for the weekend. On Sunday December 7th after the visit, the two were driving south along U.S. Route 1 headed back to Newport News. On the way, they were listening to the Philadelphia Philharmonic Orchestra on the car radio when the music suddenly stopped.

> *"We interrupt this program to bring you a special news bulletin. The Japanese have attacked Pearl Harbor Hawaii by air, President Roosevelt has just announced. The attack also was made on all U.S. naval and military activities on the principal island of Oahu. Please stand by for more information as we receive it."*

In between updates on the radio, the two discussed what the news might mean for them and their country. They both agreed the attack would most likely result in the United States declaring war on Japan. Caleb, who had been stewing over the fact he only had a few weeks left until his enlistment in the Navy was supposed to be up, suddenly blurted out, "I guess I can kiss my discharge papers goodbye now. I'll probably be in for the whole war, and Desmond, you might get drafted."

"You're right," he agreed. "I was just thinking the same thing."

April 1, 1942
I'm In the What?

One day in late March, Desmond came home after work and picked up his mail. There was only a single letter, and his attention was instantly drawn to the return address on the envelope.

SELECTIVE SERVICE
OFFICIAL BUSINESS

Despite his high lottery number, Desmond had known since Pearl Harbor that this day would eventually come. He nervously opened the envelope and read the enclosed form letter.

ORDER TO REPORT FOR INDUCTION
The President of the United States,
To: Desmond Thomas Doss
Order No. 523
GREETING:
Having submitted yourself to a Local Board composed of your neighbors, for the purpose of determining your availability for training and service in the armed forces of the United States, you are hereby notified that you have now been selected for training and service in the Army.
You will, therefore, report to the Local Board at Lynchburg, Virginia City Armory, 1219 Main St, at 7:00 A.M., on 1 April 1942.
This Local Board will furnish transportation to an induction station of the service for which you have been selected. You will there be examined and if accepted for training and service, you will then be inducted into the stated branch of the service.
Persons reporting to the induction station in some instances may be rejected for physical or other reasons. It is well to keep this in mind when arranging your affairs, to prevent any hardship if you are rejected at the induction station. If you are employed, you should advise your employer of this notice and of the possibility that you may not be accepted at the induction station. Your employer can then be prepared to replace you if you are accepted, or to continue your employment if you are rejected.
If you are not accepted, you will be furnished transportation to the place where you were living when ordered to report. Wilful failure to report promptly to this Local Board at the hour and on the day named in this notice is a violation of the Selective Training and Service Act of 1940 and subjects the violator to fine and imprisonment.
You must keep this form and bring it with you when you report to your Local Board.

14-18034 Chief Clerk of Local Board

D.S.S. Form 150

Desmond couldn't help but find it ironic. In a mere seven days, he would be going into the Army on April Fool's Day. He took the letter inside and sat down at his table to make a list of the things he would need to do before next Wednesday morning.

The week flew by before he knew it. Desmond had gone to talk to his boss at the shipyard, who assured him that his job would still be available if the Army rejected him. He then drove the 180 miles from Newport News to Washington, D.C., so he could spend a long weekend with Dorothy and more importantly to ask her if she would wait for him until after the war. She eagerly said yes and all too soon it was time for the young couple to say goodbye. On Monday night, he drove to Lynchburg, so he could spend a day with his parents. Early Wednesday morning, his father got up and used Desmond's car to drive him uptown. Desmond had already said his goodbyes to Dorothy in Washington and to his mom at home because he figured if they came along to see him off, it would just make leaving all the harder. When they arrived at the armory, his dad pulled the Ford to the curb and let Desmond out. Then he put the car back into gear and drove away, leaving his son standing on the sidewalk in front of the building with about two dozen other inductees.

Desmond walked up to the nearest man and asked, "Why's everyone hanging around outside? It's almost seven."

"Doors locked. We knocked, but no one answers."

Desmond and the other men milled around on the sidewalk for almost half an hour speculating about what was going to happen to them. Most of the men tried to put on a brave front, but Desmond could tell many of them were actually just as nervous as he was. Finally, a clipboard carrying man in civilian clothes came out of the armory and down the steps.

"Listen up all you men. When I say your name, raise your hand and answer in a loud voice, 'here'. Then form a line behind me."

Desmond looked over the draft board man's shoulder as he called out and then checked off the names on his list. Twice, no one responded even after he repeatedly called out the name. As he stood there, Desmond wondered what would happen to the men who failed to report.

An Atlantic Greyhound bus pulled up as the official was working through the roster. After the man finished with his list, he addressed the group again. "Listen up you men. This bus is here to take you to the induction station in Richmond, but first we want you to line up on the steps, so we can get a group picture for the newspaper." As they posed, Desmond made an effort to put on a smile for the photographer. After several tries, the newspaperman finally announced that he was satisfied, and the men boarded the bus for the three-hour ride to Richmond.

When the Lynchburg group arrived at the induction station, they were taken, along with other inductees from all over the state, to a large room. There, they were given a short speech by the station commander and then told to strip down to their shorts. Next they got in line to drop off their clothes at the checkroom, where they would be kept for safekeeping until the physical exams were over. Afterwards, a very long line of half-naked men formed and began to snake its way around the room. Desmond entered the line and worked his way to the first table where he was questioned by a clerk who was using a typewriter to fill out a form. When he was through, the clerk placed the paperwork in a large manila envelope, handed it to Desmond and told him to go to the next table to have his vital statistics recorded.

"Step on the scale. Height, 5 feet 6 inches. Weight, 121 pounds. Hair, black. Eyes, brown. Take your paperwork and go to the next table. Next man, step on the scale."

During the following three hours, Desmond went from table to table. In the process, he had his hearing and eyesight tested. They checked his feet, teeth, posture, balance, flexibility, and strength. They took blood and urine samples and a chest x-ray to check for tuberculosis. They looked in his eyes, nose, throat, and mouth. At one point in the line, he was told to take off his shorts and join a group of about 30 other nude men waiting to be examined to see if they had hemorrhoids, hernias or VD. All this activity took place in full sight of hundreds of other men.

Since Desmond had never graduated from high school, he was required to take a written examination to determine the functional level of his education.

Once he finished the test, he waited in another line to be examined by a psychiatrist. As soon as Desmond sat down, the psychiatrist began the evaluation by handing over a form to fill out. It contained 23 questions such as; Are you ever bothered by nervousness? Have you ever been troubled by cold sweats? Have you ever been bothered by pressure in your head? How often are you troubled by an upset stomach? Have you ever been bothered by your heart beating hard while at rest?

As Desmond filled out the answers, the psychiatrist watched closely to see if he appeared nervous or if his hands were sweating or trembling. After finishing the form, he handed it back to the psychiatrist who skimmed over it before asking a few more questions.

"Do you like girls?"

"I like most of them. In fact I plan to marry one named Dorothy."

"Do you bite your nails?"

"No, sir."

"Then why are they so short?"

"I keep 'em like that, so I won't keep snagging them at work."

"You passed. Go on to the next table."

There, Desmond was only asked one question.

"What branch of the service do you want? Army or Navy?"

"Army."

Without even looking up, the soldier staffing the table smacked a rubber stamp on his inkpad and then stamped ARMY across the top of his paperwork. He picked up another stamp and slammed it down on the form before spinning it around and sliding it back across the table to Desmond.

ACCEPTED. That last smack of a rubber stamp sealed his fate.

"Go to the next table to be fingerprinted."

Desmond had gone through the fingerprinting process once before when he started work at the shipyard, so the procedure was familiar to him. When they finished, he was told to wipe the ink off his fingers, go get his clothes and wait with the other men who had made it through the process.

After Desmond dressed, he was talking with a group of men from Lynchburg when a sergeant walked up with a handful of brooms and shoved one of them in Desmond's hand. "From now on, don't ever stand around with your hand in your pocket. You're in the Army now. Start sweeping."

At the end of the day, the station commander showed back up to give another talk to the men.

"I will now administer the Soldier's Oath, after which you will become members of the Armed Forces of the United States of America. Raise your right hand, and repeat after me."

"I, state your name, do solemnly swear or affirm that I will support the Constitution of the United States. I, state your name, do solemnly swear or affirm to bear true allegiance to the United States of America, and to serve them honestly and faithfully, against all their enemies or opposers whatsoever, and to observe and obey the orders of the President of the United States of America, and the orders of the officers appointed over me."

"You men are now officially members of the armed forces. Your enlistment term will be for the duration of the war plus six months. As of now, you will be temporarily assigned to the enlisted reserve force and given a furlough for a period of seven days. You will be provided transportation back to where your local draft board ordered you to report. Once back home, use the next week to wrap up your civilian affairs. At the end of the seven day period, you will be required to assemble at a location to be designated by your local draft board, and from there, you will proceed as a group to a reception center to begin your military service."

When the bus carrying the men arrived back in Lynchburg very early Thursday morning, they were met by a man from the draft board who gave them more instructions and told them to report to the Lynchburg Train Station on Wednesday April the 8th at 4:00 pm.

Desmond used the next week to quit his job at the Newport Shipyard, inform his landlord that he was going into the Army and make sure all of his bills were paid. He also spent some more time with Dorothy. They once again discussed the possibility of marriage. Their biggest concern was what would happen if Dorothy had a baby and Desmond didn't come back from the war. The discussion ended the same way as it always had before. They agreed that a wartime marriage was not the best idea but hoped the war wouldn't last long since they were both eager to tie the knot.

All too quickly, Wednesday afternoon rolled around, and it was time for Desmond to leave. For a second time, his Dad drove him uptown.

When they arrived at the station, Desmond's dad had a few last words he wanted to say before dropping him off. "You've been a good son Desmond. Mom and I will be praying for you every day. You know that don't you?"

"Sure Dad."

"I don't think the Army's gonna be easy for you Desmond, but if you put your trust in The Lord Jesus you'll do all right."

"Thanks Dad. I'll try."

"Bye son, I love you."

Desmond saw a tear run down his dad's face and felt one of his own. They hugged; his dad got back in the car and then drove off.

The troop train arrived at 5:30, and the men were herded into an old relic of a coach car for the trip to Camp Lee, Virginia. From the moment Desmond stepped foot on the train, he could tell that a group of men already onboard had disregarded the instruction not to party the night before, and it was obvious they had plans to keep up the celebration until the last possible moment. Some of the men were drinking whiskey, and almost all of them were smoking. This made the ride miserable for Desmond who neither smoked nor drank. After an overnight eleven-hour trip, which included stops at almost every station along the way to pick up other new soldiers, the train reached Camp Lee. The ride took so long, that some of the men complained they could have walked the distance in half the time.

As soon as the train arrived at camp, the men were lined up, given their first rudimentary drill instruction and then marched to a receiving building where army clerks began the process of turning civilians into soldiers. Desmond sat down at an open table. First the clerk typed up a records jacket envelope and physical profile form with name and date of arrival. Next he embossed two dog tags with Desmond's name and army serial number and dropped both of them into the records jacket along with the forms. Then he held up a pamphlet. "Read this when you have spare time waiting in lines. It'll answer a lot of your questions." He slid the pamphlet into the envelope before spending several more minutes using his typewriter to fill out more cards and forms, which he then placed in different stacks and baskets on his desk.

Finally looking up, he handed the record jacket to Desmond and said, "It's your responsibility to keep this with you during processing."

When the men in his group finished at the receiving building, they were marched to an auditorium and given a general orientation talk outlining what would happen to them over the next few days.

Then they marched back across camp to another building to take the Army General Classification Test, consisting of 130 multiple-choice questions. The test was not specifically designed to measure academic levels. Instead, it evaluated the recruit's ability to learn quickly. During the test, the men filled out answer sheets, which would later be graded by electric tabulating equipment. The marks a man received were of great importance. A prerequisite to being selected for officer candidate school was a score of 110 or higher, and a low score could negatively affect a soldier's initial job classification.

The test was divided into three sections consisting of, vocabulary, arithmetical reasoning problems and block counting. How well a man did in the first two sections was influenced by what he had learned, while the block-counting portions were designed to determine abstract reasoning and problem solving ability. The test was 12 pages long, and each page followed a similar format.

31. MATURE means most nearly (A) one (B) work (C) cake (D) time
32. A LATH is made of (A) cloth (B) wood (C) jam (D) dough
33. To FIGHT is to (A) fly (B) sing (C) squabble (D) whisper
34. A THUD is a (A) screw (B) pin (C) sound (D) flash
35. VIOLENT means most nearly (A) new (B) dead (C) fierce (D) ancient
36. Emily has 5 dollars, Katie has 2 dollars, Donice has 7 dollars, and Dolly has 3 dollars. How many dollars do they have altogether?
    (A) $19 (B) $17 (C) $13 (D) $15
37. A soldier attended target practice 9 times. His total score was 207. What was his average score?
    (A) 17 (B) 20 (C) 23 (D) 25
38. Six men went on a fishing trip. The total expense was $12.84, which they agreed to share equally. How much was each man's share of the total expense?
    (A) $2.24 (B) $2.14 (C) $2.92 (D) $3.24
39. Donald started work at 7:30 in the morning and quit work at 12:00 noon. How many hours did Donald work in the morning?
    (A) 2 ½ (B) 3 (C) 4 ½ (D) 4
40. A camp has 192 men in three equal groups. How many men are in each group?
    (A) 64 (B) 96 (C) 33 (D) 48

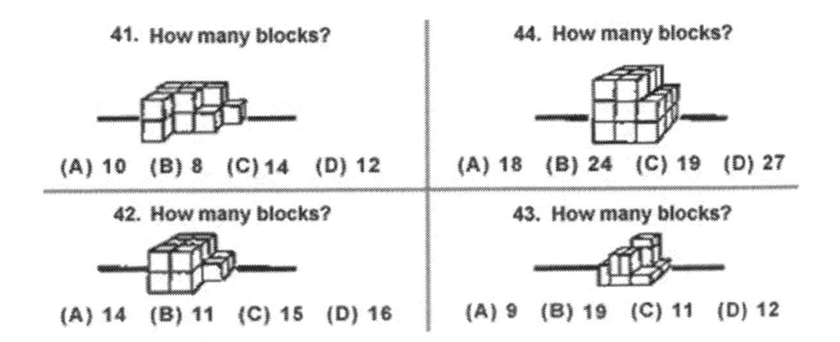

Despite having only an eighth grade education, Desmond did surprisingly well on the vocabulary section, in large part because he had read the Bible through so many times. He also had no trouble with the math section, which to him seemed to reflect the type of problems he solved in normal day-to-day life and work.

During the block test, the men were shown a series of drawings of stacked blocks arranged so that some of the blocks were not visible. To determine the total number of blocks in each stack, they had to use their imagination and reasoning power. Desmond thought the block test was fun, and he had no problem with it. Although he didn't know it, he got a perfect score on the block sections and only missed eight questions on the test.

When Desmond finished the test, he was taken next door and given a brief physical exam during which they recorded his weight, height, hair and eye color on one form. They also measured his vision and hearing, which they recorded on another form. Because of his poor eyesight, the Army said that he would be issued two pairs of regulation glasses at a later time. The doctor doing the exam reached into Desmond's record jacket and pulled out the Army dog tags, which had been stamped earlier that morning. He informed Desmond, "From now on, you are required to wear them at all times, including in the shower and while on leave." Desmond carefully checked his tags over before putting them on.

DOSS, DESMOND T
33158036

As he placed the chain around his neck, he wondered how long the war would last and when he would be allowed to take the tags back off again. *I guess if I get killed, these dog tags will be on me for the rest of my life, but at least I won't be wearing them in heaven,* he thought.

Next the men were taken to lunch. The Army maintained a Quartermaster Bakers and Cooks School at Camp Lee, and the student cooks practiced on the new recruits. Because of the depression, many of the new soldiers hadn't had a good meal in years, and their first meal in the Army turned out to be one of the best they had eaten in ages; for Desmond it didn't turn out that way. He believed and practiced what the Bible taught in Leviticus 11 concerning which foods should and should not be eaten. Although the Bible prohibited eating many animals, Desmond soon came to find out that during his time in the Army, he would experience the most trouble avoiding pork. To make matters even worse, in addition to not eating pork, he went a step further and practiced vegetarianism.

In the mess hall, the men lined up, picked up a stainless steel tray and then moved through the chow line where servers on KP duty placed a specific food in each section of the tray. As Desmond shuffled through the line, they added bread and butter, salad and a scoop of mashed potatoes. Next up was green beans, which Desmond loved. Unfortunately, they were seasoned with meat. He figured he would just eat the beans and leave the meat if they were seasoned with beef. He dreaded asking but he did.

"Is that pork in those green beans?"

"Of course it's pork. What else would it be?" the server answered.

The soldier manning the green bean ladle reached across to put some on his tray. "No thanks," said Desmond. "Could I have a second helping of mashed potatoes instead?"

Meanwhile, the mess sergeant, who had come over to see what was holding up his chow line, heard the question and gave Desmond his answer. Just to be sure he got the message, he shouted it at the top of his lungs.

"What are you, a picky eater? There's nothing wrong with them green beans, and you don't get doubles in the army 'cause that wouldn't be fair to the other men."

Desmond moved down the line with the sergeant mirroring him every step of the way. Next up was roast beef, which Desmond also turned down as well as the gravy that went with it. At the end of the line, he picked up an apple and placed it on his tray. This was too much for the sergeant. "You're insulting my food. How dare you come in my kitchen and insult my food?"

"I'm sorry Sergeant. It's nothing against your food it's just that I'm a vegetarian."

"Oh, a vegetarian are you? Well, for your information an apple is a fruit." With that, he reached over and snatched the apple back off of Desmond's tray. "Now get the hell out of my chow line, 'cause there's no dessert for you."

As Desmond walked to a table, he heard the laughter and saw that every eye was on him. Embarrassed, he sat down, said a prayer and slowly ate his food. It didn't come close to filling him up and he would have still been hungry after the meal if it weren't for the fact that one of the other new soldiers thought of a practical joke to play on him. When the man finished eating, he got up from his table, walked past Desmond, turned around and then placed an uneaten apple on his tray. Then he said in a mocking voice, "No dessert for you." The other men thought it was so funny, several of them repeated the gag. Each time it happened, Desmond said thanks and gratefully ate the apple.

After lunch, the men were taken to a large warehouse to exchange their civilian clothes for army uniforms. They lined up outside and were let into the building in groups of thirty. Once inside, a sergeant read them a set of instructions.

"The captain in charge of supply has required that the following be read to every new soldier before being allowed to proceed through the supply line."

"In this building you will be issued clothing and equipment for which you will be held financially responsible in case of loss or damage. At the end of the line is a large sign listing everything you should have been issued. As you pass along the issue line, all items will be carefully checked and all that you are not required to wear at that time will be placed in your barrack bags. Upon completion of the issue, you will be assembled in an assembly room of the warehouse and all items issued you will be checked by an officer from your company to make certain that you have received all that you are entitled to. Do not leave this building until you have checked and double-checked that you have everything on the sign. No claim can be made after you leave this building."

"Items requiring alteration should be taken to the tailor shop in this building upon completion of the issuing of your property. All clothing should be tried on as soon as possible and any ill-fitting items exchanged between 1300 and 1400 hours, (that's between 1:00 and 2:00 P.M.) the following day after the completion of all processing."

"Your appearance as a soldier is largely up to you. Cooperate."

After reading the notice, the sergeant had one last instruction for Desmond and the other men before sending them on their way. "Take off all your clothes. Take your civvies to the first table, and they'll help you ship 'em home."

Once undressed, Desmond went to a table where there were stacks of empty shipping bags. He placed all his clothes into one of them but decided to keep his Bible with him. After filling out a mailing tag addressed to his mom, he tied it to the bag and then handed it over to the soldier at the table. The soldier set the bag on a scale and wrote its weight on a shipping form. Then he tossed it out the loading dock door where it landed in a boxcar parked on the siding next to the building.

Desmond, who was now nude, began working his way down the long counter with only his record folder and Bible held in front of him to maintain some sense of modesty. As he approached the first station, he read the sign to himself. *When asked, respond with Last name, First name, Middle initial.*

He reached the head of the line, and the soldier behind the counter didn't even look up when he asked, "Name?"

"Doss, Desmond T."

The soldier turned around, opened a file cabinet drawer and pulled out a folder containing some forms, which he placed on the counter and slid over to the next station. The next soldier picked up the file, opened it to the first form and motioned Desmond over.

"Hand me your record cover. What's your name and birthdate?"

"Desmond Doss, February 7, 1919."

"From now on, when someone asks your name, it's always Doss or Doss, Desmond T. Do you understand?"

"Yes, Sir."

The corporal had been called Sir so many times by the newly inducted men, he could only shake his head.

"Serial number?"

"I'm not sure."

He reached into the folder, pulled out a typed index card and handed it to Doss.

"Read it out loud."

"Doss, Desmond T. 33158036."

"That's your Army serial number. It's also on your dog tags. Memorize it by the end of the day." Then he slid the paperwork down to the next man.

As Doss moved along, a soldier on the other side of the counter would add to his pile of equipment, call out what he had added and then push the pile on to the next station.

"Two barrack bags. One shaving brush. One toothbrush. One comb. One razor with five blades. Two towels, huck. One towel, bath. One meat can. One knife. One fork. One spoon. Four handkerchiefs, cotton. One tape for identification tags. One canteen. One cover, canteen. One cup, canteen. Move over. Next."

"Five drawers, cotton. Five undershirts, cotton." The soldier left out a set of underwear and then placed the rest in the bag. "Put on the underwear. Next."

"Three pair socks, wool, light. Five pair socks, cotton, tan. Put on a pair of cotton socks. Put everything else in the bag."

"What's your shirt size?"

"About a 14 neck, 32 sleeve."

The clerk looked at Doss to size him up and then returned with a pile of clothes.

"Two shirts, wool, olive drab. Two shirts, cotton, khaki. One jacket, field." He placed everything into the bag except one khaki shirt before he said, "Put it on and move down."

"What's your waist and inseam?"

"My waist is about 28, but I don't know my inseam."

The soldier glanced at him for less than a second before disappearing among the shelves. 30 seconds later, he returned with an armful.

"Two trousers, wool, O.D. Two trousers, cotton, khaki. Two trousers, herringbone twill. Two jackets, herringbone twill. One belt, web, waist." He placed everything in the bag except a pair of cotton pants and the belt. "Put 'em on and then up on the platform for shoes."

Doss stepped onto the platform where he was greeted by a soldier who was standing on the floor below. The height of the platform placed his feet at the soldier's chest level.

"What's your shoe size?"

"8 ½ d."

After the soldier used a device to carefully measure his feet, he left for a moment and then came back with two pairs of 9 d shoes.

"Hey, I said I wear an 8 ½."

"That was as a civilian. In the army you're a size 9."

Doss put on a pair of shoes. Then he picked up the other pair, stepped off the platform and got back into line.

"Give me those shoes." Doss handed them over. "Two pair leggings. One pair gloves. One coat. One overcoat." He stuffed it all in the bag. "Next."

"What's your hat size? "

"Size 7 sir."

"One hat, herringbone, twill. One liner, helmet with neckband and headband. One cap, garrison, O.D. Two caps garrison, khaki. One cap, wool, knit. Two neckties, Mohair." He stuffed everything in the bag except a khaki cap and necktie. At this point Doss had reached the end of the counter. He put on the cap, tied the necktie, picked up his bag and climbed up onto another platform where his uniform was inspected to determine if it needed any alterations. Doss thought his uniform fit pretty well, and the army tailor must have agreed, because he was sent on to another small room and told to take all the items out of his barrack bags and place them on the floor. There was a large sign painted on the wall listing everything he should have received along with the replacement costs. The sign also said that the total value of the property which had been issued was $80.86. A corporal in the room helped Doss double check that he had everything on the list. Once both men were satisfied, they co-signed a receipt form, and Doss repacked his bags.

The corporal told Doss to grab his bags and wait outside. When everyone from his group was outside and lined up, a sergeant gave them some more drill instruction and then marched them off toward the barracks. By the time they arrived most of them were even in step.

The two-story barracks buildings were each identical to the next. It would have been impossible to tell them apart if it weren't for a small number stenciled over the outside doors. Every inch of ground in the camp was covered with gravel, and the area was immaculately clean. Not even so much as a blade of grass grew alongside the buildings.

The men were told to memorize the barracks number and then sent inside. To reach the squad bay, the soldiers had to pass between two small rooms, which were reserved for the sergeants. The only furniture in the area where the men would sleep were rows of steel bunk beds spaced about five feet apart along the walls. The interior walls and floor were bare wood; the light fixtures consisted of a bare bulb in a porcelain socket and a heating duct ran down the middle of the room. Toward the back of the first floor was a stairway leading upstairs, and in the far back was a latrine room consisting of six flush toilets, a trough urinal, a shower area and six sinks. Doss realized there would be no privacy in the latrine as the toilets, urinal and shower were all out in the open with no partitions. To the left of the latrine was a small room, which contained the furnace.

The men were given a few minutes to pick out a bunk and drop off their barracks bags before being marched back across camp to a barbershop. There a barber spent about two minutes on Doss's haircut. First he ran an electric clipper up the side of his head before he switched to scissors to chop away at the hair on top, all while blowing smoke from a cigarette in his face. When he was finished, Doss's hair wasn't much shorter, it was just more ragged.

After the haircuts, the soldiers again lined up outside where the sergeant spent the last few minutes of daylight showing them the rudimentary elements of how to salute. It was then off for another trip through the chow line before being marched back to the barracks for the night.

After an all-night train ride and a full first day at the reception center, the men were beat. A few went into the latrine for a shower, but most of them went straight to their bunks and were asleep as soon as they hit the blankets. Even though he was as exhausted as the rest of the men, Doss knelt down by his bed, as had always been his custom, to say his nightly prayers. When he finished, he crawled into bed and instantly fell asleep.

It seemed his head had just hit the pillow when he was startled awake by the sound of a sergeant yelling and banging the lid of a garbage can. "Wake up you sleepy heads. You've had enough beauty sleep, though by the looks of you I don't think it did much good. I woke you up bright and early, so you'll all have plenty of time to shit, shower and shave. You can thank me for my thoughtfulness later. Make up your bunks, be dressed and lined up out on the street in 20 minutes."

Doss and the other men made their way into the latrine. After a quick shower alongside 30 other men, Doss found an open sink and used his new army safety razor to shave. Then he quickly used the toilet and went back to his bunk. Not knowing what to do with the wet towel, he draped it across the bunk frame to dry. He dressed and went out to the street with the other men. As he waited, he thought about how he might better work the latrine in the future. *Maybe the guys who took a shower last night had the right idea. I might sleep better after a shower and it'll give me more time to get ready in the mornings.*

While the men waited for the sergeant to show up, two corporals circulated among the men and made adjustments to their uniforms. They told Doss to straighten his hat, get his belt buckle in line with the buttons on his shirt and pants and then showed him how to tuck his necktie into his shirt between two of the buttons.

The sergeant arrived and marched the men off for breakfast. When Doss surveyed the line that morning, he was pleasantly surprised. The night before at chow, he had found even less to eat than he had at lunch, but as he looked over the breakfast food, he was encouraged. When he went through the line, his tray was heaped with pancakes, butter, eggs, cereal, milk and fruit. For the first time, he left the mess hall with a full stomach and the realization that he had better load up at breakfast because it was probably going to be the best meal of the day while he was in the Army.

After breakfast, the men were taken to a large auditorium and read the Articles of War. When Congress enacted the War Articles, they felt it vital that every enlisted man understand his military obligations. In fact, during the lecture the men learned they had specified in Article 110, that Articles 1, 2, and 29, 54 to 96, and 104 to 109, "shall be read and explained to every soldier at the time of his enlistment or muster in, or within six days thereafter, and shall be read and explained once every six months thereafter."

As the officer stood on stage explaining the Army rules and possible punishments, the men were somewhat taken aback by the number of times he uttered the phrase "shall suffer death." During the lecture, Doss leaned over and whispered to the man next to him. "I guess the Army is serious about its rules."

The group was then taken to another room, where Doss signed up for a free $10,000 life insurance policy payable to his mother in the event he should be killed in the line of duty. After he completed the paperwork, he was sent over to a soldier who was operating a dog tag embossing machine. The operator asked him to take off his dog tags and then used the machine to stamp his mother's name and address on them. Then he asked, "What's your religious preference?"

Doss answered, "Seventh-day Adventist." The soldier wanted to know if that was a protestant religion. When he replied that it was, the clerk embossed the letter P at the end of the last line. Then he handed the tags back to Doss and asked him to check them over to verify the new information.

DOSS, DESMOND T
33158036
BERTHA DOSS
1814 EASLEY AVE
LYNCHBURG VA P

Doss examined his updated dog tags and then put them back on.

Next the men were taken to a building to be interviewed and given a preliminary job classification. Once Doss was called over to a table, the officer sitting there explained what was going to happen.

"I have the results of the Army General Classification Test, which you took yesterday. That, along with the information you provide in this interview will help determine what job you will do in the army. Remember, the Army's needs come first, and you might not be assigned to a job that relates to your experience. So, let's get started. What grade did you finish in school?"

"I went all the way through 8th grade and partway through 9th."

"Okay, I'm going to count that as one year of high school."

"Did you play any sports in school?"

"No."

"Tell me about your occupation or any work you have done."

"I quit school and went to work in a lumber yard to help support my family. I painted signs for a while and then I worked as a carpenter."

"Tell me more about your carpentry work."

"I worked at Newport News Shipyard converting ships into troop carriers."

"Tell me more about the work you did at the shipyard."

"We added wooden rooms in passenger ships, so they could carry more troops. We built them in ballrooms, hallways, even swimming pools. Sometimes we enclosed outside decks to make more space for the troops."

"Can you read blueprints?"

"Yes."

"Okay, I'm going to put you down as a skilled pattern maker."

"What I really want to do is be a medic."

"You don't have any experience at that, do you?"

"No, but I went to first aid training at my church."

"Tell me about any hobbies you have. Things like ham radio, hunting or photography."

"I really don't have any hobbies."

"Any military experience?"

"No."

"Well Doss, the interview so far indicates that your classification should be infantryman, but let's go back to the idea of you wanting to be a medic. Why is that?"

"Well Sir, you see, I'm a conscientious objector, and my draft board said that is where I would probably fit into the Army best. I'm not willing to take a life, but I sure would be proud if I could save lives as a medic."

"Now I see your point. Being an infantryman is no place for a C.O. Since your test scores are very high for a man with an 8th grade education, I'm gonna go ahead and classify you as a medic."

"Thank you Sir."

"When you get assigned to a division and someone looks at this card, they'll assume I made a mistake with your classification. When that happens, just explain you're a C.O. like you did with me. Good luck Doss."

After lunch, the men went through a building where they were given vaccinations against smallpox, influenza, paratyphoid A&B, typhoid fever and tetanus. A doctor told them that during the next several weeks they would get the second and third tetanus and typhoid shots. The medics giving the shots hadn't been very gentle, and the smallpox vaccination was especially brutal. By the time they were finished, there was blood running down both arms of every man. To top it all off, blood was drawn to determine their blood type. At the end of the line, Doss handed over his dog tags where a machine operator embossed them with two last pieces of information, inoculation date and blood type, before handing them back to Doss to check over.

DOSS, DESMOND T
33158036 T42 O
BERTHA DOSS
1814 EASLEY AVE
LYNCHBURG VA P

By the time the ordeal was over, several men had passed out, and within a few hours, most of the men's arms were so sore and stiff they could barely move them.

Next the men were taken back to the auditorium and shown a film about sex morality and the dangers of contracting venereal disease and then another on the life of a soldier. Afterwards, they were taken outside where a physical training instructor led them in exercises, marched them for a while and then took them back to the mess hall for supper. After marching back to the barracks, the sergeant explained that even though they had completed all of the required processing, it was possible they might be at this camp for up to ten days until they were assigned to a unit. While they were waiting, they would be required to work details such as kitchen police or any other menial labor jobs that came up. Finally, he informed them that they were not restricted to camp and if anyone wanted to go into town for a few hours to see him for a pass.

Doss took the opportunity to find an Adventist church and attend the Friday night sundown meeting. Afterwards, he came back to camp, made his way to the barracks, said his prayers and went to sleep.

The next morning, the sergeant pulled the same trashcan alarm clock routine, which was even more annoying to the men who had been out drinking Friday night than it was to Doss. After a trip to the mess hall, the men were marched back to the barracks. Once inside, the sergeant had an announcement. "Settle down you guys. Every Saturday afternoon, the officers inspect the barracks, so here's what you're gonna do for the rest of the morning. You're gonna change into your work clothes, and then you're gonna get buckets, brushes and mops outa the furnace room and you're gonna scrub every inch of this floor. You're gonna scrub and polish the latrine until you can eat off the floor, and you're gonna shine the windows until they sparkle, and then you're gonna dust every surface in the place. Now get to work."

Doss recognized he couldn't do that kind of work on the Sabbath, and knew he would have to have a talk with the sergeant.

"Excuse me Sir, I can't do this today."

"What did you call me, boy? I know you don't know any better, but you might as well learn it right now. You don't ever, call a sergeant 'Sir.' You call me Sergeant 'cause I work for a living. Now try it again."

"Excuse me Sergeant, I'm a Seventh-day Adventist, and I can't do this kind of work on the Sabbath."

"What's your name, boy?"

"Desmond Doss, Sergeant. "

"No, it's not. Try again."

"Doss, Desmond T., Sergeant."

"Now get this clear. I don't care who or what you are, Private. You're gonna clean this floor."

"I'm sorry Sir, I mean Sergeant, if I did, I would be breaking the fourth commandment, and I couldn't allow myself to do that. I could clean the floor tomorrow, and I would work twice as hard to make up for it."

"So you're telling me, you're not gonna clean this damn floor no matter what I say?"

"I'm real sorry Sergeant I can't do it today."

The sergeant exploded into a rage, shouting so loud that spittle was flying with every syllable, and the windows were rattling with every word. He shoved Doss toward the door as he roared. "Then get the hell out of my barracks before I lose my temper and break you like a twig. I wouldn't want one of these soldiers to mistake you for a piece of trash and throw you into the garbage you filthy piece of crap."

By that time, the sergeant had backed him onto the front steps of the barracks, and then he slammed the door in his face. Desmond didn't know what to do, so he sat down on the steps, pulled out his Bible and began to read. After a while, an officer passed by. The new soldier remembered enough to stand up and salute. The captain might not have stopped if the private had been wearing his hat, but without it, the officer felt obligated to let him know that he was out of uniform.

"Where's your hat, Soldier?"

"It's back inside on my bunk, Sir. The sergeant told me to stay out here because I can't work on the Sabbath, and that, I might get in the way of the men while they clean the floor."

"You're not supposed to be outside without a hat. Get back inside Soldier."

"But Sir-"

"Don't you dare ever 'but' me or any other officer again. Now you get back inside right this instant, Soldier."

"Yes, Sir." Doss saluted. Then he turned and went back into the barracks. He wasn't two steps inside, when the sergeant noticed him and started yelling.

"What part of get outside don't you understand?"

"I'm real sorry Sergeant. An officer came by and said I wasn't allowed to be outside."

"Then get over to a corner and stay out of the way. At least you'll be some other sergeant's problem in a few days, and keep your filthy mouth shut. I don't want to hear one more stinkin' word outa you for as long as you're here. Now git."

For the rest of the morning, Doss sat in the corner while every man scrubbing the floor took turns coming near, to either splash dirty water on him or try out every cuss word they could think of. By that afternoon, he and his mom had been called every filthy name in the book. Lucky for Doss, he only spent one more night at the reception camp. The sergeant came in the next morning and told him to pack up all his gear. He had already been assigned to a camp for basic training. Later that day, when Doss boarded the train along with the other soldiers who were leaving Camp Lee, he was relieved to see that none of the men from the barracks were on the train with him.

FEBRUARY 25, 1942
77TH INFANTRY DIVISION

American strategists knew that winning the war would hinge on how quickly they could ramp up the manpower of the armed forces. The method they decided to rely on was the cadre. A cadre was a group of experienced personnel taken from previously trained units and then used as the core of a newly formed division. The theory was that these experienced men, comprising about ten percent of the new unit, would be able to quickly expand the capabilities of the division by sharing their knowledge with the green officers and recruits. The 77th along with the 82nd and 90th Divisions were to be an experiment in how rapidly the cadre method, along with other new training theories, could transform draftees into a cohesive and effective fighting force.

An order dated 14 February 1942 set the ball in motion. Major General Robert Eichelberger had just finished a tour of duty as the Superintendent of the United States Military Academy at West Point and was familiar with the newest military theories and methods. The Army decided he was the perfect man to command the newly reactivated 77th Division at Fort Jackson, South Carolina. In addition to Eichelberger, 600 other officers and 1,178 non-commissioned officers were selected from existing army organizations to fill out the cadre.

On 18 February, General Eichelberger, along with his 16 staff officers, arrived at Fort Jackson and got straight to work figuring out how to feed, quarter, supply and train almost fifteen thousand men. On 25 February, the two hundred officers selected to command the regiments, battalions and companies arrived. During the following week another 400 junior officers, mostly reserve lieutenants, showed up. Finally, on 5 March, with the arrival of twelve hundred experienced sergeants and corporals, the cadre was complete.

From his first day in command, General Eichelberger had decreed that he would hold the 77th to the highest standards of discipline, police and dress. His officers soon found out, that coming straight from West Point, Eichelberger's standards were indeed high.

Eichelberger informed his commanders that when the draftees stepped off the train from the reception centers and were taken to their barracks they were going to find made-up bunks, hot clean showers and manicured grounds and buildings waiting for them. Therefore, each company commander was faced with the task of putting four large barracks, containing a total of two hundred bunks, along with the company mess hall, kitchen, day room and about two acres of ground into order. To make it happen, each company had a work crew of five officers and 12 non-commissioned officers with no tools, vehicles or money. For the next three weeks, working together in-between classes and meetings, the officers and sergeants got down on their hands and knees, and scrubbed floors and toilets. They climbed ladders, washed windows, changed light bulbs, painted buildings, and repaired hot water heaters and plumbing. They carried mattresses, blankets, pillows and even toilet paper from the warehouse to the barracks by hand. They scrubbed pots, pans and serving trays in the kitchen. Finally, they hauled dirt and gravel in wheelbarrows to fill in eroded and bare areas in their company area. The whole time, some of the officers bellyached that General Eichelberger was forcing them to do labor better left for enlisted men, but after three weeks of working side by side, the officers and NCOs had been transformed from strangers, into a core group of men the general could use to build his division.

The Army drafted most of the men for the 77th from New York City and the surrounding area and by late March, when the trains started arriving loaded with new recruits from the reception centers, the barracks and company areas were ready for them. Upon arrival, the new men were immediately taken off the trains and marched to a regimental area. There, they were arbitrarily divided up and housed in temporary company barracks while they waited to be assigned a job in their permanent area.

One of the new methods the Army was trying out on the 77th was machine aided job classification. When the men's records arrived from the reception centers, their classification cards were sent to division headquarters to be run through an IBM tabulating machine. The machine spit out all the cards of potential cooks into one pile and radio operators in another. Every time the remaining stack of cards went through the machine it got smaller and smaller until they all were separated into bundles representing every possible job required to run a division. Of course, the largest pile was the one containing the cards of infantrymen. The machine further arranged the cards so that those of the men with the highest scores came out on top. After all the machine sorting was done, classification experts began going through the collated piles to assign each man to a specialty.

Late in the afternoon on 12 April, Doss was among the last trainload of men destined for the 77th to arrive at Fort Jackson. By that time, most of the work of assigning job classifications to the new recruits had already been completed. In fact, the division had started its training program a week earlier.

Doss was assigned quarters with an infantry company on a temporary basis while he waited to be classified. After setting his barracks bags neatly on the only unoccupied bunk, he talked with some of the other men. Doss soon found out that, not only was he the only unclassified man in the barracks, he was the only one not from New York City.

After what had happened just the day before at Camp Lee, Doss decided not to wait until the last moment to ask about getting his Sabbaths off. After supper, he said a prayer and then walked to the front of the barracks to see if he could talk to whoever was in charge. In the room on the left, he saw the back of someone sitting at a small desk. Even though the door was open, he had enough common sense to knock and wait for an answer instead of just busting in.

"Yes? What is it?"

"My name is Doss, Desmond T. Could I ask you a question?"

The sergeant knew the new private hadn't learned how to properly report to a superior, so he decided to give him credit for trying and let it go at that.

"Come in Doss. What is it?"

"You see Sergeant, I'm a Seventh-day Adventist, and we worship on Saturdays instead of Sunday. I need to find out who I can talk to about getting excused from duties and having my Saturdays off."

Doss held his breath as he waited for the sergeant to fly off the handle like the one at Camp Lee had, but he was surprised when he got a pleasant response instead.

"If you have a question about worship you need to see the regimental chaplain. His name is Captain Stanley, and he has an office at the chapel near the aid-station. Oh, and for your knowledge, a chaplain is the one officer you are allowed to go and talk to without permission. You need to get the consent of your sergeant before you go to talk with any other officer."

As he was listening, Doss thought, *Wow, this sergeant is really nice. He sure is different than the ones at Camp Lee.*

"Thank you for your help Sergeant."

"Sure Doss. You'll probably only be in my barracks for a few days, but if you need any more help, come see me again. Now to find Chaplin Stanley, turn left out the door. Go to the end of the street, then right. The chapel is at the end."

When Doss came back out of the sergeant's room, he saw that one of the other men was standing just outside the door and had been eavesdropping on the conversation. He figured the other soldier wanted to see the sergeant and was just waiting outside until they had finished. Doss waved at the man and said, "I'm through talking with the sergeant now." The sergeant, who had followed Doss out of the office to make sure he started off in the right direction, saw the soldier standing there and asked, "What are you doing out here? Did you want to talk to me Private Lane?"

"No, Sergeant."

"Then get back to the squad room. You know you're not supposed to be hanging around the sergeant's area uninvited."

Doss set off right away and had no trouble finding the chapel. Upon entering, he saw the words Chaplain Stanley, Capt. stenciled on a door to the left. After knocking, he heard a voice telling him to come in.

"What can I do for you Soldier?"

"My name is Desmond Doss, and the sergeant said you'd be able to help me out. I'm a Seventh-day Adventist and I'd like to have Sabbaths, Saturdays, off, so I can go into town for church. I ran into a real big problem at Camp

Lee last Sabbath, and I thought I'd try to settle things here ahead of time, this time, Sir."

"I'm somewhat familiar with Seventh-day Adventists and how sincere they can be about their Sabbath observance. We chaplains have a committee meeting once a week on Wednesdays with Colonel O'Brien, the division chaplain. I'll bring it up there and see what we can work out, but I have to tell you right up front there might be a problem because soldiers are supposed to be confined to camp for the first two weeks." Seeing the blank look on the private's face, Chaplain Stanley asked, "Didn't they tell you about how it's possible to spread small pox for two weeks after you get the vaccine?"

"No, Sir."

"Well anyway, come back to see me toward the end of the week, and I'll let you know what we decide."

Doss thanked Chaplain Stanley and made it back to his barracks at 2130 hours, right about the time for the men to go to sleep. Doss knelt by his bed, as he always had, to say his nightly prayers. Private Lane, the big rough looking brute from New York City, who was still sore for being caught snooping by the sergeant, was the first one to notice him praying.

"Hey fellas, look at the Holy Joe. He must think he's a priest or something. Hey Doss, do you want your mommy to tuck you in after you finish praying?"

Doss, who did not intend to cut his prayers short, tried to pretend that he hadn't heard the taunts and kept right on praying. When Lane failed to get a rise out of Doss, he took off one of his shoes and threw it across the room. It missed the praying soldier's head by inches before slamming into the wall. When Doss continued to ignore Lane's abuse, some of the other men joined in on the jeering.

"Holy Jesus."

"Holy Joe."

"Momma's boy."

Soon other shoes were flying. Doss was scared. He didn't understand why this was happening. *Haven't these men from New York ever seen a man praying?*

Before Doss could finish his prayers and get into bed, the sergeant he had talked with earlier yelled out of his room. "You men quieten down. Don't make me come out there." All the men, except for Lane were smart enough to pay attention. Unfortunately for him, he had become so caught up in tormenting Doss that he didn't hear the warning. Just as the sergeant stepped out of his office, Lane yelled, "I bet he wets the bed," then lobbed his other shoe in the praying man's direction.

Lane finally noticed the sergeant standing behind him and seeing the look on his face, realized he had pushed things too far.

"Private Lane, put on your fatigues, and wait for me, at attention, on the street in front of the barracks. Since you seem to have so much energy that you can't go to sleep, we'll see if we can find some work that'll make you a little more tired." The sergeant turned off the lights and then headed back to his room.

Hours later, after Lane had finished his punishment, he came back into the barracks and stopped by Doss's bunk on his way to the shower. Shaking him awake and making sure no one was able to hear, he quietly said, "I'll get you back for this Deacon." After being startled out of a deep sleep and then overcome with the strong smell of rotten garbage, Doss was too shocked to respond before Lane shoved him one more time then turned and headed into the latrine.

The following day, Doss tried several times to smooth things over with Lane, but the big soldier would have nothing of it. His only response was more jeers and taunts. That night, Doss decided to wait until after lights-out to say his prayers. Lane was watching, but he figured teasing Doss that night wasn't worth the risk of having to scrub garbage cans again. He decided to keep his mouth shut, at least for the time being.

The next day, Doss was sent to the supply hut, where they issued him a Soldier's Handbook Basic Field Manual, bedding, another fatigue uniform, a gas mask, steel helmet, raincoat, and some more underwear. He was also given a small bag stamped ARMY HOUSEWIFE, which contained needles, three colors of thread, a thimble, spare buttons and several 77th Division patches. Sergeant Brinkley, the supply clerk, told him to look in the handbook and then sew the patches onto the left sleeves of his dress uniforms according to the diagram. Doss had seen the blue patches embroidered with a gold Statue of Liberty on the other men's uniforms and was eager to sew his on. Then it dawned on him. *This division must have something to do with New York. That's probably why most of the men seem to come from around there.*

On Friday, Doss went back to talk to Chaplin Stanley, so he could find out what had been decided.

"Doss, the committee discussed your request. Because of your unique situation, we have decided to allow you to go into town for church on Saturdays. Of course, you will need to make up your work on Sundays while the other men have their day of rest. I have a pass here for your trip into town tomorrow, but from now on, you will need to request it each week through the normal channels."

"Thank you Chaplin Stanley."

The next morning, Doss got up early and went into Columbia where he found an Adventist church to attend. The preacher had a powerful sermon, and after the worship service some church members invited him to stay for the weekly potluck dinner. For Doss, the meal sealed the deal. He decided there was no need to look any further. He had found his Fort Jackson church home.

Sunday morning after breakfast while the other men went to church or into town, Doss was given the job of cleaning the latrine area, which took him over four hours since he was working alone. Then for the rest of the day, he raked gravel around the company area.

On Monday morning, word came that Doss was to pack up his gear. He had been classified and was being assigned to Company C as an infantry soldier. Just as the officer at Camp Lee had predicted, when his card went through the IBM machine at Fort Jackson, it came out into the pile of cards slated for infantry soldiers. The problem with the sorting system was that the cards did not contain a place to indicate if a soldier was a conscientious objector. If there would have been such a space, the machine could have sorted all the objectors' cards into a separate pile to be given special treatment. Instead, Doss had to get Chaplin Stanley's help to straighten things out.

Doss stayed with the infantry unit while headquarters filled out the mound of paperwork it took to transfer him from the infantry company to the medical detachment. While he waited on the red tape, he trained, ate and showered alongside the infantrymen. He learned marching, saluting and military courtesy, watched training films and did calisthenics. They taught him how to make a bed, hang up his clothes and store his gear. He quickly learned that for everything, there's the right way, the wrong way, and the Army way.

During one of the training sessions, Doss learned that a privilege afforded to him as a soldier was being able to mail letters at no cost. All it took was for him to write his name, rank, serial number, and organization in the return address area and "free" where the stamp would normally go. *At least I won't have to pay for stamps out of my $21 a month pay,* he thought. He vowed to take maximum advantage of the benefit to write to his mom and of course to Dorothy. In his first letter home, he told about the mix-up of having been assigned to an infantry company instead of the medics and asked everyone to pray that the situation would be straightened out soon. One week later, the prayers were answered when his paperwork was finished, and Doss was transferred to the medical unit. Right away, he sent letters to his family and Dorothy telling them to write to him at his new address, Pvt. Desmond Doss, 302nd Medical Battalion, APO 77, Fort Jackson, South Carolina.

One of the classes the medics attended told of the responsibilities and protections afforded medical personnel under the Geneva Convention. Doss learned that the rules of the convention made attacking medical personnel a war crime. In order to comply with the Geneva Convention, each medic was required to wear a medical brassard above his left elbow, which consisted of a red cross stitched onto a white armband. Every official brassard was stamped on the inside stating *"Issued by Medical Department, U.S. Army, in conformity with Article 21, International Red Cross Convention, Geneva, 1929."* A medic was furthermore required to carry at all times a Geneva Convention Identification

Card showing his photograph, fingerprints and unique Medical Identification Number, which was also stamped on the inside of his Red Cross Brassard. If a medic was captured, the accord stated that he should not be treated as a common prisoner of war but be allowed to continue in his medical duties. In return, the medic was required to treat enemy soldiers if no other care was available.

A medic was forbidden to engage in combat and was prohibited from bearing arms. If the enemy saw a medic holding a gun, his Geneva Protections were no longer in effect, and it became legal to shoot him. A medic captured by the enemy while engaging in combat and at the same time wearing the Red Cross Brassard, could be rightfully executed.

For the first half of their basic training, the medics were segregated from the combat infantrymen, but because they needed to be in superb shape, they received the same physical conditioning and training with the exception of learning how to use weapons. Instead of learning how to maintain a rifle, they were taught the uses of the items in their medical kits. While the infantryman was learning the difference between a M1 trigger guard and a follower rod, the medic studied the different uses of a bandage and a dressing. The medic also became skilled at how and when to apply a tourniquet, the correct way to inject morphine and how to carry a litter. They were taught to study the terrain and use existing cover and the lay of the land to plan their approach to a wounded soldier. They also learned about camp sanitation and malaria prevention. Some of the lectures bored the medics, but Doss tried his best to pay attention and learn the material.

One night after supper, as Doss was in the barracks reading his Bible, he overheard some of the other medics discussing the situation in Europe.

"I don't know if anyone can stop Hitler. If it keeps going the same way, Europe will end up as one big Germany."

Doss felt the Holy Spirit urge him to join the conversation and piped up, "No, it won't."

"What'a you mean no it won't," a medic named Glenn challenged. "How would you know?"

"Because the Bible says so," answered Doss.

"You telling me, the Bible says something about Hitler won't conquer Europe? Get outta here. If that was true I think I would'a heard it somewhere before. Show me where it says that, 'cause I don't believe it."

Doss turned some pages in his Bible. "It's all here in Daniel chapter 2. King Nebuchadnezzar had a nightmare, which woke him up in a panic, but then he couldn't remember what the dream was. He asked the wise men of Babylon to tell him what he had dreamed and what it meant, but they said it was impossible since he couldn't even remember his own dream. King Nebuchadnezzar got so angry, he said if they weren't able to tell him what his dream was, he would have them all cut to pieces. Are you sure you want to hear this?" Doss asked.

By that time, he had the attention of every man in the barracks.

"If this dream is about Hitler, sure we want to hear it," said Glenn.

Doss looked around at the other men who were shaking their heads in agreement before he continued. "Nebuchadnezzar gave the order to Arioch, who was the captain of the king's guards, to gather up all the wise men and hack them to pieces. But when he went to get them, one of the men, a man named Daniel, said if he could have some time to pray to the God of Heaven he would be able to tell the king his dream. Daniel prayed and that night God caused him to have the exact same dream as the king had."

"The dream about Hitler?" asked Glenn.

"Daniel told the king that he had dreamed about a great statue whose head was made of fine gold, his chest and his arms of silver, his belly and his thighs of brass, his legs of iron, his feet part of iron and part of clay. A stone, which was cut out without hands, smashed into the statue's feet that were of iron and clay, and broke them to pieces. That's right said the king. That is what I dreamed, but what does it mean?"

By that time, the men had moved closer, surrounding Doss and looking over his shoulder at the Bible he was holding. One of the other men had pulled out his own Bible and was reading along in Daniel 2 as Doss told the story.

"You and the kingdom of Babylon are the head of gold, Daniel told the king. After you shall arise another kingdom inferior to yours and then another third kingdom of brass, which shall rule over all the earth. The fourth kingdom shall be as strong as iron. You saw the feet and toes, which were part of clay, and part of iron? After the fourth kingdom, they shall mingle themselves with the seed of men, but they shall not cleave one to another, even as iron is not mixed with clay."

"But where's Hitler?" asked one of the men.

"Hitler and Germany is one of the toes, and the Bible says it won't join with the other nine toes."

"You're just making this up. This Daniel guy didn't even say what the other kingdoms were," said Glenn.

Doss turned a few pages in his Bible.

"Daniel 5:28 says that Medo-Persia conquered Babylon, just as God showed in the dream, and Daniel 8:21 says Greece succeeded Medo-Persia. Everyone knows from their history class at school that Rome conquered Greece and ruled until it fell apart into the countries of Europe. The vision that God gave Nebuchadnezzar and Daniel showed that the ten toes represented the countries of Europe after Rome fell. God knew that men would try to reunite the toes back into one empire but that no matter what they tried it wouldn't work. That's how I know Hitler won't unite Europe."

When Doss had finished his story the men just stared at him until the man who had been reading along in his Bible broke the silence. "I can't believe it. He's right. It's all right here in my Bible, just like he says, but what's the stone?"

Doss closed his own Bible before answering. "The stone is Jesus. When he comes back to earth he will destroy all nations and set up his own kingdom, which will last forever."

By the time he finished his story, it was well past time for lights out. In fact, the sergeant, who had come in to turn out the lights just as Doss made the claim about Hitler, had become interested, and paused to hear the Bible story. Once it was finished, the sergeant announced lights-out and went back to his room.

Over the next few days, the sergeant and the other men in the barracks retold how Doss had shown them a Bible Prophecy proving that Hitler would never conquer Europe, and the story began to spread throughout the medical battalion.

Even though he tried, Doss found it hard to make a friend in the army. He just had too many strikes against him. Strike one, was that he was a conscientious objector. Because of military culture, even if the other soldiers didn't have a prejudice against objectors when they came into the army, they soon developed one. Strike two, was his insistence on keeping the Sabbath while the rest of the men worked on Saturday. Doss worked just as hard on Sunday, but the other men assumed he was getting a special privilege that they were not getting. Strike three was that he refused to use profane language or tolerate the other men's crude sexual humor. Some of the men found out he was dating Dorothy and insisted on making foul sexual comments about their relationship just to give him a hard time. He would have none of it.

Doss began to look forward to and take comfort in the frequent letters from Dorothy. The few times she was able to visit him in Columbia to spend the Sabbath together, Dorothy could see how lonely and depressed Desmond was becoming and she started to rethink their marriage plans. One weekend she decided to discuss it with him.

"Desmond, I know we decided to wait until after the war to get married, but maybe we need each other to get through the war."

"What are you trying to say Dorothy?"

"Maybe it would be best if we got married now. We would have to be very careful to make sure I don't get pregnant because I wouldn't be able to support a child by myself if something awful happened and you don't come back from the war."

Desmond broke out in an ear-to-ear grin. "That would be great Dorothy. It would ease my mind so much if we were married. If you lived nearby, we could see each other every Sabbath. Let's both talk to our pastors and see what they say. I'll be due a furlough after basic training. Maybe we could get married right after that, sometime in mid-August."

The couple spent the rest of their visit talking and making plans for the wedding.

That weekend marked another milestone for Doss. The medic's training had progressed enough that the company aid-men were ready to be assigned to an infantry company. Each infantry company in the division needed to have two medics and Doss and Glenn were assigned to Company B. The aid-man's responsibility was to locate a wounded soldier, quickly assess how severely he was wounded and then immediately begin the treatment necessary to stabilize him for transport to the battalion aid-station. The doctors believed that if a severely wounded soldier was treated by a medic within the first hour, he would have about an 85 percent chance of survival.

The aid-men were different than the other medical soldiers because they lived, ate and moved with the infantry company they served. They would go into combat alongside the infantrymen and remain on the front lines with their company. An aid-man was put into a somewhat awkward and unique situation. He was still under the administrative umbrella of the medical battalion, while living with and subject to the day-to-day scheduling of the infantry.

As soon as Doss settled in with the infantry, he sent both his mom and Dorothy a post card with his new address.

"Don't write to me anymore at the 302nd Medical because I'm not there anymore. My new address is Pvt. Desmond Doss, 307th Infantry Regiment, 1st Battalion, Company B, APO 77, Fort Jackson, South Carolina. Don't worry; I'm back in the infantry but this time as a company aid-man. Praise God. This is just what I have wanted."

Desmond

JUNE 1942
THAT LONG HIKE

Doss learned that he had been designated an aid-man just before Company B was scheduled to spend a week at the rifle range. The infantrymen spent weeks learning how to disassemble, reassemble, operate and clean the M1 rifle. They practiced sighting and aiming. They learned different firing positions and how to squeeze the trigger, but the one thing they had not yet done, was to shoot their weapon. During the last part of May, the 77th Division began sending men from the 305th Regiment on the 14-mile march to a rifle range located at the far edge of the camp near Leesburg where they could teach them how to fire live ammunition. By the first week of June, the 305th had completed their training, and it was time for the 307th to start sending men there.

Even though Doss would not be qualifying with a weapon, he went along with the infantrymen. The Fort Jackson range incorporated all the newest safety features and included 400 known-distance targets for the M1 rifle. There were also additional targets for machine guns, BARs (Browning automatic rifles), and pistols. Since the men using the range stayed there for at least a week, the Army had set up a tent camp with all the necessary facilities to house them during their stay.

Every day, hundreds of shooters were scheduled to be on the range. As soon as the platoons and companies reported for the start of live firing, they were separated into relays, which corresponded to the number of firing positions available. Each relay performed a different task at different times of the day. While one relay was on the firing line, the next would be on-deck, waiting to move up for their turn to shoot. Two other relays were usually assigned to target marking duty. Their job was to stand in a trench beneath the large targets and crank them down after each round of firing. Then they would mark the bullet holes by placing a marker plug in each one and crank the target back up, so the shooter could see where his bullets had hit. Different color disks were then placed on a long stick and held up in front of the holes indicating the point value of each shot. If the shooter completely missed, the scorer would wave a red disk back and forth in front of the target.

While the infantrymen were constantly busy at the rifle range, being a medic, Doss didn't really have anything to do. In the end, he decided to just tag along and watch. Most of the time he ended up sitting and watching while the infantrymen fired shot after shot. It didn't take long for some of them to start resenting the medic. *Why should he get to just sit around while we're working so hard?* they reasoned.

About the only action he got as a medic were a few cases of Garand Thumb, an extremely painful condition resulting from the M1's bolt accidently slamming closed on a man's thumb. The soldiers had been taught to pull the bolt back smartly to ensure that it would properly latch open, but if they didn't follow the training to the letter, the bolt would catch on the follower. As soon as a soldier's thumb touched the follower, the bolt would slam forward smashing his thumb. Doss was near the firing line when he saw his first case.

"Ouch! Son of a . . ."

When the medic stood up to see what was going on, he quickly spotted Private Palmer jumping around with his thumb in his mouth. He grabbed his medic kit and ran over to help. When he got there, the training sergeant shook his head and simply said, "M1 thumb."

Doss took the man aside and examined his injury. He could see that it was not only badly smashed but also slightly cut. He opened his medic bag and got to work. First he swabbed the thumb with iodine and then used a 1 by 3 inch bandage to cover the cut. "I'm sure that hurts. If I had some ice, it would help with the pain, but there's none around here. You're probably gonna lose the nail, but other than that, you'll be okay. If it doesn't feel better by tomorrow, report to sick call."

"That's all you're gonna do?"

"All I can do. If you think it's not enough you can go to sick call right now."

After taking a moment to think, the soldier made up his mind.

"No, I'll just stay here. If I leave now, I'll miss out on qualifying today. Go on back to your shade tree, pill pusher."

The soldier's words stung. He hadn't realized how bad sitting in the shade made him look to the other men who were working in the hot sun. Doss decided that from then on, when his men were training, he was going to stay right next to them. If they were standing, he would stand also. If they were in the sun, he would stay in the sun with them. He said a quick prayer asking God to forgive him for the bad impression he had made with the infantrymen. Then he moved up close to the men on the firing line and sat down with a group of them waiting their turn.

After the men finished up their training at the rifle range, they all marched 14 miles back to the main part of the base. Even though the 77th had trucks and other vehicles, the enlisted men and even most of the junior officers had, up to that point, never ridden in a vehicle during their time in the army. The reason was twofold. The first being that the division had a limited supply of gasoline, only equal to about one gallon per vehicle per day. After allocating enough fuel to keep the essential vehicles running, there was none left over to move troops around. Secondly, the hikes were used as part of the physical fitness plan to toughen the men up. The army had started them off with short marches as soon as they stepped off the train their first day in camp. From then on, they were gradually worked up to longer and longer marches carrying more and more weight. The ultimate goal was a timed 25-mile marching test that every man was required to complete in eight hours. What made the test even harder, was that the men were required to carry a full pack and rifle, which taken together weighed over 60 pounds.

Besides going to the rifle range, two other interesting things happened in June. The 77th Division got a new commander, General Roscoe Woodruff and the 307th Regiment was selected to pass in review for Winston Churchill. Since the 307th was just back from the rifle range and the other two regiments were in the middle of training, they were the ones chosen to represent the 77th Division in the massed formation. Churchill visited the base on 24 June. After taking a tour of the fort and watching the soldiers and equipment parade past his reviewing stand, he was very impressed. He was heard to say, "If this is what an American soldier looks like after only two months of training, I'm confident, that together, we shall prevail against Hitler."

Not long after the visit by Churchill, Doss was scheduled for a day of kitchen police duty. Every enlisted man was expected to take regular turns at KP, and a schedule was posted on a bulletin board in the barracks. Normally, KP duty was a scheduled job, but sometimes it was assigned as an extra duty punishment. No one liked KP because it entailed a very full day of doing whatever dirty jobs the mess hall sergeant needed done. The work usually involved cleaning between meals, serving food, washing pots and pans, scrubbing garbage cans and of course peeling potatoes.

At 0400 hours, the Charge of Quarters woke up Doss and one other man to send them off to the mess hall. As soon as they arrived, Doss was surprised to see that Private Lane and another man from a different company were already there. The mess sergeant fed all four of them an early breakfast and then put them straight to work. All morning, it seemed the instant they finished one job, the mess sergeant would show up to give them another.

After the men cleaned up and scrubbed down the mess hall following lunch, the sergeant gave each of the four men a knife, sat them in a circle around two garbage cans labeled "vegetables only" and set them to work peeling one hundred pound sacks of potatoes. Before he left, he gave them extensive instructions. "Potato peels in the cans. Peeled potatoes in the pots." After plopping down several large 15-gallon pots, he gave them one final order. "Keep peeling till there ain't no more."

Doss was sure he had never seen so many potatoes in one place in his life. After a while, the men agreed that the only good thing about peeling potatoes was that the work was mindless, and it allowed them to carry on a conversation as they worked. Doss was in a good mood, because it seemed that he and Lane were getting along well. As soon as they filled a pot, one of them carried it to a cook who then boiled them to make mashed potatoes. Hours of peeling later, the four finally worked their way through the mountain of potatoes. After sitting around for a few minutes and when the mess sergeant failed to swoop in with another job for them, the men began to discuss what to do.

"He said keep peeling till we're done, and we're done. Let's go outside and take a smoke. You wanna come outside with us Doss?"

"No, I don't smoke. I'll just stay in here."

"Suit yourself."

While the other men were outside, Doss decided to get a broom and sweep up some potato peelings, which had missed the trashcan. After he finished that, he found a mop and was in the process of cleaning the floor when the mess sergeant came in. "What do you think you're doing with that mop?"

"Well Sergeant, we finished the potatoes and I just decided to clean up while I waited for you to come back. I learned in school that a job worth doing, is worth doing right, and I figured the job wasn't over until the cleaning was done."

The mess sergeant was surprised to find a man working without being told what to do. Normally, he spent most of his time trying to keep the men assigned to KP duty from goldbricking.

"What's your name, Private?"

"Doss, Sergeant."

"Where are the other men?"

"They went outside for a smoke."

"Okay Doss. The last part of this job is to take the garbage cans full of peelings out back. A farmer comes by every night and picks 'um up for his pigs. When you finish that, you can come back in for your supper. Oh, and tell those other men to get back in here. I've been saving up a special job for loafers like them."

Doss carried the first can out back and sent the other men back in. When he came back after dragging the second can out, he saw that the sergeant had put Lane and the other two men to work cleaning out the grease traps beneath the sinks. The foul odor emanating from the traps made Doss gag, and he held his breath as he passed by. He got a mess tray, piled it with bread, mashed potatoes and a piece of pie and sat down to eat.

The mess sergeant came over with his tray and sat down next to him. "Is that all you're gonna eat Doss?"

"Yes Sergeant, I'm sure everything you cooked is delicious, but you see, I'm a vegetarian, and I don't eat meat."

"You don't eat meat? What are you, some kind of hep cat jazz musician?"

"No, I just try to follow what the Bible says about eating."

"The Bible talks about eating? Hey, I'm a cook, and I believe in the Bible, but the Army sure never taught anything like that in cook school. Maybe you better tell me what it says about food."

"I don't have a Bible with me, but it's Deuteronomy 14 where it says some foods are unclean and we shouldn't eat them. That's where it talks about not eating pork. Some people say Jesus changed the food laws in the New Testament, but Isaiah 66 says that when Jesus comes back, he will destroy with fire those eating swine's flesh, mice and other unclean food. That's the reason I don't eat unclean food, but I go a little farther and try not to eat any meat. Did you know that God didn't allow men to eat meat until after the flood?"

"Is that why you didn't take any beans? Because they have pork in 'em?"

"Yes Sergeant. If it was beef, I would just eat the beans and leave the meat, but I gotta be especially careful with pork."

"I've never heard anything like that before. I'm gonna study up on what you said. Once you're done eating, go help wash the supper pots and pans. Then I'll be through with you."

Later that evening, as Doss left the mess hall to head back to his barracks, he passed Private Lane sitting on the back steps. He was covered in a mixture of filth from the grease traps and his own vomit. Doss felt sorry for the man, but he didn't want to linger because the smell had him on the verge of throwing up. As he passed by, Lane muttered, "Deacon, you won't live a day when we get into combat 'cause I swear to God Doss, I'll shoot you myself." Doss turned around to say he was sorry, but Lane just jumped up and raised his fists. When he tried to explain that it wasn't his fault the mess sergeant got sore, Lane became furious. Doss could tell that the man had become too irrational to reason with, so he gave up trying. He reluctantly turned away, walked wearily back to the barracks and then took a long hot shower. Seventeen grueling hours after he began his KP duty, Doss collapsed exhausted on his bunk.

Several days later, the almost 200 men of Company B had just finished breakfast. They were assembled in formation waiting at ease for the Company Commander, Captain Frank Vernon to speak to them. The infantrymen were wearing fully loaded backpacks and carrying their rifles. Doss and Glenn, identified by the Red Cross Brassards on their left arms, weren't carrying guns. Instead, they each had two large medic bags attached to a chest harness in addition to their backpacks. Earlier, when Doss had come running to get in line with the 2nd Platoon, some of the men joked that with his long legs, bouncing helmet and flapping medic bags, he looked like the scarecrow from *The Wizard of Oz*. Doss had never seen the movie. In fact, he had never seen any movie, so he had no idea if he looked like the scarecrow or not. He just assumed the men were blowing off steam and smiled.

Captain Vernon called the men to attention. "Today's the day men. All the marching and physical training we have done so far has been leading up to this. We will be making a 25-mile forced march in less than eight hours. Every enlisted man and officer is required to complete this march in the allotted time frame to graduate from basic training. Company B's pride and honor is at stake. I fully expect every man in this company to complete this march together as a unit. Company, Left FACE. For-ward, MARCH."

For the next several hours, Captain Vernon used every trick in the book to maximize the pace and minimize the men's exertion. On uphill grades, he marched them at a normal cadence and on the downhill sides, he increased the pace to double time. On level ground, he took advantage of whenever the sun went behind a cloud to step up the pace. Despite his efforts, it didn't take long for most of the men to become completely drenched in sweat. Even so, Captain Vernon kept up the quick pace until they had completed 15 miles of the march. It had taken them just slightly under four hours to make it that far.

When the captain called a 20-minute rest for lunch, the men slumped down under whatever shade they could find and took out their K-rations to eat. Doss had just opened up his, when one of the nearby men called the medic over. "Hey Doss, anything you can do for this blister? It's killin' me."

"Sure, just hold on a second."

Doss went over to the man, unfastened his medic bag and took out a metal container of iodine swabs. First he used one of them to paint the blister. Next he opened a safety pin, struck a match and ran it through the flame several times. He laid the safety pin flat on the soldier's foot and slid it up, nicking the bottom edge of the blister, after which he carefully squeezed out the water. Then he used his scissors to cut a donut hole out of some folded 3-inch gauze, making it into a cushion ring. Finally, he taped the gauze around the blister to help take off some of the pressure.

The nearby soldiers were watching him work. As soon as he finished with the first soldier, they begin calling out, asking him to work on their feet next.

Doss answered back, "Anybody who wants me to work on a blister, go ahead and take off your leggings and shoes to help speed things up. I'll get to you as soon as I can."

The medic spent his entire lunch break fixing up blistered feet. Before he had a chance to eat a bite, Captain Vernon called the men back into formation. Doss quickly placed the biscuits, gum and malted milk tablets from the K-ration into his pocket. He would try to eat them while he marched. He poured the salt and sugar along with the powdered lemon packet into his canteen and sloshed it around to mix it up. Lastly, he took the book of matches and placed it into his medic bag. He had the feeling he would need them to sterilize more safety pins on the way back.

Captain Vernon called the men to attention. "We've made good time so far, and we only have 10 more miles to go. Remember, that for the pride of the unit, I expect every man to finish together." Captain Vernon turned left and walked up to take his place at the head of the column. "Company. Right, FACE. For-ward MARCH." After a few minutes the captain gave the command, "route step MARCH," allowing the men to break cadence and talk among themselves.

The men, as a group, did well until they hit the 20-mile mark. By that time, it had reached the heat of the day, the temperature had climbed to 98 degrees, and the older men were struggling just to keep up. Many of the men had developed serious blisters, and the others were just plain exhausted. When the weaker men started straggling, a number of the younger men divvied up their equipment and carried it for them. It was not enough. Doss and Glenn had fallen back to the tail end of the column and they were doing everything they could to encourage the men, patch them up and keep them going. Despite their efforts, one of the older men developed heat stroke. He couldn't go on. Doss waited with the soldier until he was loaded into the ambulance, which was following along behind. As he ran to catch up with the rest of the column, Doss passed by Glenn who was working on another heat stroke victim. Before the end of the march, the medics had treated several other men as they fell out of line. Each time, after waiting to turn the patient over to the ambulance crew, they were forced to run to catch back up with the rest of the formation.

When Company B had completed the grueling march, and as the men were standing at attention waiting to be dismissed, another soldier fainted. Doss hurried to his aid just as Captain Vernon dismissed the rest of the men. While the medic was kneeling next to the passed out soldier, Captain Vernon came over, mad as a hornet. "What good are you medics? Eight men didn't make it through the march. You've disgraced the honor of this company."

"It was a awful hot day today Captain Vernon. Maybe, the hottest this year. We did the best we could."

From the look on his face, Doss could tell the captain wasn't in the mood to hear excuses.

"I'm sorry Captain Vernon. I'll try to do better next time."

As Vernon turned his back and began to walk away, Doss heard him mumble, "Wouldn't take much to do better than this."

Doss had felt pretty good about how he had performed during the march until Vernon cornered him and told him what he thought of him and medics in general. What he didn't know, was that even though the captain hadn't appreciated the medic's efforts during the march, the enlisted men did. They took notice of how both of them had worked their hardest to care for them, seeing them running in the blistering heat to give aid to the next downed man. Before the march, the medics were seen as outsiders, but afterwards the infantrymen began to accept them as one of their own.

Doss was still in a funk from Captain Vernon's dress down as he started through the chow line for supper. When he reached the middle of the line, the mess sergeant spotted him and came rushing out from the kitchen. He snatched the serving spoon from the soldier who was dishing out mashed potatoes and pushed him aside. At the top of his lungs he announced, "See this here man in line. His name is Private Doss, and he's a vegetarian. That means he don't eat meat."

At that moment, Doss wished he could find a rock to crawl under, but his face brightened when the sergeant began heaping his tray with scoop after huge scoop of mashed potatoes.

"From now on, when any of you men are on KP duty, this is how I want a vegetarian's tray loaded up."

The sergeant moved down the line to the navy beans and with his finger motioned Doss closer. Holding his hand up next to his ear, he whispered, "Don't worry. From now on, it's beef for all my seasoning." The sergeant winked then turned and went back into his kitchen.

With a smile on his face, Doss held out his tray to the soldier serving the beans. "Two scoops please." He was still grinning ear-to-ear as he sat down and began to eat.

One of his tablemates asked, "What gives Doss? Who do you know, a general?"

Doss didn't answer. He just ate and was happy.

After passing the milestone of the 25-mile march, Doss began to worry because the furlough he was due after basic training still had not been scheduled. He and Dorothy had tentatively planned to have their wedding in the middle of August, but without a firm date, they weren't able to make any definitive plans. Every time he asked for a date, the answer he got was that he would just have to wait his turn like the other men. Seeing Doss come into the medical office for the fourth day in a row, the top sergeant finally gave in. "Look Doss, I'd sorta like to help you out, but they still haven't made out a schedule for the enlisted men's furloughs. I even asked Major Goldman, but all he would say was that officers and non-coms come first. If you want to go talk to the adjutant officer at regimental about it, you got my permission."

"Thank you Sergeant. I sure would."

Doss went right away to regimental headquarters, but when he got there, he found that the adjutant was out of the office. While he was in the process of asking the sergeant when the adjutant would be back, Colonel Craig, the 307th Regimental Commander walked into the room and came up behind him saying, "The adjutant will be gone for a few days Soldier, is there something I can do for you?"

When Doss turned around, all he could see was a pair of silver eagles staring back at him. Colonel Craig was the highest-ranking officer that had ever spoken to him. He regained enough composure to salute the colonel before answering him. "Sir, Private Doss does not have permission from his top sergeant to speak with you, Sir."

"It's alright Doss. I'm giving you permission. Now what did you want to speak with the adjutant about?"

"Well Sir, I want to get married as soon as I finish basic training, but I need to nail down when my furlough will be, so we can set a firm date."

"When were you planning on having the wedding?"

"The night of Aug 15th, if possible, Sir."

"Got a church all picked out?"

"Yes Sir, we do."

Colonel Craig flipped the page on the calendar to look at the month of August. "The 15th is a Saturday. You're going to need a few days for travel. How about we start your furlough on the 13th? Sergeant, get me Major Goldman on the phone."

A few moments later, the sergeant handed the phone to Colonel Craig.

"Major Goldman, I have a Private Doss here. Says he wants to get married. In my opinion, if a soldier wants to get married, it's best not to stand in the way. What do you think? Good. Good. Private Doss and I feel that August 13th is an appropriate date to start his furlough. Will that work for you? Glad to hear that Major. If you run into any trouble with the paperwork, let my sergeant know, and we'll cut through the red tape."

Colonel Craig handed the phone back to the sergeant and then turned to Doss. "I've got a few minutes to spare. Why don't you tell me a little more about that future wife of yours."

Doss finished at headquarters and headed back to the medical detachment office. When he walked in the door, the top sergeant was waiting. He held a finger to his lips to make sure Doss didn't say anything and motioned for him to go outside. The sergeant followed close behind and shut the door.

"Doss, what in the world have you gone an done? Major Goldman got a call from Colonel Craig, and now he's ready to tear your head off. You were supposed to talk to the adjutant. I never gave you permission to talk with the Colonel."

"I'm sorry Sergeant. When I got there, the adjutant wasn't around, and when I was about to leave, the Colonel came up out'a nowhere and asked what I wanted. I told him I didn't have permission to talk to him, but he said it was okay. Before I knew what was happening we were talking about my wedding, he started asking questions about Dorothy, an then he picked up the phone and called Major Goldman. I heard him tell the major to give me my furlough on the 13th. Am I in trouble?"

"You can't go in there now, that's for sure. Stay low for a while until I smooth things over."

Major Goldman eventually calmed down, and Doss received his furlough papers, but he had rubbed the major the wrong way and the major had a long memory.

Desmond and Dorothy were married on Monday, August 17th. They had originally planned to have the ceremony on Saturday night but then ran into some roadblocks with the marriage license, which took a few days to straighten out. That left them with a little over two weeks to spend together as husband and wife before Desmond would be due back at Fort Jackson on September 3rd. Desmond couldn't help but think that those were the happiest weeks of his life.

Desmond and Dorothy discussed the possibility of her living close to his camp, so they could spend his off times together. The Army paid the wives of privates $50 per month, and if Desmond was careful with his $21 a month pay, they thought it might work out. Dorothy believed she would be able to pick up some part time work to help cover expenses and save the $50 a month as a nest egg to use after the war. After having made a dollar an hour at the shipyard before he was drafted, Desmond felt a little guilty at the thought of his new wife working to make ends meet. Dorothy reminded him that army wives all over the country were in the same boat, which made Desmond feel a little better but not much.

All too soon, his furlough was over, and Desmond was getting ready to head back to the base. Having to leave his new wife was one of the hardest things he had ever done. Just before they said goodbye, Dorothy pulled a small tissue wrapped box from behind her back. "Here Desmond. It's a present I got for you. Go ahead. Open it up."

Desmond took the box. "I'm sorry. I'm such a heel. I didn't get you anything."

"It's okay darling, you just take care of yourself, and come back from this stupid war. That would be the best present in the world."

Desmond unwrapped the box and opened it up. "It's a pocket Bible. Thank you honey."

"I know you have your regular Bible, but I checked with the salesman, and this one is the perfect size to fit in your uniform pocket. Now you can take it with you everywhere you go."

"Oh thank you Dorothy, this is a wonderful gift. I'll think about you every day when I read it."

"I know you will, silly. Look in the front, I wrote you a letter."

Desmond opened the Bible and began to read what Dorothy had written there. By the time he finished, tears were rolling down his cheeks.

January 15, 1943
Louisiana Maneuvers

The buzz among some of the barbers in town was that the 77th Division would soon be relocating. Doss himself heard the rumor while sitting in the chair at Tiny's Barber Shop in Columbia. Tiny was chatting away as he worked on cutting his hair, but the soldier was paying little attention to the conversation. Instead, he was studying the huge Victorian style grandfather clock ticking away in the back and wondering how such an expensive antique had found its way into a simple barbershop. His thoughts were interrupted by something he thought he heard Tiny ask him.

"Say it again. I didn't hear what you asked."

"I said, 'are you getting spiffed up for your trip to Louisiana?' "

"I'm not going to Louisiana. I'm just due for a cut."

"That's not the way I hear it. Word is that the 77th is moving out for Louisiana the middle of January to play eight weeks of war games."

Doss was surprised that Tiny's rumor was so specific.

"If that's true, how did you find it out? That kind of information is supposed to be secret."

"Think about it soldier. I don't just give haircuts to privates."

After Tiny finished the cut, he attached a shiny motorized device to his hand, turned on the switch and used it to give Doss a quick scalp and shoulder massage.

"That feels great. They sure don't have anything like that back in Lynchburg. Is it something new?"

"It's a Stim-u-Lax. Bought it about a year ago. All my customers love it."

When the massage was over, Tiny told Doss, "Since soldiers get a nickel discount, that'll be 45 cents for the shave and cut. The massage is free, but next week the price is going up a dime."

Doss paid-up and then headed back to camp. Once there, he found the grapevine in full swing. Even though Doss had heard the same rumor that was being spread all over camp, he decided not to repeat it himself because Proverbs 11:13 came to his mind. *A talebearer revealeth secrets: but he that is of a faithful spirit concealeth the matter.* Besides, the men had been given several lectures emphasizing that military activities should be kept secret, and he just couldn't bring himself to believe that a barber could have accurate information on military troop movements.

The next day, Doss's trust in the effectiveness of Army security precautions suffered a serious setback when word came through official channels that the division would in fact be moving to Louisiana.

Relocating the 77th to Louisiana turned out to be a challenge because it was the first time the entire division had attempted a rail movement. The first order of business was to produce an accurate inventory of rolling equipment within the division. The 77th had over 2,000 vehicles, including jeeps, trucks, half-tracks and trailers, which needed to be cataloged listing their exact length and weight. The division also had fifty-four 105 mm and twelve 155 mm howitzers, which also had to be moved by rail. Once completed, the detailed inventory was used to determine that it would take almost 900 railroad flatcars to move all of the vehicles.

To secure the vehicles on the railcars, sixteen thousand, five hundred 8"x12"x24" wooden wheel chocks and sixteen thousand, 3 foot long 2x4s were ordered. When the lumber arrived from the sawmill, most of it was very heavy, and many of the chocks weighed over 30 pounds each because the wood was still green. One thousand, eight hundred crossover ramps were fabricated out of 4"x12"x6' lumber, which were then used to bridge the gap between the ends of each flatcar. When it came time to load the train, a vehicle drove onto the end of a long line of flatcars and then moved forward, driving over the crossovers, until it reached its designated spot on the train.

The railroads supplied the Army with whatever random rolling stock it had on hand. Because flatcars came in lengths of 36', 40', 42', 50' or 52'6" long, careful consideration had to be given to the length of each military vehicle and its placement on the train. For example, if the flatcar was 40 feet long, it could hold three jeeps, or a truck and a jeep but not two trucks. A vehicle was prohibited from hanging over the end of a flatcar to keep it from interfering with the operation of the car's swing up handbrake. Therefore, it took at least a 50 foot flatcar to accommodate two 2½ ton trucks, which measured 22½ feet in length with a winch or 21½ feet long without.

Once a vehicle was in the correct position on the train, wooden chocks were placed against the wheels and fastened directly to the deck of the flatcar with four, 20-penny nails. Then the vehicle was tied down with heavy 8-gauge steel wire, which was first doubled then twisted together until all the slack was taken up. Next two stacked 2x4s were nailed along the outside edge of each wheel and finally the crossover ramps were taken up and nailed to the bed of the flatcar so that they would be available for offloading the vehicles at the destination.

Each such train, made up of approximately 50 cars, was assigned a steam engine and route to follow. Armed military guards were posted on the flatcars and rode along in the cabs of the vehicles they were assigned to protect. Their job was to cordon off the train anytime it came to a stop, as well as to regularly check the tension of the vehicle tie downs.

Hundreds of types of smaller equipment such as radios, typewriters, tents, medical supplies and the other things it took to supply an army division were shipped in boxcars, of which approximately 200 were required.

The Army had a policy of moving troops in sleeper cars, whenever possible, on trips of 12 or more hours. During the war, the Pullman Company struggled to meet the high demand for troop trains. They managed by pressing their mothballed heavyweight sleeping cars back into service. Before the war, these older sleepers had been gradually retired and moved into storage as Pullman worked to replace its fleet with lightweight streamlined cars.

The heavyweights could each sleep 39 soldiers. During the day, the accommodations consisted of pairs of seats, alternating forward and backward, positioned on either side of a center aisle. A restroom, located at both ends of the car, each contained several washbasins and a drop toilet that deposited the waste directly on the tracks. Located across from the men's restroom was a water cooler, which provided drinking water. At night, the seats would be converted into a lower berth, and then an upper berth was dropped down from the ceiling. This formed a section, which was screened off from the aisle by a curtain. Soldiers in standard Pullman sleepers slept two in a lower berth and one in the upper.

During the war, the Pullman Company continued to staff each sleeper it supplied to the Army with a black porter, just as it had always done when they were in civilian service. The porter's duties included converting the seats into sleeping berths and making them up with fresh sheets and pillowcases each night. In addition to keeping the cars and restrooms tidy, they were required to be available day and night to wait on the passengers. A Pullman Porter's pay was very low, which forced him to rely on tips for much of his income. Working for tips typically meant putting up with degradation and humiliation. A porter especially resented the common practice of being called George or Boy by the passengers, an allusion to being George Pullman's, the company's founder's, "boy." Shortly before the beginning of the war, the porters had succeeded in forming a labor union. Their first demand was that the Pullman Company supply a nametag for their uniforms.

A steam locomotive could pull enough cars to move about 600 men, or three companies of soldiers. The typical troop train consisted of a 4-8-2 type locomotive pulling 15 Pullman sleeping cars, three kitchen cars and three baggage cars.

The troop kitchen cars had the capacity to serve approximately 250 men each, and they were normally spaced out along the train so that food could be served from both ends. Since all cooking was performed by the division's regular U.S. Army cooks, the cars were each outfitted with two standard army coal ranges. Rounding out the equipment was a pair of 200-gallon cold-water tanks, a 40-gallon coal fired hot water tank, a bread locker, a large refrigerator, and a series of built-in cabinets and drawers. When a meal was ready, the men utilized their army mess kits and ate in their seats or bunks.

Doss, in his role as one of Company B's aid-men, was traveling to Louisiana with the infantrymen instead of the 302nd Medical Battalion. The men were formed up, standing at parade rest about five hundred feet from the tracks waiting for the order to board the train. To the far left was the division band.

"Attention."

"Right, FACE."

"For-ward, MARCH."

Moving as one, 600 men slightly shifted the weight of their body to their right foot and swung their left foot 30 inches forward. Their heels contacted the ground one-half second later. At the same instant, the division band let out the first note of *The Washington Post,* and the entire formation marched off toward the train. When the band reached the engine, it peeled off, came to a standstill and continued to play as the rest of the men passed by.

The men were halted beside the train, and while still at attention, each file was marched into their assigned sleeper cars as the band played, *This is the Army, Mr. Jones.* As soon as the train was loaded, the conductor gave the signal, and the engineer opened the throttle. The train lurched and then slowly began to chug forward. As the train passed by the band, the men recognized they were playing the tune, *I've Been Working on the Railroad.*

After a trip of 23 hours, Doss and the other men stepped off the train near the small town of Many, Louisiana where the division was being bivouacked. In the end, it had taken several weeks, 25 troop and almost 40 freight trains to move the 77th to Louisiana.

When Germany invaded Poland and started WWII in 1939, the American Army was much smaller than most European armies, and it still consisted of infantry troops supported by mounted cavalry. American war planners were shocked when they saw how cavalry troops faired against the German Blitzkrieg, so they quickly began work to mechanize their forces. The newly reorganized Army lacked experience with mechanized fighting, and the Louisiana maneuvers were set up as a series of war games designed to test new strategies and doctrines that might be used against the Germans. These games were not primarily intended to provide training to the enlisted men. Instead, they were used to evaluate the readiness level of U.S. training, logistics, and doctrine as well as the competence of upper level commanders. The lessons learned during the first maneuvers, held in 1940, resulted in the decision to eliminate horse-mounted units as well as to allow armored units to operate independent of the infantry.

The 1940 maneuvers were such a success that follow-up war games were scheduled to test out other newly developed strategies before employing them on a real battlefield. Therefore, when the Army needed to try out new scenarios involving defense and retreat, the 77th along with the 90th motorized divisions were chosen to oppose each other in a series of highly scripted war games.

The preconception Doss and the other men had of what the war games would entail turned out to be very wrong. The men had presumed that there would be lots of excitement, action and noise. In reality, the enlisted men's role mostly involved being trucked to a certain map location during the night and then marching cross-country to another map location during the day. After a certain amount of time, they would be told to move back to where they had started. Many times, on the way back they would discover that the bridge they had crossed in the morning now had a white X painted on it, signifying that it had been declared destroyed. Then the men would either be told to wade across the stream, or that the stream had been designated an uncrossable river, in which case they were to set up defensive positions and wait until the bridge had been "repaired" by the engineers. The umpires would consult their rulebooks and then inform the engineers what type of make-work they would have to do to satisfy the maneuver of the day's requirements before eventually allowing the infantrymen to cross.

Sometimes, Company B would repeat the same exact boring scenario three or four days in a row before moving on to the next scenario. It seemed to Doss that the only type of troops who were getting any hands on training were the engineers. They were constantly building corduroy roads and setting up pontoon bridges only to have them "destroyed" by Piper Cubs dropping bags of flour "bombs" on them.

The combat aid-men saw very little action. Sometimes an umpire would randomly declare that a few men had been injured or killed by a sniper or artillery attack and then they would have to pretend to treat the injuries. Depending on the umpire, the "wounded" man would be either actually transported back to the rear area or just told to stay where he was. At first, the men who were told that they had been killed in action thought they had hit the jackpot because they got to lay around for the rest of the exercise. However, after several instances when the "dead men" were accidently forgotten and left behind as the rest of the division moved down the road, most of the men didn't want to play dead anymore.

As sundown was approaching on the first Friday of the war games, Company B found itself miles from camp, and Doss began to worry about how he was going to be able to keep the Sabbath. During one of the lulls in the action, he got down on his knees and asked God to work out the situation.

Dear Jesus, I thank you for watching over me up to now during my army time. Since you have always worked it out for me to keep the Sabbath so far, I trust you to work it out again tonight. Amen.

A little while later, Company B was told to set up camp for the night in a nearby field. As the other men were hooking their shelter halves together and pitching tents, Doss noticed a farm across the road. He tapped his shelter half buddy, Lonsway, on the shoulder and pointed. "See that barn? How about you and me go ask the farmer if we can sleep in there instead of the tent?"

"I don't know, Doss. If you want to do it, go ahead. I don't want to get into trouble."

"No one said we couldn't sleep over there, but if I go by myself you'll be alone in the tent, and someone will notice for sure. If we go together, I don't think anyone will miss us."

"Okay, I'll go along if you do the talking."

The two men walked across the road and up the front porch steps. Doss opened the screen door and knocked. A few moments later, the farmer came to the door.

"Excuse me sir, my name is Desmond Doss. My buddy, Jasper Lonsway and I, are part of the war games. The thing is, I'm a Seventh-day Adventist, and I keep Friday night to Saturday night as my Sabbath, so I was wondering if it would be all right for the two of us to spend the night in your barn."

"Well now Private Doss, I sho do appreciate you coming up and askin' first. I got plenty of hay up in in dat loft. It be okay by me if you twos wants to sleep up there."

Doss reached out to shake the farmer's hand.

"Thank you sir. We won't make a mess."

The farmer was laughing as he closed the door.

"What's so funny Frank?" asked the farmer's wife.

"Couple a soldiers. Wanted to spend the night in the cow barn. Said they not gonna … make a mess."

That night, the two soldiers were warm, dry and comfortable sleeping in the farmer's hayloft. The next morning before sunrise, Lonsway shook Doss awake.

"Come on, we better get back before anyone notices."

"You go ahead. I'm gonna spend the day here."

"What? Are you nuts? You'll get caught for sure."

"Let me worry about that. If anyone asks where I am, just go ahead and tell the truth."

After Lonsway left the barn, Doss pulled out his little Bible to read. He had been at it for about an hour, when he heard some movement downstairs in the barn. *Well I guess they did miss me after all.* He climbed down the ladder, but instead of being greeted by the military police, he was met by the farmer and his wife.

"Mornin' Private Doss. Where's your buddy?"

"Oh, he woke up and went back across the road a while ago."

"My wife ask about you both last night. I told her that you say you were a Seven-day Advent. That right?"

"Yes, sir."

"You believe in Jesus?"

"Yes sir, I sure do!"

"She say, she think that you Advents don't eat meat. That right?"

"Well sir, Adventists don't eat unclean meat like pork, and most are vegetarians like me."

"So, what do a vegetarian eat?"

"The easiest way to explain it sir, is that if it can run away from me, I don't eat it."

"So, you eat eggs, cheese and milk?"

"Yes sir, I like them fine."

"Good, we be back with breakfast in a while."

Before he could say a word, the two turned and headed back toward the house.

A little while later, the couple came back out carrying a large basket. Inside was a huge platter of scrambled eggs and rice, along with fried potatoes, homemade drop biscuits, strawberry jam, fresh butter, a large hunk of cheese and a pitcher of cold buttermilk.

"Last week at church, the preacher man say we should treat a soldier nice. You the one."

"Thank you. I'm grateful to you and your pastor. If it wouldn't be asking too much, could I stay in your barn for the rest of the day? I'd like to spend it worshiping God and reading my Bible."

"Well brother, this here old barn, it sho don't look like no church but you goes right on ahead."

After polishing off the best breakfast he had eaten in almost a year, Doss spent the rest of the Sabbath in the hayloft, praying, reading his Bible and watching the rest of the soldiers maneuver back and forth along the ridge on the far side of the pasture. That night, just after sundown, he thanked the farmer and his wife, walked across the field, and rejoined his unit with none the wiser.

Doss knew he couldn't spend the next seven Sabbaths in a cow barn, because he had made plans for Dorothy to move down and find a room nearby. If they couldn't see each other and go to church together, there would be no point of her following him, so he decided to ask at the medical battalion to see about continuing to get his Sabbaths off. He first approached Captain Webster, who told him that he didn't feel like he could make a decision like that, and he would need to talk to the commander of the medical battalion. Since Doss had permission, he decided to do it right away. He went to see Major Goldman and requested that since the Army had been giving him his Sabbaths off would it be possible to continue to go to church while they were on maneuvers. The major let him know in no uncertain terms how he felt.

"Doss, I'm a Jew, and I keep the Sabbath too. I'd like to have my Saturdays off, but we're in the Army now. We've got to do things the army way."

"I'm sorry sir; I just don't see it that way Major. The Bible doesn't say that the Fourth Commandment only applies if you're not in the army. Besides the other men get Sunday off and it's the wrong day. Don't you think we should both get the real Sabbath off?"

"All right Doss, I'll give you this Saturday off, but don't make it a point to keep asking me."

That Saturday, Doss got his pass and hitched a ride with a farmer who was going to Shreveport, the nearest town with an Adventist church. His wife was waiting for him there, and they enjoyed church together. After the service, the couple was invited to eat lunch at one of the member's home. When the meal was over, Dorothy had some good news to share.

"Desmond, another army wife and I went together and rented a small room in a rundown farmhouse right across the road from your camp. The place is a real dump, but we can clean it up a little, and since it's only going to be a few weeks it'll do."

Doss was elated. "Oh Dorothy, that's great news. It's easier on me when I know you're nearby."

Desmond and Dorothy enjoyed the rest of the day together. When it started getting dark, Doss decided it was time to head back. He kissed Dorothy goodbye and walked over to the main road hoping to catch a ride back to camp. What he didn't realize was that some towns rolled up their sidewalks on Saturday night, and during the war, Shreveport was one of those towns. After he waited beside the road for 20 minutes without seeing a car, he knew that he needed to come up with another plan. *I guess if I start walking now, I can get back to camp before morning,* he thought, and then set off down the road. He hadn't even gone a mile, when two military police from the 90th Division pulled up beside him in a jeep. "Where do you think you're going Soldier?"

"I just went to church, and now I'm heading back to camp"

"Looks like we got another drunk one, Smith."

One of the MPs jumped out of the Jeep and quickly grabbed the handle of his nightstick, which was hanging from the left side of his white web belt. "You're under arrest Soldier. Get in the back of the jeep."

"But Sergeant, I'm not drunk. I don't even drink except water and milk that is."

"You better quit mouthing off to me if you know what's good for you." The MP pulled out his nightstick and smacked it against the palm of his hand a few times to emphasize the point. "Now shut up, and get in the jeep."

Doss knew he'd better keep his mouth shut around those two, so he reluctantly got into the jeep, and they drove him to their stockade. He remained locked up all night until a truck from the 77th came the next morning to pick up their men who the 90th Military Police Platoon had been holding. When he got back to camp, Doss had to take a lot of ribbing about getting locked up with the drunks. When Major Goldman found out, he let Doss have it with a lot more than good-natured ribbing.

"Private Doss, I let you have off and now you made me look bad. One of my medics getting arrested and thrown in with the drunks. I told you to get that Sabbath keeping idea out of your head, because I knew it was going to cause me trouble. For the rest of the week, when you're not attending to your regular responsibilities, you are on punishment duty."

"I'm sorry Sir. I just wanted to go to church."

"I don't care, Private. Now get out of here before I have time to think up something worse."

Although Doss suffered through a week of punishment, he still came back to Major Goldman the next Friday and asked for another pass. He quickly found out that Goldman was still infuriated over what had happened.

"Private Doss, I am not going to give you anymore Sabbath passes to go into town or allow anyone else to give you one. You do not have my permission to go to a higher authority to appeal my decision. Do you understand me?"

"Yes Sir, I do."

Even though Goldman had refused to give him a pass, the next day Desmond went across the road to where Dorothy was staying. Together, they took a picnic lunch and laid out a blanket in the hayfield where they spent the Sabbath talking, praying and having their own private worship service. When he returned to camp that evening, Major Goldman was furious.

"Private Doss, you were gone all day. How dare you go into town after what I said to you yesterday?"

"I didn't go into town Major. My wife is staying at the farm across the road. We spent the day in the hayfield. And Sir, there is a division order that I should be given Sabbaths off if at all possible."

Major Goldman was livid. He knew the farm and the hayfield were technically located within the overall boundaries of the camp and that the men were allowed to move around the camp freely if they didn't have any duties. He also knew that Doss had a point about the arrangements that Chaplain Stanley had made with division headquarters concerning his worship day. *If I try to discipline him over this and it goes to division, they might side with him, especially since he's got that order backing him up.*

"Doss, I'll be watching you, and if you give me half a chance I'll court martial you for sure."

"Sir, I'll sure try not to give you that half a chance."

Doss didn't have any trouble getting a pass the next two Sabbaths, but on the third week the entire division was out in the field on maneuvers and the war games were scheduled to continue through the weekend. When Doss asked for his weekly pass, Major Goldman put the plan he had been working on into action.

"Private Doss, since we're on maneuvers, if you want a pass for this Saturday you're going to have to talk with the colonel. He's in the command car right over there."

Major Goldman was still peeved that Doss had a division order backing him up. He figured if he could get Doss to make a pest out of himself in front of the brass they would realize how ridiculous that order was.

When Doss neared the car, he got a lump in his throat, and his knees went weak because all three Regimental Colonels were standing there, along with a lieutenant colonel, looking at a map. It was the largest concentration of high-ranking officers he had ever seen. For a second, he started to turn around and walk away but decided to be bold. He said a quick prayer and then walked up and saluted.

"Sirs, my name is Private Doss, and Major Goldman said I had to ask you to approve a pass for me to go to church tomorrow."

It was the lieutenant colonel who answered while the full colonels listened. "A pass? Why are you bothering us with this, Private?"

"Sir, I'm sorry to bother you since I can see you have important war game planning to do, but there is a division order that I should have Saturday's off whenever possible, so I can keep the Fourth Commandment. I guess Major Goldman wasn't sure if it applied while we were on maneuvers. You see, the Army classified me as a conscientious objector although I like to say that I am a conscientious cooperator, anyway because of my religious scruples I can't do regular work on the Sabbath"

"I thought Jews could do good on the Sabbath."

"Oh, I'm sorry I didn't say right up front. I'm not a Jew. I'm a Seventh-day Adventist. We keep Saturday the Seventh Day as Sabbath too, but you're right, we can do good on the Sabbath."

"Well Private Doss, you're a medic, what if someone gets hurt?"

"You see Sir, there are other medics. I take off Saturdays and then work for them on Sundays, so they can have off. Besides, we've done this same war game scenario every day this week and no one's been hurt so far, and even if someone gets hurt we just send them off to the local hospital."

"Okay, I've heard enough. I'll let Major Goldman know that the order giving your Saturdays off applies. You can go on back, and tell him that's going to be my decision."

Doss saluted, turned and started to walk away. Before he got out of earshot, he heard one of the colonels say, "What was Goldman thinking? He should have made that decision himself instead of sending that private over to pester us."

APRIL 1, 1943
CAMP HYDER

Scuttlebutt spread among the men that the 77th was being sent to Europe. This rumor was very plausible, because after a year of training the men were sure they were ready for combat. The other thing that made the rumor so convincing was that it had been true but only temporarily. Headquarters had received orders to move the division to Camp Edwards, Massachusetts as the first step to prepare for overseas deployment, but those orders were quickly rescinded and replaced with ones sending the 77th to Arizona.

The Arizona Desert Training Center had conditions and terrain similar to North Africa and was originally conceived of by General George Patton as an area where American armored divisions could learn how to fight the German Afrikakorps. The area was used exclusively by tank divisions until May 1943 when the Germans were defeated in Africa.

The 77th actually was chosen to be the first infantry division to receive training at Camp Hyder, but on 1 April, when the advance contingent stepped off the train at a tiny yellow railroad station in the desert, their initial thought was that someone had played an April Fool's Day joke on them. The entire town of Hyder, Arizona consisted of six small wooden buildings, one of them being the railroad station. On the other side of the tracks were two water tanks used to supply the Southern Pacific steam engines and a huge pile of tents and survey stakes. The advance men quickly realized that Camp Hyder existed on paper only. The division's first job would be to build it from scratch.

The advance party sent back word that the 302nd Engineers and their equipment should be given first priority for transportation. While waiting for the engineers to arrive, they began measuring, surveying and pounding stakes into the dusty desert ground to designate where Camp Hyder would soon become a reality.

As soon as the engineers reached Hyder, other units began to load aboard troop trains in Louisiana for the 1,500-mile trip west to Arizona. Most of the men enjoyed the trip because the trains were made up of new, comfortable, air-conditioned, Pullman cars unlike some of the other museum pieces they had endured in the past. While in route, the rumor mill was active. The most often heard theory being that the men would be staying at a comfortable holding camp for a few months while waiting to be assigned combat duty.

As each packed troop train pulled up to the little yellow station in the desert, the soldiers were invariably shocked when they looked out the windows to see their new army home. Camp Hyder was just starting to take shape as a tent city, which would eventually cover four square miles of broiling, dusty desert floor. There were no roads whatsoever in the camp area. Vehicles moved along paths marked out only by survey stakes, throwing up clouds of dust everywhere they went. Each company had been assigned an area to erect double rows of six man tents. The tents were supplied with cots and hay filled sleeping mats but nothing else.

After the men arrived, one of the first things they learned was that the nearest drinking water was six miles away and had to be trucked daily into the camp. Not only was there no running water for washing or showers, there were no latrine facilities at all. In fact, there were no permanent buildings whatsoever.

The Army had scheduled the men to begin training as soon as they reached the camp, but they quickly realized the soldiers required a period of inactivity to acclimate to the oppressive temperature, which regularly reached 110 degrees in the shade. The problem being, there was no shade.

Because they were the first infantry division to train in the desert, the Army planned to use the 77th to find out the minimum amount of water a foot soldier required to function. Entire regiments were sent on cross-country marches with only one canteen per man. Doss and the other medics were not issued any extra water, and when a man fell ill from dehydration, they felt compelled to share some of their own.

During one of the marches, Doss came upon a confused soldier who was obviously suffering from heat stroke. He had a rapid heartbeat, shallow breathing and his body was not sweating despite the heat. The medic allowed the man to drink from his canteen and while they waited for the ambulance, which always followed along at the rear of the column, he used the rest of the water to wet down the stricken man's uniform in an attempt to cool him off. As they were waiting, several officers drove up in a jeep to see what was going on.

"This soldier has heat stroke, Sir. I gave him all my water. Can I refill my canteen from your water can?"

"I think you're lying, Medic. I think you drank all your water, and now you see an opportunity to get some more. You just hike the rest of the way back to camp without any more water, and then maybe you'll learn to ration it more carefully next time. Do you understand me, Private?"

"Yes Sir, I do," he answered.

With that, the officers drove off, their jeep throwing up a cloud of dust and sand, which settled on Doss and his patient.

By then, the rest of the regiment had moved almost out of sight. Doss knew that he could not make it back to camp alone without any water, so when the ambulance finally arrived, he climbed in with his patient and rode along with him back to camp. As far as he could recall, during his entire time in the Army, this was the first time he had ever disobeyed an order that didn't have something to do with breaking the Sabbath or bearing arms. He knew he couldn't let going against orders become a habit, but he also realized obeying that order would have probably cost him his life.

Dorothy was able to follow her husband to Arizona, and she soon found a room to rent from an Adventist doctor and his wife in the nearby town of Buckeye. Doss was still regularly receiving a pass every Sabbath and was eager to spend the time with Dorothy. He knew the train, which passed by Camp Hyder, also went through Buckeye. He would like to ride it but there was just one problem. When the division first arrived, a few of the men had gotten drunk while on leave and damaged the Hyder train station and some of the Southern Pacific passenger cars. Because of the incident, the division had banned all army personnel, including officers, from boarding the train at the Hyder station. Now when the men went on leave, they were forced to ride army trucks across more than 100 miles of desert roads to reach Phoenix or Yuma. If not for the ban, Doss knew the train would be the ideal way to travel when he went to visit Dorothy. He decided to see what could be done about the situation. Doss worked his way up the chain of command until he reached regimental headquarters. There, he was finally allowed to make his case.

"Sir, I would like permission to ride the train to Buckeye, so I can go to church on Sabbaths."

Coming from any other private, the request would have seemed strange, but by then most of the officers were very familiar with the medic's worship habits.

"Doss, that rule came from the railroad not the Army. You're going to have to ride the trucks just like everyone else."

Doss knew that if he was forced to ride the truck to Phoenix on Saturday mornings and then take a train 50 miles back to Buckeye, he wouldn't have much time left to spend with Dorothy.

"Sir, could I have permission to talk to the stationmaster to see if he'll make an exception for me?"

"If you want to waste your time go right ahead. Better men than you have tried and failed to get the railroad to reverse that rule."

Doss went back to his tent, shaved and then cleaned his uniform as best as he could before he walked over to the little yellow station to talk to the stationmaster.

"Excuse me sir, my name is Private Desmond Doss. I'd like to talk to you about riding the train to Buckeye."

"Hold up there Soldier. Before you go any further, the answer is no. I made it clear to the Army that I won't stand for destruction of Southern Pacific property. A few of your buddies ruined it for everyone."

"Would you at least hear me out? I'm a Seventh-day Adventist, and my wife has a room with a doctor and his wife in Buckeye. I only want to ride the train, so I can go to church with her on Saturdays."

The stationmaster eyed Doss to size him up and then hesitated for almost a minute before he replied.

"Well now Private, it just so happens I know a few Adventist folk from up around Needles way, and I ain't never heard of one of them getting drunk and acting a fool. I guess there'd be no harm in selling a ticket to a soldier who just wants to take his wife to church."

"Thank you so much sir, this will mean a lot to my wife and me."

"Just one more thing Soldier. Are there any more of you Seventh-day Adventists that might be askin' to ride the train?"

"No, sir, I'm the only one."

"Thanks Private, that's all I need to know. See you Saturday morning."

After Doss had bought a ticket and left the station, the agent chuckled to himself as he grabbed a broom and began sweeping the ever-present sand back out the door.

I wonder how many new converts will be walking in here with some cock and bull story after they find out I let that boy ride? Not gonna do them any good though, nosir.

The extreme heat and primitive conditions that the desert inflicted on the men were quickly tearing apart the camaraderie, which had developed during the year they had spent together. Tempers were growing short, and the slightest provocation was likely to result in an altercation.

It only took a few trips by Doss on the train to elicit envy in the other men. Some of the officers were especially peeved and let it be known among themselves.

"Can you believe that Doss?"

"Yea, he gets more damn perks than a general."

"The nerve of that private. Riding the train, with air-conditioning, while the rest of us bounce our butts off in the back of a stinkin' hot army truck."

Another situation that was eating at the men was the constant shortage of water. This was especially taking a toll on Doss because each man's water allotment was calculated to include the coffee served in the mess tent, and Doss did not believe in drinking coffee.

Every morning, water trucks would arrive in front of each company area to top off their water storage containers. Captain Vernon had come up with a scheme to allow the men to fill their canteens and kitchen barrels each day just before the water trucks showed up. That way, the big storage containers would be as empty as possible when the water trucks arrived, allowing the company to always get the maximum amount of water possible.

For days, the anger over the lack of water had been boiling beneath the surface and about to explode into the open. One morning several men rushed up to Doss in a tiff.

"Doss, Vernon's gone, and the lieutenant's in charge and he's just sitting around. The water truck's due, and he ain't let us fill our canteens yet."

"Yea, he's just sittin' on his ass doin' nothing."

"You gotta do something Doss. They owe us that water."

Even as they begged, the men could tell that the medic was hesitant to make waves with the lieutenant, so they tried another tact. "You're responsible for our health. Without that water we won't stay healthy."

"And what about sanitation? The manual says medics got to watch out for sanitation. Ain't that right Doss?"

He knew the men were right about what the manual said. *Maybe the lieutenant just forgot about the water delivery. It couldn't hurt to remind him.*

"Okay guys. I'll go talk to him."

Doss approached the lieutenant who was chatting with a group of men and saluted.

"Sir, I just wanted to remind you the water trucks will be here soon, and you haven't let the men fill their canteens yet."

"Don't worry about it Doss, I got it covered."

"Yes Sir," he said.

Doss walked away but just far enough to keep a casual eye on the lieutenant and the men he was talking with. He could see the group laughing and glancing in his direction, but the lieutenant made no move to let the men fill their canteens. After a few minutes, the group broke up, and the lieutenant walked back into his tent.

At that moment, Doss made the decision to take the matter further, so he went to talk to the officer of the day in the medical unit.

"Sir, Captain Vernon's gone for the day and the lieutenant in charge hasn't distributed the water to the men yet. I reminded him the trucks are due, but he still hasn't done anything."

"That's really none of your business Doss."

"But Sir, we're responsible for the men's health. Without enough water, they won't stay healthy. And what about sanitation? The field guide says one of the responsibilities of medics is to watch out for sanitation. Sir, I really think we're obligated to do something about the situation."

The medical officer didn't like being told what to do, especially not by a private. "Doss, I told you that's none of our business. If men start passing out from dehydration, come talk to me again. Otherwise, that's the end of it."

By the time Doss made his way back to the company area, the lieutenant had already distributed the water to the men, and the truck had come and gone. The same men who had egged him on earlier now came back to talk with him again.

"Sorry Doss. You missed the chance to fill your canteen. The lieutenant waited until after you left, and then, as soon as you were out of sight, he came out and told us to fill ours up. We found out the jerk knew all along the water trucks were coming late today, and that's why he was waiting. Let me have your canteen."

After Doss handed it over, the soldier unscrewed the cap. Then he held it out while each of the other men poured in a share of their water until the medic's canteen was filled to the top.

"Thanks," said the soldier. "We'll never forget how you stood up for us today."

Although what the medic had done succeeded in winning points with the enlisted men, it hadn't helped his situation among the brass. In fact, the water incident was the last straw for the officers. They decided to get rid of their "pain in the butt," once and for all.

The next Friday, when Doss went to the medical battalion tent to get his Sabbath pass, the top sergeant handed it over with a smile on his face.

"Here you go Doss. By the way, we arranged for you to have all your Sabbaths off from now on."

"What do you mean, Sergeant?"

"Oh, you'll find out soon enough."

"Find out what?"

"Why, it's good news. The officers have been discussing your case, and they decided that you'll be getting out of the Army soon. Turns out you qualify for a Section 8 discharge."

"Section 8?"

"That's right Doss, in a few days you'll be out of the desert, back with that pretty little wife of yours, and you'll be able to spend all your Saturdays together. Won't that be nice?"

Doss just stood there, too dumbfounded to speak. Finally, one of the officers came up to him and said, "Go back to your tent Doss. When the discharge board meets in a little while, we'll call for you."

Doss was so taken aback, he didn't even salute before he turned and walked out in a daze.

On the way back to his tent, he started to think. *Maybe I should just take the discharge. I sure would like to get out of this desert. Who wouldn't jump at the chance? But a Section 8? They said I could have all my Sabbaths off. That must mean they think I'm crazy because I want to follow the Ten Commandments. I can't accept that. What would God think if I did?*

By the time the medic reached his tent, he had decided that he would do everything he could to fight back against the Section 8 discharge. He took out his little Bible and got down on his knees to read and ask God to give him the wisdom he knew he would need when he faced the discharge committee. That was how the sergeant found the medic when he came looking for him over two hours later.

Doss followed the sergeant to the medical tent where he could see that the "discharge committee" consisted of three doctors. They had set up a table and chairs out in the open, and many of the enlisted men were hanging around to see the action.

"Private Doss," the chairman of the committee said, "after extensive discussion, we have concluded that you are eligible for an administrative discharge from the United States Army under Section VIII AR 615-360, 26, Nov. 1942."

Holding up a pen, he said, "We have the paperwork all filled out. All you have to do is sign it, and you'll be on your way home."

"Sir, do you have a problem with my work?"

"No, it's not that Private Doss. We have no comeback on the quality of your work. It's just that we feel you do not possess the required degree of adaptability for military service. While everyone else is training seven days a week, you're away at church every Saturday. We feel you might miss something important."

"Sir, I'm adaptable. Private Glenn and I worked out a system where we trade duty. He takes my duty on Saturday while I take his on Sunday. That way we can both go to church. It must be working out okay because Company B has the lowest rate of men lost to sick call in the entire regiment. You can check the records, and I don't feel I've missed any important training on Saturdays, because Saturdays are normally just inspection and review days."

Holding up the pen again, the chairman said, "Doss, can't you see we just want to give you all your Sabbaths off?"

"Sir, it seems to me that since you have no comeback on my work, what you're saying is you think I'm crazy because I want to go to church on God's Sabbath-day of the Fourth Commandment. I would be a poor Christian indeed, if I accepted a Section 8 discharge off my religious convictions. I'm sorry Sir. I'm not going to sign that paper under any circumstances, but believe me when I say, I know God will give me the wisdom to be a good medic on just six days a week training, and I'll prove it if you give me the chance."

The doctors realized they had lost. Their only chance had been to get Doss to voluntarily sign the paperwork. If they tried to take the matter further, a psychiatrist would have to be called in. His findings and recommendations would be reviewed by the next higher level of command who would then forward it to Major General Bruce, the new commander of the division, for final action and discharge. The doctors could not take the risk of pushing the matter up the chain of command. They were not familiar enough with Bruce to chance how he would react to a Section 8 discharge based solely on a soldier's religious convictions.

When word spread about how Doss had beaten the trumped up charges, it made the doctors in the medical battalion even more determined to get rid of him.

SEPTEMBER 15, 1943
DOSS VS. DOLLENMAYER

Lieutenant General Lesley McNair was the commanding general of Army ground forces. His role was the overall organizing, training and preparation of U.S. Army forces to get them ready for combat. One of the training methods he had formulated was the use of division scale exercises. These were used to help Army commanders gain experience controlling large forces in simulated combat. On 15 September, he came out to the desert to inspect the division.

When McNair arrived, he found that the regimental combat teams were just returning from the mountains east of the camp, where they had completed a demanding six-day field exercise and final examination. During the exercise, they were observed and graded on all the skills that they had learned during the previous six months at Camp Hyder.

The men and officers had been expected to demonstrate their competence in long marches, moving by vehicles at night and desert camouflage. During the war games, the reconnaissance teams had been given a chance to exhibit techniques of observing and reporting on the movement of other units while attempting to remain undetected. Doss and the rest of the medics not only rehearsed their medical skills on simulated injuries, they also treated and evacuated soldiers with real wounds ranging from snake bites, to heat exhaustion, to broken bones accidently inflicted during the course of the training.

The final course scheduled for the division following the field exercise, was a daylong class dubbed aircraft operation. When the men heard the lesson's title, some of them joked that after all the time the Army had spent making them infantry soldiers, only Uncle Sam would be stupid enough to try to retrain them as pilots. They pretended to be disappointed after they were told that a transfer into the Army Air Corps was not in the works. Instead, the training would actually consist of close air support coordination, aircraft recognition, and ground to air communication.

Although the Marine Corps had already embraced the concept of close air support, the Army had always relied exclusively on artillery fire to support their infantry. In late 1943, the idea of air support was just starting to be implemented. Although the instruction they received was somewhat rudimentary, the 77th became one of the first Army divisions assigned to take close air support training. General McNair was there in part to observe how this new initiative was working out.

During the training, one of the skills the ground forces practiced was the proper use of brightly colored panel markers to identify friendly troop positions. The men expressed hope that in actual combat the markers would be enough to keep them from being accidently bombed by their own aircraft. The pilots on the other hand, prayed the infantrymen would pay enough attention during the aircraft recognition portion of the training to prevent them from firing indiscriminately at every plane that flew overhead once they got into combat.

That afternoon, after the men had completed their training, they were gathered together to watch a massive demonstration of close air support, which McNair had arranged. At the conclusion of the exhibition, General McNair gave a speech to the entire division, where he said in part, "No army can be fully effective unless it is properly organized, correctly equipped, adequately led, and completely trained. Today's demonstration by the Army Air Force shows that with the proper training and coordination, close air support can be an effective and safe addition to the infantry division."

Once General McNair had finished talking, General Bruce stepped up to the microphone to make an announcement to his assembled division.

"Congratulations. Your training at Camp Hyder is now complete and-"

No one heard what he said next because the cheering was so loud it drowned out the rest of his words. After waiting a few moments in vain for the noise to die down, General Bruce leaned over and said to General McNair, "Oh well, they heard the most important part anyway."

The men were still cheering as Bruce folded the paper containing the rest of his short speech, shoved it into his pocket, turned, and followed General McNair off the viewing platform. General Bruce got into his car. As he was being driven away, he couldn't help but think, *I know they're happy to get out of this hellhole. So am I, but I wonder if they'll even be this excited when the war is finally over.* As he drove through Camp Hyder's gate for the final time, he had one last thought, *Good riddance to bad rubbish.*

That night, after leaving behind orders directing the division to prepare for a move to their next destination, Indiantown Gap Military Reservation, Bruce and his top aides departed by plane and headed east to Pennsylvania.

Soon after General Bruce's departure, Doss was walking back to his tent when he was intercepted by the top sergeant of the medical unit.

"Doss, pack up and turn in all your medical gear. You're being transferred to Headquarters Company."

"What'a you mean Sergeant? Headquarters doesn't have a medic."

"Oh, you're not gonna be a medic anymore. You've been reassigned to the Ammunition & Pioneer Platoon. You're going to be an ammo bearer from now on."

As the sergeant walked off he heard Doss mutter in disbelief, "I can't be an ammo bearer."

Standing there, Doss thought, *I know some things the A P platoon is responsible for. Laying mines, I can't do that. Finding and removing mines, that would be alright but stringing barbed wire, carrying ammunition, and blowing up obstacles, God wouldn't want me to do any of those other things.*

As he was thinking about what to do, one of his friends, a technical sergeant from the medical battalion came up to him.

"Hey Doss, I just made a ten dollar bet with Lieutenant Dollenmayer from the pioneer platoon. He said he'd have you carrying a carbine within 30 days. I said no way. I figure the bet was easy money for me, but I wanted to let you know what you're in for with the jerk."

"I'm sorry you made that bet Sarge, 'cause you know I don't like gambling, but God willing I don't think he'll be collecting from you."

"That's what I was hoping you'd say."

Many of the other men in the medical battalion had been around Doss long enough to come to believe that he could not be forced to compromise his religious beliefs, so it was easy for the A & P lieutenant to find men willing to cover his bets. By the end of the day, he had well over a hundred dollars riding on whether or not he could persuade Doss to carry a gun."

The medic went back to his tent to gather up all the medical equipment that had been issued to him. He knew this new assignment meant nothing but trouble and that once again he would have to trust God and his faith to see him through. Just as he had done countless times before, he went to his knees to read his Bible and ask the Lord for guidance.

After he had finished his prayers and turned in his medic bags, Doss went to Headquarters Company to report to his new unit. Waiting for him was First Lieutenant Robert Dollenmayer, commander of the pioneer platoon. Dollenmayer believed himself to be a model soldier. Even though he was a replacement officer transferred in from the Ohio National Guard, he looked like something from an Army recruiting poster. He stood over six feet tall in his perfectly tailored uniform. Unlike the other officers, he wore the strap of his polished helmet liner between his lower lip and chin. Dollenmayer had played football in high school, and his physique showed it. The lieutenant had trained as an explosives disposal expert in Ohio, but after he was transferred to the 77th, he was given the assignment to command the A & P Platoon.

Dollenmayer had been told that a troublemaker medic was being transferred into his unit. The lieutenant had no patience for troublemakers because he feared that a foul-up in his command would undermine his chance to finagle a transfer to commander of the explosive disposal squad. While waiting for the troublemaker to arrive, Dollenmayer, never short on confidence, was certain he would be able to whip the miscreant into army shape in short order.

All this lowlife needs is someone with enough determination to apply an adequate amount of pressure and discipline to break his spirit. No wonder the doctors in the medical battalion couldn't control this private. They're just as pathetic as he is.

When Doss reported to the pioneer section, Lieutenant Dollenmayer was ready for him.

"Doss, stand at attention. All members of the Ammunition and Pioneer Platoon are required to carry a M1 carbine rifle."

The lieutenant picked up a carbine from his desk and held it out toward Doss.

"Private, take this rifle."

Doss realized if he even touched the rifle, the lieutenant would use that small action as a wedge to eventually force him to violate his convictions. He also recognized that he could not openly refuse a direct order from a superior officer without facing the possibility of a court martial, so he had to be very careful.

"Sir, if you look in my records you will see that I am classified 1AO, conscientious objector. Because of my religious convictions I cannot bear arms."

"Who said anything about bearing arms, Private? I just want you to hold the rifle."

"Sir, because of my religious convictions, I cannot bear arms."

"Private Doss, new Army regulations require that ammo bearers carry a M1 carbine, but because of your convictions, I think I can make an exception in your case."

Placing the rifle back on the desk, he picked up a holstered M1911 .45 caliber semiautomatic pistol.

"Here you go Private, it's only a pistol. Just strap it on. That way you won't technically be bearing arms. You might even be able to go through the entire war and never have to use it."

"Sir, because of my religious convictions, I cannot bear arms."

Lieutenant Dollenmayer exploded, "Damn it Doss. I've heard that three times already. Is that the only answer I'm going to get from you?"

"Yes, Sir."

"Damn you Doss. Everyone in this platoon has to qualify on a M1 carbine. You're no use to me if you don't. Until further notice, I am placing you on continuous KP duty. If any crappy jobs come up, I'm saving them for you. I don't want to see your face again until you decide to come back in here and tell me you're willing to qualify with a rifle. Do you hear me Private?"

Before Doss could answer, Dollenmayer screamed, "Now get out of my sight."

Doss endured day after day of unremitting punishment duty until his standoff with the lieutenant was interrupted later that month when troop trains begin arriving to move the 77th to their next location. Lt. Dollenmayer had made it perfectly clear that he was restricted to base until he qualified on the M1 carbine, so Doss and his wife decided it would be of no use for her to follow him to the new camp back East. Instead, Dorothy went home to stay with her parents until the situation worked itself out.

There was confusion among the enlisted men about the division's destination after some units were ordered to the A.P. Military Reservation, Virginia while others were sent to Elkins, West Virginia. Doss and the 307th received orders to travel to Indiantown Gap and from there, proceed to Camp Pickett, Virginia.

Rumors ran rampant that the 77th was being broken up and used to supply replacements to other combat units. The misunderstanding was finally cleared up when the men were told that the plan was to rotate the regiments through three separate locations for month long training sessions. The three courses would consist of mountain, amphibious, and finally marksmanship and combat training.

After arriving at Indiantown Gap and while waiting for the training rotation to begin, Lt. Dollenmayer once again placed Doss on KP duty. He had scrubbed so many floors and washed so many pots, that the constant exposure to harsh lye soap had his hands raw and bleeding. It was during this time that he received a letter from his mom.

Dear Desmond,
Your brother has finished up his Navy training. He will be home on leave for three weeks starting October 10th. It sure would be nice if you could come home to see him before he ships off. Do you think you could arrange leave to come home? Let me know if you can come.
Love,
Mom

Doss knew this might be the last chance to see his brother alive, and it would mean a lot to his mom if she could see her boys together one last time before they shipped off to war. He also knew that he was due a 15-day furlough before the end of the year, so he decided to inquire at company headquarters to see if he could arrange leave. After talking with the sergeant on duty, he found that he was in fact among the next group up for a furlough. The sergeant assured him there would be no problem getting leave and that the paperwork would be ready next Monday.

That evening he started to plan the trip in his mind.

Lynchburg is only about 300 miles away. If I show my furlough paper, I know I can ride the train for a special rate of one and a half cents per mile. The round trip ticket will cost me about nine dollars. Even though the ticket is going to be expensive, I have enough money on hand, so that's not a problem. I can save money by picking up free food along the way at one of the trackside canteens. I should probably count on the train ride home taking at least 12 hours.

That night, he wrote a letter to his mom telling her of his plans and that he should be home late Monday night or early Tuesday.

On Monday morning, Doss went to headquarters to pick up his furlough paperwork. As he waited, he noticed Lt. Dollenmayer standing at the back of the room. When Doss reached the front of the line, the sergeant sorted through the stack of forms, found the completed paperwork and handed it over. As soon as Doss had the form in his hand, Dollenmayer made his move.

"What's that you got there, Doss?"

"It's my furlough paper Lieutenant."

"Let me see it."

Doss reluctantly handed it over.

"I just remembered something, Private. Army regulations say that no man may receive a furlough until he has completed all scheduled training. I don't think you have qualified on the carbine yet, have you Doss?"

"No, Sir."

With that, Lieutenant Dollenmayer slowly ripped the paperwork in half before handing it back.

"Now look, I'm a reasonable man. You agree to carry a rifle; I'll go ahead and let you go on your furlough. Otherwise, I don't think you'll be stepping foot off an Army base until this war is over."

Dollenmayer walked back to where he was before and returned with a carbine. Holding it straight out he said, "Doss, take this rifle."

Then he let go of it. Doss did not make the slightest move to take the rifle, and Dollenmayer had to awkwardly grab back hold of it to keep it from hitting the floor.

"Sir, my conscience will not allow me to bear arms. All that is on my record. I don't touch guns Sir, but if you'll give me a chance, I'll try to be as good of a soldier as you, without using a gun."

Dollenmayer's face turned a bright shade of red.

"Private Doss, I'm giving you a direct order to take this rifle."

Once again, he held the rifle out toward Doss and let go. Once again, the lieutenant was forced to grab the rifle to prevent it from hitting the floor.

"Doss, I am now court marshaling you for refusing to obey a direct order."

During the exchange, a major had come in to headquarters and was watching the standoff.

"Lt. Dollenmayer, what's going on here? You know Private Doss is a conscientious objector and is exempt from carrying weapons. It's right in his records."

"I just don't understand this Major. It's not right."

Instead of answering the lieutenant, the major turned to Doss.

"Go on back to your quarters Private."

When Doss walked out of the room, none of the other enlisted men would look him in the eye. He assumed that they hated him for his beliefs, but in reality, the soldiers were embarrassed from having witnessed the way Dollenmayer had mistreated him.

As Doss was heading back to his quarters, he passed by the PX and saw that one of the phone booths was empty. He hesitated a second before stepping inside to get change from the clerk. Then he came back out again, entered the phone booth, picked up the receiver, dropped in a nickel and dialed 0.

"Operator."

"I'd like to make a long distance call."

"One moment please."

"Long distance."

"I'd like to make a call to Lynchburg Virginia."

"Number please."

"One, nine, eight, one."

"Would you like to hold while I make the connection or shall I call you back?"

"I'm at a phone booth, so I'll wait."

"One moment please."

His mind wandered during the ten minutes it took for the call to be connected. At last, he heard his mom answer before the operator came back on the line.

"Deposit two dollars and eighty cents for 10 minutes please."

After listening for him to place the coins into the phone, the operator disconnected, and Doss could hear more clearly.

"Mom, it's me."

"Desmond. What in the world? Why are you calling on the telephone? Is something wrong? Are you alright?"

All he could choke out was, "Mom, I can't come home."

The weight of everything he had endured in the Army seemed to come crashing down on him at once. For the first time during his military service, he began to cry.

"Desmond what's wrong? Desmond. Please answer me Desmond."

Doss could only stare at the payphone as his mother repeatedly called his name. This continued until his dad interrupted her to ask something in the background.

"It's Desmond. Something's terribly wrong. He's crying."

Then he heard his dad ask, *"Do you want me to talk to him?"*

"Not yet," his mom replied. *"Let me try one more time."*

"Desmond you've got to answer me." Then she too began to cry.

Hearing his mom sobbing on the phone was the thing that forced him back to reality. He proceeded to pour out the whole story of what was going on with Lt. Dollenmayer and the fear of how he might be facing a court martial. He ended the call by saying, "I love you Mom. Please pray for me." After the call, Doss went back to his quarters feeling a little better. He always did, after talking with his mom.

After they hung up, Mr. and Mrs. Doss got down on their knees and began to pray for their son.

"Dear Heavenly Father, You know Desmond is in trouble. We trust that you have only good planned for our son's life, so we ask that you protect Desmond and intervene in this situation. In Jesus name Amen."

After they finished praying, Desmond's dad said to his wife, "Maybe I should contact the National Service Commission in Washington. I read somewhere that Elder Haynes is a board member, and since he's an Adventist, maybe he can help us out."

The next morning the 307th Infantry Commander, Colonel Stephen Hamilton, received a call from Washington, D.C.

"Colonel Hamilton? This is Carlyle Haynes, Chairman of the War Service Commission. I've received word that you're having some sort of problem up there with a Private Doss. Is there a need for me to come investigate or do you think you might be able to straighten the situation out on your own?"

Colonel Hamilton realized he needed to think quickly before he answered. *Whatever the War Service Commission is, it sounds important. I better be careful not to get on the wrong side of this Haynes fellow.*

"Thank you for calling Chairman Haynes. We were just working on the situation you called about. I'm certain I will have it rectified by the end of the day."

"I'm glad to hear that Colonel Hamilton. I'll be sure to mention your name when the topic comes up again. Thank you for your help in the matter. Goodbye."

As soon as Colonel Hamilton hung up the phone, he called out to his aid.

"Captain West, come in here."

"Yes, Colonel."

"Find out who Private Doss is and what in the world is going on that would rate a call from the War Service Commission."

"The War Service Commission, Sir?"

"That's right. Now whatever's going on, use my name to straighten it out by the end of the day. Ream out whoever caused this foul-up. Make sure they understand I don't want any more calls from Chairman Haynes."

"Yes Sir."

Later that day, Doss was on his hands and knees scrubbing the kitchen floor when he received word to report back to the medical unit. Waiting for him was Captain Webster.

"Doss, you're back in the medics, and this time it's for good."

"Thank you Captain."

"Don't thank me. Thank that big shot you know with influence in Washington."

"Captain, I'm due a furlough, and my brother is about to ship off to the Navy. Can I take it now?"

"As in now, do you mean today?"

"Yes, Captain."

"I'm sorry Doss, there's no way I could arrange a furlough that quick. You can have one before the end of the year, but since you just transferred back, you'll have to go to the end of the line. About the best I could do is give you a pass, but it'll count toward the days the Army owes you and then you won't be eligible for a furlough anymore."

"I guess I don't have much choice. I'll take the pass. Can you at least give me five days?"

"For a man with connections like you've got, that shouldn't be a problem. Come on. We'll take care if it right now."

When Doss returned from his five-day leave, he found that in his absence Chairman Haynes had sent a letter signed by President Franklin Roosevelt to Colonel Hamilton. Haynes had also sent a copy of the letter to Doss.

Dear Colonel Hamilton,

The President has explicitly defined noncombatant service in Executive Order No. 8606, dated December 6, 1940. I have enclosed a copy.

1. By virtue of authority contained in section 5 (g) of the Selective Training and Service Act of 1940, approved September 16, 1940, whereby it is provided:
Nothing contained in this Act shall be construed to require any person to be subject to combatant training and service in the land or naval forces of the United States who, by reason of religious training and belief, is conscientiously opposed to participation in war in any form.

Any such person claiming such exemption from combatant training and service because of such conscientious objections, whose claim is sustained by the local board, shall, if he is inducted into the land or naval forces under this Act, be assigned to noncombatant service as defined by the President. I hereby declare that the following military service is noncombatant service:

(1) Service in any unit which is unarmed at all times.
(2) Service in the medical department wherever performed.
(3) Service in any unit or installation the primary function of which does not require the use of arms in combat provided the individual's assignment within such unit or installation does not require him to bear arms or to be trained in their use.

"I further declare that noncombatant training consists of training in all military subjects except marksmanship, combat firing, target practices, and those subjects relating to the employment of weapons.

2. Persons inducted into the military service under the above act whose claim to exemption from combatant training and service because of conscientious objection has been sustained will receive noncombatant training and be assigned to noncombatant military service as defined in paragraph one.

Franklin D. Roosevelt
The White House
Dec. 6, 1940.

If I can be of any more assistance, please contact me.

Carlyle B. Haynes
Chairman, War Service Commission

Doss returned from leave just as the 307th was starting their first training cycle with amphibious training. The course began with lectures about the differences between boats and ships, where the soldiers learned that boats are small enough to be carried on ships. They were told about day-to-day shipboard life. They learned the navy called the floor of a ship a deck, a latrine a head, and that food aboard a ship is prepared in a galley not a kitchen. After a series of lectures, they began to practice climbing up and down elevated platforms using cargo nets. Finally, they traveled to Camp Bradford, Virginia to practice all they had learned with real landing boats.

The final stage of amphibious training was held at Solomon's Bay, Maryland where the entire regiment was loaded onto transport ships. The men went through several exercises during which they made practice landings, "captured" beachheads, unloaded their supplies on the beach and then moved inland where they set up camps using only the supplies landed from the ships. By the time they finished their amphibious training, it was well into November, and the water was starting to get cold. The men realized they were lucky to have been scheduled to go through amphibious training first. They felt very sorry for the groups who would have to practice beach landings in December.

Next the 307th was transported by open top trucks to the mountains of the West Virginia Maneuver Area. When they arrived at the tent camp near Elkins, West Virginia, they were still wearing the same summer weight cotton khaki uniforms that they had been issued at Camp Hyder. As soon as the trucks came to a stop, the freezing soldiers jumped out and landed in over 7 inches of fresh wet snow.

After being allotted warm weather clothing and artic sleeping bags, the training began. The goal was to give the men some practical experience in mountainous terrain, not to make them into elite mountain troops. In 1943, the United States did not possess enough soldiers to have the luxury of developing specialized divisions equivalent to the German 1st Mountain Division or Italian 3rd Alpine Division, both of which were dedicated to mountain combat. Instead, the American Army relied on familiarizing "general purpose divisions" with diverse combat environments. After they completed their stateside training, it was hoped that the American soldier would be able to perform reasonably well in whatever theater of war they were sent to.

During their time in the mountains, Doss and the other men learned how to load and carry packboards weighed down with up to one-hundred pounds of gear and then lugged them up and down steep trails. They also camped without tents at high elevations, utilizing only their sleeping bags on the snow covered ground. During one of the overnight camping trips, when the temperature dropped below zero, one of the men was heard to say that he wished they were all back at Camp Hyder. His suggestion was quickly shouted down by the majority.

While in West Virginia, the men spent several days learning how to tie knots. This was a very important part of mountain training because a man's life would depend on his knot tying skills later in the course as he used ropes to descend from cliffs or cross ravines.

On the first day of rope training, the lieutenant in charge was watching Doss and noticed that he was able to quickly tie each knot on the first try.

"Doss, come over here."

"Yes, Sir."

"You're pretty good at knots. Were you an Eagle Scout?"

"No, Sir. I learned to tie knots in the Junior Missionary Volunteers, which is sort of like the Boy Scouts, and then later when I worked as a carpenter at Newport shipyard I used ropes almost every day."

"Well, anyway, I can see you already know your knots. Look around, and help out Sergeant Brock with the men who are having problems."

"Yes, Sir."

Doss spent the rest of the day demonstrating and coaching the other men as they struggled to learn how to tie the specialized mountaineering knots. Two man teams paired up to share each end of a long rope, which they used to practice. As Doss went from team to team, he would double up the middle of their rope and use it to demonstrate the knot they were working on. Doss was helping two men who were having trouble learning how to tie a bowline. First he doubled up the middle of their rope, made a bight and then said as he demonstrated, "This is how I remember the bowline. A rabbit comes out of his hole, goes around the tree, and then back down his hole."

His students saw the puzzled look on his face, when what resulted was a bowline with two loops instead of just the one he had expected. Of course, the men used the opportunity to give Doss a little good-natured ribbing.

"What's the matter? Trying to make a pet rabbit out of your rope? That knot looks like a cute little bunny with two floppy ears."

"Okay guys, go ahead and laugh it up, but just tie your knots on the end of the rope like I showed you and it'll come out alright."

As the other men continued to practice, Doss was intrigued with the knot he had just tied.

I've never seen a knot like that before, he thought.

As he continued to circulate and demonstrate different knots among the men, Doss couldn't get the strange double loop bowline out of his mind. He tied it over and over until, by the end of the day, he could do it without even thinking.

After they had finished rotating through all the training locations, General Bruce assigned each regiment an area or camp to clean up. The 307th was sent back to the Solomon Island Maneuver Area. There, they spent several days removing cans and other junk, which the 77th had left behind. They also worked to fill in foxholes, repair every fence they had damaged and finally to clean up the buildings that had been used by the division.

It was during this time that, because of General Bruce's obsession that the men always wear their leggings and helmet liners and carefully clean up every camp before leaving, he acquired the nickname "Old Man Leggings, Liners and Landscape."

The 307th coat of arms consisted of a broken chain in front of a mailed gauntlet grasping crossed oak branches, which symbolized the drive through the Argonne Forest in World War I and the rescue of trapped American troops. The motto across the bottom of the shield was "Clear the Way." After working for a week cleaning up the Solomon Islands, some of the men suggested they change the coat of arms to crossed brooms and rakes but leave the motto the same.

By February, the entire division was back together at Camp Pickett, where they worked to complete the Preparation for Overseas Movement requirements. The men were instructed to pack up and ship home all radios, cameras, civilian clothes and electric razors as well as other personal belongings, after which, they went through a series of showdown inspections to make sure they still possessed all of the government issued equipment that had been assigned to them and none of the prohibited items. All equipment and clothing was then marked with the first initial of the soldier's last name and the last four digits of his Army serial number. If any government issued equipment came up missing, the men were required to purchase replacements. They received shots, underwent dental and physical inspections and attended courses on censorship rules. There was a weapons check and they tested their gas masks in a tear-gas chamber. The men were offered forms for filling out a Last Will and Testament. It was not a requirement to fill one out, and most of the unmarried men chose not to. They were advised to write final uncensored letters to their love ones explaining they might not be heard from for a period of up to 30 days.

The men attended farewell parties both off and on the base. Doss and some of the other married men were allowed to say goodbye to their wives during a scheduled overnight visit in one of the camp guesthouses.

On 6 March, military police surrounded the base, and all the men were restricted to camp. No phone calls or letters were allowed, in or out. Two days later, the first empty troop trains arrived to start the men on their way to war.

March 18, 1944
Headed to Camp Stoneman
Replacement and Reclassification Depot

The 77th Infantry Division had become so proficient at moving cross-country by train, that this time, it almost seemed routine. When the men of the Statue of Liberty Division boarded the troop trains at Camp Pickett, they were happy because they were made up of comfortable, modern passenger cars unlike some of the other antiques they had been subjected too in the past. After the loaded trains passed through the switchyard, they headed west.

As the train chugged along, Doss was in one of the kitchen cars along with some other soldiers on KP duty. They were peeling potatoes and looking out the door watching the scenery go by, when Doss realized the train was entering his hometown of Lynchburg, Virginia. He knew the tracks ran right next to his dad's house and that he regularly stepped out onto his front porch to watch the trains pass by.

"I don't believe it," he told the other soldiers. "My dad lives right next to the tracks. I might get to see him!"

Hastily, the men gathered up brooms, mops, and towels, anything they could find to wave out the door in hopes of drawing the attention of Doss's dad. "I see him," he shouted. Sure enough, his dad was standing out on the porch, looking up in their direction as the train passed by. Doss starting jumping up and down and yelling, "Dad, it's me, Desmond!"

Even though he had waved back at the crazy acting soldiers, Desmond could tell by the perplexed look on his dad's face that he had not recognized his own son. At that instant, he had the terrible feeling he might never see the people he loved again. Desmond desperately wanted his dad to know that it was him who had been waving. He grabbed a paper napkin and quickly wrote, "Dear Mom and Dad, It was me. I'm on my way now. Pray for me." He tied his handkerchief around it, and a small potato for weight, and then wrote, "Deliver to: William T. Doss, 1814 Easley Avenue" on the outside. Hoping that if he tossed it off the train, someone would find the note and take it to his dad, Desmond decided to wait until the kitchen car passed over a road crossing. Seeing a man standing on the sidewalk, waiting for the train to pass by, Desmond waved, pointed at the note and lobbed it underhand to the man's outstretched hands.

After the excitement of passing through his hometown, Doss used his free time on the train to sleep, read his Bible and catch up on his Sabbath School Study Guides. The men enjoyed loafing during the trip, and some of them even made a game out of trying to trick the railroad porters into telling them where the train was headed. Of course the porters were sworn to secrecy, and the only answer they got from them was, "I'm sorry sir, that's the only thing I'm not allowed to answer." After a while, the porters grew tired of the soldier's game and decided to put a stop to it. From then on, if asked about the train's destination the porter would put on an exaggerated Uncle Remus dialect and answer, "They don't tell us where were going, but I heard some of the officers talkin' about Camp Hyder. Maybe that's where you all headed." The mere mention of Camp Hyder was enough to put an end to the soldier's amusement.

The men were on the train for five days before it arrived at Camp Stoneman, California. The camp had 346 barracks and could process 20,000 troops at a time. It was the largest troop staging area on the west coast and was the last stop in the United States for most soldiers headed to war in the Pacific.

The arrival of a troop train set off a flurry of activity. Soon after they arrived, the men were given a complete medical exam to determine if they were fit for overseas duty. Some of them needed to have their immunizations updated and any other last minute medical care they needed was provided. Each man was required to go on at least one 10-mile hike to check his fitness level and the condition of his feet. If a soldier needed new glasses, he was issued two pairs. The dental department's forty-five chairs were kept busy almost around the clock pulling teeth and filling cavities because the Army had learned that something as simple as a bad tooth could knock a soldier out of commission. For this reason, every man was given a very complete dental examination.

The accounting department made final pay allotments, and the soldier had one last chance to draw-up or revise his Last Will and Testament.

Next came a complete clothing and equipment inspection. Shoes were carefully examined for signs of wear, and even the shoelaces were checked. Any shortage or defect was made up from the camp stock. Every soldier's weapon was test fired by an expert armorer. It had to work without a hint of malfunction or it was repaired or replaced.

The men attended refresher lectures on mail censorship, security regulations, and how to conduct themselves aboard a troop ship. Demonstrations were given showing the correct way to abandon ship. Every man was required to attend a first aid class each day. After four days of frantic activity, the men were ready. The next day they would leave Camp Stoneman and head off to war.

MARCH 24, 1944
SAN FRANCISCO EMBARCADERO AT FORT MASON

Early in the morning, just before sunrise, the troops were marched down Harbor Street to the Pittsburg waterfront where they entered a covered dock after passing beneath a huge sign which read, "Under this portal pass the best damn soldiers in the world." There they boarded army harbor boats for the three-hour trip down the San Joaquin River to the San Francisco Embarcadero at Fort Mason.

Although they had not been specifically told, the men had figured out they were heading to war in the Pacific because it was only logical that a ship leaving from San Francisco was headed toward Japan and not Germany. Most of them were apprehensive. Surprisingly, many were also excited, not only about finally being headed into combat but for a more simple reason. For almost all of them, this would be their first trip aboard an ocean going ship.

Private Byran, a tall lanky soldier from the mountains of Tennessee, was particularly enthusiastic because as a boy he had loved to build model boats. "I wonder if we'll git to ride the Queen. You know they're a use'n' her to transport troops now. Wouldn't it be somethin' if the Army pays for me to git a ride on the *Queen Mary*?"

Tennessee's obsession with the *Queen Mary* started a lively discussion about what life would be like aboard a troopship. They would find out soon enough. As the ferry pulled up to the dock, an announcement came over the loudspeakers: *"Attention all troops. Prepare to disembark. Attention all troops. Prepare to disembark."*

After they left the ferry, the soldiers found themselves standing on Pier 45. "Hey, where's our ship?"

"Shut up Byran. You'll get to see your stinkin' ship soon enough."

"Come on guys, I'm just a mite excited. That's all."

The troops were marched less than a mile to a huge warehouse building at Fort Mason. When they arrived, the Red Cross was waiting inside with coffee and donuts. Many of the men tried, unsuccessfully, to chat up the Red Cross girls while they waited. It was hard for them to be charming because every soldier was wearing a helmet, which had been chalked with an embarkation number, berthing location and bunk number before they left Camp Stoneman. In addition, each man was carrying the rest of his personal gear, which in the case of an infantryman, included a backpack, duffle bag, and rifle. All this equipment added up to almost 100 pounds.

After about an hour, word came to begin boarding. A line of soldiers was formed, which then snaked out of the building, up a steep gangplank and onto the ship. The line wound its way through the ship, down stairways and past doors. Every so often, a sailor would stop the line and send the next group of men with the same chalk marking into a certain berthing area. As

Doss got near the front of the line, he could hear a sailor reading the bunk numbers written on their helmets. "190, 191, 192. You're the last one," he said to Doss. "Welcome to your new home for the next week or so."

When Doss descended the stairs, he saw that he was in a room about 60 by 60 feet square. He noticed that there weren't any lockers or a storage area. There were bunks of a sort made out of pipes. Each section was four bunks high with about 18 inches of vertical clearance between bunks. Doss counted 48 of the 4-bunk assemblies in the room. There were no mattresses, just pieces of canvas laced to the pipes with ropes. Since he was the last person in the room Doss ended up with the top bunk furthest from the stairs. To climb up he had to use the lower bed frames as a ladder. Once he got into the rack, another soldier handed up his gear. Doss and the other medics, of course, did not have a rifle like the infantrymen, but they did have their medic bags, which took up more space than a rifle.

As Doss was beginning to think about where to store all his equipment, a sailor came down the stairs and yelled, "Listen up army. This ship is the USS *General W. M. Black,* and it's going to take you wherever it is you're going. Right now that's a Navy secret, but you'll find out once we're underway. You're located on the third deck, forward troop berthing. Remember that. Now get all your gear off the deck and into your rack. Always keep the passageways clear of gear. If you have to get off the ship fast, you don't want to be tripping over anything. Also, the troop head is through the two doors in the front of the berth. That's what you army boys call the latrine. Until you hear otherwise, you are to stay in this berth or the latrine. Nowhere else. Your officers are getting the drill on everything you need to know, and you'll find out the rest from them." When he finished, the sailor went down the stairs to the next level, and Doss could hear him repeating the same speech to the men below.

One of the soldiers had already returned from exploring the latrine area. "Good news, they got forty toilets in there. There won't be any waiting in line for us." What the soldier didn't know was that their berth had the only direct connection to the latrine. The men in other berths had to climb stairs to a higher deck and then come down a different set of stairs to reach it. Instead of 200 men sharing this one latrine it would have to serve closer to 1,000.

Before long, the same sailor came back up the stairs. "Hey sailor, are we gonna be stuck down here for the entire trip?"

He laughed then answered, "This isn't a slave ship. Soon as we get all you army pukes squared away you can come up on deck." His comment set off an eruption of cussing. "Hey, what's that all about?" he asked.

"Say Popeye, what'a'ya mean, calling us army pukes?" yelled back one of the soldiers.

The sailor, who was already retreating up the stairs, stopped and shouted down, "You'll find out soon enough, army."

The men were eager for the ship to get underway, but as it turned out, it was not scheduled to leave until the next morning.

After a long night of trying to sleep, Doss began to feel vibrations and hear noises indicating that they were moving. The ship's horn sounded several times during the next few minutes, rousing anyone who was still asleep.

Suddenly, the sailor from the day before came down the stairs and shouted, "Whoever wants to go on deck-" Before he could finish, the men pushed him aside and rushed up the stairs. Men streamed out of doors all over the ship. Soon, the deck became so tightly packed that it was hard to move.

Doss arrived on deck just in time to see the ship make a left turn toward the Golden Gate Bridge. As the *General Black* passed beneath the bridge, the captain sounded a long blast on the ship's horn. Doss imagined that the ship was roaring, *Watch out Japs here we come!*

March 25, 1944
At Sea aboard USS General W. M. Black

After the *General W. M. Black* cleared the Golden Gate Bridge and began to pick up speed, Doss and the other soldiers set out to reconnoiter the ship. With so many soldiers on deck, moving around was difficult, so some of the men decided to head down and scout the lower levels. Doss chose to remain on deck, because he wanted to breathe as much fresh air as possible.

For much of the morning, Doss wandered around and explored the top side of the ship. He quickly learned that many areas were restricted and army personnel were not allowed. He had rightly assumed the bridge was off limits, but he also found out that soldiers were not allowed onto the gun platforms. It was likewise forbidden to enter the engine room, and the lifeboat deck was reserved for use by officers only.

From his observations, Doss discovered the ship had four large and many smaller guns. By listening in on a conversation between some infantrymen and the navy gunners, he learned the big guns were referred to as 5"/38 caliber or just five thirty-eight for short. The sailors had explained that 5-inch, was the diameter of the projectile and caliber described how long the barrel was. One caliber equaled one projectile diameter, so 38 calibers meant the gun barrel was 190 inches long. They also said that by choosing different shells, the big gun could be used against aircraft or surface targets. The gun crew explained that hitting a fast moving plane with the five thirty-eight was so difficult it took, on average, almost 1,000 rounds to score a hit. That was why so many smaller anti-aircraft guns were scattered around the ship.

While listening to the discussion, Doss noticed it was almost time for him to return to the berthing area because his group was scheduled to eat at 1000 hours. He had to hurry to be on time. After a short lecture and receiving a meal ticket, the men formed a line and headed toward the galley. They followed a path up the stairs leading out of the berth, then across the deck, before starting down another set of stairs, which led to the mess room. Before long, the line slowed and eventually stopped. As the men moved forward one step at a time, they began to detect the smell of food. Since the last thing the soldiers had eaten were the donuts passed out by the Red Cross girls, their mouths began to water in response to the delicious aromas. As they passed through the serving line, their trays were loaded with a variety of food. Grinning navy cooks piled them high with fried potatoes, bacon and eggs, and pancakes with butter and milk.

As the cooks dished out food they also dished out comments. "Here soldier have some more bacon."

"Make sure you eat plenty of potatoes."

"Don't forget to use a lot of fresh butter on those pancakes."

After receiving their food, the men proceeded to long stainless steel tables, which were constructed with rolled up edges on all sides to keep the trays from sliding off in rough seas. There were no chairs, so eating was strictly a stand up affair.

Soon after the men sat their trays down and began to eat, a strange thing started to happen. The men, who had felt famished moments before, started to feel something different. The slight rolling motion of the ship combined with the smell and taste of food began to take its toll on a few of the soldiers. Before long, the sound and smell of vomit was detected. As soon as the first man threw up, soldiers all around the galley instantly lost their appetites. They abandoned their food trays and rushed upward toward the open deck, trying to reach the ships rails before they too became ill.

Doss felt fortunate. He was not feeling seasick. He reasoned that except for the bacon, which he had turned down in the serving line, this meal had a lot of good food he could eat. He had always made it a point to "eat while the eatin' was good." Since there was no telling what would be served for the next meal, he decided to stay and polish off his breakfast.

By the time he had finished eating, cleaned his tray and made his way onto deck, the ship was encountering bigger waves. It wasn't long before Doss started to feel weak. A sweat broke out on his forehead, and he noticed a gurgling in his stomach. He began to feel quite queasy. His legs felt like they were made of rubber as he made his way over to the rail. He leaned over. That was when Doss realized the mistake he had made. Eating breakfast had done nothing more than provide him with some food to feed the fish. As he leaned over the side, about to heave his guts out, he heard some of the sailors laughing, and then he knew. The last thing he remembered hearing before spewing his food out all over the side of the ship was a sailor jeering, "Look at all the army pukes. First sign of waves and they're hugging the rails."

MARCH 26, 1944
TROOP SHIP TO HAWAII

After spending considerable time leaning over the rail, Doss figured the entire contents of his stomach was now floating in the Pacific, so it might be wise to go back to his bunk and lie down. By the time he made his way back to the troop berth, it became obvious that most of the other soldiers were just as sea sick as he was. Looking around, he saw that half of the bunks were occupied by pale, sweating soldiers. There was a fair amount of vomit on the floor, and several unaffected men on mop duty were trying to clean it up. It was clear that some of the men had been below decks when their seasickness hit by the noise coming from the adjoining latrine area. Doss shuddered when he imagined what it was like in there right now. He sure didn't want to have to find out. Lucky for him, his bunk was far away from the smell emanating from the entrance to the troop head.

After Doss made it to his bunk, he climbed up and laid down. Unfortunately, being located near the front of the ship amplified the movement of the waves. Every time the transport headed down and slammed into the next wave, it felt like an elevator was dropping out from under him. He found that keeping his eyes closed gave him some relief and praying gave him a little more. One of the ventilator openings was located over his feet, so he changed position to allow the air to blow directly on his face. The cool air helped and since he was exhausted from all of the vomiting, he fell asleep. When he woke up several hours later, he felt a little better and decided to try a sip of water from his canteen. Doss was glad for the rule requiring soldiers to keep their canteens at least half full at all times while on a troop ship. Otherwise, he would have to venture into the latrine for a drink and that was a place he would rather not go right then.

As soon as he swallowed a capful of water, the seasickness hit again. Now Doss felt he had no other choice than to head for the latrine. After he made his way inside, he was greeted by a sight and smell that he would never forget. Puke covered much of the floor. The two urinals were full and overflowing with it. As the ship rose and fell with each wave, a mixture of vomit and water sloshed from one end of the floor to the other. Several soldiers and sailors with mops were working in vain, trying to keep up with the mess. Doss wondered if the mop-wielding sailors were being punished for some infraction of Navy rules. He could not imagine anything short of mutiny that would justify vomit cleaning duty. Doss decided that if he had to throw up, he would just use his helmet and clean it out later. He quickly turned around and headed back to his bunk.

The next day, several of the unaffected soldiers took pity on the suffering men and brought them a box of soda crackers, which they had smuggled from the mess room. They said some sailors had told them the crackers would help settle their stomachs. When the bunk bound men recalled the sadistic way the navy cooks had smiled as they piled food on their trays, knowing full well they would soon throw it all back up, they were reluctant to say the least, to try the cracker cure. Because Doss was a medic, several of the men asked him what he thought.

"Well, I guess we have to start eating again sometime, and crackers seem safe enough to me. I'll tell you what, I'll try 'em first."

Doss took several crackers and slowly started nibbling on them but then shook his head in disbelief when he heard several of the men trying to bet on whether or not he could hold them down.

"Fifty cents says he throws up."

"I'll bet a quarter he can't eat 10."

Doss supposed some people would gamble on anything. "What's wrong with you guys? Don't you know that when you win a bet, the other guy gets sore at you? Besides, if I can hold these crackers down, we'll all win."

His admonishment tamped down the gambling talk a little and besides, the way the men's stomachs felt, no one was willing to cover the bet anyway. When the excitement of wagering on the outcome fizzled out, the men began to observe Doss as if he was some kind of science experiment. One man kept time. "A minute. Two minutes. Five."

After he had been able to tolerate the crackers for ten full minutes, someone piped up, "Give me some of those."

Others joined in.

"I'll take a few over here."

"I want some."

Soon the cracker supply was depleted, and a few men offered to go and try to get some more. Doss was starting to feel good enough to leave his bunk, so he decided to tag along. As they approached the galley, he wondered how they were going to finagle more since it was not a mealtime.

When they walked in, Doss was surprised to see several cooks standing behind large open crates of crackers. The cook who seemed to be in charge piped up, "Sorry about the fun we had at you soldier boys expense, but if you're prone to sea sickness, there ain't nothing you can do to stop it. Don't feel too bad though, most of us got sick our first time at sea. Most people start feeling better in a day or so, but you got to let the puking run its course. Now, it's strictly against Navy regulations to take food out of the mess room, but I bet you army boys are starting to get your appetite back. Who's to say how many crackers you might eat once you get out of my sight over by them mess tables, if you know what I mean. Spread the word that the cook has plenty of crackers, and for today only, he ain't gonna pay no attention to the rules."

Doss and the other soldiers just stood there until the cook bellowed, "Well, what are you boys waiting for? Load up and move out!"

By the end of the third day, most of the troops were over their seasickness and back to roaming. Doss was able to finish exploring the ship, and since his stomach had settled down, he was enjoying the navy chow. He reckoned he had lost at least five pounds from his bout with seasickness and was eager to see if the navy food could put some of that weight back on. What he didn't enjoy, was the long wait in line to reach the mess room. Most of the men had gotten their appetite back and were spending more time eating to make up for the meals they had missed.

April 1, 1944
Hawaii
Jungle Warfare Training

General Bruce had traveled ahead by air and was waiting at the Honolulu docks for the ships to arrive. On 1 April 1944, the first of his troops reached Hawaii. He watched them debark the ships and then board trucks and trains, which were standing by to transport them to camps on the northeast side of Oahu.

The 305th Regiment was housed at Camp Pali, while Division Headquarters and the 306th Regiment quartered at Fort Hase. Doss and the 307th Regimental Combat Team, along with the 504th Anti-aircraft Artillery Battalion, boarded an OR&L Co. steam train for the six-hour, 40-mile trip to the Army Air Base at Kahuku, near the northeast corner of Oahu.

Kahuku Air Base consisted of a two-strip landing field located within feet of the beach. During their stay, the 307th was responsible for patrolling the beach and manning some of the static defense works, which included machine gun pillboxes and anti-aircraft guns. They also worked to improve the fortifications by clearing brush and stringing barbed wire.

While in Hawaii, the 77th Division rotated its companies through a two-week course at the Unit Jungle Combat Training Center. There, they practiced jungle first aid and evacuation, hand to hand combat, assault with bayonets, patrolling and ambushing, hip shooting at pop-up targets, construction and passage of wire entanglements, booby traps and demolitions, stream crossing, and jungle living.

Then they went through a refresher course on how to attack pillboxes and fight in the close quarters of towns and villages. During the training, they worked with live ammunition and high explosives, which presented a real possibility of death or injury if a mishap were to occur, but with almost two years of instruction under their belts, the men felt comfortable around the danger. General Bruce was impressed with the readiness of his men. As they casually went through the training exercises, nearby explosions and bullets whizzing overhead didn't seem to bother them in the least.

While at the jungle school, Doss and the other medics were told that they should not wear the Red Cross insignia in combat. Reports had come back from the front lines that, unlike the Germans, Japanese troops did not honor the Geneva Convention. In fact, experience showed the Japanese actually went out of their way to kill medics. It was for this reason the Army made the decision to arm medical personnel operating in the Pacific theater. The instructors made one last appeal, trying to get Doss to agree to carry a weapon, but he refused.

After completing the Jungle Training School, the troops reviewed amphibious assault procedures by making three practice landings on Makua beach. Although the men had already received beach assault training in Virginia, no one complained about repeating the drill in the warm clear waters of Hawaii. There they were introduced to the new LVT (Landing Vehicles Tracked), which was a tracked boat that was able to climb out of the ocean over coral reefs or other obstacles using its tank-like treads.

Soon after arriving in Hawaii, division headquarters sent word to begin freely issuing passes to men who wanted to visit nearby towns. They also organized large group trips to Honolulu and many of the spectacular beaches. During this time, Doss approached his sergeant with a request for a pass to go over to the nearby air base.

"Doss, why in the world would you want a pass to go visit some other Army base?"

"Well now Sergeant, I got the idea I might find another Seventh-day Adventist over there who could tell me where the nearest church is."

"Okay Doss, I'll give you a pass, but I doubt you're gonna find one of your kind of churches in Hawaii."

When Doss took the pass from his sergeant, he thought about saying that since he had grown up reading stories about Adventist missionaries in Hawaii, he was sure he would find a church, but in the end, he decided not to.

Doss set off down the dirt road toward the ocean and in a short while reached the air base, approached the military policeman on duty at the gate and handed over his pass. The MP looked over the pass then looked over Doss.

"Privates from a different division don't normally just walk up to my gate and try to get in. What's the deal? You got a brother or a buddy stationed here?"

Doss answered, "I'm looking for someone, but I don't know a name. I'm trying to find another Seventh-day Adventist, so I can ask him if he knows where our nearest church is."

"Sorry Soldier, I don't even know what a Seventh-day Adventist is, so I can't help you out."

"How about this? Do you know someone who has a pass to leave almost every Friday night or Saturday morning and always comes back to base sober?"

"Since you put it that way, there are a few like that, from the hospital and one's a fireman. The fire station's near the beach and the hospital's at the end of the road to the left."

Doss decided to try the fire station first since it was closest and besides, he had always liked fire trucks. As he walked inside the station and looked around, he noticed a soldier with his head in the engine compartment working on one of the trucks.

"Excuse me. The guard at the gate said one of you firemen might be a Seventh-day Adventist."

The man didn't bother to look up from his work as he called out, "McCoy, some guy out here lookin' for an Adventist."

A soldier walked out of a side room and approached Doss, "You an Adventist?"

"Sure am, I'm Private Doss, and I'm looking for someone to tell me where the nearest church is."

"Well, I'm the one to ask. You've got three choices. They're all okay, but the biggest is the Keeaumoku Street church in Honolulu. That's where I go the most."

"How'd I get there?"

"You have to take the Friday evening train 'cause the ride takes too long to leave on Sabbath morning. The church will feed you and let you stay overnight for free. If you can get a pass, meet me here Friday, and we'll go together. But the thing is, I've got to head back a little before sundown on Sabbath, 'cause I've got to be on duty at midnight."

"Sounds okay. I trade duty with a Sunday keeper, so I'll come back with you. What time Friday?"

"1800 would be good. We can meet at the fire station, if that's okay by you."

Doss said good-by to McCoy and headed back to camp. Before he returned to his quarters, he decided to swing by to see the sergeant about a church pass. When he was about to knock on the door, the sergeant walked out. "Say Doss, how was your trip to the air base?"

"Well Sergeant, I was just coming to talk to you about that. I found a fireman who's an Adventist. He said there's a church in Honolulu, but I have to take the train on Friday night to make it in time for Saturday morning church. You know Glenn and I always trade, so would it be okay for me to have a pass for Friday night and all day Saturday?"

"Doss, I guess by now it shouldn't surprise me that you found a church in Hawaii. I know what your orders say, so come back tomorrow and I'll have your pass."

The next day, he picked up his pass and met McCoy for the trip into Honolulu. During the train ride, the fireman introduced Doss to several other Adventists from the air base. This was a nice surprise for Doss, since as far as he knew, he was the only Adventist in the 77th Division, and he was not used to going to church with other men from the Army. It was a pleasant change to be able to talk with other soldiers who shared his beliefs during the ride to church.

Once they arrived in Honolulu, McCoy led the way to the church. Even though they arrived very late Friday night, a deacon was waiting there to assign the soldiers a place to spend the night. Since the nearby church school was already filled to capacity, Doss and the other men from the air base were directed to go to Jon and Lena Bowman's house.

When McCoy heard the name Bowman, he got a big smile on his face. "Boy Doss, did we ever get lucky. Sleeping on cots in the school is okay, but the Bowman's treat us just like family. I can't wait for you to meet them."

When the five men arrived at the house, Brother Bowman was on the front porch, sitting in a chair waiting for them. "The deacon called ahead to tell me you men were on the way. It looks like most of you have been here before. You know where the sleeping room is. Too late for talk tonight. See you in the morning," he said, as he got up from his chair and went back inside.

The next day, the men woke up bright and early, so they wouldn't have to rush to be on time for church. When McCoy introduced Doss to the Bowmans, Sister Bowman asked Desmond if he would do her a favor. "Whenever you visit would you please sign my military guest book, and write a little something about yourself. We get so many fine young Adventist soldiers and sailors visiting with us. We want to pray for all of you, but without my little book I'm afraid I could never remember all of your names."

Doss glanced through the book and saw that there were several hundred names written there. He took a clue from the other entries and signed. *"Private Desmond T. Doss, Army Medic from Lynchburg, Virginia. Thank you for your hospitality. April 22, 1944"*

While he was looking at the book, the others had gone ahead to where the food was laid out for breakfast. Brother Bowman was waiting on him to come in, so he could say the prayer. As soon as Doss joined them, he began. "Dear Heavenly Father, we thank Thee for the privilege of having these fine young men visit with us on Thy beautiful Sabbath morning. We ask that Thou bless this food so that it may strengthen and nourish our bodies that we may better serve Thee. We further ask Thee for a special blessing on these men in this time of great turmoil and if it is Thine will, that you protect them from harm. In Jesus name, Amen."

The soldiers filled their plates with fresh fruit and oatmeal before moving outside to eat on the lanai. They especially enjoyed the pineapples as none of them had ever had a fresh one before arriving in Hawaii. When they had almost finished eating, Sister Bowman came outside and teased. "Don't get too full Private Doss, or you might fall asleep in church. Besides, you have to save lots of room for the special potluck dinner. There's plenty of poi waiting."

Doss leaned over and whispered to McCoy, "Is that what they have at potluck? Poi?"

"No. She tells that to all the new men."

The other men were watching, always eager to see the reaction when Sister Bowman played that joke on a new man, and after seeing the relieved look on Doss's face, they burst out in good-natured laughter.

After breakfast, they all walked together the short distance to the Keeaumoku Street church.

As the soldiers entered, the pastor was there to greet them. "Hello men. I see you brought a new friend with you this Sabbath." Extending his hand, he said, "Aloha, Happy Sabbath. My name is Pastor Melvin Goodwin."

"Nice to meet you Pastor. My name is Desmond Doss. Lately, I've been the only one wearing a uniform at church, but today I've got lots of company. I'm really enjoying it."

"Yes Desmond, God has blessed us with many visiting soldiers and sailors. We average over a hundred Adventist military men each week. I hope you have a good Sabbath, and remember we have a special potluck dinner after church for the service men."

The soldiers standing around Desmond tried to keep from laughing, but they had a hard time holding it in.

Pastor Goodwin thought, *I wonder why they always seem to laugh when I mention the word potluck?*

Doss and McCoy went together to one of the Adult Sabbath School classes and spent the next hour discussing the Bible lesson with the local church members. That week, the lesson was about the book of 1st Kings. The study involved the story of King Ahab's initial victory over his enemies, and how later, Ahab met his fate in battle after he and Jehoshaphat chose to continue their battle plans in spite of the definite warnings received from the Lord.

After Sabbath School, Doss moved into the sanctuary, and while he waited for the service to begin, he looked around at the crowd. The servicemen were seated intermixed among the civilians, who seemed to be mostly of Hawaiian decent. By counting the pews, he estimated there were more than 600 people in attendance. Doss supposed this was the largest congregation he had ever attended. While he sat there, he thought about how much Dorothy would love Hawaii and decided that after the war he would try to come back with her.

Pastor Goodwin's sermon title was, "*I Can Do All Things Through Christ, Which Strengthen Me.*" He preached about Ephesians 6:10-18, discussing the armor of God and how the primary focus of Scripture is the battle between Christ and Satan. He also related that like Hawaii, whether or not they chose to be, every single one of them is involved in the battle. He explained that the battleground Christ and Satan fight over is not Europe or the Pacific but the human heart. He said Satan is tremendously interested in winning control of our minds and that to protect ourselves and win eternal victory we must put on the entire armor of God. Pastor Goodwin ended his sermon with three Bible quotes "Finally, my brethren, be strong in the Lord, and in the power of his might." Jesus said, "Without me ye can do nothing." However, he also promised, "You can do all things through Christ, which strengthens you."

Doss decided he would try to return to the Keeaumoku Street church as many times as possible before being shipped off to war.

JUNE 1944
WAITING IN HAWAII

By the beginning of June 1944, all of the men of the 77th Division had cycled through the jungle training school and participated in several practice amphibious assaults. After two years of training, the war department determined that the division was prepared for combat, but for the time being, they were to be held in Hawaii as a land based reserve force in the event they were needed in the Marianas Operation.

The intelligence section of Headquarters Company spent its time in Hawaii drawing up contingency plans in case the division was called upon to deploy to Saipan, Guam or Tinian. At the same time, G-4 and the quartermasters requisitioned additional vehicles, weapons and equipment suitable for use in the Pacific Theater. Once the material arrived, it was sorted into small mountains of rations, water, ammunition and other supplies. After it was organized, the equipment was stacked onto pallets. Then came the decision of how it would all be combat loaded onto the troop transport assault ships.

A combat loaded ship was arranged so the materials and supplies that would be needed first in a battle were loaded into the ship last. The result was that the most essential materials ended up at the top center of the cargo holds and were unloaded soon after the troops went ashore. The less urgently needed supplies were loaded on the ship first, which placed them at the bottom and sides of the cargo hold. If 80 percent of the supplies were loaded in this manner, the ship was said to be combat loaded. By mid-1944, combat loading transport ships was standard operating procedure for beach assaults, and the method was fairly well refined.

Late in June, the 305th Regimental Combat Team and the Advanced Headquarters received orders to move out and were hastily loaded onto assault ships. On 1 July, they left behind the majority of the 77th Division and sailed for Eniwetok. There they received orders, which attached the 77th Army Infantry Division to the Third Marine Amphibious Corps. Their mission was to take back the American Territory of Guam from the Japanese.

Meanwhile two additional convoys of empty ships had reached Hawaii, where the remainder of the 77th Division was standing by to be combat loaded onto the transports. As soon as they were aboard and ready, the convoys steamed off toward Guam, almost 4,000 miles away, eager to catch up with the 305th, which had departed days earlier.

Before daylight on 21 July, the 305th Combat Team arrived off the coast of Guam. The Marines were scheduled to make the initial assault at 0830 hours. At the same time as the marines were landing on the beach, the 305th 2nd Battalion was climbing down cargo nets to load into flat bottom LCVPs (Landing Craft, Vehicle–Personnel). Since they had been ordered to be on call at the line of departure as soon as the Marines had secured and moved off the beach, the landing craft were forced to circle near the departure line for four hours until finally, at 1300, they received word to move in and land their troops.

Guam was completely surrounded by a fringing coral reef varying in widths of between 400 and 800 yards. The beach assault planners had assigned both tracked landing vehicles and six-wheel-drive amphibious DUKWs for use in the initial assaults. This gave the Marines a vehicle which had the ability to climb over the reefs and onto the beaches. The hope was that once the marines secured the beachheads, the majority of the troops and supplies could be brought ashore at high tide in the normal LCVP landing boats. Unfortunately for the army, even when the water was at its highest, there was not enough clearance for the boats to cross the reef.

The navy coxswains maneuvered the LCVPs carrying the 305th toward the beach until they ran up against the coral almost a quarter of a mile from the shore. Having no choice, they dropped their ramps and unloaded the soldiers into water up to their waist. Upon exiting the boats, the troops dispersed to the left and right, like they had been taught in training, and began to move toward the beach. Almost immediately, several soldiers stepped into potholes in the coral and disappeared from sight beneath the water. With the weight of the equipment they were carrying, there was no possibility of swimming back to the surface. They drowned before nearby men could pull them out. From then on, the troops followed single file behind a lead soldier, who had removed his heavy gear and carefully traced a narrow but shallow path across the coral.

Wading ashore single file caused the troops to lose their dispersion and resulted in most of them exiting the ocean at the same spot on the beach. Men from the same landing boat were able to make it to shore together, but platoons and companies became intermingled by the time they reached shore. Fortunately, while the mishmash of soldiers were crossing the reef and reassembling into units, the enemy was too busy dealing with the marines, who had pushed several hundred yards inward, to direct much fire toward the beach. By midnight, the 1st Battalion of the 305th had landed and the entire regiment was ashore by 0600 the next morning.

The ships transporting the remainder of the 77th Division arrived later on the 22nd and began landing the 306th Regiment the next day. On 24 July, Doss and the 307th prepared to come ashore. A storm at sea was raising heavy waves as the men began to climb down the cargo nets into the waiting LCVPs. While Doss was waiting his turn to descend the net, he saw a soldier lose his grip and crash onto the deck of a landing boat bobbing below. Just as he reached the rails and was about to climb over, two navy corpsmen headed for sickbay passed by carrying the wounded man on a stretcher. Doss saw bones protruding from the skin and knew the soldier had suffered compound fractures in both legs.

Even though he had said a lengthy prayer before assembling on deck, Doss decided another quick prayer was in order before swinging over the side. *Dear God, please give me the strength to not slip off this net and give comfort to the soldier who broke his legs. Amen.*

Doss concentrated to recall all of his training. He unfastened the straps of his packs and helmet, so he could quickly shed the heavy gear if he fell into the water. Ready to descend, he swung his left leg over the rail first. To prevent the soldier above him from accidently stepping on his hands, he remembered to grab hold of the wet vertical ropes, leaving the horizontal ones free to be used like ladder rungs. As he climbed down, he could see the landing craft rising and falling several feet with each wave.

When he had almost reached the LCVP, he could hear Lieutenant Munger directing the men when to turn loose of the net and step into the boat. "Doss you're next. Wait till I tell you." The lieutenant paused long enough for the landing boat to almost reach the peak of the next wave before yelling, "Jump."

Just as he let go of the net, the boat reached the crest of the wave, hesitated, then started down into the trough. The lieutenant had timed it so perfectly that Doss barely felt an impact when he landed. As soon as the boat was fully loaded, it pulled away from the ship and headed off toward the beach.

The waves were running very high, and the LCVPs circled at sea for several hours before they began the run ashore. By the time the boats made it to the reef, most of the men had already vomited up everything the Navy had fed them that morning.

When the 307th reached the coral, they found that the landing area was secure, and a safe path from the beginning of reef to the beach had been marked with flags by engineers. The officers and men made the long wade to shore burdened down with close to one hundred pounds of equipment. This included a helmet, gas mask, backpack, rifle, bayonet, grenade launcher, a pouch of hand grenades, ammunition, a machete, K-rations, two canteens of water, and a life belt that, in theory, enabled them to float while weighted down with all of their gear. As the men trudged along through the surf, they could only imagine the terror it must have been to wade ashore while under enemy fire.

Doss was not carrying any weapons of course, but his equipment weighed almost 70 pounds, and considering the extra weight of his two medic bags he was loaded down as much as the infantrymen.

The exertion of fighting the waves had worn out the men by the time they reached shore, but they still had several miles to hike to reach the company bivouac area. As he moved off the beach, Doss began to come across dead Japanese bodies. Some were half buried in the sand and mud, and many of them were blown in half, missing limbs or even headless. As they passed the bodies, the men slowed down to look. This was not only the first time they had seen Japanese soldiers, it was also the first time they had seen men who had been killed in combat. After looking at the bloated bodies, Doss was grateful he had lost his meal on the landing craft because if there had been anything left in his gut, he would have surely puked it up after viewing the mangled corpses.

The so-called road to the bivouac area was in reality more quagmire than road. So many tracked vehicles had passed over the same ground that it had been churned into mud ranging from ankle deep in most places, to others where it almost reached the men's waists.

After the strenuous slog through the mud, Doss was famished, so as soon as he reached the bivouac area he pulled out one of his K-rations. As was his custom, he said a prayer before eating.

Dear Lord, thank You for this food. You have taught that there are certain things that are biblically unclean and that we should not eat. These K-rations contain many of those things. That is why I need Your help. Please provide me with enough clean food to survive. I put my trust in You. In Jesus name Amen.

After the prayer, he began to sort through the contents of his K-ration. The entrée was a can of cheese and ham. "Pork," he said with a disgusted look on his face. *Well I can't eat that,* he thought, as he placed the can in his pocket. He hoped to be able to trade it later for a can of plain cheese. He ate the GI biscuits and malted milk tablets right away. Then he took out his canteen, mixed in the orange powder, salt and sugar cubes and drank it down. Next he placed the book of matches in his pocket before throwing the 4-pack of cigarettes into a nearby puddle. A soldier, who had been watching him, cried out, "Hey, you didn't have to throw them cigarettes away. I would have smoked 'em."

"That's why I did it. I don't want people smoking. Tobacco is a poison."

"Come on Doss, that's crazy talk. Everyone knows that smokin's good for ya. Otherwise, why would the Army give 'em out for free? Anyway, I would'a traded you something for 'em."

After Doss finished eating, he was still hungry. He needed to figure out how he was going to get enough food to keep from starving. Unfortunately for him, almost every K-ration contained pork and he knew he would not compromise and eat a biblically unclean meat. By the time he finished thinking about it, he had come to a decision. Since he had already decided to trade food containing unclean meats, he would start saving the cigarettes and trade them but only as a last resort. As he sat there, he worried, *How many men will die from tobacco poison after they get addicted to free army cigarettes. Oh Lord, have I made the right decision?*

JULY 1944
GUAM

Word came down that Doss and the men of the 1st Battalion were being held in reserve. Since they knew they would be spending at least another day where they were, the men had a lot of work to do before nightfall. First a perimeter was set up around the bivouac area. Then foxholes were dug in groups of three, arranged in inverted-v shapes with the tip pointing outward. Trenches were dug between the holes. That way, one man was able to remain on watch while the other two slept. When it was time to change the guard, the men would switch positions by crawling through the trenches. For the first few nights in combat, the officers expected the men to be very trigger happy and liable to shoot at any noise or movement. They knew it would not be safe to expose the men after dark during guard changes until they calmed down.

War planners had expected Guam to be defended by between 20,000 and 40,000 enemy troops. During the landing phase, American troops had encountered far less than half of the anticipated defenders and there had not been much organized enemy activity since the 307th landed. Most contact with the Japanese occurred when groups of five or 10 infiltrated into the American camps at night. Many times, the first indication of trouble was a grenade that dropped out of the darkness. Other times, a lone enemy soldier would walk boldly toward the American lines only to be shot down by gunfire from multiple nervous GIs positioned along the camp perimeter. It didn't take long for the GIs to figure out that the solitary soldiers were sacrificing themselves to give their artillery spotters a chance to see the muzzle flashes and target their positions.

By 28 July, intelligence officers suspected the enemy was moving to the north end of the island where they intended to make a last stand. Suspicions weren't enough. General Bruce needed conclusive evidence of where the Japanese force was located before he could decide on his next course of action. The 307th had already cut the island in half, but if any sizeable hostile force remained in the south, Bruce would have to leave a substantial number of troops behind to guard his rear. If no organized Japanese troops remained to the south, he felt it might be safe to utilize the entire division to pursue the enemy north.

Because of the dense jungle foliage, planes could not make conclusive observations. To gather the intelligence he needed, Bruce sent out several four-man patrols to the east and south. Sending out such small squads was a risk. Even though the patrols were told to remain in radio contact and call in artillery support if they encountered any Japanese troops, there was a good chance they would be wiped out if they encountered a substantial concentration of enemy soldiers.

While General Bruce struggled to obtain the intelligence he needed to decide where to move his division, another struggle was occurring on the beaches. The broad reef that surrounded Guam was severely hampering efforts to move supplies from the APAs (Assault Transport Ships) to the beach. The original plan was to bring supplies ashore on landing boats then use bulldozers to drag the palletized equipment off the boats and directly to supply depots. This plan proved unworkable because the landing boats were unable to cross the reef under any tide conditions. Instead, floating barge cranes were positioned to transfer all the supplies from the landing boats onto waiting DUKWs or LVTs, which then drove over the reef and onto the beach. Heavy equipment such as tanks, artillery, construction machinery and vehicles that would not fit into the DUKWs, were unloaded at low tide by crane and set directly onto the reef. Then they were either driven across the reef or in many cases, hooked to a long cable and dragged to the beach by shore-bound bulldozers. Despite the waterproofing equipment attached to the vehicles, many of the engines were drowned out or damaged by salt water during their trip across the reefs.

Once ashore, the equipment still had to be moved almost 600 yards to the supply dumps. The road between the beach and the dump had become so rutted and filled with mud that it sometimes took a truck three hours to make one round trip. Early in the operation, it became apparent the transports would not be unloaded in a reasonable amount of time if the work was restricted to daylight hours. Since the threat of enemy airstrikes against the beach had been largely eliminated, floodlights were set up to illuminate the area at night, and the work continued round the clock. Every available man including the division band was utilized in the unloading process. After five days, the APAs were 80 percent unloaded. By the end of a week, the 302nd Medical Battalion, 95th Surgical Hospital and 36th Field Hospital were all set up and operating. Enough supplies and support had been built up ashore to allow General Bruce to move his division out of the bivouac area and into combat.

Bruce had hoped his construction troops could cut a road from the west coast to the east side of Guam before he needed to move his troops. Unfortunately, during a quick survey, the engineers located a ravine along the proposed route, which could not be bridged or filled in a reasonable amount of time. They reluctantly told the general that by the time they could complete the road, it would probably no longer be needed.

By 30 July, the reconnaissance patrols had supplied Bruce with the information he desired. None of the scouts had located any sizeable concentration of Japanese troops in the southern sector of Guam. Furthermore, friendly native Chamorros confirmed that they had seen them moving to the north and in several gruesome instances, graphically demonstrated that they were able to deal with any enemy stragglers left behind.

Meanwhile, the infantrymen of the division had spent five miserable nights huddled in their foxholes waiting for General Bruce to give the order to move out. They tried stringing ponchos over their holes in an attempt to keep them dry, but even when it wasn't raining, water continually seeped in. Almost constant bailing was not enough to stop mud from accumulating in the bottom of their foxholes. After a while, the men just gave up and sat down in the slimy red mud, which then oozed through their clothes and eventually covered every part of their bodies.

Bruce finally made the decision to use the entire division to pursue the enemy north. Before sunrise on the morning of the 31 July, the 307th Infantry, along with the 3rd Battalion of the 305th moved out, having been given the objective of reaching the Pago River in two days. The march was through jagged terrain covering steep slopes and ravines. Vehicles followed along for a short distance, but they were soon blocked by terrain so rough that even the jeeps could not pass. Due to the lack of resistance, the troops made unanticipated progress, so early in the afternoon of the first day, a spotter plane dropped orders from Bruce to press on and try to make it to the objective by nightfall. Late that afternoon, the 307th reached the banks of the Pago. Elements of the 3rd Marine Division, which were traveling with the Army, crossed over the river and scouted the far side. They had expected to find strong defensive positions, but the patrols returned without finding any sign of enemy troops.

Information coming in from many sources convinced General Bruce that the Japanese were still moving north where they intended to make their last stand. He decided to change his strategy from attack to pursuit. He thought that if he could move quickly enough, he might get the chance to engage the main force in the north before they had time to reorganize and set up an effective defense.

There was just one problem with General Bruce's plan to have the 307th chase down the enemy. His troops had set out with minimal supplies, and now their rations were running low. If they kept up the quick movements, the resupply situation would quickly become critical. To solve the problem, General Bruce worked out a deal to share a road, which the Marines were using. It ran up the west side of Guam along the shoreline, but before it would be useful to the 77th, they needed to capture the connecting road, which ran from Agana on the west coast and crossed over the island to Pago Bay on the east.

The morning of 1 August, the 307th crossed over the Pago River and turned north. By midday, they ran low on rations. The ammunition supply wasn't a problem since they hadn't encountered any resistance, but lacking clean drinking water, the men were forced to fill their canteens from creeks.

Not trusting a halazone tablet's ability to disinfect the muddy water, some of men drank coconut water instead.

By the end of the day, the troops had almost made it to the Agana-Pago road. They had also run out of food, so they requested permission to delay the next day's advance to allow time for more K-rations to be carried up by hand from the rear. General Bruce sent back word reminding them how close they were to the road. He promised that if they captured it first thing in the morning the resupply trucks would be there by breakfast time.

At first light, on the morning of 2 August, the 307th captured the Agana-Pago road, and while they were regrouping, supply trucks arrived with rations and clean water. General Bruce was good to his word. The men were allowed time to sit and eat their breakfast.

Their next objective was the crossroads village of Barrigada, where intelligence indicated the enemy had set up a roadblock. The Japanese plan was to use the village to slow down the American troops and give the rest of their forces time to prepare for a final stand. General Bruce intended to smash through the roadblock before the enemy had a chance to regroup in the north, but he also had another reason for wanting to capture the village. There was a well and reservoir at Barrigada, which could produce almost 20,000 gallons of water a day. Although army engineers had piped clean water to the troops on the west side of the island, there was no other safe drinking supply under American control. General Bruce desperately needed clean drinking water for his troops.

AUGUST 2, 1944
BARRIGADA

After breakfast, Bruce sent the M5A1 Stuart light tanks of Company D, 706th Tank Battalion toward Barrigada to see if they could draw enemy fire and locate their positions. As the tanks approached the village, they received a smattering of small arms fire, but after they failed to pinpoint any concentrated defense, they withdrew. G-2 section relayed the findings to Bruce. The general sent back orders for the tanks to try again, and "this time attempt to pass through the village and reconnoiter the far side."

For the second time that morning the armor headed into the village. Upon reaching the road junction, the twelve tanks turned left and headed up the road to the northwest. They passed by a pillbox but drew no fire. About 500 yards up the road, they encountered a rickety roadblock, but instead of crashing through, they decided to bypass it by driving through the jungle. As they continued up the road, they blindly swept the jungle on both sides with machine gun fire. After traveling another 1,000 yards they encountered a more substantial obstruction consisting of three trucks and about 35 Japanese troops. The three leading tanks spread out and engaged the roadblock with machine gun and 37mm cannon fire, destroying the trucks and killing all of the enemy troops.

After demolishing the roadblock, the column turned around and headed back toward Barrigada. As they passed through the village, they machine gunned the jungle, houses and any likely hiding places in an attempt to draw return fire. Upon reaching the road junction, the tanks made another left turn, this time heading up the road to the northeast. That section of the road was very narrow, passing through dense jungle which reached all the way to the edge of the road. The clearance was so tight that foliage was scraping both sides of the tanks as they proceeded up the road. After traveling only 200 yards, one of the lead tanks became hung up on a tree stump, which forced the entire column to come to a halt.

Now the tankers were in a very dangerous situation. At a standstill, with limited visibility and no infantry protection, was a tank commander's worst nightmare. Almost instantly, their nightmare became reality as Japanese troops hidden in the jungle opened fire on the stalled column. Grenades thrown by unseen enemy soldiers began raining down all around. Troops swarmed out of the jungle and tried to crawl under or climb onto the tanks in attempts to set off demolition charges. The enemy sappers were unsuccessful, because as soon as one of them approached a tank, another nearby tank used its machine gun to cut them down. After the tanks blindly poured machine gun and cannon rounds into the jungle, the incoming fire began to slow. When the stuck tank finally worked itself free, the company commander radioed back to headquarters, *"Can I come home?"*

"Why?" demanded the intelligence officer.

"Damn-it-to-hell, I've got a hundred and fifty Japs swarming all over my tanks. They got machine guns, a 20mm cannon and plenty of grenades. Anything else you need to know? So, can I come home now?"

The G-2 officer had heard enough. He radioed back, "Okay, come on home."

While the scout tanks were pulling back, the infantry was moving up. The plan was to move the 307th in on the left side of the village and the 305th on the right. Together, they would surround and attack the village on a wide front. On the far left, Company C, 307th was to cut through the jungle, pass the village and then swing right and hit them on their flank. The job of Companies A, L and K of the 307th was to hit the village straight on while Companies I, A, B and L of the 305th moved in on the right. Doss and Company B were held back as a reserve.

About 0930, the point of the 305th reached the extreme southern edge of Barrigada. As they came out of the jungle, the scouts could easily see the water reservoir and a two-story building. Only the roofs of the other buildings were showing because the ground sloped downward. At first, all was quiet, but then, several enemy soldiers came out of the jungle and crossed the trail ahead before disappearing back into the foliage on the other side. Just as two GIs scouts moved forward to investigate, enemy snipers opened up and shot them both down. The firing seemed to be coming from the front, and also from the left, in the direction of the village. It was difficult to pin down its source. As a sergeant motioned the rest of his men toward cover, he was struck in the arm by a bullet. 1st Platoon's lieutenant tried to move his men around to the enemy's flank, but as they were crossing a small grassy area, a machine gun opened up on them, killing four men and wounding several others almost instantly. Snipers hidden in the trees began firing down on the trapped Americans. When Private Rowe saw the company machine gunner hit by an unseen sniper, he rushed forward, picked up the still smoking machine gun and screaming at the top of his lungs, fired blindly into the nearby treetops, shredding the foliage until a hidden sniper's, bullet-riddled body tumbled out. Company I was stopped dead in their tracks by the ambush and the other companies moving up on the right were forced to slow their progress because of the heavy fire.

On the other side of the village, the 307th was having a different kind of problem. When Company C headed toward the left flank, they became disoriented in the thick jungle and ended up far to the northwest of their objective. Company A veered too far to the right as they approached the village and ran into Company L, which in turn shifted to the right and ended up where Company K was supposed to go. The result was that the entire concentration of American forces ended up on the right side of the village leaving a thousand yard gap on the left. Company C, which was supposed to close in on the left flank, remained hopelessly lost and out of the fight.

While Company B was waiting in reserve, Doss observed the action from a shallow hole he had dug at the edge of the jungle. As he watched men from another company crouch low, then sprint one by one across the nearby road, one of them suddenly lurched forward and fell. At first, Doss thought the soldier had tripped, but when an officer stood up, ran straight to the fallen man and began yelling for help, Doss knew he had been hit. The circling officer was obviously distraught or in shock, because he seemed oblivious to the danger, as he waved his arms and called out the fallen soldier's name. Doss crawled out of his hole and with a combination of crouching and creeping, cautiously approached the wounded soldier.

When the medic reached the injured man, he did not recognize the dismayed officer, but he knew the first thing he needed to do was to get him calmed down and under control.

"Captain. Captain! Get down! I need your help. If you don't get down you'll get us all killed."

The officer suddenly realized the danger he was in and dropped to the ground. "Okay, you're right medic. What do you want me to do?"

"First thing, help me roll him on his back."

After they turned the wounded man over, Doss saw the horrible chest wound that he had suffered. The damage was severe, and he had already lost so much blood that the wound was no longer actively bleeding. Doss knew there was no hope of saving the man, but seeing the pleading look in the captain's eyes he opened up his left side medic bag and selected the largest dressing he carried. With his left hand, he pressed it in place over the gaping wound and using the other hand felt for the pulse he knew would not be there.

Looking up at the distraught officer, he said, "I'm sorry Captain. He never really had a chance. We did what we could, but now we have to turn him over to God. Come on Sir, we've got to get back under cover." He and the captain lunged for the relative safety of the jungle.

As Doss carefully made his way back to his unit, he said a silent prayer. *Dear Lord, thank you for protecting me and the captain. You know this is the first soldier that's gone and died on me. I ask that You give me the strength and wisdom to carry on with my job. Please comfort that soldier's family when they find out about his death. In Jesus name, Amen.*

While Doss was dealing with the wounded soldier, Colonel Coolidge made the decision to deploy Company B from their reserve position by moving them into place on the left side of Company A. His intention was to use them to fill in some of the thousand-yard gap on the left of the misaligned units by locating them about dead center of the village.

Lieutenant Munger guided Doss and the 2nd platoon through the jungle and around the back of Company A to the edge of a cleared field along the Finegayan-Barrigada road. From there, he spotted a large green, two-story house on the other side of the road. After using his binoculars to study it, he could tell that the first floor was made of concrete, and it appeared to be located in a good tactical position. Munger spoke to Sergeant Adams, "Our objective is going to be that green house. Have your men cross the field two or three at a time, and hold up in the ditch on this side of the road."

Once all of the men had made it to the safety of the roadside ditch, Lt. Munger was ready to order the final sprint to the green house. Before he could, a machine gun opened up from the woods just beyond, forcing 2nd platoon to hunker back down in the ditch. At about the same time, observers near the village temple pinpointed another hidden machine gun. It was coming from a grass shack near the back of the village. American machine guns and mortars opened up on the hut, setting it on fire.

Just when they thought they had put the machine gun nest out of commission, the side of the shack burst open, a tank crawled out and then headed for the road. Three ill-fated Japanese soldiers, who were riding on top and firing their rifles, were shot off before they had traveled 100 feet. When the tank reached the road it turned to the right, drove a few yards and then stopped. Directly ahead and in plain sight was 2nd Platoon. The tank paused for a few seconds as if trying to decide what to do. By then, GIs from all around the village had opened up with rifles, machine guns, and rifle grenades. The small caliber bullets didn't faze the tank, but they did pose a deadly danger to the men in the ditch. Bullets were grazing off its armor and ricocheting in every direction. To avoid the friendly fire, some of the platoon crouched down lower in the roadside ditch while others made a mad dash for the green house.

The men's sudden movement seemed to spur the tank into action. It started to pursue the men running toward the house, killing one and wounding two, before Pfc. Shank, who was manning a heavy machine gun next to the village temple, targeted the rear of the tank and opened fire. After moving only a few feet, the continuous hits from Shank's gun seemed to get the tank's attention, causing it to change its mind, turn 180 degrees and lumber back toward Shank. As it roared back across the village, the tank machine-gunned anything that moved. Shank held his ground and continued to fire on the approaching monster as it headed directly towards him.

When the enemy tank reached the temple, it collided with the wall, shifted into low gear and smashed through, missing Shank by less than a foot. It continued through the temple and smashed out the back, causing the thatch roof to collapse onto the tank and momentarily pinning Shank to the ground. Even though the tank was blinded by debris covering its vision port, it continued on, ran over another machine gun position, knocked down a tree and then became stuck when it ran up the trunk.

With the tank hung up, three bazooka teams tried to destroy it. The first two rockets failed to launch and the third hit the tank but did not explode because in the excitement, the loader had forgotten to remove the safety pin from the detonator.

The tank continued to fire as one tread spun wildly in the air trying to free itself from the log. Finally, the other tread found a grip, and the tank backed down off the fallen tree, turned around and headed back down the road. The thatch which was blocking its vision finally fell free.

The rest of 2nd Platoon, still lying in the ditch, saw the tank headed back their way and thinking it was returning to finish them off ran for the perceived safety of the green house. When the tank once again reached the road junction, instead of continuing toward 2nd Platoon, it turned left and headed down the road toward the 307th's rear area. It raced along the road, firing all the way, as it smashed through the aid-station, the battalion command post and the 307th Regimental Command Post.

As the tank passed through the last command post and headed deeper into the rear area, two Stuart light tanks roared off in pursuit. Since the Japanese tank had expended all of its main gun ammunition in Barrigada, the Stuarts were able to destroy it before it could cause any more mayhem, although the situation it left behind was bad enough. The American positions were now more disorganized than ever and 2nd Platoon, holed-up inside the green house, was cut off and in serious trouble.

The concrete walls of the first floor provided the platoon protection from small arms fire, but if the enemy decided to use mortars or artillery, it would drop right in through the tin roof. While Lieutenant Munger and Sergeant Adams discussed their next move, a machine gun opened fire on the house from a pillbox less than 60 feet away.

Lieutenant Munger said, "If anyone wants to bug out I won't blame you, but I'm sticking. I think, maybe with some artillery support, we can hold this house."

Sergeant Adams volunteered to go back, explain the situation and try to get some help. He ran from the house, jumped in the ditch and crawled through a drainage pipe under the road. Then he raced across the open field back to Captain Vernon. After hearing of the situation, he told Adams to tell Lieutenant Munger to forget about it. Possession of the green house wasn't that important. Vernon promised to have Company A provide cover as they fell back.

Sergeant Adams had made the dangerous return trip back to the green house and was just relaying Captain Vernon's orders, when several heavy artillery explosions hit nearby.

Munger yelled to be heard over the explosions, "Okay men let's get the hell out of this house before one of those Jap shells drop through the roof." The men poured out of the house and back across the road. Sergeant Adams was wounded as he crossed the road for the fourth time that day, and Lieutenant Munger was killed when he dashed out of the door.

Pfc. Shank was hit as he continued to man his machine gun position near the demolished temple but remained to provide cover fire as Doss and the other medics dragged the wounded men from the field. Only when the last injured man had been pulled to safety did the injured Shank quit firing his gun. *Thank God they're safe,* he thought. He turned and began to crawl his way toward the rear. Pfc. Shank made it almost 10 yards before a sniper noticed him and shot him dead.

August 2, 1944 Evening
Barrigada Second Try

At 1330, Company K, 305th Infantry, along with five light tanks, attacked the right side of Barrigada in the general area where the scout tanks had been ambushed and forced to turn back earlier that morning. The correct procedure would have been to use medium tanks in an assault of that sort, but they were held up along the Agat-Agana road because of concerns over the ability of the bridges to support their weight. A Sherman medium tank weighed over 30 tons, so each bridge had to be load tested before the engineers would allow them to cross.

Each light tank making the assault had infantrymen spaced around it for close in protection. When the formation reached the draw where Company I had been stopped that morning, the tanks began crossing one at a time. The first four tanks made it across without incident, but when the fifth began to cross, Japanese artillery and machine guns opened fire. Bullets and shell fragments ricocheted off the side of the tank killing a sergeant and wounding two others. The tanks returned fire, but like so many other times that day, they were unable to precisely locate where the enemy was located, making their return shots ineffective.

The light tanks did not have sufficient armor to stand up to such heavy fire and were soon forced to withdraw to a less exposed position, but the infantrymen didn't dare move. With such dense fire pouring in, they had no choice but to hunker down utilizing whatever protection they could find.

2nd Lt. Haggard volunteered to lead a tank back to an enemy position he had discovered earlier that morning when he and 1st Platoon, Company I had been stopped by enemy fire in the same area. His hope was that he could use the tank to create enough of a diversion so that Company K would be able to withdraw.

Lt. Haggard climbed into a light tank and directed the driver to within 15 feet of the position, but even at close range, it was so well hidden that nothing was visible. The tank opened fire anyway raking the brush and trees with its machine guns. An antitank gun returned fire, hit the tank and knocked off one of its tracks. Another shell punched a hole clean through the side armor, narrowly missing the driver. Haggard and the tank crew were forced to bail out and rush for cover. Once again, the light tank design had proven itself unsuitable for the task of assaulting enemy positions.

The Japanese had stopped another advance in the draw. Normally, artillery would have been utilized to support a pinned down unit such as Company K, but the situation was so confused it could not be employed for fear of accidently hitting friendly troops. Most worrisome, was the chance of inadvertently dropping artillery on Company C, which had been lost and out of contact all day. Colonel Chalgren the 3rd Battalion, 305th Regiment

Commander, had no choice but to order Company K to fall back without being able to supply tank or artillery support to cover their withdraw. As a result, several men were killed as they retreated.

A platoon of M4A2 Sherman medium tanks finally arrived on the scene late in the afternoon. Lt. Haggard eagerly volunteered to lead them back to finish the job he had attempted to accomplish with the light tanks earlier. With Haggard directing, the tanks formed up four abreast and moved out. Lt. Haggard had been frustrated all day, but now he wished he could see the look on the Jap's faces when they realized they were about to be destroyed by a platoon of Shermans.

As each tank came up out of the draw, it opened fire with its machine guns and main cannon. They fired blindly into the jungle as they slowly approached the location that Lt. Haggard had been itching to destroy ever since he had spotted it that morning.

Haggard was about to get some gratification as he leaned over and yelled to make himself heard over the roar of the tank's engine. "See that large tree just behind the wrecked American tank. The Japs are about 10 feet to the right."

The tank commander reached for his radio, *"Target in jungle. 10 feet to right of Stuart. Open fire!"*

His gunner was the first to respond, sending a high explosive shell toward the hidden target. The round exploded, knocking a piece of camouflage loose, which exposed a tank dug into the side of a hill.

Excited chatter erupted over the tanks' radios.

"Is that a tank?"

"Hell yes!"

"One of ours?"

"Hell no that's a damn Jap!"

The other three tanks fired almost simultaneously, destroying the enemy tank and setting it on fire. For the first time that day, Lt. Haggard had a smile on his face.

Over on the left side of the village, the 307th was ready to make one more attempt to close the gap created when Company C had gone too far to the left and gotten lost in the jungle. They began by ordering the 2nd Battalion to move up on the left of the 1st Battalion.

Just as men from Company G started to cross the open field, the American tanks that had been covering medics as they evacuated the wounded, started to pull back. With the tanks no longer in sight, the enemy felt brave enough to open up again with machine guns and rifles. Some of the men of the 1st Platoon hit the ground while others started toward the roadside ditches. Realizing they didn't have a chance to make it to the road, they all dropped for cover in the open field. Some of them found shell holes to crawl into but most lay exposed in the short grass.

The 2nd Platoon of Company G was heading toward the green house when the hostile fire started back up. Two men dashed into the house, but the four others who tried to go around the right side were all hit. The 3rd Platoon also made a dash for the same house, and when they arrived, they too were pinned down by heavy enemy fire. Now two platoons of Company G found themselves trapped in the green house under the same circumstances as Doss and the 2nd Platoon had been just hours before.

Sergeant LaCoste volunteered to go for help just as Sergeant Adams had done earlier. LaCoste explained the situation to the Company G commander who then called for the tanks to return and cover the withdraw of his men. When the tank commander received orders to screen another withdraw from the green house he couldn't believe it.

What the hell is going on with those infantry boys? We just finished covering one withdraw from that damn house and now another group gets their asses trapped there.

Reaching for the radio, he keyed the mic., *"All tanks. Fuel up and rearm as quick as possible. We're headed back to the green house."*

All the way on the left, 1st Platoon was in serious trouble. Most of the men were lying exposed in grass, which was only a foot high. Their backpacks, that stuck up above the grass, made perfect targets for the Japanese firing from the woods. One by one, the exposed men were hit. The only ones who escaped were those lucky enough to have found a shell hole to crawl into. Very late in the evening, the rearmed and refueled tanks finally arrived and provided enough cover fire to allow the wounded men to be dragged off the field. Thc 1st Platoon alone had suffered 26 casualties. During the day, the 77th had suffered 29 killed and almost 100 wounded.

As sundown approached, the fighting ended, and men all along the line dug in for the night. After reviewing the day's action, General Bruce was heard to say, "There was a lot of individual bravery shown today but not much tactical skill. We better get our damn act together or we're all in for one hell of a messed up war."

The next day General Bruce spent the morning realigning his troops. When every unit was in the correct position, they made the assault on Barrigada the way he had intended it to happen the day before. Artillery pasted the jungle on the far side as infantry and tanks advanced in a coordinated manner. The troops passed through the village with no opposition. Apparently the Japanese had suffered enough the day before. During the night, they had removed their dead and wounded and left Barrigada undefended.

When the enemy pulled out, they neglected to destroy the well. Army engineers jury-rigged a jeep to supply power to the pump and the costly water began to flow into the reservoir. General Bruce now had a secure supply of clean water. His next move was to run down and kill the remaining enemy troops before they had a chance to set up another organized defense.

August 3, 1944
Cleaning Out Guam

After the village was secured, Doss and his pal Glenn were walking past the collecting area where all the dead native and American bodies had been laid out. Doss paused.

"Glenn, hold up a second. I thought I heard a sound coming from one of those dead natives."

"Maybe it's a ghost," his friend laughed.

"Quit joking around Glenn. You know there's no such thing as ghosts. I think one of those guys just moaned."

Doss and Glenn moved closer to where the bodies were stacked. Even though they both listened intently, neither could detect a sound.

"It must have been your imagination, I don't hear a thing."

"I don't hear anything either, now, but I'm gonna check all these natives just to make sure."

"Get outta here. You really wanna go and cause yourself all that work? Don't you think someone made sure they were dead before they stacked them here?"

"Maybe so, but it won't take that long to double check especially if you help me out."

Doss bent down and began to feel the first body for a pulse.

"You really gonna to do this? How you know these natives are even worth saving?"

"I don't know, but I'm gonna try. Jesus does everything he can to save each man. Don't you think he wants us to do the same? Are you going to help me or not?"

"Okay buddy, you win. I'll help."

After examining several bodies, Doss thought he detected a very weak pulse in one of them.

"Glenn! I think I found him."

Glenn came over and felt for a pulse. "I don't believe it. This guy's really alive. I'll go for a stretcher."

While Glenn raced off toward the aid-station, Doss continued to examine the native. Someone had already applied dressings to his wounds, and since nothing else could be done for the man except wait for the stretcher, the medic decided to check the rest of the bodies. He had finished the line of natives and was checking the Americans on the other side of the road when Glenn returned with the stretcher-bearers.

"You think you'll find another one?"

"I don't know. Maybe."

Glenn had knelt down and was helping to check the American bodies when he suddenly called out, "Hey Doss, you're not gonna believe it. I got another live one here."

Word quickly spread that the medics had found a GI someone had left for dead but who was actually still alive. A small crowd formed around Doss and Glenn as they moved the man back to the aid-station.

One of the men in the group called out, "Hey Doc, you think he'll live?"

Doss answered back, "I don't know, but I promise you guys I'll never give up on a man as long as there's hope he can be saved."

The 77th spent the next four days chasing and hunting down the remaining concentrations of enemy troops. The division's massive firepower could never be properly utilized because of the lack of open space to maneuver its units. Instead of advancing on a broad front, the division was reduced to moving in separate disjointed columns. Because of the thick jungle growth and lack of trails or roads, they were forced to hack their way through the undergrowth. Even though they attempted to maintain contact with the units on each side of them, they invariably lost sight of each other and became separated. Dealing with inadequate maps and the thick cover, they also had a very difficult time determining their precise location. It was in these conditions that Doss made the decision to accompany 2nd Platoon on patrols instead of following the standard procedure of remaining in the company area until a medic was called for.

The first time he asked to follow the platoon on a patrol, the lieutenant had to be persuaded to allow him to come along.

"Doss I'm not so sure letting you go out on patrol is such a good idea. It's too dangerous for an unarmed man to go along. I think it'd be better if you just stayed behind like the other medics."

"Look Lieutenant, here's how I got it figured. If you need a medic, you need him right away. Besides, I think it's more dangerous for me to come up to your position than to just keep out of sight and follow along. That way, if a man gets wounded, the platoon can close in and protect us while I start treating him right away. I thought about just following along without telling you, but I figured you had to know, so you can make sure the guys don't mistake me for a Jap."

"Okay, I give. I'm willing to give it a try and see how it works out. Maybe the men will be more at ease knowing a medic is close by in case they get hit."

The next day, when the 2nd Platoon went out on patrol, Doss went along with them. Using the system he and the lieutenant had worked out the day before, Doss followed along, staying just close enough to keep in sight of the last man in the platoon. When the platoon stopped, he crouched down and waited for them to move again. Even though Doss was covering the same ground that the platoon had just passed over, he still had to remain vigilant to watch for booby traps and enemy soldiers that might try to sneak up from behind.

The patrol was nearly complete when Doss heard an explosion from up ahead. He resisted the urge to rush forward to see if anyone had been wounded. Instead, he dropped down and waited for the signal from the platoon leader that would indicate it was safe for him to move up. After several minutes, he got the OK sign and moved forward. When he arrived, he found that one of the men had tripped a booby trap. The other men had already spread out and formed a perimeter.

Doss unslung his medic bags and got to work. First he carefully looked the soldier over to assess the extent of his wounds. Several shrapnel injuries were apparent on the man's left leg. He ripped open two sulfa packs and sprinkled the contents directly into the wounds. None were bleeding seriously enough to require a tourniquet, so he applied compression dressings instead.

Doss had to decide if he should give the man a painkiller. Since they were relatively close to friendly lines and the man was in considerable pain, he decided to go ahead and administer morphine. Doss removed one Syrette from the box in his kit. He then used an iodine swab to clean an area the size of a silver dollar on the wounded man's arm. Next he removed the clear protective cover from the morphine tube, pushed down on the loop wire to break the inner seal and then removed the wire from the hypodermic needle. Finally, he slowly inserted the needle at an angle into the man's arm and squeezed the tube until all the morphine was injected. The last thing the medic did was to pin the empty Syrette to the soldier's collar. It would help alert the aid-station that the man had already received a dose of morphine in the field.

"There you go Gorska. You should feel less pain in ten or fifteen minutes."

"Thanks Doc. Am I going to be okay?"

"You'll do fine. If you start feeling drowsy from the morphine just go on to sleep. You'll wake up in the aid-station."

While Doss waited for the litter bearers to arrive, he filled out his portion of a form 52b Emergency Medical Tag, detailing the injuries and treatment he had given and tied it on through a buttonhole of the injured man's jacket. By the time he was through, the stretcher had arrived, and the platoon began to make its way back. Once they reached friendly lines, the rest of the platoon headed back to the company area. Doss followed his patient to the aid-station, so he could restock his medic bags before rejoining 2nd Platoon.

As he was getting supplies, Doss was approached by his friend Tech. Sergeant Joe Lawrence.

"What's this crazy talk I hear from the litter bearers that you went out on patrol today? Did Captain Vernon order you to go along or did you just think up this stupid stunt on your own?"

"It's not crazy talk, and I don't even think Captain Vernon knows I went along. Those guys are my friends, and when they get hurt I want to be nearby, so I can help them."

"Look Doss, you know I can't give you an order, but it's not your duty to go along on patrols. It's to stay in the company area until you're needed. You won't be doing your buddies any good if you get yourself killed."

"I know it's not my duty, but it's what I want to do."

Even after the conversation with Sergeant Lawrence, Doss continued to go along with 2nd platoon when they went out on patrol. Word of the medic's actions soon filtered its way up to Captain Vernon. After a while, the captain began to believe that it was Doss's duty to accompany the men on patrol, but he also started to question why he was sending so many men back to the aid-station for treatment. One day, when Vernon saw Doss passing by, he decided to set the medic straight.

"Doss! Get over here!"

"Yes, Captain Vernon."

"Why are you babying the men so much? That man you sent back to the aid-station today wasn't injured badly. He could have stayed on the line and kept fighting."

"Captain Vernon, some men are injured worse than I can deal with, but even a slight injury can become infected if it's not treated right. Then we'd lose the man for good. Besides, they usually get sent back in a day or so. If a man goes on patrol with a fever or a bad case of trench foot, he can't think straight. He'd liable get himself and the rest of us killed."

"Doss, I'm getting damn tired of you pill pushing, blister poppers babying my men. This is a war we're in the middle of, not some soap opera hospital."

When Doss returned to the aid-station that afternoon for supplies, he got grief of a different type from Captain Stanley Webster the chief medical officer of the battalion aid-station.

"Doss, is the rumor I hear about you going out on patrols with your platoon true?"

"Yes, Captain Webster. It is."

"Were you not paying attention when we taught you the role of an aid-man? You're supposed to stay in the company area until called. Don't you know the Japs try especially hard to kill medics? I want you to quit going on patrols and stay in the company area like the other medics."

When Doss returned to Company B's area, he found that 2nd Platoon had been sent on another patrol. Despite what Captain Webster had told him, the medic set out after them. He hadn't gone far when an officer saw him.

"Where are you going Doss?"

"I'm trying to catch up with my men Lieutenant. They left on a patrol while I was gone to the aid-station."

"It's too late. I just came from their direction. There's Jap snipers all along that path. You'll never catch up with them now."

In spite of what the lieutenant had just said, Doss continued walking in 2nd Platoon's direction.

"Doss, didn't you hear me? Get back to the company area right now. That's an order!"

Doss knew he couldn't disobey a direct order, so he reluctantly turned around and headed back to the company area. As he was walking toward his foxhole, Captain Vernon called to him.

"Doss, come over here."

"Yes sir, Captain Vernon."

"2nd Platoon's on patrol. Why aren't you out with them?"

"They left while I was at the aid-station."

"Well, go catch up with them."

"It's too late now Captain. There's snipers all through the jungle, and if they don't get me, the green replacements might just mistake me for a Jap and shoot me. They aren't expecting me to show up now."

"Are you refusing to go?"

"Captain, I'd just end up getting killed if I went now, besides I'm under orders not to take that kind of risk anymore."

Captain Vernon exploded.

"Doss, you're refusing an order! You just bought yourself a court martial! You blister poppers have to take orders, just like real soldiers do. Now get out of my sight."

Doss hurried back to the aid-station and told Captain Webster what had happened.

"You're right to come to me with this. We've got to get this straightened out once and for all. Even though you're assigned as an aid-man to Company B, your chain of command runs through me, not Captain Vernon. I've been hearing from other medics about Vernon's degrading slurs, and I'm going to try to put a stop to it. For now, go on back to Company B, and try to avoid Captain Vernon until he cools off, and try not to worry. I'll see what I can do."

After Doss left, Captain Webster sent a report of the incident up to regimental headquarters. Because of Webster's report, there was no court-martial, and headquarters reminded Captain Vernon that the medics took their orders from the medical battalion not the officers of the infantry company where they were assigned. As far as regimental headquarters was concerned, the incident was officially over, but Doss knew Captain Vernon would not be so quick to forget.

By 10 August, combat operations were winding down. Although Guam had been declared secure, troops were still encountering small pockets of resistance, and the 77th continued mop-up operations for several weeks. By the end of the campaign, the 77th Division had killed almost 3,000 Japanese troops while they themselves suffered 248 dead and 663 wounded.

By late August, the entire division had been moved to a large bivouac area on the hills near Agat. The soldiers found little comfort there. The division had left a rear detachment on Oahu along with tents, extra clothing, vehicles and all the other supplies necessary to establish a semi-permanent camp. The supplies were not sent to Guam because the original plan was for the 77th to be moved to Guadalcanal and then to New Caledonia as soon as the battle ended. In the end, the division was not moved from Guam as planned, and there was no available flat area that the 77th could develop into a camp. The division was instead parked up in the hills. Troops spread out over the ridges and pitched their pup tents or built shacks out of bamboo and palm leaves. The men had to improvise almost everything they needed. Worst of all, without camp kitchens, they were forced to continue eating combat rations.

One day, Captain Webster called Doss to the aid-station.

"Doss, I'm transferring you out of Company B. I know you're still having problems with Captain Vernon. If he doesn't appreciate having one of the best aid-men in the Army, I sure do. I'm making you a litter bearer. You'll be working out of my aid-station from now on."

Doss packed up his things and moved them back to the medical battalion. He had several friends there including a litter bearer named Herb Schechter. Schechter observed the Sabbath like Doss did, but instead of being an Adventist, Schechter was a Jew. The two men liked to discuss theology, and they had discovered the Adventist and Jewish religions had many things in common.

When Schechter heard that Doss had been reassigned he went looking for him.

"Boy, I sure am glad to see you. I bet you're happy to be out of Company B and away from Vernon."

"I guess so," he said.

"You don't sound so sure buddy. What's the problem?"

"I can't help feeling I could serve my country better as an aid-man, but I guess God must have some other plan. I'll just have to wait and see what it is."

November 3, 1944
Headed to New Caledonia

Late in October 1944, a squadron of transport ships arrived off the coast of Guam. They had orders to convey the 77th Division to New Caledonia for rest and refurbishment.

On 1 November, with the ships tied up at the pier, the 77th Division soldiers began the work of packing up their equipment and loading it aboard. The 77th was ordered to leave behind all their ammunition, rations and many of their best vehicles. Since the division was not heading back into combat, the ships were not being combat loaded. Instead, the supplies and equipment they were taking with them were arranged in the holds commercially, meaning similar supplies were placed in the same hold. For example, all the cots went into one hold, and all the radio equipment went into another. This was a more efficient method of shipping supplies that made it easier to keep track of the inventory, but it would never have been used for an assault landing.

Once the ships were loaded, there was one more task to complete before the troops could board. The whole area had to be cleaned up. The men had hoped General Bruce would forget about his obsession of leaving a camp cleaner than he had found it, but just as he had done every time before, the general ordered the men to meticulously police the area. They all set to work filling in foxholes, tearing down the shacks they had built and picking up every piece of trash. Things left behind that might possibly be useful, such as logs and lumber, were neatly stacked in piles. Everything else was either burned or buried.

Mid-morning on 2 November, after the men finished policing the area, they headed off toward the ships. Doss was grinning ear to ear as he marched along. As the men left the perfectly cleaned area, they passed by a sign that some jokester had erected. Painted on the sign was the 307th Infantry motto "Clear the Way." Below the motto was a perfect reproduction of their coat of arms, but the mischievous sign painter had replaced the crossed oak branches with crossed brooms.

The troops were eager to get aboard the ships for a very good reason. Food! The GIs had been living on combat rations for the last four months, so they were all salivating over the navy food, which they knew was waiting for them. As the troops approached their ships, they talked about the food they wanted most.

Schechter started off the wish list. "All I want is a big juicy steak. About two or three of them and for dessert another steak."

"Not me," said Doss. "I want a tray piled full of mashed potatoes and some corn or green beans on the side. Then for dessert, lots of fruit or better yet, ice cream!"

"How about breakfast?" shot back a nearby soldier. "Aren't you hungry for bacon?"

"No," shouted Doss and Schechter, at the same time.

After seeing the bewildered look their reply caused, both medics broke out laughing.

As they moved closer to their ship, Doss could finally make out the name painted on its side, *USS Barnstable* (APA 93). After boarding the *Barnstable,* he and the other men quickly settled down on their bunks and began to talk about their plans for the immediate future.

"I'm gonna take a long shower then eat until I'm stuffed," said Schechter.

"Me too," said Doss. "I don't care if the showers are seawater. I might take one twice a day if they let me. Then I'm gonna sleep for at least a day or maybe two."

As it turned out, the ship stayed in port until the next day, during which time the men made the most of the chow line. By the time it pulled out of port, the men had eaten three filling navy meals. It seemed to Doss the food was even better than he remembered it.

After leaving port, the *Barnstable* waited off shore for the other ships of the transport division to arrive and form into a convoy. *Barnstable* took its place, second in line in the center column just behind *USS Harris* (APA 2). The other ships maneuvered into their assigned positions, 1000 yards between columns and 600 yards between rows. When the convoy was properly formed up the ships headed off together, their next stop, New Caledonia.

During the passage, Doss planned to do three things, eat, sleep and read his Bible. While on Guam, he had never been able to get enough food. He had been forced to survive on "dog biscuits," chocolate bars, and canned cheese from his k-rations. Sometimes he had been able to add a coconut to his meal or trade a can of pork for an unwanted can of cheese or a dried fruit bar, but the lack of adequate nutrition had taken a toll on him, and the medic had become very weak.

After just a few days of regular meals and plenty of sleep, Doss felt the strength coming back to him. Soon, he began to spend more time on deck, where he spent hours reading his Bible or talking with Glenn and Schechter. Doss had not seen much of Glenn after he was transferred to the aid-station, but aboard ship the two men regularly sought each other out.

Many times, as Doss was reading, a passing soldier or sailor would notice his Bible and stop to ask him a question about what it said on a certain subject. This happened so often, he took to writing out answers to the most common questions and keeping those sheets of paper tucked in his Bible. Word soon got around the ship that if anyone needed a Bible question answered Doss was the man to see.

After eight days on the open sea, the convoy made a sharp turn to the northwest. Rumors quickly spread throughout the ship. Because the men had been hearing discouraging radio reports about lack of progress in the battle for Leyte, most of them assumed they were being sent directly back into combat.

On 17 November, the convoy put into Seeadler Harbor at Manus Island where ammunition and supplies were waiting to replace those left behind on Guam. All the ships were unloaded, and then the cargo and men were rearranged and combat loaded back onto the transports.

While the ships were being reloaded, most of the men were able to spend at least a day on a nearby recreation island, but that seemed a poor consolation for the men who had been promised a stay in New Caledonia.

By 19 November, the ships had been reloaded and replacement troops were aboard. Late in the day, the convoy steamed out of port and headed for the Philippine Island of Leyte.

November 23, 1944
East Coast of Leyte

Before sunrise on 23 November, the 77th arrived off the east coast of Leyte in the midst of a driving rainstorm. The heavy rain was a blessing because as long as the downpour continued, Japanese planes could not operate. To take advantage of the storm, troops immediately began moving ashore. Most of the division was landed at Tarragona, but the 307th Regimental Combat Team went ashore further south near the town of Dulag, having orders to proceed inland to La Paz.

The ships were able to move very close to shore and land the troops directly on the beaches, which had already been captured and secured by the Sixth Army; therefore, the men faced no resistance from the enemy. Unloading the equipment was more difficult, because there were no piers and many of their vehicles had been left behind on Guam with the expectation of obtaining replacements from the huge supply depot on New Caledonia. To make matters worse, the vehicles the 77th had been allowed to bring along were not in good condition.

Once ashore, the 307th was charged with protecting the roads and passes leading to La Paz and also the airfields and supply dumps on the eastern coast of Leyte. It wasn't long before the men who had been cheering the rain when they first arrived, switched to cursing it. Unfortunately for the 77th, they had arrived during the rainy season, and water was everywhere. Rice paddies were flooded and overflowing. Wherever the men walked, they had to slosh through water or mud. The GIs discovered that trying to keep their feet dry was useless. The constant traffic on the roads turned them into mud pits, and repeated attempts to improve them had failed.

After patrolling the rear areas for two weeks, the 77th Division received orders on 1 December to prepare for a beach assault on the other side of Leyte near the town of Ormoc. At the time it received the orders, the division was spread out over half of the eastern side of Leyte.

On 2 December, the separated units of the 77th began the complicated task of packing up, moving to and reassembling at a staging area near Tarragona. The 307th Combat Team had the most difficult route to the loading area. Days of continuous tropical rainstorms had converted the La Paz-Rizal road, over which they must travel, into a soupy strip of slime with several huge mud pits so deep that trucks could not cross them unless being towed by bulldozers.

On 3 December, the 307th began their move toward the beach, but they soon bogged down after the churned up road became impassable. The 232nd Engineer Battalion arrived on the scene in the midst of a blinding downpour and using their heavy equipment began towing the mired vehicles through the mud. By that evening, the engineers had been able to free about a third of the 307th vehicles.

Men and equipment continued to arrive and assemble on the beaches and by mid-morning on 5 December, it became apparent that all the units of the 307th would make it by the deadline. That night the loading operation commenced.

The Navy warned General Bruce that they did not have control of the ocean off the west coast of Leyte; therefore, its ships would only be able to remain near the landing beach for two hours at most. There was no reef blocking access to the beach, so equipment and men could be unloaded directly onto shore. General Bruce decided to preload all the vehicles with supplies instead of troops. That way, instead of having to fill landing boats with supplies and then unload them on the beach, as was standard procedure, the loaded trucks could be driven directly off the ships.

The Navy only had 47 small transport ships available for the operation, which included 8 Assault Destroyers, 25 LCIs (Landing Craft Infantry), 10 LCMs (Landing Craft Medium), and four LSTs (Landing Ships Tank). These ships had to hold all the men along with supplies for two days. In the space left over, the 77th was able to cram 269 of their remaining vehicles.

Doss and many of the other members of the medical team were assigned transport on LCI-746. The Infantry Landing Craft was designed to hold about 200 troops, but on this trip, it carried more than 300. At less than 160 feet long, LCIs were the smallest Navy ships capable of serious ocean voyages under their own power. The ships were so small they were not even named. Their only identifying mark was their hull number.

As Doss boarded the ship, he noticed a word neatly painted above the armored porthole windows of the bridge.

Turning to his friend Schechter he asked, "Is that word what I think it is?"

"Yea, it's FUBAR. You know what that means don't you?"

"Of course I know what it's supposed to mean, but when I see it, I just think 'Fouled Up Beyond All Recognition' instead. I sure hope FUBARS's just a joke and not the reputation of the ship."

For other men, boarding a ship nicknamed, "FUBAR" might have been considered a bad omen, but it did not overly concern Doss or Schechter. Doss did not believe in bad or good luck but instead that he should put his trust in the Lord. If he happened to be killed, he believed he would receive eternal salvation because of God's grace. Schechter, on the other hand, believed in predestination, the idea that "the destiny of a man is determined beforehand by God." In his view, God had already pre-determined when he would die and since there was no changing His decision, there was no need to worry about it.

Early in the morning on 6 December, the loading was complete, and the convoy of small ships steamed away toward the southern tip of Leyte. Shortly after leaving, several destroyers joined the transports to escort them on their 225 mile journey around the bottom of the island and then up the west coast.

Once the ships were at sea, the men learned the nature of their mission. Seven battalions of infantry and one of artillery would be landed a few miles south of the main Japanese base located near Ormoc. To do this, they would have to sail up the west coast of Leyte through Japanese dominated waters and then land on beaches where the enemy maintained air superiority. In contrast to the assaults on the beaches of Guam, where battleships and cruisers had softened up the shoreline with days of heavy bombardment, this landing counted on the element of surprise.

The convoy arrived at its destination about an hour before sunrise on 7 December. It was decided to postpone the landing until it became light enough that the four accompanying destroyers could accurately hit targets near the beach with their 5-inch guns. Meanwhile, two LCIs, which had been converted into rocket ships, maneuvered into firing position.

At sunrise, the assault began with the rocket ships firing continuous salvos of 5-inch rockets at the beach. The ships each carried four hundred rockets, but since the launchers were bolted to the deck, the entire ship had to be turned one way or the other to aim them. Consequently, the rocket ships provided a lot of firepower, but targeting was not very accurate. The large volume of incoming rockets was intended to keep the enemy under cover while the destroyer's 5-inch guns were used to engage individual targets.

During the rocket bombardment, the troop LCIs raced straight for the beach. Several hundred feet before reaching the shore, each ship dropped its stern anchor and let the cable play out. The LCIs continued on until they grounded on the sand. Then the port and starboard ramps were lowered and the troops streamed off. Doss and Schechter went ashore by racing down the port ramp and then wading less than 50 feet in knee deep water to reach the beach. In addition to their normal equipment of rations and medic bags, each man carried several canvas litters. It took only minutes for each ship to unload their troops. Once empty, the LSIs freed themselves from the beach by shifting their twin variable pitch screws into reverse, hauling in on the stern anchor and violently moving the rudder, all while applying full power from their eight diesel engines.

Once he made it ashore, Doss wondered why the enemy had not put up much resistance to the landing. What he did not know, was the Japanese Commander at Ormoc had been expecting a friendly convoy to land reinforcements that day. When the American ships arrived offshore before sunrise and then took no offensive action, the commander assumed they were Imperial Navy ships waiting for better light to land their troops. It was not until the rocket ships opened fire that the commander realized it was American troops coming ashore. He did not live long enough to learn that all the ships bringing his reinforcements had been intercepted and sunk.

DECEMBER 7, 1944
END RUN TO ORMOC

The 307th infantry landed to the left of the 305th, and after meeting little resistance, they quickly captured their objective, the Boad River Bridge.

General Bruce's initial plan was to capture and secure a beachhead and then hold it until the transport convoy returned two days later with more supplies and reinforcements, but because of the light resistance put up by the enemy, he decided to press the attack. At 0900, he ordered the 307th to move north along Highway 2 toward Ipil.

While the 307th was preparing to move out, several amphibious DUKWs of the 902nd Field Artillery Battalion, each loaded with a howitzer, ammunition and gun crew drove out of the LSTs, into the ocean and then lumbered onto shore. Knowing the 307th might need fire support at any instant, the gun crews set up their howitzers right on the sand of the beach. The artillery was in place, zeroed-in and firing on targets less than three hours after the first infantrymen came ashore.

Enemy resistance picked up as the troops moved north toward Ipil. The Japanese had positioned machine gun nests under native huts which had to be destroyed one by one. Even so, by afternoon the 307th had killed 83 soldiers and captured Ipil. At 1640 hours, orders came down to consolidate and dig in for the night.

As soon as a defensive position had been established, General Bruce ordered several patrols sent out to obtain the information he needed to plan the next day's attacks. Bruce had two possible courses of action. He could play it safe and capture a large semi-circle with a radius of about five miles around the beachhead. This would provide enough distance to keep hostile artillery from firing into his position. However, controlling such a large area would require all his troops. If he took the safe option, he would have to wait for reinforcements from the 7th Infantry to arrive overland from the south before he could go on the attack. The problem with this plan was that although the 7th was moving north they were still seven miles away and meeting stiff resistance. If Bruce decided to wait for them to show up, it might give the Japanese time to get their defenses organized.

Bruce's second option was to maintain a half-mile beachhead. That was barely enough to keep long-range enemy machine gun fire off the beach but then he would be able to use the majority of his troops to go on the offense.

Just as he had done on Guam, Bruce decided to go on the attack. He reasoned it would be foolish to waste the element of surprise achieved during the landing by tying down all his troops just to secure a beachhead. He gambled that if he could create enough havoc in the enemy's rear area, it would bring a quicker end to the overall battle for Leyte.

The next day, 8 December, General Bruce put his plan into action. The entire division began crawling up the west coast like an inchworm. In a series of steps, the 307th would first attack to the north and then after gaining a foothold, the 305th, which was guarding the rear, would pull in close behind. In this way, Bruce maintained a narrow moving beachhead, which slowly inched its way up the coast toward Ormoc.

All that day, Doss had been working out of the 1st Battalion Aid-Station. In his new role as a litter bearer, he was not positioned up front with B Company as he had been when working as a company aid-man. Instead, the aid-station served A, B, C and D Companies. If a man was wounded in any of those companies, the litter bearers would move up to where he was being treated by the combat medic and then bring him back to the aid-station for further treatment. Doss missed living with the infantrymen from Company B, but at least in his new role, he still had some contact with them.

Late in the afternoon, one of the litter bearers returning from the front lines brought back word that a combat medic had been hit. When Doss heard the rumor, he had a sick feeling in the pit of his stomach. He searched out the litter bearer and asked, "Who was it?"

"I'm sorry Doss, it was Glenn."

"What happened? Where is he?"

"A machine gunner was hit in the head while covering Company B as they pulled back across a creek. They must have thought he was dead, but after they all pulled back, he came to and started calling for a medic. Glenn said he couldn't just leave him out there. Before anyone could stop him, he jumped up and ran out after the guy. A filthy Jap sniper waited until he got close and then shot him."

"Is he still alive?"

"Hasn't moved an inch since he got hit."

"We can't just leave him out there. I'm gonna go get him."

Schechter had been listening to the conversation. "Remember the guy Glenn was going after. There's two men out there. I'll go with you."

Both men strapped on medic bags. After receiving better directions as to the location of the wounded men, they set out.

As they approached the area, Doss spotted both men lying in some grass near the crest of a hill just on the other side of a small creek. It looked like they would have to cross several hundred yards of no man's land to reach them. Just beyond the injured men was thick brush and then jungle where the enemy was probably hiding.

The two medics worked their way across the creek, then after crawling up a shallow gully, they were able to get fairly close to the wounded soldiers. After a few more minutes, the medics were able to reach them. Doss crawled up next to the wounded machine gunner while Schechter moved in next to Glenn.

Doss could see his patient had a deep gash across his forehead. The wound had bled quite a bit, and there was a lot of dried blood crusted in the man's eyes. Blood had also coagulated in the gash, and the bleeding had almost stopped. Because of the amount of blood and location of injury, he could understand how a non-medic might have assumed the head wound had been fatal, especially since whatever had made the gash on his head probably knocked the soldier unconscious at the same time. Doss took out a dressing and using the water from his canteen, he began to soak the dried blood out of the man's eyes and then wipe them clean.

When he had finished, the soldier opened his eyes and with a big smile on his face said, "Thank God, I thought I was blind. When I came to I was alone, and I started yelling for a medic. After a while, I heard someone getting closer and then the shooting started back up. That's when I decided to shut up and play dead. I must have passed out again until you showed up."

"Are you able to crawl?"

"Sure. I think so."

"Then head off downhill and across the creek. I've got to go help another man."

Doss called quietly to Schechter, "How is he?"

"He's alive," Schechter yelled back.

Enemy soldiers, hiding in the jungle, heard his voice and began firing in the direction of the sound. Schechter jumped up and started to run.

"Down, get down. Quit running. Play dead."

Schechter hit the ground so convincingly that Doss thought he actually had been killed. After he crawled up next to him, Doss was relieved to see that he really had just been play-acting.

"From now on, no more talking," Doss whispered. "Let's go get Glenn."

Doss crawled over to his buddy. He decided that since the enemy knew where they were, he couldn't take time to examine his best friend. Instead, he took Glenn's poncho and spread it out next to him. Schechter crawled up on the other side and helped roll the injured medic onto it. Just as they got Glenn positioned, a machine gun opened up and began firing blindly into the tall grass.

The medics knew that with the machine gun firing, they dare not carry Glenn. They each grabbed hold of a corner of the poncho, crawled a few inches downhill and then pulled the poncho along behind. After repeating the process several times, they came upon a dead enemy soldier. Instead of taking the time to go around, they dragged Glenn right over the body. It took more than a half an hour of crawling before they were able to drag Glenn across the creek and behind some bushes. Schechter examined him more closely while Doss used his machete to cut two long straight branches and fasten them to the poncho to make an improvised litter.

"He's still alive Doss."

"Thank God."

By the time Doss had the litter ready, Schechter had finished treating Glenn as best as he could.

"He's ready to go."

As both men started to lift him onto the litter, Glenn opened his eyes and began to moan. Doss reached down and held his buddies hand. "Glenn, it's me."

Doss looked for some sign that his friend recognized him and then with tears streaming from his eyes he said a prayer. "Dear Lord, if it is your will please save this brave man." Doss choked up before he could say any more, but he believed God already knew everything else he had wanted to say.

The two medics picked up the homemade litter and started back for the aid-station. Glenn was a big man and even with the aid of the litter, their burden was extremely heavy. The machine gun had shifted its fire to their side of the creek, and bullets started whizzing overhead. The two men were able to carry Glenn about 100 yards before they had to set him down to rest for a minute. While they caught their breath, Doss checked Glenn's pulse. He was still alive. As they prepared to move out again, a squad of soldiers showed up.

"Captain Vernon heard you two fools were out here alone, so he sent us as a rear guard."

Two of the infantrymen grabbed hold of a litter handle while the other men spread out to give them cover. Even with four men carrying the litter, the going was rough. They managed to cross two more hills and another stream before they all had to stop for a short break.

Doss checked Glenn again and saw he was still alive. He figured they might be able to make it all the way back to the aid-station on the next trip. It was just coming into sight when the men were forced to rest one more time. Doss reached out to check his friends pulse, but he could not feel it.

"Glenn. Glenn! Clarence!"

He felt for the pulse one more time; it was not there. His best friend in the world was dead.

DECEMBER 9, 1944
THE MISSING NIGHT

Doss knew Glenn was dead, but his mind refused to accept it. The combination of exhaustion, dehydration and the shock of his friend's death had immobilized him. Doss froze in place, kneeling in the middle of the road, looking straight ahead, his face gone blank.

Concerned about the medic, Schechter and the other men attempted to talk him back to reality.

"Come on Doss, let's go, we're almost to the aid-station."

"Get up. You can't stay here in the middle of the road."

No matter what the men did or said, he would not respond. After struggling for several minutes to get through to Doss, Schechter decided to run ahead while the other two men finished carrying Glenn's body the rest of the way. Schechter was out of breath when he reached the aid-station, but he saw Captain Webster and told him what had happened.

"Glenn died…while we were…bringing him in…and now…I think…Doss is in shock."

"Where is he?"

"He's kneeling in the middle of the road…and won't move. We tried to talk to him,…but he acted like…we weren't even there."

"Okay. Show me where he is."

Schechter guided Webster back to where they had left the medic and found him still kneeling in the road. By that time, a small crowd had gathered around.

As Webster approached, he said, "You men get back. We'll take care of Doss."

Webster got down on his knees next to the grief stricken medic.

"Doss can you hear me?" He snapped his fingers in front of the medic's face. "Private Doss, this is Captain Webster, answer me."

Getting no answer, he turned to Schechter.

"Come help me get him up."

Each man took hold under an arm, lifted Doss to his feet and then all three started back.

As they neared the aid-station, Doss began to talk.

Ironically, a correspondent for *Yank* magazine had been at the aid-station all day working on an article and included part of the incident in his story.

> "As the trucks pulled out, a company aid-man was brought in suffering from battle fatigue. His denims were several sizes too large, making him look very tiny. His hands were shaking badly. "I feel okay," he kept saying. "I feel okay, but I can't stop trembling. What's the matter with me?" He looked as though he was going to cry. The other medics tried to comfort him but it didn't do any good."

After they reached the aid-station, Captain Webster brought a hand full of pills for Doss to swallow. Then he took him over to a cot and told him to lie down.

"You rest here for a while Doss. I'll come back and check on you in a minute."

Webster knew the sedatives he had just given Doss would kick in soon, and he hoped a forced rest would be enough to bring him out of it.

When Doss woke up the next morning, he was disoriented. The last thing he remembered was realizing Glenn had died. Somehow, he was now lying on a cot in the aid-station without his helmet or medic bags. One of the other medics saw he was awake and came over to talk to him.

"How you feeling?"

"Okay, I guess, but what am I doing here?"

"After Glenn died you sort of went into shock. You were laying in the road and wouldn't move. They brought you here and shoved some pills down your throat, and you've been zonked out on that cot ever since. Webster said he wanted to talk to you when you woke up. He's right over there."

Doss went over to Captain Webster. "I'm sorry for how I acted Captain. I don't know what came over me."

"How are you feeling now, Doss?"

"I'm not sure. Okay I guess."

"Do you think you're ready to go back on duty?"

"Yes sir, Captain Webster but I'd like a little time to pray first, if that's alright with you."

"Sure Doss, sure that's okay."

Doss went over to a corner of the aid-station, took out his Bible, got down on his knees and began to read and pray. He realized he needed the strength only God could give him if he hoped to carry on. He also knew he would have to figure out some way to protect himself from ever again going through the shock of emotions he had experienced with his friend's death. After some thought and prayer, he decided that in the future he would make an effort not to learn the identity of any man he treated. From then on, he wouldn't look a wounded man in the face if he could help it. He would just try to treat every man as fast and best as he could. He knew he would probably see more friends die before the war was over. If he kept letting it affect him as much as Glenn's had, he would end up in an army psych ward. After about 20 minutes of reading and praying, he felt ready to return to his duties.

When Doss went back to Captain Webster and told him he was prepared to go back to work, the captain had other ideas.

"Doss, I want you to spend the rest of the day helping move patients from the aid-station to the mobile hospital at Deposito."

"But Captain, I feel ready to go back on litter duty right now."

"Listen here Doss. I'm not asking your opinion, and I don't appreciate you 'buting' me. Today you are going to evacuate men to the clearing station. If you do okay, we'll see about putting you back on litter duty tomorrow."

The medical battalion was using two captured trucks to transport the wounded men back to Deposito. One of the medics had painted crude white stars on the doors to warn the American troops that the trucks were not being driven by the enemy. He didn't add the Red Cross insignia because experience showed that such a marking tended to draw Japanese fire instead of providing the protection called for in the Geneva Convention.

The previous night, infantrymen of the 307th had reached the high ground just short of Camp Dawnes. From there they could see the former Philippine Army base consisting of several wooden buildings laid out along the top of a ridge. Coastal Highway 2, a ten-foot wide sand and gravel road, ran between the camp and the ocean. It was there the 307th held up for the night to give the 305th enough time to pull in close behind them and consolidate the gains they had made during the day.

On the morning of 9 December, at about the same time as Doss was starting his first evacuation run, the 307th attacked Camp Dawnes. During the night, the enemy had strengthened their positions, and the Americans faced heavy fighting, but by the evening of the ninth, the 307th had fought their way into the camp and captured the two most southern buildings.

While the 307th battled for Camp Dawnes, Doss made several round trips, helping to move men to the collecting station where they would be prepared to be evacuated by ship. In between one of the trips, he spotted a plantation of coconut trees, loaded with nuts. Previously he had tried to supplement his K-rations by eating coconuts he found lying on the ground, but every time he did, it gave him diarrhea. The last time he got sick, he promised himself he wasn't going to eat any more. In the meantime, he had noticed that the native men gathered coconuts from the trees instead of off the ground. After seeing the grove of trees, he decided he would climb up one and pick a nut to see if his stomach would tolerate a fresh one better.

As he neared the trees, he could see the natives had cut notches in the trunks to make them easier to climb. As he stood pondering the trees, several soldiers from a nearby engineering battalion walked up.

"Hey mac, you thinking about climbing that tree?"

"Yea, I guess so, but those notches look too far apart."

"Haven't you ever seen a native climb a palm tree? They can reach the notches because they aren't wearing pants. Now, if you took your pants off, you could probably climb it too."

"Very funny, Ha Ha. I'm not taking my pants off."

With a determined look on his face, he grabbed hold of the tree. After a little trial and effort, he made it to the top. Once there, he held on with one hand and used the other to twist off a nut. As soon as he had the coconut free he realized he couldn't hold it and climb back down. He called out, "Look out below." Then he dropped the nut to the ground.

The soldiers called back up, "While you're up there, how about throwing some more down."

Doss twisted a dozen more free and dropped them to the ground. That was when he recognized he didn't really know how to get back down. He had seen the natives sort of slide down the trunk, so that is what he tried. When he reached the bottom of the tree, he realized he must have done something wrong. His clothes had slid up, and the bark left cuts on his legs, chest and hands. To make matters worse, the engineering troops were gone, and the coconuts he had dropped were nowhere to be found.

When he returned to the truck the other medics took one look at him and asked, "What happened to you?"

He just looked at them and replied, "I don't want to talk about it."

Later while working to unload casualties at the clearing station he overheard some of the other medics talking about how three surgeons had been operating nonstop for over fifty hours. Doss could not imagine how the doctors were able to hold up to such a strain, but their actions helped him realize that the war was testing every man to the extreme. He decided that if they could handle the pressure then with God's help he could also. By that night, he was thankful Captain Webster had assigned him a day of light duty and felt confident he would be able to return to work as a litter bearer the next day.

December 10, 1944
Moving into Ormoc

So that he could keep closer contact with his front line troops, General Bruce ordered the division command post relocated to a hill just south of Camp Downes. His men had the command post ready to be moved so quickly, that when the forward team arrived at the hill, they found themselves in the middle of a battle between the 307th and some stubborn holdouts. Fortunately, by the time the command staff arrived, the enemy stragglers had been eliminated.

The new location gave General Bruce a clear view of the town. From his vantage point, he could see that Ormoc was situated directly on the coast, bound on the west by the ocean, on the northwest by the Antilao River and on the southeast by the Ormoc River. It was a large town. Not like the villages the 77th had captured thus far in the war. The main road passed through town, mirroring the coastline, about 300 feet from the beach. Ormoc's other streets were arranged in a grid pattern, creating about 36 city blocks, with one of the streets leading to a large concrete pier, which extended westward into the ocean. The pier looked large enough to accommodate an American cargo ship, and it would come in handy once the city was in American hands. Bruce made a note to remind the artillery that he wanted them to avoid shelling the pier.

After verifying the layout of the town was correctly depicted on his maps, Bruce issued orders for the plan of attack, which he scheduled to begin the next morning. The 307th was to make a frontal attack by moving northward into town between the beach and the Ormoc-Tambuco road while the 306th would move around to the northeast, in an attempt to flank the enemy.

The morning of 10 December, before General Bruce's plans could get underway, a large group of Japanese fighters and bombers appeared over the area. They made a bombing run and then flew away. The air raid did nothing to disrupt Bruce's timetable and at 0930 hours the artillery opened up on Ormoc. At the same time, LCM rocket ships approached the town from the ocean. Once in range they let loose with a thunderous salvo of rockets. The ship's crews got in on the action by firing their .50 caliber machine guns at the enemy soldiers defending the pier. The combined artillery and rocket barrage set most of the buildings in town on fire and detonated several ammunition dumps, which sent great clouds of concrete dust and smoke into the air.

Using the cover of the smoke and explosions, the two regiments moved into position. As the 307th approached, they were met by enemy troops firing from dugout holes beneath houses in town. When such an emplacement was located, it was first blasted by mortars or self-propelled guns and then the infantry would move in to finish the job. In that manner, the men fought house to house through Ormoc. By the end of the day, the 307th had made it to the other side of the town and linked up with the 306th. Despite very heavy fighting, the division's losses were surprisingly low. The 77th ended up losing only 13 men in the battle.

Once the town was in American hands, General Bruce decided to take a day to reorganize and resupply his troops. December 11th was spent making limited attacks to straighten up the front lines. The supply depots and hospital, as well as one battalion of artillery, were moved forward to Ormoc. Bruce planned to turn the defense of the area over to the 7th and 11th Divisions as soon as they arrived and then continue toward Valencia in pursuit of the enemy. The general was chomping at the bit to continue the chase, so that evening he sent the following radio message to the commanders of the 7th and 11th divisions.

"Have rolled two sevens in Ormoc. Come on 7 and 11. Bruce."

During that time, Doss and the other litter bearers were moving wounded men back across the Ormoc River. Despite the almost constant rain, the river was not very deep, being only up to their knees or hips at most, but it was about 100 feet wide at the area where they were crossing. Moving casualties across the river was dangerous because while the men were in the water they were exposed to snipers hidden along the banks.

To make carrying the stretchers easier, each medic had a harness, which went over his shoulders. Attached to the rig was a loop that fit over the handle of the litter. Four medics were used to move a litter with one man on each corner. Doss was positioned on the front left while Schechter carried the front right.

The litter-bearers had just crossed the river and were struggling up the bank when Doss heard the sound of a bullet whiz by behind him followed by the wet "thunk" of it impacting flesh. Schechter pitched forward and the wounded man they were carrying tumbled from the stretcher. At the same time, the crack of a gunshot reached their ears.

Doss and the other two medics dragged Schechter and their patient over the crest of the hill where they would be shielded from the unseen sniper.

Doss removed Schechter's jacket, ripped open a packet of sulfa and sprinkled it in the wound. Then he took two large compression dressings and tied them tightly over the bullet entrance and exit holes. Leaving Schechter alone for a few minutes, the three medics carried the original wounded man the rest of the way to the waiting jeep ambulance and fastened the litter to one of the pipe racks. Then they ran back with an empty stretcher to get Schechter. When they returned, they saw that Schechter was still alive but unconscious. As they were placing the wounded medic onto the stretcher, Doss tried to comfort him, and also to reassure himself.

"Don't worry buddy, we got you now. You'll be okay."

The three medics had carried their friend back to the jeep and were starting to place him on a rack when a machine gun opened fire. Enemy bullets impacted all around and before they could secure Schechter, the driver panicked and hit the gas. Doss shoved the stretcher forward with all his might as he ran to keep up with the jeep. Machine gun rounds were splashing up mud at his heels as he lunged forward and grabbed hold of the spare tire. Doss, who was being dragged behind the jeep, held on for all he was worth as his shoes plowed two furrows in the mud. After the driver rounded a curve in the road that took them out of sight of the machine gunner, he finally came to his senses and stopped. Somehow, Schechter's stretcher had remained on the jeep despite all the bumping and swerving and they continued on to the aid-station without any further incident.

After the medics removed Schechter from the ambulance and placed him in the triage area, Doss waited by his friend while one of the doctors looked him over. The doctor saw him waiting, and after finishing his examination, he just looked at Doss and shook his head. The medic knew they would try everything humanly possible to save his pal, but the look on the doctor's face said it all. He later learned that Schechter never regained consciousness. Doss had now lost two good friends in less than a week.

DECEMBER 12, 1944
RICE PADDY RESCUE

Just a little way up the road from Ormoc, at the Cogon road junction, the enemy had established a strong roadblock. General Bruce's first preference was to bypass it and continue on to the division's objective at Valencia. Before he could seriously consider that option, he needed to send a patrol into the area to gather information. He decided to allow one more day for the men to regroup while the patrol had a look around. The division used this extra day to build up supplies at the depot they had established near the Ormoc pier and to reposition the artillery closer to the front lines.

When the patrol returned, they brought news that Bruce did not want to hear. The enemy troops at Cogon had enough firepower to deny them the use of the highway. From their position, they also controlled the surrounding countryside. The Japanese had established a fort in a large concrete building and placed many machine gun positions in spider holes to protect the approach. It would be impossible to isolate and bypass Cogon. If the division wanted supply convoys to follow them north, they would have to eliminate the roadblock.

Bruce had no choice but to devise a plan to take Cogon. The 305th would make the main thrust of the attack by moving up the left side of the highway. The 307th would protect the left flank and the 306th would protect the right. As the battle progressed, the 306th would try to move around to the right and cut the road north of Cogon to prevent the enemy from retreating.

Before the attack could begin, aerial artillery observers flew over the area. From the air, many dug-in positions, which were not visible from the ground, became apparent. The observers called in artillery fire, which blasted away camouflage revealing even more enemy positions.

General Bruce delayed the infantry assault until the area could be softened up by some more artillery fire. A 105mm howitzer was brought up on the south side of the Antilao River to a position where it could fire directly across at the concrete building. From there it fired over 100 rounds at almost point blank range. Even after firing every shell they had, the howitzer was unable to destroy the stronghold. After running out of ammunition, the big gun pulled back.

As the infantry moved up, they were met by repeated counterattacks, but by early evening they had managed to reach the last ridge before Cogon. Every time the Americans tried to cross over, the Japanese defenders were able to force them back. In one attempt to advance past the ridge, hostile fire reduced an American squad of 52 men to 11 in less than a minute. When the enemy tried to counterattack, the Americans were able to hold them at the ridge. By the end of the day, the Americans had tried to cross the ridge five times, and each time they were met with a counterattack. A stalemate had developed.

General Bruce ordered his troops to hold their positions for the night and then continue the attack the next morning. Around 1700, as the men of the 305th were digging in, Captain Hufnagel noticed a group of Japanese soldiers moving up a ravine toward Cogon. He radioed back a request for artillery support, but headquarters was reluctant to agree because they had sent a patrol up that same ravine earlier and were not sure of its current position. While waiting for headquarters to approve the artillery strike, Hufnagel moved several machine guns into position to fire down into the ravine once they got word the patrol was in the clear. The captain, growing impatient, radioed back to headquarters again.

"This is Hufnagel calling. What's the hold-up? I know those are Jap troops in that ravine. I can see them in the Snooperscope."

By the time headquarters had confirmed that the American patrol was out of the ravine and given permission to open fire, it was well past sunset. Several machine guns immediately opened up spraying tracers back and forth into the gulley. Within minutes, artillery began dropping on the far side, and as the firing angle was adjusted, the explosions moved down the slope. The barrage continued for almost 20 minutes until it seemed every square foot of the area had been pounded. The next morning, when Captain Hufnagel sent men to investigate, they found the bodies of more than 350 enemy soldiers.

The orders for 14 December were the same as the day before. Continue the advance toward Cogon. At first light, spotter planes flew over the area again. From the air, they spotted a large network of soldiers hidden in foxholes directly in the path of the 305th. Bruce ordered another artillery barrage on the enemy position to soften it up further. Then he sent motorized guns and armored D7 bulldozers into the area. The dozers lowered their blades and roared off into the midst of the emplacements. As dozers scraped off the tops of foxholes, drivers leaned out of their cabs and shot the exposed soldiers with their carbines. Other drivers used their blades to bury alive, enemy soldiers crouching in their holes. The motorized gun crews devised a tactic of driving over a foxhole and then dropping a grenade through the floor escape hatch as they passed over the terrified men cowering below.

While the 305th was engaged in the direct attack, the 307th encountered relatively little opposition as they continued to move forward protecting the left flank.

Doss was working in the aid-station when a call came back from the front lines that a lone man had been hit while trying to cross a rice paddy and was crying out for a medic. They were warned that the area was not secure, and there was still an unseen sniper operating in the vicinity. When the medics heard the situation, nobody spoke up volunteering to go after the man. They knew the Japanese often set traps by wounding an American and letting them cry out to lure medics into the area. The snipers would wait until a medic arrived, and then kill both him and the original wounded man. The enemy set a high priority on killing medics because they knew it was a sure way of breaking down the morale of the infantrymen. Standard procedure in such an instance was for the medics to wait until the area was secure before attempting a rescue.

When Doss heard of the wounded man, he spoke up.

"We can't just leave him out there. It could take hours to get that sniper. He might bleed to death in the meantime. I'm going after him."

Doss waited for a moment to see if anyone else would volunteer to go along. When he heard nothing but silence from the other medics, he strapped on his medic bags and hurried off alone. As he neared the front line, Sergeant Brock motioned him over.

"I figured it'd be you Doss. The man is about halfway across the rice paddy. He got hit by a sniper hidden somewhere up on that hill. The Jap hasn't fired again. I think he might be hunting medics. You sure you want to go after him?"

"I'm willing to give it a try. Give me about a minute to say a prayer then I'll go get him."

"Okay, let me know when you're ready."

The sergeant listened while Doss got down on his knees. "Lord, please forgive my sins. A soldier needs help out there, and I feel you want me go after him. I ask that you send your angels to protect me as you have before. If I get killed, please look after Dorothy. In Jesus name, Amen."

"Okay Sarge, I'm ready now."

The medic looked over the area one last time, plotted his route and then set off. At first, he crawled toward a low rock wall, which ran from right to left along the edge of the field. When he reached the wall, he followed it to the left until it ended. Then he slid down into the water and mud of the rice paddy and inched his way deeper into the field. As soon as he entered the field, other GIs moved in behind the wall and began firing at the opposite hill in an attempt to keep the unseen sniper's head down. As Doss crawled through the water and mud, deeper into the field, Sergeant Brock used his binoculars to watch the medic's progress. Suddenly he spotted a hidden machine gun directly in his path. It was impossible to fire at the position because Doss was directly in the line of fire. It seemed obvious that the medic, who was concentrating on reaching the fallen man, was not aware of the danger.

The sergeant watched, anticipating that at any moment the Jap machine gun would open fire. Doss had crawled within 40 feet of the enemy position when he heard the injured man moan. Now having an exact location of the downed man, he veered slightly off to head directly for him. Doss had come so close to the enemy gun, that at first, Brock had believed it was unmanned.

That is, until the medic veered to the left and the machine gun barrel moved to follow him.

When Doss reached the casualty, he found that the snipers bullet had badly broken his right leg, and he had lost a lot of blood. Crawling up next to him, Doss tightly bandaged his leg and then began dragging him back the way that he had come. By that time, other GIs were watching the machine gun track the medic, but they were unable to fire at it because Doss and the wounded man were still blocking their shot. When the medic neared the wall, he stood up, holding the injured man under the arm and called out.

"Hey, someone help me with this guy."

The shocked soldiers began motioning for Doss to get down, but he just stared back with a puzzled look on his face. Within moments, one of the infantrymen jumped over the wall, ran out to Doss and quickly helped him carry the wounded man back to safety. Once they were out of the way, the other men begin firing at the area where the machine gun had been hidden, but they soon realized it was no longer there.

Brock crawled over to the mud-covered medic.

"I can't believe you made it out of there alive. Didn't you see that Jap machine gun? You passed within 30 feet of it. He had you in his sights the whole time. The good Lord sure must have heard your prayer."

After Sergeant Brock finished telling what he had seen, the medic went weak in the knees. The story the sergeant had told him seemed almost unbelievable, but as Doss numbly followed the litter-bearers back to the aid-station, other soldiers kept coming up to him telling the same story.

"Hey Doc I saw the whole thing from up on the hill. You're lucky to be alive!"

"Praise the Lord," Doss mumbled.

"I can't believe that Jap didn't shoot," said another.

"Praise God."

"He sure took care of you today, Doss."

"Praise God," he said again.

When the medic reached the aid-station, he began to think about why the enemy machine gunner hadn't opened fire. That day, a scripture he had read many times in his little Bible kept returning to his mind again and again.

Thou shalt not be afraid for the terror by night; nor for the arrow that flieth by day; Nor for the pestilence that walketh in darkness; nor for the destruction that wasteth at noonday. A thousand shall fall at thy side, and ten thousand at thy right hand; but it shall not come nigh thee.

Doss believed the things he had read in the Bible and took them seriously. During the last two years, he had stood firm on his understanding of the Ten Commandments and the Army had finally come to realize that he was unmovable in his convictions about God's law, but what about God's promises? Could God's promises be literal also? The Bible passage that talked about thousands falling certainly seemed to apply to the situation Doss found himself in. After some more thought, he decided that he would have to study what the Bible said about the whole subject of God's protection, and for the next several days he spent every spare moment doing just that.

DECEMBER 15, 1944
FORWARD TO VALENCIA

For the 307th, there was a temporary lull in the action as they remained in position to protect the left flank while the rest of the division continued the attack at the Cogon road junction. Doss was using whatever spare minutes he could find to study what the Bible said about God's protection. It was during one of those times that a runner from Company B came to the aid-station with a request. Since their company aid-man was sick, Captain Vernon asked that they send someone else to take a look at his feet.

When the medics at the aid-station heard the message, their response was not very sympathetic to put it mildly. In fact, each man tried to outdo the others as they vented their pent up frustration with Captain Vernon to the messenger.

"You can tell the jerk, that after all the crap he gave us about being blister poppers, he can sit there and suffer for all I care."

"Maybe his feet will rot off, and then he won't have to worry about them anymore."

"Tell him to crawl back here, and then we'll take care of him. Oh, I forgot, real soldiers don't go to the aid-station when they get sick."

Doss was the one medic who more than any other, had the right to be sore at Captain Vernon, but instead it sickened him to hear the other men react that way. He silently strapped on his medic bags, and then said to the messenger, "Come on, let's go."

When Doss arrived at Vernon's tent and stepped inside, he saw that the captain had taken off his shoes and propped his legs up. His feet were red and swollen and there were several oozing sores. Doss knew right away he was dealing with a case of jungle rot.

When the captain looked up, he was surprised to see that it was Doss who had come to help him.

"Hello Doss," mumbled Captain Vernon.

"Hello Captain Vernon," answered Doss.

No more was said as he opened up his kit and went to work on the captain's feet. First he knelt down and used a canteen full of clean water and some soap to thoroughly wash Vernon's feet. Captain Vernon felt uncomfortable with what Doss was doing, but he would have been surprised if he knew the medic felt no such awkwardness. The medic knew Jesus had washed the feet of his disciples as an act of humility, and he himself had ceremoniously washed the feet of other men at church each time before he took part in the communion service.

Once Doss had the captains feet as clean as possible, he applied Frazer's Solution, a mixture of alcohol, iodine, salicylic and boric acid and then wrapped his feet loosely with clean gauze. He knew Captain Vernon should have had his own personal foot care kit that included a small bottle of Frazer's Solution, because every infantry soldier had been issued one, but because of his past dealings with the captain, he suspected Vernon had not thought the kit was important enough to keep track of.

When Doss was finished, he stood up. "I'll leave my big bottle of foot ointment in case yours is already used up. You should stay off your feet as much as possible and keep them warm and dry. Wash your feet every day and use the Frazer's afterwards."

Doss knew Captain Vernon had heard all this before; every infantryman had been repeatedly told how important it was to take care of his feet. Even so, he had felt obliged to go through the foot care instructions again. Doss turned to go.

Captain Vernon called out, "Doss I'm …." His voice dropped off before he finished the sentence.

Doss figured it was hard for the captain to express his gratitude, especially to someone he had caused so much grief. Whether Vernon had finished what he started to say or not, the medic knew the captain appreciated that he had come to help, and for the medic, that was thanks enough.

Later that day, back at the aid-station, Doss learned that the sick medic who had replaced him as aid-man for Company B had died of pneumonia. When Doss heard the news, he immediately went to Captain Webster and asked to be transferred back to his old job.

"What's up Doss? Why would you want to go back there?"

"I just want to be with my men Captain. It feels wrong with someone else taking care of them."

"Okay Doss. Who knows, maybe Vernon will treat you better this time around. If you're sure that's what you want, I'll fill out the paperwork and send you back up there tomorrow morning. But I don't need any problems between you and Captain Vernon like last time. Is that clear?"

"Yes sir, and thank you Captain Webster."

The next morning, Doss went to get his transfer orders and then set off for Company B. When he arrived, he reported to Captain Vernon.

"I've been sent back as the replacement company aid-man. Here are my orders, Captain Vernon."

Vernon took the paperwork, grunted and then after he looked them over, turned to the medic.

"If there's ever anything you see that's not right with the company you come to me, and I'll set it straight. Now get out of here and go to work."

Other men might not have seen it that way, but Doss took the words from the captain as a welcome back to the company.

"Yes sir, Captain Vernon. I'll do just that."

Doss had arrived back at Company B just as they were preparing to move out. The Japanese stronghold at the Cogon road junction had finally been overcome and the division was ready to move on to Valencia. Although the 305th was now able to move north following the road, the 307th had to move cross-country, first to the west and then turning north to attack Valencia. The 306th would initially follow the 307th then at the halfway mark turn to the northeast and cut Highway 2 between the villages of Catayom and Dayhagan. This plan required the 307th to make about an eight mile trek through the jungle. Since the terrain was too rough for normal vehicles, four amphibious tanks had been assigned to help carry supplies. However, when they failed to show up on time, all the equipment and supplies needed for two full days ended up having to be hand carried. To help make up for the loss of the tanks, about 100 natives were recruited to carry ammunition and other supplies.

At 0730 on 16 December, the division moved out. They were led by the 2nd Battalion, followed by Doss and the 1st Battalion, with the 3rd Battalion bringing up the rear.

Even with 100 natives helping to carry the supplies, each soldier had to carry something extra in addition to their normal equipment. Doss volunteered to carry a case of M16 smoke grenades, since many times they were needed to screen the movements of medics as they moved to rescue downed soldiers. He figured it was in his best interest to make sure they had plenty along. The grenades weighed about two pounds each and were packaged 25 to a box.

The men had put up with almost constant rain since the day they landed on Leyte, but as they prepared to move out that morning the weather cleared. By midmorning, there was not a cloud in the sky. The troops started off, tromping under a clear sky through mud that ranged from ankle to knee deep. By noon, they were broiling under the hot tropical sun. Every step they took stirred up clouds of biting insects and added more sticky mud to their shoes.

Doss, who had never had trouble keeping up before, found himself struggling and dropping further and further back in the column. By the time the troops reached a chest deep stream, he was in danger of falling behind. The other men tried to urge him along because they knew how dangerous it was to become a straggler.

"Come on Doss you got to keep up."

"Don't fall behind or the Japs 'll get you for sure."

After marching all day in the scorching sun, weighed down with pounds of mud on their clothes, the other men were eager to plunge into the cool stream. All Doss could think of as he watched the other men cross while holding their burdens above their head was how tired he was. When Lieutenant Colt saw him sitting on the box of grenades staring at the stream, he became concerned.

"What's wrong with you Doss? I've never seen you like this before."

"I don't know what's come over me Lieutenant. I just feel so weak today."

Colt knew he couldn't leave Doss sitting there. Suddenly he had an idea. Ever since they had started out that morning, more and more natives had shown up to follow alongside the troops. The soldiers joked among themselves that maybe the natives thought they were coming along on a picnic. Colt motioned a group of five of them over and pointed to the box, which Doss was carrying. The men were so eager to help, two almost got into a fight over who would carry it. Several others helped steady Doss as he waded to the other side of the stream. The native men stayed by the medic's side until that evening when the 307th reached the village of San Jose about two miles west of Valencia. By that time, he was feeling like himself again.

When the 307th entered San Jose, they surprised two platoons of enemy soldiers who were fixing their supper. Instead of escaping to warn the troops at Valencia as they should have, the Japanese stood their ground and fought. They were eliminated within minutes.

An aid-station was set up along a narrow road, and the few casualties incurred that day were gathered together to await evacuation. The medical team had planned to use the amphibious tanks to evacuate the wounded, but they still had not shown up. Instead, the artillery's Piper Cub spotter plane landed on the dirt road and flew some of the most serious cases back to Ormoc. The plane could only take one man at a time, and the round trip took about half an hour, so after several trips, the plane had to revert back to its role of artillery spotting. Sundown was coming, and it was needed to zero in the protective artillery fire before it became too dark for the spotter to see.

The next morning on 17 December, General Bruce flew to San Jose in the spotter plane. Once the pilot dropped off Bruce, he made several other round trips to fly out all of the remaining casualties.

Meanwhile, Bruce informed the 307th commander that although he was letting the other regiments continue toward their objectives, the 307th would remain in San Jose until Valencia could be softened up with artillery and an air strike.

All morning, the artillery continued pounding Valencia until around 1400, when aerial observers saw what they estimated to be 2,000 enemy troops leave the town and head east toward the mountains. At that point, General Bruce gave the go ahead for the 307th to move out. They had only gone a short distance when the forward scouts spotted a large group of Japanese soldiers heading toward them on the San Jose-Valencia road. They radioed back a warning, which gave the Americans a chance to set up a crossfire with machine guns placed along both sides of the road. The enemy troops continued down the road, and when they eventually spotted the Americans, they demonstrated no military discipline whatsoever. Instead, they charged forward wildly screaming and waving their swords. Though shocked at the enemy's actions, the Americans wasted no time mowing them down with concentrated automatic gunfire.

As the GIs continued up the road, they met periodic resistance. Doss was moving forward along with the rest of the men. He normally maintained a position about two thirds of the way back in line. That way, he was far enough forward to reach wounded men at the front of the column quickly but not so far forward to be an easy target for Japanese snipers who were always on the lookout for medics to shoot. That day, Doss was not paying enough attention and found himself at the front of the column. Just when he realized where he was, the soldier who was standing next to him carrying a BAR (Browning Automatic Rifle) was shot in the foot. Doss opened up his medical kit and began to work.

"Don't worry Sarge, you're not hit bad."

Since the wound was pumping a lot of blood, the medic took out a tourniquet and applied it just above the ankle.

"That should take care of the bleeding. I'll give you some morphine to help the pain while you wait for the stretcher bearers."

As soon as the sergeant heard that Doss wanted to use morphine, he began to argue.

"I don't need no morphine, and I don't need to wait around to be carried back on no stretcher. The aid-station's not far. I can make it back there myself."

"Look Sarge, there's no need for that."

"Forget it Doc. Go worry about someone who's really hurt."

Despite Doss arguing to the contrary, the sergeant got up and began limping his way back toward the aid-station.

While Doss had been trying to deal with the sergeant, another soldier was wounded by a heavy caliber bullet, which split open the man's abdominal wall and spilled his intestines out all over the road. When he reached the man, another medic who was already there, looked up at Doss and shook his head. It seemed obvious to him that the man had no chance of surviving such a serious wound. Doss had to agree with the other medic's unspoken assessment, but he also had a personal motto that he tried to live by.

While the other medic looked on, Doss gathered up the man's intestines and stuffed them back inside. Then he used a large battle dressing to push the wound back together and hold it closed. The stretcher-bearers waited until he was finished to load the man and then set off for the aid-station.

When Doss stood up, he had expected the other medic to give him some grief about "wasting his time treating a dead man." Instead, the other medic looked at him and said, "I know, I know. You don't have to say it again. Where there's life there's hope." Then he shook his head, turned and walked away.

By sundown, the 307th had made it to the southwest corner of the Valencia airport where they dug in for the night.

At 0830 the next day, the attack continued, and after 30 minutes of fighting, the 307th had taken both the entire airfield and the town of Valencia. While the men spent the rest of the day mopping up sporadic resistance, the regimental commander sent a strong patrol southward down Highway 2 toward Cogon to meet up with the 306th. Once contact was made, the road was opened up, and a waiting supply convoy moved north into Valencia to resupply the 307th. The men were ecstatic to see the trucks roll into town because they had been surviving for four days, on the two days' worth of supplies they had brought along.

Doss went over to the aid-station to restock. While he was there, he asked Captain Webster about the patient he had sent back the day before.

"You're not gonna believe it, but he was still alive this morning, so we evacuated him back to Ormoc. Last I heard, he's holding on. Oh, but the sergeant you treated with the foot wound. You wrote on the 52b he refused morphine? He staggered in mumbling something about not needing a stretcher. He died right after he got here. Probably shock. Happened when we loosened up his tourniquet."

DECEMBER 19, 1944
FINISHING UP THE BATTLE FOR LEYTE

General Bruce's orders for 19 December were to continue the attack up Highway 2, secure the Tagbong River Bridge and capture the road junction at Libungao. To accomplish this, the order of battle required the 305th to move up and take over the defense of Valencia, allowing the 307th to continue the advance north along the highway. Meanwhile, the 306th would swing around to the west moving cross-country to capture the Tagbong Bridge.

That morning, the 307th moved out and headed north along Highway 2. They were using a wedge formation with the 2nd Battalion in the lead. The 3rd Battalion was a little back on the right and the 1st on the left. The road north of Valencia was crossed with many streams and ridges, which ran perpendicular to the highway. At some time previously the ground along both sides had been cleared for use as farmland and planted with sugar cane, but for the last several years the neglected fields had grown up in wild grass, which was in most places higher than a standing man. That native grass made it difficult for the advancing troops to spot hidden defensive positions.

At first, the 307th made good progress meeting only scattered resistance as they moved north, and by 1700 hours the leading troops had covered three miles. However, when they reached the area near the Naghalen River, they began encountering strong resistance. It was estimated that about 2,000 Japanese were defending the approach to Libungao, and soon it became apparent that the 307th had run into the most heavily defended strongpoint since Camp Downes. Because it was getting dark, there wasn't enough time for the 1st and 3rd Battalions to envelop the position, so instead, Colonel Hamilton ordered the men to dig in for the night.

All that night American mortars and artillery blasted the enemy in an attempt to soften them up before morning. The next day the regiment assaulted the position using the same wedge formation they had been using the day before. After the 2nd Battalion was fully engaged, the 1st Battalion moved in behind them and snugged up next to the 3rd Battalion's left flank. They all continued forward in this new configuration.

At 1000, the 2nd Battalion had just fought their way to the high ground and were about to overrun the position when the enemy launched a counterattack.

"Banzai, Banzai," they screamed, as about 200 Japanese troops jumped up from a hidden position just to the north of the ridge. Several screeching officers waved their swords over their heads as they led the charge screaming "Banzai" at the top of their lungs.

The word Banzai, roughly translated, means long live the Emperor or just long life. The militaristic leaders of Japan had perverted and corrupted the samurai conception of Bushido to condition the Japanese people to be ideologically obedient to the emperor. Since the samurai would rather commit suicide than endure a great humiliation, the government brainwashed its soldiers to believe it was a greater humiliation to surrender than to die. At the beginning of the war, they worked to convince the troops that if they ever faced the likelihood of being captured, a Banzai attack would be an honorable alternative. They also exaggerated the effectiveness such an attack might have against American infantry troops. When the Banzai strategy was being devised, Japanese war planners never dreamed that America would equip every infantryman with a M1 Garand semi-automatic rifle. The M1, which was able to fire eight rounds as quickly as the soldier could pull the trigger, gave the American infantryman a tremendous firepower advantage over the Japanese troops who were still using bolt-action single shot rifles.

That advantage invariably played out the same way during a Banzai attack. For the first one or two seconds the frenzied hoard of onrushing soldiers paralyzed the Americans into inaction. Then the GI's reflexes, honed by numerous hours of rifle training, took over. A wave of two or three hundred Japanese infantrymen attacking in the daylight over open ground was usually mowed down within moments.

This was exactly what happened to the suicide wave that attacked 2nd Battalion. The enemy troops were cut down so quickly, that in the aftermath their bodies ended up in a huge pile. It looked as if they had run into an invisible lethal wall. When the leading soldiers were hit, their bodies slowed down the ones in the rear of the charge and allowed the American troops to stop them as they tried to maneuver past their fallen comrades. The more Japanese that fell, the bigger the obstacle became until finally they were forced to climb over a pile of bodies in an attempt to continue the charge.

The 2nd battalion had just stopped the first Banzai charge, when moments later, another one erupted a slight distance away. The result of that charge was the same as the first.

Within a span of less than 20 minutes, the 2nd Battalion had killed over 400 enemy soldiers. Later when the infantrymen came to realize a Banzai attack was such a quick and effective way to kill Japanese, they began trying to think of ways to provoke them into making one.

After taking a short pause to reorganize after the two suicide attacks, the 307th continued on until that afternoon, when they reached another strong enemy position about 1,000 yards south of Libungao. There the Japanese had set up a defense similar to those the 77th had encountered several times before, and it was robust enough to stop the forward momentum of the 2nd Battalion.

Colonel Hamilton ordered a double envelopment of the position. The 1st Battalion would move around to the left and cut off the highway just to the rear of the enemy while the 3rd Battalion would go around the right, bypassing the strong point and continue on to the original objective at Libungao.

Despite a maximum use of mortars and artillery support, the enemy defenses were so strong, all three units failed to reach their objectives.

The 3rd Battalion was moving through tall grass just before dark when Company K, which was leading, ran into a hidden enemy position. The resistance was so fierce, they were forced to withdraw without retrieving their wounded.

Meanwhile, the 306th had successfully captured the bridge at the Tagbong River. Since they could not evacuate their casualties by road until the 307th cleared the roadblock, they left one battalion behind to guard the bridge while the other two began heading east toward the Highway 2 intersection at Libungao to help with the battle there.

The 306th arrived in close proximity to the road junction at about sunset, just as K Company, 307th was being forced to retreat from the tall grass on the other side of the road.

General Bruce was eager to push through this last roadblock, open up Highway 2 and link up with X Corps, which was fighting its way down the highway from the north. In an effort to break the Japanese resistance, he ordered an all-night artillery barrage followed by a maximum effort 30 minute barrage to occur just before sunrise. This was followed by an infantry attack at 0700 on the morning of 21 December, which began with the 1st Battalion completing their encirclement of the enemy position and cutting the highway just north of the stronghold. Then the 2nd Battalion moved into the crossroad. Resistance was very light because the few enemy soldiers, who were still alive after the all-night barrage, were too dazed by the artillery to offer much resistance.

The next morning, when Company K returned to the grassy area where they had been forced to leave behind their wounded, they discovered that overnight the Japanese had bayoneted every one of the injured soldiers.

After the battle, Doss was at the aid-station to get supplies, when he noticed a wounded Japanese prisoner being brought in under guard. This was the first POW he had seen on Leyte. Although the 307th killed more than 4,000 enemy soldiers in the Leyte campaign, the wounded man Doss saw, turned out to be the only prisoner captured by them during the entire campaign. The medic looked around at the wounded Americans at the aid-station and seeing that they all had been treated or were being attended to, he opened up his aid kit and headed outside toward the wounded enemy soldier.

Several walking wounded with minor injuries were waiting outside and saw what he was about to do.

"Doss," one of them yelled, "if you touch the filthy slant eyed devil, I swear to God I'll kill you."

When the medic turned around to face the man who had yelled at him, he found himself staring down the barrel of a M1 rifle being held by Private Lane. He also noticed several other nearby soldiers were starting to bring up their rifles. "Doss, after what those devils did to K Company I really mean it. Don't touch that Jap!"

He had no idea what Lane was talking about, but by the look in his eyes, the medic knew he meant business. Doss was too frightened to turn his back on the enraged soldier, so he raised his hands and started walking backward. "Okay buddy, take it easy. Just take it easy."

After Doss had moved a dozen steps away from the Japanese soldier, one of the other wounded infantrymen placed his hand on Lane's shoulder. The human contact seemed to trigger something, which caused him to lower his rifle. The medic breathed a sigh of relief and hurriedly stepped back into the aid-station. Inside, one of the doctors came up to him.

"I just saw what happened. Guess you didn't hear? K Company had to leave some wounded men behind. The Japs bayoneted them all. We'll take care of that Jap, but not like they took care of our wounded men. Doss, there's something else I need to talk to you about. There's a rumor going around that you're treating wounded Japs out on the battlefield."

Doss started to speak up, but the doctor cut him off.

"I don't want an answer from you, but if you're doing such a thing, I want it stopped. As medics, we're only obligated to treat them after they're captured or surrender and you know that never happens. Besides, if our men catch you treating one of those Japs, I'm afraid they really might kill you. Do we understand each other?"

"Sure, Captain."

Doss finished filling up his medic kit and headed back to Company B.

After pushing through the crossroads at Libungao, the 77th continued north on Highway 2 until they linked up with the 1st Cavalry Division late in the afternoon. The road between Ormoc and Carigara Bay was finally under control of the Americans.

On Christmas Day, after the 1st Battalion, 305th Infantry had made a successful amphibious assault and captured the enemy port at Palompon, General Bruce sent a radio message to General MacArthur.

"The 77th Division's Christmas contribution to the Leyte campaign is the capture of Palompon, the last main port of the enemy. We are all grateful to the Almighty on this birthday of the Son and the Season of the Feast of Lights."

The capture of the port denied the enemy on Leyte the last opportunity for them to reinforce or evacuate their troops, thus ensuring their eventual total destruction.

Later in the day, General McArthur declared that all organized resistance on Leyte had been broken.

December 26, 1944
Mopping Up Leyte

When the men of the 77th heard that General McArthur had declared an end to organized enemy resistance, the consensus among the foot soldiers was that the headline might sell some papers back home, but they also doubted many Japs had subscriptions to American newspapers. They knew there were still plenty of soldiers on Leyte who would rather die fighting than surrender.

Since Leyte was a day ahead of the United States, General Bruce decided it would be best for the troops to eat their holiday meal a day late, so they could celebrate on the same day as their families' back home. On 26 December, the division cooks prepared a special turkey dinner for all the men. It didn't bother the troops much to wait an extra day for their meal. Besides, they had been a little too busy on Christmas to enjoy it.

Even though there was no alcohol within miles of the party, that night, some of the men lit huge bonfires and sang Christmas songs while pretending to be drunk. Their idea was to encourage any nearby concentrations of enemy soldiers to commit a Banzai attack. Although they carried on like that for several hours, to their disappointment, no Japanese were stupid enough to fall for the ruse. Never ones to give up, the men vowed they would continue to try out ideas to encourage them to commit mass suicide.

Just after midnight, the 307th participated in a Christmas miracle of sorts. One of the radio operators intercepted a message from a group of American planes that was in trouble after returning from a bombing run. They were low on fuel, and an intense storm over the airfield at Tacloban, on the east side of Leyte, made it impossible for them to land. Word of the airmen's plight was relayed to the 307th, which was still in the vicinity of the Valencia airstrip. Within minutes, jeeps, ambulances and trucks moved to line the runway, and they illuminated the strip with their headlights allowing five fighter planes and one B25 bomber to safely land. The soldiers were in such a festive mood they even shared some leftover turkey with the 11 grateful airmen.

General Bruce ordered the 307th to remain near Valencia, occupying the captured area while he used the other two battalions to run down and destroy the remaining pockets of resistance.

Each day, the 307th sent out several patrols to look for and eliminate enemy stragglers. Doss was along on a patrol to check out a road in the area southwest of San Jose, when they came across eight native women who the Japanese had raped and bayonetted. The medic checked each body and found that one woman was still alive. While he was working on her injuries, a young native girl of about 8 or 10 came out of hiding and approached the men. She began speaking in Spanish, which as luck would have it, one of the men in the patrol could understand. As she talked, he translated.

"My name is Rizza. The Japanese soldiers took the most beautiful women from the villages and forced us to watch as they raped them. They told us this is what the American soldiers would do to us. We know what the Japanese say is a lie. Then as the women are crying, they use the bayonets and left them here to die. They have done this same thing many times. Thank you for helping my friend Maricris. Will she live?"

Doss was barely able to hold back tears as he answered. "She is hurt very badly. I don't know if she will live, but she is still alive, so there is hope. I will send her back to our hospital."

The radioman had already sent back word requesting a jeep be sent right away and was just now getting a reply.

"Doc, they say they can't spare a jeep."

"Then send back a message to Captain Vernon. Tell him what is going on and then say, 'Doss says this is something that is not right.'"

"I'll send it, but it'll be your butt in a sling when Vernon gets that message."

"Go ahead, and send it."

It wasn't long before an answer came back over the radio.

"Hey Doc. I don't know how you did it. A jeep is on the way."

While they waited, the medic was continuously praying that God would spare the life of Maricris. Soon, the jeep arrived with stretcher-bearers who loaded Maricris aboard and headed back to Valencia. Rizza watched until the jeep was out of sight, and then she ran to Doss and gave him a big hug.

"Gracias doctor médico Doss. Gracias." Then she turned and ran away.

"Hey, how did she know my name?"

The Spanish-speaking soldier spoke up, "Chiquita asked; I answered. Looks like you made a friend Doc."

That night, Doss and the patrol had returned to the division area at Valencia when a procession of Filipinos, being moved along by members of the Philippine Civil Affairs Unit, began to stream through the area. They were of all ages, babies to grandparents, men and women, boys and girls. Some were riding caribou, others were on scrawny cows or ponies, but most were walking. Their clothes, if they were wearing any, were ragged.

When the Japanese took control of Leyte, the natives fled into the hills and survived the best they could. Now that the enemy had been forced out of the cities and into the hills, the people were returning to their towns and villages.

The 77th Division's Judge Advocate and Civil Affairs Officer, Lieutenant Colonel Darrell Stephens, was watching the procession. He estimated there were at least 150,000 natives whose homes were in his operational area. As he observed the group shuffle past, he realized that caring for them would be an almost impossible job for his small unit.

Doss was standing next to the road along with many other soldiers watching the crowd of skinny but smiling natives pass by when he heard a familiar voice call out, "Hola, doctor médico Doss." He searched for the source of the voice, and after spotting the waving girl, he returned the wave, calling back, "Hi Rizza." As Doss smiled and waved, it seemed as if every nearby head turned to look directly at him. Many of the Filipinos walking close to Rizza called out and waved, "Gracias doctor Doss." A priest in the group stopped, and said, "Dios os bendiga a vosotros y a vuestras familias, y guíe vuestros esfuerzos." Another Filipino, knowing English and seeing the bewildered look on his face translated, "He say, 'may God bless you and your family and may God guide you in your work doctor Doss." Apparently, Rizza had shared the story of how the medic had cared for Maricris, and now they all wanted to see what médico Doss looked like.

The Civil Affairs Officer was watching the exchange with great interest when a plan started to form in his mind, but before he could decide if it was workable, he had to find out what the medic had done that caused the natives to express such admiration. He approached the medic and questioned him about the incident. Doss related the story of the Japanese brutality and told how he and the other men worked to try to save the life of the one survivor. By the time he finished, Colonel Stephens had enough information to feel that his plan, which he began sharing with the medic, just might work.

"Doss, your simple act of kindness may have done more to get these local Filipinos to trust the United States again, than all the work my Civil Affairs Unit has done so far. As soon as we finish mopping up most of the Japs in our operational area, I'm going to arrange for the medical units to spend some time helping out the local population. In the meantime I'll talk to the company commanders about giving you medics a little leeway to treat local civilians, but of course, only as long as it can be done without hampering your ability to treat our soldiers first."

"Thank you for the opportunity Colonel. I always admired medical missionaries. This might be as close as I'll ever get to being one."

Over the following days, the 307th continued to send out patrols searching for any remaining enemy forces. They typically came across less than ten soldiers a day, unlike the other two regiments who were still regularly encountering and destroying groups of 100 or more Japanese in their operational areas.

On the last day of 1944, the 307th made a surprising discovery. A patrol uncovered several tunnels about 1,000 yards west of Valencia, near the airstrip, which held drums containing over forty thousand gallons of aviation gasoline, and around six hundred, 500 pound bombs along with other assorted ammunition. It was decided to keep the fuel, but the bombs and ammunition had to be disposed of. That task fell to Captain Robert "Remo" Dollenmayer and the seven men of the 92nd Bomb Disposal Squad.

Ever since he was a boy, Dollenmayer had been attracted to fire and explosions, so the captain was one soldier who could honestly say that he loved his job.

Finding such a big cache of explosives on New Year's Eve presented an opportunity Remo could not pass up. Dollenmayer knew he could not destroy all of the ordinance at once, but if his men and their Filipino labors worked hard all day, he felt he could put on a New Year's fireworks show the men would never forget.

Normally, when the bomb disposal squad destroyed ordinance, they did it during the day with controlled explosions of 100-ton lots. The spectacle Remo had planned would require only about 25 tons or so. After looking over the ordinance, he selected 41 bombs and 14 drums of gasoline. He then directed the Filipino work gangs to transport the material to several trenches the engineers had dug for him about a mile west of the airstrip. Meanwhile, he set another native crew searching through the tunnels for cases of tracer ammunition normally used in the Japanese airplane's machine guns.

Dollenmayer placed four bombs in a shallow pit at the bottom of a trench along with an electrically detonated shaped charge of C3 plastic explosive. Next he lowered a drum of gasoline on top of the bombs. He had his men repeat this same assembly nine more times spread out among the other trenches. In a separate trench, he placed almost a hundred cases of tracer ammunition and the remaining four drums of aviation gasoline. The last bomb was placed in a hole dug a short distance away from all the other explosives.

After working all day, Captain Dollenmayer had his display wired up and ready to go before sunset. Of course, Remo knew it was against regulations to set off an ordnance disposal explosion at night, so he had not informed his crew of his scheme. His men on the other hand, not being stupid, figured out the captain had some mischief planned the instant he told them to load the gasoline drums. Once he instructed them how and where to place the enemy ordnance in the blasting trenches, they knew it could be trouble. Like in similar times past, they decided it was best to keep their suspicions to themselves and their mouths shut. That way, they could always claim ignorance if something that Remo did caused trouble.

That night, a little before midnight, Dollenmayer went out to the disposal sight and opened the bungs of four of the gasoline drums allowing 200 gallons of fuel to flow into the trench full of tracers. Then he retraced his steps to the foxhole where all the detonator wiring terminated, took out his 10-cap blasting machine and hooked it up to the first set of wires. At precisely 2358, he twisted the T-handle, setting off a 500-pound bomb and igniting the gasoline in the trench. The first bomb was just to catch the attention of the nearby men and get them looking in the direction of the show since he figured it would take about two minutes for the tracer rounds to get hot enough to start going off.

As the fire burned among the cases of ammunition, Remo connected the second set of wires to the blasting machine and then begin staring at his watch. The closer the second hand moved to midnight the more he began to laugh. He didn't know how much trouble this stunt would get him into, but he figured it would be worth the price. At about 15 seconds to midnight, the tracers started to cook off and soar by the hundreds into the night sky leaving trails of yellow lights as they ascended.

When the second hand reached midnight, he again twisted the handle of the machine, simultaneously setting off all forty 500 pound bombs and sending 10 blazing drums of gasoline over a thousand feet into the air. As Remo lay on his back looking up at the most extraordinary New Year's display he had ever seen, he could only imagine how impressed all of the nearby troops would be. He was laughing so hard he couldn't catch his breath, and tears were flowing down his face. Remo decided this was one of the grandest stunts he had pulled since the time he and his buddies had accidently set a coal train on fire as boys living in Ohio. If only his old Price Hill Gang could have been there with him, he knew they would have been impressed.

Remo had no idea how he could ever top this stunt. Unfortunately, he would never have a chance to try. Through bad luck or bad planning, one of the flaming drums of gasoline dropped directly into Remo's foxhole, killing him instantly.

The 307th spent the first month of 1945 going on patrols and engaging small, scattered groups of enemy soldiers. As the intensity of the conflict ramped down, Doss found more and more time to help out sick and injured Filipinos. Word continued to spread among the natives that the medic named Doss was a kind man who truly cared about their well-being. Early one Saturday morning, he was asked to treat an old man in a nearby village with a severe leg gash. When the medic arrived and saw how infected the leg was, it didn't take him long to realize the old man needed far more care than he could provide. He would have to be sent to the army hospital if he were to have any hope of surviving. Unfortunately, the man didn't speak English, and Doss had to communicate through a family member, who was interpreting. The old man was stubborn and said he didn't want to go. After a lot of persuasion, the man still refused to leave. Finally, the medic gave up, treated the wound as best as he could and then asked if he could pray with the family before he left. After praying, the medic got up off his knees and prepared to leave when the old man finally agreed he would go to the hospital. Doss left, to arrange for the Civil Affairs Unit to have the man taken to the hospital and then returned a few hours later with the ambulance to make sure the old man didn't have a change of heart.

After helping to load the man into the ambulance, he stayed awhile to visit with the family. During their discussions, it came to light that Doss was a Seventh-day Adventist.

"Oh we know some Seventh-day Adventists not far from here. Would you like to visit with them?"

"I sure would."

"Our son can take you there. It's not that far."

Doss hurried back to the company area to get a few things and restock both of his medical bags. As he was leaving, Lieutenant Colt saw him and asked, "Where are you off to in such a hurry?"

"I'm going to church," was his reply. "Is it okay?"

The lieutenant thought the medic was kidding around and decided to play along.

"Sure it's okay, Doss. Sure. I suppose there's one of your churches right up the road. Be sure an say hi to the pastor for me."

"Thanks Lieutenant I will. Don't worry. I'll be back before sundown"

He turned and left Colt standing there with a blank look on his face. *No. There couldn't be. Could there?*

In late January, the situation along the west coast of Leyte was under enough control that the 77th was ordered to prepare for the move back to the east side of the island. On 5 February, the X Corps took control of the 77th Division's area of operations in the west of Leyte. The division discontinued their patrolling and concentrated all their efforts on moving back to Tarragona. By 9 February, the 77th had made the move and were settling in at the bivouac area.

By the end of the Leyte campaign, Doss was so exhausted he spent days sleeping off and on in his tent. He was so tired that, many times he didn't even have the strength to go to the chow line and some of his friends would bring him back something to eat. After two weeks of rest and regular food, he felt his strength coming back to him and before long felt like his old self again.

During the battle for Leyte, the division records showed that they had killed 19,456 Japanese soldiers. No one had kept track of how many of the 2,000 killed or wounded American GIs Doss had treated, nevertheless, for his actions, he was awarded the bronze star.

MARCH 5, 1945
USS *MOUNTRAIL* (APA-213)
COMBAT LOADING THE 307TH

The day finally came when the 77th Infantry Division would be leaving Leyte. Earlier, their hopes for rotation out of combat had been dashed when the quartermasters begin staging their vehicles and equipment on the beach in preparation to be combat loaded onto attack transport ships. Trucks and trailers were being preloaded with the ammunition and supplies that would be needed in the next assault and then parked in designated areas near the beach. To the troops, this could only mean one thing.

After being on this island for five months, the men were eager to get off of Leyte. Even though they knew they would be sent back into combat, they still dreamed about showers, navy food, sack time, and looked forward to the relative ease of shipboard life.

During the daylight hours, landing craft began making trips between attack ships and the beach. Coral obstructions had been blasted out of the water and the beaches improved with steel matting, which made the roundtrips relaxed, compared to activity that had taken place months before.

The placement of material in the ships holds was carefully thought out. Each boat picked up a prearranged load in the reverse order it would be needed in the next landing. The things thought to be needed first had to end up at the top of the holds so the less urgent supplies, that were to reside in the bottom of the holds, were offloaded from the beach first. Some of the last things to be loaded were vehicles filled with ammunition and fuel. Since it had worked so well before, these preloaded vehicles would be driven from the landing boats directly into the next battle.

Doss and the other men of the medical detachment were busy crating up equipment, taking down tents and preloading their ambulances, trucks and trailers with supplies. These medical vehicles would not be the first equipment landed during an assault, but they would follow very quickly. The first to go ashore would be the fighting men, and, as Doss well knew, the medics who accompanied them.

On 13 March, the transports moved from their position just off shore, to Hinunangan Bay on the southern side of Leyte. In a stroke of good fortune, a beach resided there, which very closely resembled Kerama Retto, the next objective of the upcoming campaign. The plan was to use it to practice landings for a few days before heading off to Okinawa.

Doss, who was still attached to the 307th, followed his infantry company aboard the Haskell-class attack transport, USS *Mountrail* (APA 213). On 16 March, the *Mountrail* made a practice landing with the 307th, but before the exercise could be completed, the weather took a turn for the worse, and the rest of the landings had to be canceled. Because of that, the 307th was the only infantry regiment that got a chance to practice a landing at Hinunangan Bay.

On 21 March, the *Mountrail* departed San Pedro Bay. After two days of steaming, it sighted Okinawa in the distance late in the day of the 23rd.

American military tacticians relied on the strategy of holding one third of their fighting force in reserve. That way, if a unit got into trouble, the reserve could be thrown into the fight. For the assault on Okinawa, the 307th infantry regiment had been designated as the reserve force.

The men of the 307th had mixed feelings when they heard the news. Some felt they had finally gotten a break and were happy to stay aboard the ships for a while. Others were of the opinion that the reserve force would only be sent in if things had gone terribly wrong, which destined them to face hard fighting. Despite their differences, the entire group agreed on one thing, at least on dry ground, they could dig foxholes, but aboard ship, they had to trust their safety to navy antiaircraft gunners and the accompanying destroyers. After spending two years learning to trust each other, the men of the 307th didn't particularly like trusting their safety to anyone else.

MARCH 26, 1945
OPERATION ICEBERG
KERAMA ISLAND GROUP

The Ryukyu Islands were located about 350 miles southeast of Japan; therefore, the Japanese people considered them to be part of their homeland, not captured or occupied territories. Because of this, Allied planners assumed the Ryukyu Islands would be very heavily defended, and an attack on them would enrage the populace and defenders.

The plan to take Okinawa was named Operation Iceberg. Admiral Raymond Spruance commanded the Fifth Fleet task force, the largest naval armada ever assembled. Task Force 51, the Joint Expeditionary Force containing all the amphibious forces was commanded by Vice Admiral Richard Kelly.

Kelly wanted to start Operation Iceberg by capturing the Kerama Retto Islands located about 20 miles southwest of Okinawa. The Kerama group consisted of eight main and several very small islands contained in an area of about 32 square miles. The islands were so small none of them even had a road and the natives who lived there survived by fishing instead of farming.

Kelly insisted he needed these islands as a staging area and secure harbor for ship anchorage and repairs. He maintained that having the ability to refuel and resupply as well as make emergency repairs close to the action would save many lives. He also planned to establish a seaplane base, from which navy planes could be sent on antisubmarine and search and rescue operations. Kelly's plan met stiff resistance from the other planners who feared that ships operating in the restricted waters of the islands would be vulnerable to air attack launched from Okinawa or Japan.

In the end, Kelly won out. The opening landing of Operation Iceberg, began Palm Sunday, 25 March, following three days of diversionary shelling directed against the southeast side of Okinawa by five battleships and twelve destroyers. On the 26th, the Statue of Liberty Division stormed ashore with four almost simultaneous assaults on Kerama Retto. During the next five days, the 77th Infantry would make fifteen separate landings to secure the islands. They ran into less resistance than anticipated because many of the Japanese troops had been withdrawn to Okinawa to strengthen defenses there. The enemy left behind less than 1,000 troops of questionable combat value to defend the Kerama Rettos.

After two days of operations, General Bruce was ready to mop up and he spent the 28th and 29th doing just that. As the 77th searched the islands, they discovered its secret. They found 350 suicide boats hidden in many small caves. Their mission had been to destroy the American invasion transport ships as soon as they anchored in Hagushi bay off the coast of Okinawa.

The Army had developed the tactic of placing artillery on small, undefended islands nearby their main objective. While the big guns of battleships were useful in pre-invasion bombardment, the Army depended on stable, zeroed-in guns for close infantry support. The island of Keise Shima located five miles to the west of Okinawa made the ideal platform for those guns. While the 77th was securing the Rettos, navy frogmen blasted a channel through the reefs of Keise. Early on 31 March, elements of the 306th Infantry landed on Keise to double check that the island was still undefended, as earlier scouts had reported. Soon after, the 155mm guns of the 420th Field Artillery Group came ashore. By that night, the big guns were hurling shells across miles of ocean to rain down fire on southern Okinawa.

The securing of Kerama Retto and the placement of artillery on Keise were the last two objectives that needed to be met before the invasion of Okinawa could begin.

APRIL 1, 1945
EASTER SUNDAY. OKINAWA.

The operation to take Okinawa was the largest gathering of men and material in World War Two. It involved over half a million men, including 180,000 assault troops of which 60,000 were landed on the first day.

Doss and the 1st Battalion, 307th infantry were not in the group that went ashore on L-Day, because they were being held in reserve. In fact, they were designated as the reserve of the reserve. Their mission was to remain on the troop transports, ready to be inserted into battle any time a tactical opening might occur. On the first day of the Okinawa invasion, all Company B could do was watch, wait, and in the case of Doss, do a lot of praying for the safety of the troops swarming ashore. Although some of the men felt guilty about remaining in reserve on the ship and not going ashore with the rest of the division, they soon found out that being on a ship during the battle for Okinawa was more dangerous than assaulting the beaches.

In a plan that they had named Operation Ten-Go, the Japanese decided not to contest the Okinawa beach landing. They knew having their troops endure the relentless naval bombardment American battleships would inflict on the coast with days of shelling, would make it hard to put up an effective defense when the assault finally came. Instead, their plan was to let the Americans come ashore unopposed and then destroy their transport and supply ships. The Japanese war planners felt if they could block resupply and evacuation of the American troops, they would have a good chance to trap and destroy them. They further believed that even if they couldn't totally destroy them, the horrendous casualties they would inflict would cause them to lose the will to invade the home island.

Part of their plan had already been thwarted with the capture of Kerama Retto and the destruction of the 350 bomb laden, suicide boats assigned to target the troop transports. Perhaps, if the commanders had taken the initiative to use the Kamikaze boats to attack the transports when they had arrived off Kerama Retto, the outcome might have been different. However, the Japanese military did not operate on local innovation. The high command had assumed the Americans would move directly for Okinawa, so their plan called for the suicide boats to target the troop transports only after they had anchored off the beaches of that island. Local commanders had not been given any leeway to target American transports if they passed directly in front of their boat bases, so no mass suicide boat attack ever occurred.

Ever increasing American air power was beginning to convince Japanese pilots that they had no chance of surviving the war. It was that condition, which helped give rise to the development of the Kamikaze. Japanese pilots decided that since there was little chance of surviving the war, their death would have more meaning and honor if they could die inflicting damage on one of the hated American ships.

A Japanese aircraft could endure massive damage and still complete a successful Kamikaze attack. On the other hand, if a pilot's concern was to make it back home safely, relatively minor damage would force him to break off a conventional attack. As a result, the only way to stop a Kamikaze attack was to kill the pilot or destroy his plane before it slammed into a ship.

The Kamikaze was trained to go after aircraft carriers or troopships. When targeting carriers, the pilot was taught to aim for the deck elevator. A hit there would cripple the carrier's ability to launch planes, and because American carrier decks were made of wood, there was a good chance it would catch on fire.

When attacking troop transport ships they were trained to aim for the bridge, in an attempt to take the ship out of action by destroying its ability to maneuver.

In actual practice, many Kamikaze pilots simply attacked the first ship they saw. That ship usually turned out to be the radar picket destroyers located between Japan and Okinawa. The picket's job was to warn the rest of the fleet of impending air attacks and to form the first line of air defense. When a picket ship opened fire, many Kamikaze pilots took the opportunity for an honorable death by attacking them instead of continuing on to their assigned targets. Because of this, destroyers had a very short life on picket duty. Some lasted less than six hours before they were forced to withdraw because of battle damage.

It was in these conditions that Doss found himself on the evening of 2 April 1945.

April 2, 1945
Kamikaze Attack

Transport Squadron 17 consisted of 16 attack transport troop ships and several other escort ships. Doss was aboard the USS *Mountrail* along with fifteen hundred other members of the 307th infantry. On the morning of 2 April, Squadron 17 returned to Kerama Retto to pick up the last members of the 77th Division still remaining on the island and then headed out to open sea toward their nightly retirement area.

As they left the islands, the ships aligned into a defensive formation of three columns. This formation allowed each ship's guns to support the other ships during an aerial attack. The convoy's flagship, USS *Chilton* (APA-38), was at the head of the center column. The columns were 1,000 feet apart, and the ships were separated by 600 feet row to row. *Mountrail* was two miles behind the *Chilton*, second row from last in the starboard column.

Doss, along with most of the other men, liked to go on deck to watch the sunset. Since smoking was prohibited in the troop berthing area, many of the men took the opportunity for a last smoke of the day. Some of the men reread letters they had read dozens of times before. Others gazed at pictures of wives or girlfriends. They all wanted to stretch out their deck time until the last possible moment before they were sent below to their stifling bunks.

Doss sat with his Bible in his lap gazing at the sunset with a faraway look on his face.

Tennessee Byran walked up and sat down next to him.

"What'a you thinkin' 'bout?"

"Oh, just how out here, on these ships, we got no control over any part of our lives. The navy cooks our food and tells us exactly when to eat. We go where the ship goes. We have to trust those navy gunners with our lives."

"What's so danged new 'bout that? I don't ever remember the Army giving us much say so the last two years."

"This is different all right. At least on dry land we get to decide how deep to dig our foxholes."

Both laughed.

"Yea, got a point there."

As they talked, both men were watching planes circle and land on a nearby escort carrier.

"I sure am glad those planes are on our side," said Doss.

As soon as those words came out of his mouth he noticed another group of planes that were headed straight for the convoy.

Tennessee noticed them too.

"That's strange. I ain't never seen friendly planes fly straight over before. I thought there was rules against that. If they keep a heading this way they might git shot at!"

Of course, *Mountrail's* radar had detected the incoming planes, as had every other ship in the formation, but they had also received a message from the flagship *Chilton* that the planes heading their way were friendlies. What *Mountrail's* captain didn't know was that the identification signals emitted by the American planes circling the carrier had confused *Chilton* and allowed Japanese planes to slip through unrecognized.

At about the same time as Doss noticed the planes heading inward, the ship's lookouts began reporting the planes to the bridge. Word came back through the gunner's headphones. *"Hold your fire. Those planes are friendlies."* Knowing that friendly planes were restricted from flying directly overhead, the gunners on *Mountrail* and throughout the convoy became confused.

That confusion ended when a navy F4F Wildcat roared up behind one of the two engine planes and shot it down. At about the same time a second plane dived at *Chilton,* striking a glancing blow before hitting the water and exploding. Gunfire erupted from ships all along the front of the convoy. A klaxon began to blare.

"General quarters! General quarters! Man your battle stations. Army troops clear the decks."

As the troops rushed down the stairs and into the berthing compartments, Doss couldn't help but wish he had somewhere to dig a foxhole. Instead, all he could do was put on a lifejacket and climb into his bunk. That's all any of the troops could do. During an attack, they were required to remain in their bunks and keep out of the way. They had no way of knowing what was happening above. No hint if a suicide plane was about to strike the ship and end their lives in an instant. What's more, during general quarters, hatches were closed, and the blowers that ventilated the ship were turned off as a precaution. If an explosion occurred while the ventilators were operating, fire could be sucked into the system and spread instantly throughout the ship. The lack of ventilation made it even more unbearable than usual in the troop compartments. With so many men packed together, temperature and humidity quickly rose, adding to the men's misery.

Within moments, the troops heard the sound of airplane engines approaching. The guns on *Mountrail* opened fire. Soldiers in the troop compartment began moaning. The fact they didn't know what was happening with the battle going on outside was almost too much for them.

Doss began praying aloud. "God I realize I have no control over my life, but I also know that You control everything. If it is Your will, I ask that you protect my life and the men aboard this ship. Please give the captain wisdom to command the ship. If I should die tonight, I ask that you watch over Dorothy and my family while I sleep in wait of the resurrection. Amen."

When Doss finished his prayer, he heard several "Amens" echo from throughout the compartment. He looked around, smiled and thought, *I guess the men have permanently given up on throwing shoes.* From his top bunk, he could see that many of the men were praying.

APRIL 2, 1945
USS *MOUNTRAIL* BRIDGE

Captain Philbert Scott had been concerned about the threat of air attack all day. Twice, earlier that morning, single planes had broken through the destroyer screen and made it all the way to the transports before being shot down at the last second by the transport gunners. With the reports of intense suicide attacks coming from the picket line, it would only be a matter of time until a coordinated group of Kamikaze planes made it through to the troop ships.

The men of the *Mountrail* had yet to come under air attack, and Scott had long been concerned with the limited amount of live fire, air defense practice they had received. He was also worried that the 5"/38 crews had not been able to practice rapid loading since the ship had been commissioned. There was nothing Captain Scott could do about increasing the amount of live fire training against air targets, so he had done the only other thing he could think of. Months before, he had issued a standing order. Even though the gun crews obviously were not to fire at friendly airplanes, they were to take advantage of them to practice tracking and range setting whenever they were in the vicinity.

Captain Scott's thoughts were interrupted by the bridge talker.

"Bridge - Bow Lookout. Multiple planes closing. Zero four five. Position angle 30. Moving right to left slowly."

At that same moment, the executive officer, Lieutenant Jim Koch was handed a radio message from the flagship, which he proceeded to read aloud.

"Captain, message from *Chilton* to all ships. Planes operating in the area are friendlies."

Captain Scott was now faced with a dilemma. On one hand, *Chilton* was reporting that the closing planes were friendly. On the other, was the strict rule that prohibited friendly planes from flying directly over a convoy. He knew he would have to defer to the judgment of the flagship. Perhaps there was some emergency they knew of that required the planes cross over the convoy.

"Thank you Mr. Koch."

Captain Scott turned to the bridge talker.

"Gun Control – Bridge. Hold fire. Flagship indicates planes are friendlies. Have all guns track and range set approaching planes."

Captain Scott thought, laughing to himself. *The men think I don't know they call me "Captain point your guns" behind my back. Wouldn't they be surprised if they found out I'm quite fond of that nickname?*

Laughing aloud this time, Scott turned to his executive officer, "This is a good opportunity for the gun crews to get in some more practice, pointing their guns. Right, Mr. Koch?"

"Yes, it is Captain," answered Koch. *I wonder if he knows?*

From where the captain was standing, he could see that the forward quad 40mm gun mount had already been tracking the approaching planes. Looking through his binoculars, he estimated the planes would pass directly over the forward ships in the convoy. Just as he started to turn away, he noticed a smaller plane racing up behind the leading aircraft. Now, watching more intently, he saw the trailing plane open fire causing the other plane to burst into flames.

"What the hell is going on? Sound General Quarters."

Just as Captain Scott had almost concluded that a Jap fighter had somehow snuck into the formation and shot down one of the American planes, the other leading plane nosed over and began a strafing run on *Chilton.* The pilot released a bomb, which missed the ship, striking the water moments before the plane clipped *Chilton's* rigging. The plane erupted into a fiery ball, showering burning gasoline on the deck before continuing on and exploding in the water on the other side of the ship.

Now the situation became clear to the captain. Those planes crossing the convoy were Japs that had somehow tricked the American radar and made it this far undetected. Captain Scott was transfixed by the drama playing out before his eyes. Forcing himself to turn away, he looked around the bridge. He was shocked when he realized all eyes were focused on the developing air battle instead of paying attention to their duties.

Scott stepped out onto the bridge wing as he shouted, "Bring me the ships microphone."

General Quarters had just finished sounding when a sailor appeared with a microphone and handed it over to the captain.

"This is Captain Scott. Well it looks like you gunners are finally going to get a chance to shoot down some Japs. I want you all to pay attention to your jobs. Lookouts, watch your assigned sectors. Jap planes might sneak in from any direction. Gun crews, quit watching what's going on at the front of the convoy. Follow the direction of your mount captains. Loaders, load. Trainers, train. Calm down. Pay attention to your own job. Trust your training and trust your gun sight. Good luck and good shooting."

Scott returned the microphone and stepped back inside the bridge. As he looked around, he could see that his speech had the intended effect on his bridge crew at least. Now, it was just a matter of moments to see if it had worked on the rest of the crew as well.

Scott raised his binoculars to get another look at the battle raging at the front of the convoy. He could see that by then, all of the forward ships had opened fire.

Looking at the port column, he noticed that the USS *Henrico* (APA-45) was on fire. *It must have happened while I was on the starboard wing. What a mess*, he thought. *Caught with our pants down.*

The bridge talker spoke up.

"Bridge - Radar. Plane zero nine zero. Position angle ten. Closing directly."

Well here it comes, thought Scott. *This one's headed straight for us. At least he's on our beam. That'll give almost every gun a chance at him.*

Mountrail's guns opened up. Cones of tracers were converging in the distance. There it was. Captain Scott could see the enemy plane as it skimmed just above the water. It was coming straight in towards the ship. Rounds were impacting the water, throwing up splashes all around.

"Great," he yelled. "Easy target. No need to lead. Just pour it on boys."

Of course, the gun crews could not hear their captain. The only sounds they heard now, was the thunder of their guns.

The captain knew they were getting hits because some of the 40mm tracers deflected away after passing through the plane.

"Blow up you filthy Jap! You're not getting my ship!"

Now, many more rounds were hitting. A well placed string of 20mm slugs chipped off pieces of the wing, but the plane still came on, not veering from its path in the slightest.

What's it gonna take to knock this Jap down? Knock him down! Kill him! Knock him down!

The stern five thirty-eight finally got on target and fired. A black puff of smoke exploded directly beneath the Jap bomber, setting it on fire. The 5 inch fired again, this time blowing the plane's tail completely off. It rolled to its right, continued on a few more seconds and then hit the water, exploding about 400 yards off *Mountrail's* starboard bow.

Cheering erupted all over the ship.

Captain Scott was shocked. Of course, he knew about the new 5 inch VT fused proximity shells, but he had never seen them in action before. The new shells were able to sense when they were within 30 feet of a plane and then explode automatically. Two shots from the five thirty-eight were all it had taken to blow the plane out of the sky.

That shell is like something out of a Flash Gordon movie, he thought. *It might change the course of warfare.*

As the cheering continued, Scott turned to his exec. "Shoot down one plane and those guys act like they just won the World Series. To tell the truth, I feel the same way. I'm damn proud of them."

Scott thought, *Maybe we can use those gee whiz shells to help out some of the other ships.* He turned to face the bridge talker.

"Gun Control – Bridge. Engage with 5"/38 any plane that presents, even at maximum range."

Almost instantly he heard the five thirty-eight open up.

The talker reported.

"Bridge - Gun Control. Engaging Betty Bomber. One four zero. Position angle twenty. Range eight thousand."

Captain Scott realized the plane planned to come right up the tail of the USS *Telfair* (APA-210), located two rows forward in the same column. To do that, the pilot would have to pass parallel down the starboard side of *Mountrail* right to left. This would present an awkward firing solution for *Mountrail's* gunners because the speed of the plane, as it passed by, would make it very difficult to traverse the guns fast enough to keep up. The 5"/38 got off three poorly placed shots before it could no longer keep up with the enemy bomber. As it zoomed past, the 20mm Oerlikon and 40mm Bofors gun mounts had opened up and gotten a few hits.

The guns aboard *Telfair* and USS *Eastland* (APA-163) had better firing angles, so they were having more effect. By the time the plane reached *Telfair*, it was very badly damaged but still flying. It passed over *Telfair*, glanced off her port side and exploded in the water.

At the same time, another Betty was closing in on the *Telfair* from off her starboard bow. Intense fire forced the pilot to veer off to his left and begin to fly parallel down *Eastland's* starboard side from bow to stern. The *Eastland* was between *Telfair* and *Mountrail*. This gave *Telfair* a two-dimensional shot from her stern five thirty-eight. It fired up the Betty's tail at the same time as *Mountrail's* 5-inch gun fired a shot towards its front. Both proximity rounds exploded at the same time shattering the Betty into a thousand pieces, which showered down harmlessly in the ocean directly abeam of *Eastland*.

Meanwhile, two more Betties were approaching from the starboard. One was headed for *Mountrail* while the other aimed for the USS *Montrose* (APA-212) at the rear of the column. This presented both ships' gunners with easier targets since the planes were coming in straight toward their guns. Just like the first plane *Mountrail* had shot down, this one began to disintegrate with the pounding of multiple 20 and 40mm hits. The five thirty-eight fired three times before the last shot took off the Betties wing and it cartwheeled into the ocean. *Montrose* hit the last plane, which turned and splashed into the ocean at almost the exact spot where *Mountrail's* had ended up seconds before.

The ship's guns went quiet. Scott looked at his watch. It read 1900 hours.

My God it's only been 20 minutes since the attack started. I could have sworn it was at least an hour. "Report Mr. Koch."

"No damage and no injuries Captain. Radar reports no further air contacts."

"Very well Mr. Koch. Remain at General Quarters until further notice. Oh, and Mr. Koch, when things calm down, have someone paint a set of three Jap flags on both sides of the bridge. I want everyone who sees *Mountrail* to know this ship can kill Japs."

APRIL 3, 1945
ABOARD USS *MOUNTRAIL*

For some men, the stress of being confined to the troop berths of the ship during an air attack was almost unbearable. Although most of the men followed orders and remained in their bunks, others couldn't stand the confined space. The lack of ventilation, poor lighting and increasing temperature pushed several men into severe claustrophobia attacks. Those men paced back and forth, staring at the walls and ceiling of the ship. They labored to breathe and felt as if the walls were closing in, trying to crush them. One man resorted to crawling into a corner and hiding his head between his legs. Another was so distraught that he ran up the stairs to the open deck and sat down just outside the door. Once out in the open, he found instant relief from his anxiety and stayed there calmly observing the anti-aircraft battle.

Doss, though normally quiet, became very talkative when under stress.

Other men handled the stress in a very different way. They fell asleep. Although he didn't know it yet, Tennessee Byran was one of those sleepers.

"Hey Byran, I was just wondering. Do you think these sailors would be as miserable on dry land, as I feel right now, trapped on this ship? I'll bet if they had to tromp through the mud and meet up with Japs face to face, they'd be crying to get back on their ship. It's strange isn't it? Here I want to get off this ship and them sailors probably couldn't stand it on dry ground. I guess you couldn't exactly call it dry ground when it's mud up to your knees, but you know what I mean. So, what do you think? Byran? Are you listening Byran?"

Doss looked down over the edge of his bunk to see why Tennessee wasn't answering.

I'll be, he thought, *he's sleeping like a baby.*

As Doss looked around to find someone else to talk to, he noticed the firing had stopped. Doss spent the next few minutes waiting for the guns to start back up and when they didn't, he observed that the other men around him were beginning to relax. He reached down and tried to shake Tennessee awake.

"Hey Byran, wake up. It's over."

No amount of prodding would rouse Tennessee. For a moment, Doss became concerned, thinking that maybe there was something wrong with him."

To allay his concerns, he reached down and felt Byran's pulse.

No, he's still alive, thought Doss. *I've never seen anyone sleep so deep in all my life."*

At that moment, the ships speakers came to life and announced, *"The Jap air attack is over for now. Captain Scott congratulates the gun crews for their fine shooting. We will remain at General Quarters until further notice. That is all."*

The announcement broke the tension of the troops who had been in the dark about what was occurring above decks. Cheering broke out in troop compartments from one end of the ship to the other.

The next morning when Doss awoke, he could tell the ship was no longer at General Quarters by the air blowing from the ventilation duct above his bunk. Per normal, the men were required to be on deck before dawn. After the nerve-racking night, Doss, like everyone else, was eager to get outside as early as possible but knew there was something he needed to deal with first. He must thank God for preserving his life and the lives of the others on the ship. *After all,* he thought, *when God answers prayers it's only fair to thank Him.*

After Doss had finished his morning prayer and arrived on deck, the first thing he wanted to do was to question the nearest sailor about the battle he had only heard and imagined the night before. Gathered all over the deck were clumps of soldiers with the same idea. They surrounded sailors who were telling their version of how the battle had played out. Some of the sailors were better storytellers than others, using hand gestures and imitating battle sounds. One was particularly popular. The budding comedian related the battle from the point of view of a Japanese pilot complete with accents and facial expressions.

As soon as a sailor finished up his story, the surrounding group pressed in with grateful "thank yous" and "at-a-boys," handshakes and back slaps, then moved on to hear a different take on how the battle had played out.

As the sun began to rise, the men noticed it was coming up on the wrong side of the ship. The pattern had always been for the convoy to head out to sea at sunset and then back toward the islands at sunrise, so the men had grown used to seeing the sun rising and setting on the same side of the ship. Today, it had risen on the opposite side from which it had set the night before. After thinking about it for a while, the troops figured out what the sailors already knew. Instead of returning to Okinawa, they were steaming further out to sea.

Vice Admiral Turner had decided that since the 77th Division reserve force would not be needed to reinforce the troops on Okinawa for at least the next several days, it didn't make sense to subject them to the increasing menace of Kamikaze attacks. Instead of continuing to have the ships return to Okinawa each day and then retire to open sea at night, he ordered Squadron 17 to proceed 200 miles south of the islands. After arriving there, they were to follow a 500-mile racetrack shaped course until they were needed. The oval course was so large it took almost a day and a half to make it around one lap. Admiral Turner felt certain his reserve troops would remain safer on transports, alone in the open sea, then with the main concentration of ships around Okinawa.

Doss and the other men were able to relax quite a bit as the ships steamed around in huge circles. They had very little to do each day besides waiting in line for meals and an occasional lifeboat drill. No enemy had been sighted since they reached open sea, so the men were able to remain on deck most of the day. They could even come up top at night as long as they didn't smoke, wore their lifebelts and observed the blackout restrictions.

That day, Doss planned to use much of his free time to read and study the Bible Dorothy had given him. He sat down on the deck with his back leaning up against a wall. First as he did every time before he started to work on his studies, Desmond reread the short letter which Dorothy had penned him on the front page of his little Bible. He always drew comfort from the last line in which Dorothy professed her belief that if he should be killed, God would reunite them in heaven.

Next he opened his Sabbath School Quarterly to review the topic of the week. Just as he was about to start in on the study, Tennessee Byran ambled up. "Howdy Doss. I know you like reading your Bible, but what's that other little book you got there?"

"Hey Byran, sit down, and I'll show you. This is called the quarterly. It comes out four times a year, and each one covers a different topic in the Bible. Seventh-day Adventists all over the world use it as an outline for their weekly study. Then in Sabbath School, that's like Sunday school except it's on Saturday, we discuss the lesson. That way, no matter where I attend church, I know they'll be discussing the lesson I studied in the quarterly. This time, it's about the book of Ephesians." He handed the quarterly over to Tennessee, so he could take a closer look.

As Tennessee looked it over, he noticed that Doss had not signed the Daily Lesson Study Pledge and decided to question him about it.

"It says here on page two, '*As one who greatly desires to improve my knowledge of the Scriptures, I pledge myself to the careful and prayerful study of some portion of my Sabbath school lesson each day of the week.*' I notice you ain't signed that yet. Ever time I see you, you got your Bible out. You done already put check marks on the first six days, so I'm guessin' you studied it ever day this week. Are you gonna sign or not?"

Doss thought for a while before answering.

"Byran, it's like this. If I sign that pledge, it's like me making a promise to God. That's not something I take lightly. When I was on Leyte I wasn't always able to spend as much time on my studies, as I wanted to. Some days I only had time to read my Bible for a little bit and I didn't even look at the lesson guide, so that's why I didn't sign."

Byran and Doss both sat quietly for a few moments before Tennessee again spoke up. "I can sort'a see where you're a commin' from, but don't you think God knows when you're busy gettin' shot at all day, that you ain't gonna have enough time to study your Bible as much as you ought'a? How 'bout this? Read some of them there lesson things ahead a time and then if you miss a day you ain't gonna get behind."

"Byran I like your idea. That's what I'm gonna do. If I make every effort to do my lessons, I think God will work it out somehow for me to keep up with them. Hand me back my book."

Doss took out his pencil, signed the pledge and then handed the book back to Tennessee.

"Thanks Byran. I believe God used you, to encourage me to sign that pledge."

Tennessee looked at the book and read the signature.

Pfc. Desmond T. Doss. "Hows about that. Now I know your first name."

Sticking out his hand and laughing, Tennessee said, "I'm mighty glad to meet you Desmond, my name's Michael."

Doss grinned while shaking Byran's hand. "It's nice to meet you too Michael."

April 7, 1945
Battleship *Yamato*

Transport Squadron 17 had been steaming in circles for three days when they received word of a new threat. Vice Admiral Turner learned that a group of enemy ships, led by the battleship *Yamato,* had been sighted heading for Okinawa. Even though the *Yamato* was the most powerful battleship ever built, Turner doubted it would be able to break through the concentration of American ships and planes arrayed around Okinawa. Although there was little chance of it reaching the reserve troops circling to the south, in an abundance of caution he ordered his task force carrying the 77th division to move even further away from the danger that *Yamato* posed.

Admiral Ito and Captain Aruga onboard the *Yamato,* did not know the Allies had intercepted and broken the Japanese radio code and knew the details of Operation Ten-Go.

In March, the Japanese Imperial Military leaders had briefed the emperor about the Army's plan to utilize Kamikaze air attacks during the battle for Okinawa.

After hearing of the plan, Hirohito replied, "What about the Navy? Have they no more ships left to defend Japan's honor?"

Hirohito's reply shamed the Navy commanders, who then felt pressured to participate in some kind of action to aid in the defense of Okinawa.

The operation that Commander-in-Chief of the Combined Fleet, Admiral Toyoda Soemu, conceived was a Kamikaze style attack utilizing *Yamato* and any other remaining ships that could be thrown together into a battle group. His plan was to have Admiral Ito fight all the way to Okinawa, then purposely run *Yamato* and the other ships aground on the beach. Once there, they would act as shore batteries until they could no longer function. Undoubtedly, once grounded, the Americans would destroy the *Yamato.* When that happened, her sailors were to abandon ship and fight on Okinawa as infantry troops.

To insure Admiral Ito followed through with the suicide attack, Commander Soemu ordered that *Yamato* only be loaded with enough fuel for a one-way trip.

When *Yamato* and her nine accompanying ships left Japan the evening of 6 April to proceed toward Okinawa, two American submarines, the *Threadfin* and *Hackleback*, sighted them almost immediately. They were not in a position to attack but were able to shadow the Japanese ships and send reports of their course back to the U.S. Fleet.

Early the next morning, U.S. reconnaissance planes located the *Yamato* and began tracking it.

U.S. Fifth Fleet commander, Admiral Raymond Spruance, ordered his battleships to move into a position to intercept the enemy ships. Meanwhile Vice Admiral Marc A. Mitscher, who commanded the aircraft carriers of Task

Force 58, decided on his own initiative, to launch a massive air strike from his flattops. Mitscher did not inform Spruance of his decision until he had already launched almost 400 planes. After learning Mitscher's planes were airborne, Spruance reluctantly agreed to allow the air attack to proceed, but as a contingency, he ordered the American battleships to continue toward *Yamato* and engage it on the surface if the air attack should fail.

The first American planes to arrive over *Yamato,* at around 1200, were navy fighters. The F6F Hellcats and F4U Corsairs had been sent in first to eliminate any enemy fighter protection. It quickly became obvious to the American fighter pilots that *Yamato* had no defensive air cover whatsoever. When the bombers and torpedo planes began to arrive, they were able to circle outside the range of *Yamato's* guns and meticulously set up their attack formations without the fear of disruption from Japanese aircraft. At 1230, the first American planes attacked. Torpedo planes engaged *Yamato* mainly from the port side in hopes that by concentrating damage on one side of the ship, they would increase the chances of capsizing it. For the next hour and a half, wave after wave of American planes pounded *Yamato*, until finally at 1405, she was dead in the water. Admiral Ito and Captain Aruga refused to abandon ship with the rest of the crew and after 20 minutes, *Yamato* rolled completely over and then blew up in a huge explosion. Tears were rolling down his eyes during Captain Aruga's last thought. *I hope the emperor is satisfied when he hears what the Yamato achieved in her "glorious" Kamikaze attack on the American Navy.*

In one of the most lopsided battles of the war, only 10 U.S. aircraft were shot down, at the cost of 12 men, while the Japanese Navy lost their most powerful ship along with over 4,000 sailors.

APRIL 13, 1945
DEATH OF ROOSEVELT

Doss and the other men had enjoyed days of peace and quiet as their ship steamed circles in the ocean. There had been several suspected submarines detected by the sonar gear of their escort vessels, although after further investigation they turned out to be false alarms. Even though no actual submarines were spotted, the men were still required to wear lifebelts as part of the uniform of the day and to muster on deck at dusk and dawn as a precaution against possible attack. Requiring the men to be on deck at the times of most vulnerability was, in reality, just a formality as the men already spent every possible moment there. Even though the open deck was hot, the internal spaces were hotter, and at least on deck there was always a fresh breeze blowing.

Allowing the troops to spend so much time on deck caused an unexpected problem for the navy doctors. They were beginning to see cases of severe sunburn among the men. On one day alone, they treated several soldiers who were so severely sunburned that huge blisters covered almost 50 percent of their bodies. In response, the doctors immediately issued a directive that army personnel must wear shirts at all time while on deck. Even though they grumbled, the men generally obeyed the rule. However, shirts did not protect their entire bodies and more and more men were reporting to sickbay with blistered faces and arms.

Many of the soldiers came to Doss asking him to treat their sunburns. Since he did not have the necessary medical supplies, he was forced to send them on to the ship's sickbay. After turning away multiple men, he decided to go and offer to help the ship's doctors. After all, he was a week ahead on his Bible studies and was getting bored just lounging around. Besides, he considered the medical care of his men his responsibility and it seemed wrong for him to be sitting around while someone else took care of them.

Doss was taken aback when he approached the sickbay and saw several dozen soldiers lined up in the passageway waiting to be treated. Squeezing past the line, he entered and approached the navy doctor working there. "Excuse me Sir, my name is Private Doss. I'm one of the company aid-men. I came to see if I could help treat some of these men."

Lt. Abrahamson looked up from the man he was working on and replied, "Sure Doss, I'll take any help I can get. With all those sunburned men outside, it's starting to look like a gall-darned epidemic. Find one of the corpsmen and ask what kind of help he needs." Then Dr. Abrahamson went back to work.

During the time he had spent on the ship, the medic had already made friends with most of the corpsmen and one of them, who was standing nearby, motioned him over. "Hey Doss, I hear you want to join the Navy."

"Wait a minute. I don't want out of the Army. I just want to help out my men, if I can."

"Okay Doss, I'll give you a quick lesson on how the navy treats army guys stupid enough to let themselves get sunburned, and then, you can get to work. For the mild cases with reddened skin and small blisters, use tannic acid ointment. The more severe cases, with large blisters, get boric acid ointment covered with sterile gauze. Don't open the blisters. Zinc oxide if the skin is cracked or peeling. If they have a fever, send them to bed rest, and have them drink plenty of water. We only have a few medical beds, and we can't fill them up, so restrict the more severe cases to bed in the troop berths. When you get done with one, send him over, and I'll do the most important part. Fill out the paperwork. If you don't have any questions, have at 'em."

Doss thought it sounded pretty straightforward, and he pitched right in. As the infantrymen came in to be treated, they would spot Doss and almost invariably say something like, "Hi Doc." Then ignoring the navy personnel, they would head straight to him for treatment. The first few times Dr. Abrahamson heard a soldier say "Doc" he instinctively looked up to see who was addressing him, but after it happened a few times, he realized they were talking to the army medic. Some doctors, with less self-confidence, might have bristled at hearing a private being addressed as "Doc," but instead, Abrahamson was impressed with the respect these men showed their medic. Doss, on the other hand, felt self-conscious in front of the navy doctor and started to worry about angering him. When the next soldier addressed him as doc, he glanced nervously at Dr. Abrahamson before replying, "I'm not a doctor. I'm just a medic."

The next soldier standing in line outside the door was watching, and he recognized the tension. Always one to instigate a prank and seeing that the navy doctor had just finished up with his patient, he formulated a plan as he walked over to him.

The prankster stopped in front of Dr. Abrahamson and said in a voice loud enough to be heard by everyone, "Sir, would it be okay if I waited for the army doctor to treat me?"

Everybody stopped what they were doing, to see how Dr. Abrahamson would react. Doss was mortified. His face turned redder than his patient's sunburn. The navy corpsmen working in sickbay knew Dr. Abrahamson had a quick wit and keen sense of humor, and they were eager to see if he would get the best of the army prankster.

Without missing a beat, Dr. Abrahamson replied, "Soldier, I don't think I've ever seen a case of army sunburn as bad as you. I doubt I can even save your life." Then turning toward the medic, he said, "Doctor Doss, do you think you might be able to cure this man?"

Thinking quickly, he replied, "Sir, I doubt it, but I'm willing to try."

The soldiers and sailors in sickbay broke out in riotous laughter, and as the put-on was recounted by those close enough to have heard it, the laughter rapidly spread down the passageway.

Just as the laughter was dying down, the ship's speakers came to life.

"Attention men this is Captain Scott. I have an announcement from the Secretary of the Navy to be read to all ships. The message is as follows."

Captain Scott looked down at the radio message he was holding in his still shaking hands. He took a breath to calm himself and began to read.

13 APRIL 1945
I HAVE THE SAD DUTY OF ANNOUNCING TO THE NAVAL SERVICE THE DEATH OF FRANKLIN DELANO ROOSEVELT, THE PRESIDENT OF THE UNITED STATES, WHICH OCCURRED ON 12 APRIL. THE WORLD HAS LOST A CHAMPION OF DEMOCRACY WHO CAN ILL BE SPARED BY OUR COUNTRY AND ALLIED CAUSE. THE NAVY, WHICH HE SO DEARLY LOVED, CAN PAY NO BETTER TRIBUTE TO HIS MEMORY THAN TO CARRY ON IN THE TRADITION OF WHICH HE WAS SO PROUD. COLORS SHALL BE DISPLAYED AT HALF-MAST FOR THIRTY DAYS BEGINNING 0800 13 APRIL WEST LONGITUDE DATE IN SO FAR AS WAR OPERATIONS PERMIT. MEMORIAL SERVICES SHALL BE HELD ON THE DAY OF THE FUNERAL TO BE ANNOUNCED LATER AT ALL YARDS AND STATIONS AND ON BOARD ALL VESSELS OF THE NAVY, WAR OPERATIONS PERMITTING. WEARING OF MOURNING BADGES AND FIRING OF SALUTES WILL BE DISPENSED WITH IN VIEW OF WAR CONDITIONS.
JAMES FORRESTAL

"End of message. That is all."

The men who had been laughing just moments before were now stunned into silence. For many of the younger men, FDR had been president for as long as they could remember. As the shock started to wear off, the men realized they were not sure who the new president was. Secretary Forrestal's message had made no mention of the new president's name. Several of the men thought the vice-president was Henry Wallace, but others were sure Roosevelt had switched his running mate to Harry Truman in the last election.

The argument spread throughout the ship until Captain Scott announced over the ship's speakers, *"Now hear this. Word has reached me as to some confusion over the name of the new president. The name of your new Commander in Chief and President of the United States of America is Harry S. Truman. That is all."*

April 15, 1945
Back to Okinawa

As Doss emerged on deck the morning of the 15th, he realized the transport ships had returned to Okinawa during the night and were now anchored about a mile off the beach. He was surrounded on all sides by uncountable warships of every variety. Several miles down the coast to the south, was a cloud of smoke that marked the front line of the ongoing battle. Looking directly ashore, he saw two marine fighters take off from the captured Japanese airfield at Kadena and head off to intercept three enemy planes that were coming in from the other side of the island. Two were almost immediately shot down, but the third escaped after safely flying through the incredibly dense anti-aircraft fire thrown up from the ships offshore.

On 16 April, the 307th regiment received word they would be participating in a demonstration landing the next day. In hopes of drawing enemy troops away from the front lines, the sham would simulate a full-scale attack of the southern shore of Okinawa. It was anticipated, that if the Japanese pulled troops away from the capital city of Naha, the Army would finally be able to break through and capture the airfields surrounding the city.

Before sunrise the next morning, Transport Squadron 17 got underway and arrived at dawn about eight miles off the landing beach. Closer to shore, battleships were blasting the coast with their huge guns. Even closer in, smaller ships were launching wave after wave of rockets. As the troops stood massed on deck, waiting to climb down into the landing boats, they watched the shells and rockets detonating on the hills just beyond the beach. The Navy's bombardment created a rolling wave of fire and thunder that surpassed any fireworks show the men had ever seen.

When it was finally time for the troops to board the landing boats, Doss climbed down and settled in among the infantry troops. As soon as the boat was loaded, it pulled away to head to the rendezvous area. Even though the landing was a deception, the division was using it as a training exercise, so the men were all carrying their normal combat load. As the boat picked up speed, most of the men became seasick, and as was always the case, once the first man threw up others quickly followed. Before long, the bottom of the boat was sloshing with a mixture of vomit and seawater.

The landing boats formed up in straight lines two miles from shore and idled their engines, waiting for the signal to begin the dash for the beach. When the signal finally came, the coxswain gunned their engines, and the boats surged forward. At the same time, squadrons of fighters and bombers roared overhead to rocket and strafe the beach.

When the first wave of boats was two thousand yards from shore, it made a sharp left hand turn and headed back out to sea. The battleship bombardment stopped, and the planes flew home. The feint was over. Now it was time for the soaked, seasick and tired troops to head back to be picked up by the transport ships. Arriving back aboard, the navy was waiting with hot meals and almost warm showers for the exhausted troops. As soon as all the landing craft were hoisted back aboard and stowed away, the convoy headed back to the Hagushi beaches and in the late afternoon dropped anchor about a mile off shore.

Mountrail spent four miserable days at anchor waiting for word to unload her troops. On the first day, the men received word that beloved reporter Ernie Pyle had been killed on Le Shima while on his way to report on 77th Division infantrymen fighting on the front lines. The news of Pyle's death was especially hard to take coming only a week after Roosevelt's passing.

When the picket destroyers sent word of approaching enemy planes, all the ships in the harbor would begin to make smoke. In addition, each transport ship had been ordered to have at least two of their landing boats in the water at all times for smoke duty. The boats were equipped with Patterson generators, which produced a dense grey artificial fog by injecting a special oil mixture into the hot exhausts of their motors. Since Patterson smoke was heavier than air, it hugged the ground, but unlike normal smoke, it was nontoxic. Even though it was not dangerous to breathe, it was still hard on the nerves to be engulfed in a fogbank for days on end, as heard but unseen planes passed overhead. If the smoke started to disperse, a bullhorn-amplified voice would shout out the order, *"Smokey make smoke."* Often times, the smoke boat was unable to comply because it had either become lost in the fog and was nowhere near its mother ship or its smoke generator had caught fire and blown up. As enemy planes came closer, amplified voices from all over the fleet became more insistent and seemed to echo *"Smokey make smoke. Smokey make smoke...."* Eventually, the Hagushi harbor became known to the troops as "Smoky Hollow."

Finally, on 23 April, *Mountrail* received orders to debark her troops and unload her cargo. After being aboard for a month and a half, Doss and the other men of the 1st Battalion, 307th Regiment, 77th Infantry Division, were about to set foot on dry land again. The landing beach had been secured for days, so the troops did not have to worry about hitting the beach under fire. The only interruption to unloading was the inevitable one or two air attacks per day; otherwise, the crew of the *Mountrail* worked around the clock, shuttling troops and supplies ashore. Since they knew that as soon as they had emptied their ship of men and supplies they could head home, every sailor pitched in with a passion. The following day, the final load went ashore.

The 1st Battalion had spent so much time aboard the *Mountrail,* her sailors almost considered them shipmates. Even so, they were glad to finally see the last man leave. As the sailors watched the men and equipment move off the beach and disappear into the jungle, many of them said a silent prayer for their safety.

On 26 April, USS *Mountrail* raised anchor, joined up with a convoy headed away from Okinawa and steamed for home.

April 30, 1945
Hacksaw Ridge

By 24 April, the Americans had succeeded in breaking through the first line of defense in the battle for Okinawa. The enemy troops then pulled back to where they had prepared a classic reverse slope defense along an area the American mapmakers had named the Maeda Escarpment. However, the grunts who had to take the escarpment came up with a different name for it. They called it Hacksaw Ridge, because the Japanese defense which was dug in there cut through assaulting American soldiers like a hacksaw. The escarpment formed a natural barrier dividing the island at one of its most narrow points. It rose 400 to 500 feet above sea level with the last 100 feet ascending at an angle of almost 45 degrees. On top, the enemy had constructed heavy fortifications. To reach the summit, American troops would be forced to climb a final shear vertical rock face of about 40 feet.

The Japanese dug interconnecting tunnels and built pillboxes all throughout the reverse slope of the area. They planned to make their last stand at the rugged southern end of Okinawa, and the escarpment was to be their front door. With artillery and tank support, it was not difficult to capture and occupy the forward slope of the escarpment, but the advantage switched to the enemy when the Americans tried to cross over the ridge.

On 26 April, the 96th Division had the extreme misfortune of being given first crack at breaking through the defenses at Hacksaw Ridge. Every time they tried to advance over the ridge, they were ambushed and cut down by short-range fire from enemy troops hiding in pillboxes, caves and tunnels on the reverse slope. After three days of trying to kick down the door, the defenders had inflicted over 1,000 casualties on the 381st infantry Regiment of the 96th Division. This reduced their fighting strength to less than 40 percent, which rendered them militarily ineffective. Although the 96th didn't gain any ground in their four day battle, they did kill a lot of Japanese soldiers. Such were the conditions the 77th Division faced when they were ordered to relieve the 96th.

On 29 April, the 307th moved into place and relieved the 381st. The next day, the rest of the division moved up to the line. When the 77th arrived at the front, they found battle weary soldiers who were so exhausted, many of them didn't even have the energy to carry their own equipment back down the hill. It was all they could do to shuffle down the slope to the trucks waiting to move them to the rear area. Even though they were all dog-tired, the soldiers still had enough strength to talk. As they passed by the fresh troops, mumbling with blank, shell-shocked looks on their faces, the comments invariably started off one of two ways. "Welcome to Hacksaw Ridge" or "This place is hell on earth."

After relieving the 96th, the first thing General Bruce did, was to order scouts to the top of the escarpment to assess the situation. Four 307th scouts used several ropes, which the 96th had secured to the top of the escarpment, to climb up and take a look. The enemy waited until three of them had crawled onto the plateau and moved about five feet from the ledge to open fire. A fourth scout, who was about to crawl up over the edge, watched in horror as bullets from a heavy Japanese machine gun decapitated the first scout and hit the second one in the chest, knocking him back off the ledge and over the precipice. The third lay obviously dead, his lifeless body continuing to be hit repeatedly with machine gun rounds. The final scout wormed the rest of the way up over the edge and slid down into a depression behind a huge boulder where his rope was anchored. From there, he could easily spot three large concrete pillboxes further down the reverse slope, but beyond that, no other enemy positions were readily apparent.

Because of previous bombings and artillery barrages, there were jagged stumps, broken tree trunks and thousands of large pieces of shattered limestone rock littering the landscape. The surviving scout spent about half an hour on top of the escarpment gathering up as many pieces of large rock as he could reach from his protected position. Then he slid them one by one out from behind the boulder to form a crude low wall that extended several feet to the left. By the time he finished, he had formed a protected area behind which at least three soldiers at a time could lie undetected by the enemy.

When Captain Vernon and the other company commanders heard the scouting report, they realized it would be suicide to send their men up onto the ridge in groups of just two or three. What they needed was a way to move a lot of firepower up the cliff wall quickly. After some discussion, they decided to ask the navy to loan them a few cargo nets like the ones they had used to climb down from the troopships into the landing boats. Meanwhile, they sent small groups of men up the escarpment to work on extending the rock wall the scout had started building. By the end of the day, they had managed to build thirty feet of low rock wall about five feet back from the edge of the cliff.

The next morning, a truck carrying cargo nets and three fifty foot ladders arrived. After the nets were unloaded, Lt. Colt needed someone to secure them to the cliff. Spotting his medic, he said, "Doss, I guess you're about the best man I got when it comes to rope work. Would you be willing to climb up and tie the nets off?"

"Sure Lieutenant, but I'll need some other men to help me haul 'em up."

In a few minutes, Colt came back with three soldiers. "You guys help Doss. Do what he tells you."

Doss had been promoted to Private First Class while he was aboard the *Mountrail.* Joking with the other men, he said, "Whaddya know, it's my first chance at command. I guess they expect me to earn that extra four dollars a month."

The four men each tied a rope around their waist while other soldiers raised the wooden ladders against the cliff wall. Doss was the first up a ladder with the other three men following close behind. Just before reaching the peak, he came to a small outcropping. He judged the ledge was wide enough for him to step off the ladder, where he remained, out of sight of the enemy pillboxes. He waited for the three armed men to pass by and crawl over the lip, before he stepped back onto the ladder and joined them at the peak. "You guys pull up the net and hold the ropes. I'll tie 'em off."

Captain Vernon was anxiously watching them work from below, knowing that once the nets were secure, he would have a way to send an entire platoon up the escarpment at the same time. After they finished, the four men waited at the top for the rest of the platoon to come up. Doss sat with his back against the boulder, looked out across the island and tried to count the ships anchored off shore. After counting several hundred ships, he noticed Lt. Colt motion for them to come back down.

While Doss and the other men were working to secure the net, Colt had assembled a squad of men from throughout Company B to make the assault on the nearest pillbox. He had gathered a bazooka team, two BAR men, along with a two-man machine gun team, three men to carry demolition packs, a flamethrower and several riflemen to provide cover. The group numbered about 20 men in all. At the same time, Company A had a squad ready to send up the escarpment in hopes of capturing the high ground at Needle Rock on the left. After Doss heard Lt. Colt lay out the plan, he volunteered to go along.

"Doss this is going to be dangerous work. You stay down here for now. We'll call you up if we need you."

"At least let me come up and wait behind the wall. If anyone needs my help I'll get to 'em faster that way and Lieutenant, I think prayer is the best lifesaver there is. Could the men have a moment to say a prayer before they go up?"

"Men, gather round, Doss wants to say a prayer for you."

"But Lieutenant…" Doss had wanted the men to say their own prayers, but as they moved in close, some removing their helmets, others with their heads bowed waiting for him to begin, he could see they expected him to pray for them all. Doss removed his helmet and began.

"Dear gracious Lord in heaven above, I pray for the safety of the men standing round who Lt. Colt chose. I also ask that You give the lieutenant wisdom. Guide his orders so they will be the correct ones, orders that will keep us from harm. If it is in Your will, we ask that every man standing here come back down off the cliff alive. Lord, you know the hearts of each man standing round here. If any man has not spiritually prepared himself for the possibility of death, I ask that You impress him to take a moment to pray for himself. In the wonderful name of our eternal Savior and protector, Jesus Christ, Amen."

After the prayer, Doss felt a remarkable sense of peace pass through his body. "I'm ready now Lieutenant." Several of the other men chimed in that they felt ready too. With the lieutenant taking the lead, his team began the climb up the nets and ladder. Reaching the top, they squirmed over the ledge and crawled up behind the protection of the rock wall. Lt. Colt extended the antenna on a handi-talkie, which he was using to communicate with two Shermans about a half mile away. When the entire squad was in place, he radioed for the tanks to open fire on the pillbox with their main guns. Even though the rounds didn't penetrate, they were enough to encourage the occupants to keep their heads down.

The machine gunner, who had set up to the right of the boulder, opened up, directing a stream of bullets into the pillbox observation slit. The BAR teams split up and moved right and left. Lt. Colt tapped the bazooka man on the helmet, the signal for him to open fire. The gunner rested his launcher on the wall. "Load," he called.

The loader confirmed he had heard the gunner by replying, "Load." He then depressed the retaining clip on the back of the bazooka tube. Using his left hand, he took one of the rockets out of his carrying pouch and inserted it halfway into the launcher tube. With his right hand, he pulled out the safety pin and dropped it on the ground. He then pushed the rocket the rest of the way into the tube until the clip clicked into two notches on the rocket fins completing one leg of the electrical contact. Carefully stretching out the coiled rocket motor igniter wire, he wrapped it around the side contact post at the rear of the launcher to complete the circuit. In less than 15 seconds, the rocket was loaded and armed. As the final step, the loader made sure he was clear of the rear of the launcher, announced, "Ready," and gave the gunner a pat on the back.

The pillbox was less than 20 yards away. It was so close the gunner reminded himself to aim low; otherwise, it was an easy shot. He pulled the trigger, igniting the rocket. A split second later, it hit the pillbox and exploded. It took the bazooka team two more rockets to blast open a hole. As soon as the smoke and dust from the final rocket had cleared, the machine gunner ceased firing. One of the men ran up with a demolition pack, pulled the pin to light its fuse and threw it into the opening. Seconds later, a huge explosion blew the top off the pillbox. The flamethrower rapidly moved up and hosed down the inside with a stream of flaming gasoline to finish the job. The whole operation took less than five minutes.

Lt. Colt motioned his team forward, and Doss moved up to join the other men as they took cover behind the destroyed pillbox. When all his men were in place, Colt used his signal mirror to flash Company A the sign to cover them from their position on the high ground. He was surprised and aggravated when he didn't get a response. Maybe he would have been more understanding if he had known that the first five men who attempted to climb up Needle Rock were killed as soon as they stepped off their ladders. Several other men lay wounded waiting to be rescued. After more than a minute of fruitless signaling, Lt. Colt gave up and came to the realization that he and his men were by themselves on that section of the escarpment. They would have to go it alone.

For the next hour or so, Doss followed the demolition squad as it moved from bunker, to pillbox, to cave, using the same procedure on each of them. Every time they moved forward, other troops climbed up the net onto the escarpment and moved in behind them. By early afternoon, Company B had almost 150 men up on the escarpment, and it appeared that they had control of not only their assigned area but also much of what had been assigned to Company A. Captain Vernon decided it was a good time to bring the demolition squad down off the escarpment, so they could rest.

The captain was amazed when the original group came down, and Lt. Colt reported only one injury. The bazooka gunner's hand had been slightly injured by a falling rock as he was climbing down the net. When Colonel Hamilton read the morning report, he thought that there had been a typo in Company B's casualty figures. He sent a message back by runner, asking Captain Vernon to explain how he had managed to capture so much ground without any casualties while Company A had been cut to pieces. Captain Vernon read the message, turned it over, wrote two words on the blank side, signed it and then handed it back to the messenger. "Here, take this back to Colonel Hamilton." When the runner returned with the message, the colonel looked at it and read it to himself. Then with a perplexed look on his face, he repeated the message aloud, "Doss prayed?"

Since men were still fighting on top of the escarpment, Doss had stayed behind under the cover of the rock wall to wait for casualties. What the men were about to find out, was that the Japanese had developed a tried and true strategy during their previous encounters with the 96th Division. They would allow the Americans to come up on the cliff in the morning, and then inflict some casualties by using snipers hidden in caves and other places. Once a sufficient number of GI's, wounded men and medics were on the escarpment, enemy reinforcements would move into position through interconnecting tunnels and caves. Once in place, they would swarm out of the hidden openings, kill as many Americans as possible and force the rest back off the top. All at once, just after Colt's squad had come down from the top, enemy soldiers seemed to appear out of nowhere all over the escarpment.

From his hiding place, Doss saw dozens of Japanese rush out from a cave. They spread out as they ran, throwing grenade after grenade. The Americans shot down several, but most of the group made it to cover behind a large rock formation. From there, they continued to throw grenades. The GI's threw grenades back. After a while, it became obvious the enemy troops were somehow being resupplied because there was no way they could have carried the amount of grenades that had already been thrown.

Meanwhile, more and more Japanese soldiers seemed to magically appear all around and even among the Americans. It soon became all too obvious that these enemy soldiers preferred throwing grenades to using their rifles. There were so many flying back and forth that, for a moment, it reminded Doss of a snowball fight. While he was occupied watching the battle, a soldier he didn't recognize appeared at the top of the net with a box and slid it toward him. After the surreal scene he had just witnessed, Doss was having trouble processing reality.

"Hey Soldier. Grenades. Pass 'em on."

To the medic, it seemed that time had shifted into slow motion. He could see explosions all over the escarpment, but he could not hear them. On the other hand, he did plainly hear the soldier at the top of the net. He looked around for someone else who could pass the crate over the stone wall. There was no one close.

"Hey Dilbert," the soldier yelled. "They need these now. Pass 'em forward." Then he disappeared back down the net. Doss looked around again. All the nearby men were under cover and out of grenades. If one of them tried to crawl back over the wall for the box, there was a good chance that he would be killed. Doss made a split-second decision. He picked up the 30-pound box and threw it over the wall toward the nearest man. The soldier opened the lid and underhanded grenades to the nearby GIs, keeping the last three for himself. Just as he pulled the pin on one of them and stood up to throw, something struck him in the leg causing him to fall with the armed grenade still in his hand. When he hit the ground, it rolled free and exploded.

At the sound of the blast, the medic's senses seemed to come back into focus. Time started moving at a normal rate, and he could clearly hear the sounds of battle once again.

"Medic!"

"Medic!"

The calls for help were coming from all around. Doss jumped over the wall and ran to the aid of the grenade victim. When he got there, he found that the fumbled grenade had not only blown the soldier's own arm off at the elbow, it had also injured some other men. He opened his medical kit, took out a tourniquet and applied it to stop the arterial flow. As he worked to halt the bleeding from several other wounds, he felt a tap on his back. "I'm a replacement medic. Just got sent up. Captain Webster told me to come up here and give you some help. Whatcha want me to do?"

Without even looking up, Doss shouted, "Start on those other men. I'll finish this one."

After Doss had gotten the bleeding under control, he dragged the soldier back to where several litter bearers were waiting. Working together, they lifted the injured man over the wall. He didn't stick around to help secure him to the stretcher and lower him down the cliff because he could hear other calls for help coming from all over the escarpment. He did pause for a moment as he crawled past the new medic to see how he was doing. Doss saw that he had already patched up one of the men and sent him crawling back toward the litter bearers. Now he was bent over another soldier, giving a morphine injection. Since the new guy seemed to be doing okay, he continued on toward the next casualty.

The battle raged all around as Doss went from victim to victim. The Americans were finally throwing enough grenades that they had pinned most of the Japanese down. Even so, Doss could tell that a sniper had spotted him because every time he moved to a new spot, bullets would impact nearby.

Some of the less wounded men were still able to crawl, and Doss told them to head back to the litter team without treating them. It was more important for the medic to stabilize the critically wounded than to bandage a flesh wound. He left it up to the litter team to decide whether to apply a dressing before sending the man down the cliff and on to the aid-station. Others were so severely wounded he had to drag them back through the heart of the battle to reach the litter bearers.

The Japanese were slowly but surely forcing the front line back toward the edge of the cliff. Doss was unwilling to leave any injured man behind, and twice he dashed behind enemy lines to pick up and carry a wounded soldier back to the American side.

They couldn't hold. Before darkness started to fall, the 307th was ordered off the cliff for the night. Just as he was about to head back down the net, Doss noticed the body of the replacement medic. He rolled him over. The front of his head was missing. Doss thought as he climbed down the net, *Oh Lord, I didn't even ask his name, and now I'll never know what he looked like. All this fighting and killing and it accomplished nothing.*

When he got down from the escarpment, Doss started to look for somewhere to hole-up for the night. It wasn't long before he ran into Tennessee. "Hey Byran, I've been up on Hacksaw Ridge all day. You know some place I can spend the night?"

"Sure 'nough buddy, I found me a little cave. You wann'a share, it's okay by me."

Doss was so exhausted; all he could think about was sleep. He followed Tennessee, and they both squeezed their way through a narrow opening in the cliff face. Once his eyes adjusted, he could see that he was in a space about six feet wide and eight feet long. The floor was covered in loose dirt.

Byran could see how tired the medic was. "Hey Doc, I'll take the first watch. Git some sleep, and I'll wake you up in a couple hours."

Somewhat later, Doss was startled awake. At first, he thought he had been dreaming, but then he realized he really was hearing Japanese voices. He reached in his pocket and took out a pack of matches, struck one and shielded it with his hand. In the dim light of the flame, he could see that Tennessee Byran was fast asleep. The voices seemed to be coming from a narrow crack that angled downward toward the back of the cave. He blew out the match and shook Byran, whispering, "Wake up, I hear Japs."

Byran pushed the medic's hand away. "Leave me be. Go asleep Doc."

Doss knew he couldn't leave the cave in the middle of the night because if he did, he was liable to be mistaken for an enemy soldier and get his head shot off. After pinching, kicking and holding Byran's nose, he gave up. He had tried everything he could think of to wake up Tennessee, with the same result. *Please Lord, please get me out of here alive, and I'll never be stupid enough to buddy up with Byran again,* he prayed. Almost in a panic, he lit another match. In the dim light, he could see that Tennessee had several hand grenades attached to his backpack.

If I just drop one of them down the crack, it'll seal up the hole, and we'll both be safe for the night, the medic thought. He started to reach for a grenade but stopped. *What's got in me? I could'a killed someone. Please forgive me for even thinking about it Jesus.*

On and off for the rest of the night, Doss heard voices coming from the crack. At first light, Byran woke up. "Hey buddy, why'd you let me sleep all night? You should'a done woke me up when it was my turn to pull guard duty." Doss was so furious he crawled out of the cave without answering, leaving Byran alone to wonder what he had done to upset his friend.

May 1, 1945
Hacksaw Ridge Over and Over Again

Later that morning, Colonel Hamilton ordered the 307th to make another go at the escarpment. When Company B went back up the nets, they found the situation much the same as the day before. Getting a foothold on the ridge was a little easier the second time around because several of the pillboxes and caves had been sealed shut with high explosives the day before.

The problem the 307th faced was that they didn't have a handle on how extensive the underground network was. They didn't realize that when the front of a cave was destroyed, the Japanese might lose one or two men, but the rest of the troops were able to retreat through tunnels and then move to another location.

Doss was sitting at the base of one of the nets, doing his Bible study as he waited for casualties, when a colonel from the artillery approached him. "How's it going up top?"

Doss stood up before he answered. He knew better than to salute an officer on the front line, but he wanted to be respectful. "I'm sorry I don't know Sir. I haven't been called up there yet today."

"Well I need to find out what effect my guns are having. I'm going up to take a look."

Doss sat back down and continued to work on his Sabbath School Lesson. He had grown accustomed to and was able to tune out the constant noise of battle, but in a little while, he heard the one sound that always got his attention. "Medic! We got a injured man up here. Hurry up. He's hurt bad."

Doss quickly climbed the net. When he got to the top, he saw the colonel sprawled on the ground about 50 feet away with both legs blown off above the knees. Two soldiers were trying to stop the bleeding by applying their full weight on the pressure points of each leg. Japanese knee mortars were still landing all around, and an enemy machine gun was firing in their direction.

Doss made his way over and applied tourniquets to both of the man's stumps. Then he reached under the colonel's arms, picked him up and carried him to a low spot, which offered some protection from the enemy bullets but not the mortars. Doss had observed just about every way an injured man could react and the colonel was a perfect example of one of them. Up until the time he passed out from shock, apparently unaware he had lost both of his legs, the colonel was still carrying on a normal conversation with the medic.

Just after the colonel passed out, two litter bearers slid in beside them. "One of you run back to the aid-station, and bring me back some plasma," Doss said. Neither of the bearers really wanted to make an additional round trip with the amount of lead flying, but the fact the wounded man was a colonel influenced them not to argue with the medic. When the runner returned with the plasma, it was ready to use because the aid-station had mixed it together, and enough time had passed for it to reconstitute during the return trip.

The medic took the bottle and inserted the large gauge needle into the colonel's arm. To keep the plasma flowing, he had to get up on his knees and hold the bottle above his head. This exposed him to the enemy. Knee mortars started to impact closer and bullets were whizzing and ricocheting all around. While he was on his knees, both stretcher-bearers were hugging the ground, amazed that none of the bullets had hit the medic. Before all of the plasma had drained into the colonel, a very close explosion knocked Doss off balance. As he fell, the needle pulled free. The medic tried for several minutes to reinsert it, but the colonel's blood pressure had dropped so low he could not find a vein. "Go… run tell the aid-station… to send a doctor. Tell 'em… I got a injured colonel up here… and I need help... restarting the plasma," panted the medic.

A little less than five minutes later, one of the doctors from the aid-station appeared. He was carrying two more bottles of plasma. Together, he and the medic worked in vain trying to restart the IV. "It's no use Doss, we're wasting our time. I'll take him back to the aid-station, but I think he's had it."

Doss was watching the stretcher-bearers strap the colonel to the litter as they prepared to lower him down the cliff when he heard another cry for a medic. He looked around and saw a soldier waving him over. Doss crawled over to where several men were crouched down behind a blown up pillbox. One of the men pointed. "Sergeant Brock got hit trying to throw a satchel charge in that cave." The medic peaked over the pillbox. The cave was over 100 feet away.

"I don't see him."

"We think he fell in the cave," the soldier replied.

Before the men could stop him, Doss walked around the pillbox and headed directly for the cave. The medic didn't even make an effort to conceal himself. To the other men it looked like he was headed out for an evening stroll. "Get back here you damn crazy fool," shouted one of the men. Mortars and bullets struck all around the medic. The men watched in amazement as he walked up to the cave, calmly stepped inside and came back out carrying the wounded man over his shoulder. As the medic retraced his steps, the Japanese opened up on him. Dozens of rounds impacted nearby. All up and down the American side of the line, soldiers stopped firing to watch the crazy medic walk unscathed through a swarm of enemy bullets.

When the medic made it safely back to the pillbox, he shrugged Sergeant Brock off his shoulders and into the arms of the waiting men who helped lay him gently on the ground. He knelt down and removed the wounded man's helmet. With a glance at the frozen look on Brock's face, Doss assumed he was dead. After failing to find a pulse, he was positive.

"Doss, are you insane? You risked your life for a dead man."

The medic didn't even seem to hear the comment. He walked back over to the net, climbed down, took out his Bible and Sabbath School Quarterly and continued where he had left off. He had fallen over a week behind in his lessons and was determined to catch up.

Lesson 3, for the week of April 21, 1945
SEED THOUGHT: We are to trust in His promises. When we come to Him in faith, every petition enters the heart of God. When we have asked for His blessing, we should believe that we receive it and thank Him that we have received it. Then we are to go about our duties, assured that the blessing will be realized when we need it most. When we have learned to do this, we shall know that our prayers have been answered. God will do for us 'exceeding abundantly,' 'according to the riches of His glory,' and 'the working of his mighty power.'" – The Desire of Ages," page 200.

Question 1. Read Ephesians 2:10 and tell about how this verse applies in your life.

Doss struggled with the question. He had always disliked when the lesson study asked him to tell how a verse related to his life. He could never seem to think of anything that fit.

While he was working on the lesson, a signal corps photographer came up to him. "You Private Doss, the medic?"

"That's me," he replied.

"They sent me up here to get your picture. Said you helped hang this net, and because you prayed, no one got hurt in the first assault."

"Really? That's what they're saying?"

The photographer moved around and took several photos. "Hey, how about taking a picture of me reading my Bible?" Doss asked.

"I'll make a deal. Let me get you climbing up the net first, and then I will." Doss scrambled up the net and stepped off on the ledge just below the ridge, so that he could turn around. Then he smiled and waved down at the photographer. "Come on up, the view's great."

"The view's just fine from down here," shouted back the signal corps man. *What a loon,* he thought. *But, it'll make a great picture if he doesn't get killed.* Doss laughed to himself. He knew that as long as he stayed on the ledge his head was below the summit and the enemy couldn't see him, but from the camera's angle it would look like he was standing in plain sight. When the photographer was satisfied, he came back down, and the war correspondent used the last exposure in his roll to capture the medic reading his Bible.

The 307th was able to hold the peak overnight, but by the next morning, enough Japanese reinforcements had arrived to force the men back off the top again.

Later in the day on 2 May, after the 77th artillery softened up the plateau, the 307th went back up the nets again. From where they were parked on Highway 5, several tanks were in a position to support the infantrymen with their main guns. The tanks were concentrating their fire on a large cave, which the Japanese had reinforced by building a concrete wall across its opening. After managing to blast away the concrete, one of the tanks fired six rounds of white phosphorus into the cave. A small amount of smoke rolled out of the cave, but it was nowhere near the volume they had expected. A few minutes later, white smoke started venting from dozens of concealed openings all over the escarpment. For the first time, the infantrymen realized how extensively the Japanese positions were interconnected by tunnels.

Right around midnight, the enemy counterattacked and forced them back off the top again.

The next morning, the 307th went back up the escarpment for the fifth time. One scout squad was able to sneak all the way across the plateau and look down at the reverse slope. Just below their position was a group of soldiers cooking a meal under the cover of a rock overhang. The scouts threw down several grenades and then ran back to the American line. After hearing the report from the scouts, the 1st Battalion decided to try out a new tactic. Box after box of hand grenades were hauled up to the peak. Each man was given a satchel bag that would hold about 25 grenades. Then they spread out in a long straight line. The men were told to move forward and throw a grenade into every hole or crack no matter how small it might appear.

When they had cleared out a wide stretch of the plateau, the infantrymen proceeded down the reverse slope. This was the area where the enemy had prepared their strongest defense. A horrific grenade battle ensued. Men would throw a whole satchel bag of grenades in less than five minutes while the Japanese were throwing back grenades of their own. The casualties on both sides were extremely high. GIs came back in tears, swearing they would never go back over the ridge again.

Doss had dragged one wounded man into a depression just below the ridgeline on the American side of the battle. When his fellow soldiers saw him working on the casualty, they quit throwing grenades in his direction out of fear that one might fall short and kill the medic. The Japanese, who were hunkered down on the other side of the hill, took advantage of the lull in the action and started throwing grenades back across at the Americans. Doss yelled out, "What are you doing? Don't stop now." The GIs realized they needed to keep the heads of the enemy down, so their medic could work. For several minutes, the medic tended to his victim while live grenades, thrown by both sides, flew back and forth less than five feet over the top of his head.

Just as he finished bandaging up his patient, a fresh group of soldiers ran past him and rained down grenades on the Japanese side, giving him the opportunity to drag the wounded man back toward the cliff.

About halfway there, Doss turned his victim over to a litter team, which had come to meet him. As he was cramming supplies the litter team had brought along into his medic bag, he felt someone grip his arm. It was Lane. Doss had not seen him since Leyte. He was crying. "Doss you're the only one can help me. I can't go back over that ridge again. My luck's run out. I'll get killed for sure."

"What'a you want me to do Lane?"

"Pray for me, Doss. You're the only one's got any real faith. It's all over the division how you prayed an it kept everyone in your platoon from getting hurt. Please pray for me."

"I'll do it, but you need to pray for yourself, Lane. If you get killed, you need to be right with God. You need to do it right now. You can't risk putting it off."

"Sure, sure, but you gotta promise me you'll pray too. Right Doss? 'Cause if I make it out of here alive I'm coming to your church. It's a promise."

After the medic and Lane had prayed together, Lane took off toward the cliff. The last time Doss ever saw him was a few minutes later when he was heading back toward the ridge with a satchel full of grenades.

Later in the day, Doss was told that four men had been injured near the mouth of the same cave where Sergeant Brock had been killed. The medic made his way over to the destroyed pillbox. From there he could see that the wounded men were lying about 25 feet in front of the entrance to the cavern. There were machine gun muzzle flashes coming from deep within the cave. He took a few moments to weigh his options. He could try smoke grenades, but with four men to rescue, the smoke might just draw the attention of every sniper within range. A team was setting up a machine gun next to the pillbox to cover the wounded men, and he hoped they might be able to persuade the Japs in the cave to clear out. He decided his best option was prayer and then covering the open ground as quickly as possible.

Doss prayed then he crouched down low and sprinted to the group of wounded men. He bandaged up the most seriously injured one and carried him back to the pillbox. Some litter bearers had moved up and he turned the soldier over to them. It was during his second trip that Doss was spotted by the enemy. A machine gun opened up on him, sending mud and splinters of rock flying all around the medic. By the time he had made it back to the other wounded soldiers, the Japanese were also firing knee mortars in his direction. It took Doss over an hour to rescue all the men. Soldiers on both sides of the battle watched, astonished, each time the medic ran the gauntlet without being wounded.

MAY 5, 1945
THE ONLY ONE LEFT

Lieutenant Colonel Gerald Cooney thought he had the perfect plan to demolish Sergeant Brock's cave once and for all. Since the sergeant had been killed, Cooney had sent men from his 1st Battalion three separate times in attempts to destroy it. Each time had ended in failure. The cave was the one remaining stronghold preventing the Americans from holding the top of Hacksaw Ridge.

Colonel Cooney directed the A & P Platoon to construct a tin trough that could be easily taken apart and then quickly reassembled. His idea was to lay the trough on the escarpment and use it to channel gasoline into Brock's Cave.

When the trough was ready, Cooney scheduled the entire battalion to make another coordinated assault on the ridge at 0900.

Colonel Cooney was not the only one who had made plans for that day. General Ushijima, commander of the 32nd Japanese Army, had ordered all available men to begin to move into the tunnels of Hacksaw Ridge at 0900 in preparation for a surprise counter attack, which he scheduled to take place at 1000.

It was Sabbath and Doss was up at first light to pray and work on his Bible lessons. By then, he was only a day behind on his studies and eager to finish one more lesson so he would be caught up and back on schedule. As always, the first thing he did after taking out his Bible was to reread the letter Dorothy had written him. Then he unfolded his quarterly and opened it to the lesson for May 4th. After he had worked for a while, he overheard Colonel Cooney and Captain Vernon talking. "I can't ask him to go back up on the ridge today. It's his Sabbath."

"You've got no choice Captain. He's the only medic we have left to cover the entire battalion. The men need a medic, and he's all we have left."

As they were talking, Doss moved up behind the two men. "Excuse me Sirs. I'll go up, but could I have a few minutes to finish my Bible lesson first?" Colonel Cooney looked at his watch. It was almost 0900 and the entire battalion was on station and waiting for him to give the word to go. Then he looked at the medic. His uniform was crusted from head to toe with the dried blood of all the men he had rescued. Cooney looked back at his watch and then at Captain Vernon. "Okay, give him whatever time he needs. Let me know when he's done." *How am I going to explain to Colonel Hamilton that I let one medic hold up the entire operation?* thought Cooney. The colonel began to pace nervously as the medic went back to his rock to work on his lesson.

Doss picked up where he had left off.

Lesson 5, for May 5th
Seed Thought: "Jesus says. 'Lo I am with you always even unto the end of the world.' . . . We must always take comfort and hope as we think of this. . . He thinks of us individually, and knows every necessity. . . . I entreat you to have courage in the Lord. Divine strength is ours; and let us talk courage and strength and faith."

The medic was so engrossed in his study, he didn't even notice that every nearby soldier was watching and waiting for him to finish. They all heard when he paused to reread part of the last sentence aloud, "Let us talk courage?" He took the pencil out of his pocket, licked the lead and used it to make a note in the margin. *Talk? Typo? Maybe means take?* Then he finished reading the last part of the introduction.

"Read the third chapter of Ephesians. Practice the instruction given. Bear a living testimony for God under all circumstances." – Testimonies to Ministers Page 391

The medic opened his Bible and turned to Ephesians chapter three. After reading it, he copied verse 20 in the margin. *"Now unto him that is able to do exceeding abundantly above all that we ask or think, according to the power that worketh in us."*

The medic closed his Bible, folded up his lesson and placed them both back into his breast pocket. After he buttoned the flap, he got down on his knees to pray. "Dear Lord, thank you for being with me and protecting me. I want to have the Divine strength and power Paul is talking about. Please direct me, so I can always do your will, not mine. In Jesus name, Amen." When he finished praying he went over to Captain Vernon. "I'm ready Captain, but could the men have a few minutes to pray before they go up?"

"I'm sorry," said Vernon, after glancing at the colonel who was tapping his watch. "We're already almost 20 minutes behind schedule. I'm sure any man who felt like it has already prayed." Cooney motioned for Captain Vernon to hurry up and then took out a whistle and sounded a long blast. The 155 men that had gathered nearby heard the signal and began to swarm up the nets. Once the infantrymen had reached the summit and set up a defensive perimeter, other men climbed the net carrying the disassembled trough system. Still others followed with five gallon gasoline cans strapped to their packboards. As soon as all the combat men had reached the top, the medic followed close behind. Since Doss was the only medic, he was carrying his normal medic bags, plus two others. He also had stuffed all his pockets with dressings and tourniquets.

By the time Doss had reached the top and settled in behind the boulder, the men had been struggling for several minutes trying to assemble what they had nicknamed Cooney's gutter. They could already see it was not going to work. The ground was too uneven for the gasoline to flow through the trough even if they could get it put together. Finally, Lt. Colt told the men. "Forget the stupid thing. Just go throw the damn cans in the cave."

As the men worked, they were puzzled as to why the enemy was not putting up a defense that morning. What they didn't know, was that directly below their feet were over 1,000 Japanese troops in the tunnels waiting for the signal to attack. At 0950 five GIs ran up to the cave, unscrewed the caps of their gas cans and hurled them as far back into the cave as they could. The men could tell the cave extended far underground, because it took a few seconds for them to hear the sound of the cans hitting bottom. Then they heard shouts in Japanese coming from far below. The last man pulled the pin on his satchel charge, heaved it into the cave and then ran like hell. A few moments later, a tremendous tongue of flame lashed out of the cave and smoke puffed out of hidden openings located all over Hacksaw Ridge. Less than a minute later a secondary explosion occurred deep below ground. The ridge shook so violently that many of the men were knocked off their feet. The burning gasoline had set off an underground ammunition dump. After what felt to Doss like a minute-long earthquake, the ground surrounding the cave gave way and slumped down, leaving a crater filled with rubble.

With the collapse of the cave the Americans cheered, but soon their cheers were drowned out by another sound. "Banzai!" The heavy underground smoke and flames had forced a swarm of Japanese soldiers to emerge from numerous holes located all around them. The Americans were vastly outnumbered and quickly overwhelmed. Captain Vernon yelled for the men to retreat. Some, who were close enough to hear his command, ran for the nets and scrambled down in a panic. Others, who stood and fought, were run over by the wild Banzai mob. For some reason, once the enemy had overrun the position, they didn't follow up on the attack. Instead, they scattered, screaming as they ran back in the direction of the reverse slope and disappeared beneath the ridgeline.

The medic peeked around from his hiding place behind the boulder. What he saw were wounded men strewn all over the battlefield. These were the men he had come to love, and now he was the only uninjured man left among them.

Down below, Captain Vernon was taking a head count. Of the 155 men he had sent up, only 57 made it back down. The captain was sick. He was sure he had just lost almost a hundred men. Vernon had the urge to go back up, but it would be suicide for the remaining men if he sent them to face what almost surely had been at least a thousand enemy soldiers.

Just then, he heard a voice calling down from the top of Hacksaw Ridge. "Heads up below." Captain Vernon looked up and saw a boot pushing a wounded man tied to a stretcher off the edge of the cliff. It fell a few feet until the rope holding it pulled taut. Then it jerked lower a foot at a time until one end became snagged on a tree root that was protruding from the face of the cliff. The stretcher tilted, almost causing the wounded man to fall off. By the time it reached the outstretched arms of the men waiting below, the wounded man was dangling upside down, tangled up in the stretcher. Doss appeared at the edge of the cliff and yelled down. "Send him straight to the aid-station. He's hurt bad. Untie the stretcher. It's not gonna work."

"Doss, get down here or you'll get yourself killed," yelled one of the men. The medic acted as if he didn't hear. He pulled the rope back up then disappeared from sight. Several men started for the net, but Captain Vernon stopped them. As much as he wanted to let them go back up, he knew they didn't have the firepower to stand up to the Japanese. They would roll over his remaining men with ease.

While he was lowering the first man, an idea had come to the medic. *That knot I tied back in West Virginia, that double loop bowline knot, I could use it to lower the men.* He dragged another wounded man over. First he played out about 30 feet of rope, enough to reach the ground, and then tied the double bowline. Next he slipped each of the injured man's legs into a loop, wrapped the rope around his chest and tied it again. Finally, he threw the bottom end of the rope over the cliff and wrapped the top part several times around a tree stump, which he planned to use as a capstan. Holding the free end of the rope taut, he used his feet to shove the wounded infantryman over the edge. A soldier below grabbed the dangling rope to hold the wounded man away from the cliff face. The medic slacked off his end of the line. With the rope wrapped around the tree trunk, it took almost no effort for the medic to smoothly lower the man to the ground. By then, a team of litter bearers had arrived from the aid-station. They untied the chest knot, slipped the wounded man's legs out of the bowline loops and gave the rope a flip to signal the medic it was ready to be hauled back up.

Doss was grateful. While he had been waiting for the injured man to be taken off the line, he silently thanked God that he had been allowed to rescue two men. Then out loud, he prayed, "Please Jesus let me save just one more."

Captain Vernon had sent a runner to Colonel Cooney with a message to inform him of the situation and to ask for reinforcements. Cooney sent back word that there were no reserves available. The enemy was counterattacking all along the line, and there were no men to spare. He said the best he could do was to get the artillery to lay down a smoke screen. He also forbade Captain Vernon from sending his men back up on top of the escarpment until he could arrange to reinforce them.

Private Lonsway, along with two other injured soldiers, had managed to make their way over to the edge of the cliff where Doss was lowering wounded men down by rope. The three decided to stay on top and provide whatever cover they could for him. It was a good thing they did because the Japanese had started to notice him pulling wounded men to safety. Every time the medic made another round trip, he drew increasing fire. "If you men want to stay on top, I can't stop you, but I sure do appreciate it," said Doss.

Then the medic crawled off. As he disappeared into the smoke the men heard him call out, "Please Jesus, let me save just one more."

While Doss was gone, one of the wounded infantrymen saw the form of two Japanese soldiers when the smoke momentarily thinned. He fired several shots, and the men went down. A few seconds later, they heard the medic's voice coming from about 10 feet to the left. "It's me, don't shoot." Then he emerged out of the smoke dragging another man who had lost a leg and hand. Lonsway noticed that Doss had used two tourniquets to stop the bleeding before moving him.

By this time, the medic had been at work for more than an hour, and his supplies were almost exhausted. He rigged the soldier to the rope and then tied two empty medic bags to the man's belt before rolling him over the edge. The litter bearers could not see Doss through the smoke but heard him call down. "Fill up those bags with tourniquets and send 'um back up."

The medic made trip after trip over the next few hours dragging casualties to safety and then lowering them down the cliff. By afternoon, the wind coming in off the ocean had picked up enough that it blew away the smoke screen. The artillery fired several more smoke rounds but it was useless. The wind was too strong for them to be able to maintain the screen. With the smoke gone, the medic could see there were still at least 30 casualties waiting to be rescued. "Please Jesus, let me save just one more."

Senior Private Shigeru Takeshi was the best sniper on Hacksaw Ridge. He had been credited with over 60 kills and was especially proud that several of them had been medics. Takeshi had glimpsed Doss several times in the previous hour but never long enough to take aim. *It is a divine wind that has cleared the smoke. Now I will end the life of the American medic.* Once the smoke cleared, he didn't have to wait long before he spotted the medic dragging a wounded American toward the edge of the cliff. He thought, *The American is less than 100 shaku away. An easy shot. Should I shoot him in the left eye or the right?*

He decided that once he had killed the medic, he would take his time and put a bullet into the head of each wounded man left on the battlefield.

Looking through the 2.5X scope, Private Takeshi took careful aim with his Arisaka Type 97 sniper rifle. He took a deep breath, slowly let it out and then squeezed the trigger. At least he tried to squeeze the trigger. It seemed to be jammed. No matter how much force he applied, the trigger would not budge, and the gun would not fire. Takeshi carefully checked over his weapon but could find nothing wrong with it. He aimed at one of the wounded Americans and fired. The rifle worked perfectly. Takeshi relaxed and waited. He knew where to watch for the medic to reappear. He planned to kill him as soon as he did.

Doss still had almost 20 men waiting to be rescued in addition to the three wounded men who had stayed behind to cover him. The medic followed the same routine with each rescue. Just before he headed out to bring in the next victim, he would call out, "Please Jesus, let me save just one more." Several of the wounded men were moved to tears as they witnessed the faith of their brave medic. Private Takeshi had also heard the medic call out. He recognized the word Jesus but nothing more.

As soon as the medic reappeared in his scope, Takeshi pulled on the trigger but it wouldn't budge. It felt as if it had been welded into place. Takeshi tried again. This time he pulled with all his might, but the gun would not fire. He had never had anything like this happen before. *What is this?* Takeshi thought. *Is Jesus protecting this man?*

Private Takeshi suddenly felt as if he had been paralyzed. His finger remained on the trigger but except for his eyes, he was unable to move for the next hour. All he could do was watch the American medic make trip after trip, pulling the wounded soldiers to safety. As soon as the smoke screen had cleared, the Japanese began raining down artillery and knee mortars. Every time the medic showed himself, a machine gun opened up in his direction. Takeshi knew in his heart that only a miracle kept him from being hit. Time after time he observed mortars impact within feet of the working medic, enveloping him in smoke, only to see him emerge, covered with dust and dirt but carrying a hurt enemy soldier. Several times Takeshi's fellow soldiers rushed toward the medic. They intended to bayonet him since their mortars and bullets had proven ineffective. Each time, they were shot down by unseen protectors before reaching the medic.

Private Takeshi had no idea how long he watched the spectacle, but eventually he realized the American medic was gone, along with every wounded enemy soldier. The only ones left alive on Hacksaw Ridge were the Japanese. Takeshi was now able to move. As he used his scope to search the battlefield, his gaze was drawn to an injured Japanese soldier. One of his legs had been blown off at the knee. Around his thigh was an American tourniquet.

MAY 6, 1945
THE MEDIC GETS A REST

Doss had spent over six hours singlehandedly dragging injured men off the battlefield and lowering them to safety. When he was positive there were no Americans left alive on Hacksaw Ridge, he came down. While Doss was working alone on the plateau, the rest of the division had been busy beating back the surprise counterattack. Unfortunately for General Ushijima, his plan did not turn out as he intended. Instead of crushing the Americans, his own troops had been decimated. Most of the officers that he had designated to lead the surprise attack were instantly killed in the underground ammunition dump explosion. When the smoke and flames forced the rest of the Japanese soldiers out of the tunnels ahead of schedule, they emerged directly in the path of their own artillery barrage. Those circumstances taken together caused General Ushijima's plan to come unraveled. During the evening of 5 May, the 77th Division killed more than 800 enemy soldiers. In a two-day period, the Japanese regiment that was defending Hacksaw Ridge lost more than 2,000 men, after which they were no longer a cohesive fighting force. The American side had also suffered. In fact, the 307th was so badly mauled in the fight that some rifle platoons had only two or three men left. Company B had been hit especially hard. They were reduced to about 50 men, which was an almost 75 percent casualty rate.

As soon as the medic came down from Hacksaw Ridge, Captain Vernon ordered him to go back to the medical battalion. "Take a rest, Doss. I don't want to see you back up on the front line for at least two days," he said. The medic stopped back at the aid-station and told Captain Webster what Vernon had said. "He's right, you deserve a rest. It's all over the division what you did on Hacksaw Ridge. Go on back to the field hospital, and take it easy for a while."

When Doss reported to the hospital, the first thing the other medics forced him to do was to take a shower. They told him there was no way they were going to allow him to hang around smelling as bad as he did. As he headed off to the showers, a swarm of flies followed him because he was literally covered from head to toe with blood and everything else that could come out of an injured man.

It was obvious his uniform could not be salvaged, so while Doss scrubbed himself clean, the men burned it. It took the other medics awhile, and some questionable work outside the normal procurement channels, but they were eventually able to put together a complete replacement uniform. When they gave it to him, Doss thought it was a little strange that it didn't have any division patches or other insignia, but he was glad to have a clean uniform. He was especially happy they had found him a brand new pair of double buckle combat boots. Most of the other men were still wearing service shoes and leggings but the combat boot, with its double sole and more ankle support, provided much better protection in the tropical environment.

Once he was cleaned up, the medic found a secluded spot away from the hospital where he could pray and give thanks to God for having kept him safe. While he was out praying, General Bruce showed up at the hospital. After hearing the story of a medic who stayed behind and singlehandedly rescued 100 men, the general had decided he needed to meet and congratulate the man in person. The only problem was that no one knew where to find the medic. General Bruce stayed for a while as they searched in vain trying to locate him. While they searched, he decided to visit some of the injured men waiting to be evacuated. As he went through the hospital ward, the patients told him story after story of the medic's heroics.

By the end of the day on 6 May, the 307th had captured and cleaned up Hacksaw Ridge and the front lines had advanced to the bottom of the reverse slope. In seven days of fighting, the regiment had lost 87 men killed in action and 525 injured along with three enlisted men that went missing and were never found. The general decided that it was time to pull the 307th back for a few days to give them time to rest and pick up replacements.

The division had built a rest camp in the rear area near Chibana, and that is where the 307th was sent. It had a portable kitchen, which gave the men a chance to eat something other than K-rations. There the men could clean up themselves and their equipment. They could watch a movie in a theater tent or go to the mobile library to read somewhat up-to-date magazines. If they wanted to, they could catch up on their letter writing or even just lie around and do nothing.

After a few days of hanging around the field hospital, Doss started hearing rumors about how good the food was at the rest camp, so he asked and got the okay to move back with his men at Chibana. When he arrived at the rest camp, one of the first persons he saw was Tennessee Byran. "Hey there, 'buddy', glad to see you made it off Hacksaw Ridge alive," Doss said. "What'a you do, sleep through the whole thing?"

"I'm sorry Doc but it ain't my fault. Sometimes, when I git stressed, I fall asleep."

"It's okay Byran. Just show me where the chow line is, and we'll call it even."

Doss had been lounging around the rest camp for several days when the signal corps photographer showed up again. "General Bruce said he wants us to write a story about how you saved a hundred men and send it to the newspapers back home. I need to get a good picture to go along with it."

"Couldn't have been a hundred men, there wasn't enough time. It was fifty at most," he protested.

"I'm not here to argue the point. I just take the pictures. What I need today is a head shot." The photographer tried out several different poses and backgrounds, but he wasn't satisfied. "The problem is your uniform. Without any insignia, it looks too plain. What we need is something to add interest. Put on your medic bag, and let me see how that looks." The signal corps man still wasn't satisfied. "Maybe if you were holding something."

"I know," said Doss, "what if I was eating something?" Before the photographer could answer, Doss ran off to the field kitchen. When he spotted his friend the mess sergeant, he said, "General Bruce needs a picture, and the photographer wants to take it of me eating something."

"Eating what?"

"I'm not real sure. How about a can of fruit?"

The cook figured Doss was trying to pull something, but he also had heard about the medic's heroics on Hacksaw Ridge. "I got an idea," said the cook. "How about you take back a couple cans of each type, and he can decide what looks best."

The medic got a big grin on his face. "That oughta work out just fine," he answered.

While the 307th was at Chibana, replacement troops started to trickle in. When Captain Vernon saw the new men, he was appalled at the quality of the soldiers being assigned to Company B. The demand for replacements had gotten so critical the Army was forced to cut the training schedule down to bare bones. Most of the men in the 77th Division had trained together for almost two years before they had been sent into combat, so they were shocked to find out the men arriving from the replacement depots had only been given eight weeks of basic training. Colonel Hamilton ordered each of the company commanders to start the new men on an emergency catch-up course. Even before the order, the platoon leaders and old hands had already been at work, using every daylight hour trying to bring the green men up to speed. With the 307th now comprised of 80 percent green troops, the experienced troops realized their lives depended on how much they could teach the new guys before they were all sent back into combat.

As it turned out, most of the replacements had only been with the 307th for five days when the unit was sent back into action. General Bruce wanted to try a series of simultaneous pre-dawn raids, one of which would require a two-pronged attack on the "Three Sisters" hill formation. The plan required several companies to move 350 yards in the dark to get into position. Company A was to move up on the left flank while Company B followed a line of telephone poles to get into position on the right.

The two company commanders were extremely nervous about the decision to make the move in the dark. American infantrymen were not adequately trained to attack at night. Even if they had the proper training, there were still the green men to worry about. All men are trigger-happy during their first time in combat. The old hands had been when they landed on Guam, and they knew that the new guys would be no exception. Since this attack depended on the element of surprise, the company commanders made the decision to order the replacements to unload their guns. They were told that only when they were safely in position, would they be allowed to reload their weapons.

Doss was just as nervous about the replacements as the other old timers were. Before they moved out, the medic went from man to man placing strips of white medical tape on their backs. The experienced men got two pieces of tape while the replacements got one. He hoped, that as the men moved to their objective in the dark, they would be able to see the tape on the man in front of them. He prayed they would not get separated from the group.

MAY 21, 1945
THE THREE SISTERS

At 0100 hours as both companies set off toward their objectives, the weather was causing problems. It had been raining continuously and conditions had taken a turn for the worse the day before. As the men moved out, the combination of rain and darkness made it impossible for them to see the next person in line. Even the white tape Doss had placed on the men's back didn't help. In an effort to maintain their position as they struggled forward through the sticky mud, the soldiers resorted to holding onto the back of the man in front of them.

When Company A had advanced about 150 yards, they reached an area directly to the left of the lines of the 96th Division. Even though the 77th had gone to great lengths to inform the 96th that some of its units would be passing through during the predawn hours of the 21st, a slipup occurred, and word was not passed down to one of the platoons. Unfortunately, that platoon mistook Company A for infiltrating enemy troops and opened fire. Many of the replacements became confused, scattered and then ran back the way they had come. The friendly fire also alerted the Japanese, which spoiled the element of surprise. After the enemy picked up on the mistake, they began showering down mortars on the Americans. Fortunately, a first sergeant who was bringing up the rear managed to corral most of the confused men and get them under cover before the mortar barrage arrived.

Company B was nowhere near its objective when the friendly fire incident alerted the enemy that something was up. They fired illumination shells and the Japanese quickly spotted Doss and the other men while they were still out in the open. Enemy machine guns opened up. The well-placed interlocking fire pinned down Company B. Luckily, there were plenty of shell craters in the area, so Doss and the other men took advantage of them to take cover and dig in. Even the inexperienced replacements knew enough that once the element of surprise was lost, it was time for them to reload their weapons and return fire. Almost immediately, the GIs started taking casualties.

The medic could hear men calling for help. Now he faced a dilemma. If he left his shell hole and went out looking for wounded men, there was a good chance the trigger happy replacements would mistake him for the enemy. Even so, he figured some of the injured men were hurt badly enough they couldn't wait until morning. He had always said minutes could be the difference between life and death. Now he would have to trust in the Lord's protection and hope for the best. He said a prayer and then crawled out of his crater. This was one time when the medic decided stealth might not be the best plan of action. He began calling out, "It's me, Doss, the medic. I'm out of my foxhole. Don't any of you trigger happy repple depples shoot me."

While he crept from one injured man to the next, he kept up a running commentary, figuring his southern accent would help convince the men he was not a Jap infiltrator. As he crawled along, he heard someone call out, "Hey Doc. Over here. The captain's hurt bad." The medic headed in the direction of the voice. When he located the captain, the first thing he did was determine the extent of his injuries. It was not an easy task in the pitch dark, but the Japanese illumination rounds provided some sporadic light to work by. Doss could tell Captain Vernon had received some sort of head wound. The medic needed more light to see how bad it really was, so he spread his poncho over the captain, crawled underneath and used his flashlight to get a better look. In the brighter light, he could tell that some sort of shrapnel had entered the captain's mouth and then ripped out the left side of his jaw, knocking out most of the teeth on that side as it exited.

Doss used a compression bandage on the outside and stuffed gauze on the inside of the captain's mouth to control the bleeding. "It's a serious wound Captain, but it's too dangerous to call for the litter bearers until sunrise." The medic could tell Captain Vernon was in great pain. "I'll give you a shot of morphine to hold you over until we can get you out of here."

"No way," mumbled the captain. "Until someone relieves me I need to stay conscious."

"At least promise me you'll go back to the aid-station when it gets light."

"Sure Doc, now get outta here. Go take care of our men."

The medic crawled up over the lip of the crater and disappeared into the night. He didn't hear any more calls for help, so he decided to hole up. As soon as it was daylight, he would call for the litter teams and begin evacuating the wounded. The medic saw a nearby bomb crater and crawled in. He found it was already occupied by two of the replacements. "Hey guys, mind if I stay here till morning?"

"You're Doss right? They say you're good luck. We sure need some of that tonight." As Doss settled in, he was glad to see that both of the new infantrymen had enough sense to be laying just below the top of the crater on the alert for infiltrators. At that very moment, one of the men cried out, "Japs." Both men fired at unseen targets and at the same time, a hissing hand grenade flew overhead and landed right between the medic's legs. Time started to move in slow motion. He scrambled, trying to get out of the hole, but the slippery mud caused him to slide back down. The medic could see the glow of the fuse as it burned. Out of reflex, he stomped down on the grenade as hard as he could with his combat boot, forcing it deep into the mud. It went off with a muffled thud. Doss felt himself being lifted into the air by the explosion. The impact with the ground knocked the breath out of him. He couldn't hear, and he felt numb all over. He looked up. The replacements were nowhere in sight, and a Japanese soldier was standing on the rim of the crater. Doss heard him pull the pin of a grenade and smack it against his helmet. As the brief flash of the primer illuminated his face, Doss could see that he was smiling. The grenade was hissing. *He's gonna hold till the last second then drop it on me.* Doss prayed. *Lord, please forgive me.* Just as the enemy soldier reared back to throw, he was hit in the chest and head by a whole clip of rounds fired by one of the replacements. The impacts knocked him backwards, killing him instantly. His grenade rolled free but failed to explode. It was a dud.

After he lay there for a few minutes, Doss ignored his pain and climbed out of the hole. He remembered that just before they had been ambushed, he was moving up hill. The medic started to work his way back down the hill in the dark toward what he assumed was the rear line. Within a short while, he started to feel faint and stumbled headfirst into another shell hole. In the moments before he passed out, the medic squirmed around so that his head was lower than his legs hoping to force more blood to his brain. When he came to, he had no sense of how long he had been out and therefore had no idea how long it would be until sunrise. He listened. The sound of the battle had slacked off. The medic reached up and felt of his legs. His pants were shredded, and both hands came back sticky with blood. He thought about calling out for a medic, but he didn't want to expose them to danger in the dark. He took off his pants to get at the wounds. He opened his medic bag and used most of the remaining compression bandages on his left leg, which seemed to be bleeding much worse than the right. Then he passed out again.

A short while later, excruciating pain caused him to regain consciousness. Someone had been shaking him. "I'm glad it's you Doc, I got shot in the shoulder. Is it bad?" Doss looked at the wound.

"I can't get up. Lay down next to me, so I can work on it." The medic took out a package of Sulfanilamide, ripped it open and sprinkled it into the wound. Next he used his last compression bandage to help slow down the bleeding. "That's all I can do for you. Head on back to the aid-station. Tell 'em to send a litter for me when it's safe."

"I can't leave you Doc."

"Sure you can, but before you go, I need you to give me a shot of morphine." The medic reached into his bag and took out the Syrette. There wasn't anything else left in the bag, so he tossed it away.

Doss coached the soldier through the steps of giving the injection, but the infantryman was so nervous, he started squeezing the tube before shoving the needle into his arm. More of the morphine ended up on the medic's skin than in his body.

Over the next hours, the medic slipped in and out of consciousness several times. In his delirium, he thought he heard Jesus calling. *Wake up Doss. I've come to take you home.* Instead, when he opened his eyes he saw that it was Corporal Jewell the aid-man and his litter team. The medic smiled and said, "You'll do." Then he passed out again.

The next time Doss woke up it was light, and he was being carried on a stretcher. Jewell and his team had managed to carry him a short distance when a Japanese tank crawled up the back of one of the Three Sisters and began firing in their direction. When the litter bearers dropped to the ground, the shock of the impact brought Doss fully back to consciousness. The enemy tank and its crew didn't survive very long. They were pulverized within minutes by American artillery. While the medic was on the ground, he looked around and saw an injured soldier nearby who was suffering from a head wound. "Jewell, that guy's hurt bad. Take him back instead of me."

"Are you insane? We'll come back for him after we get you out of here." Doss wasn't in the mood to argue. Instead, he just rolled off the stretcher.

"You know a head wound has priority. The sooner you get him to the aid-station the sooner you can come back for me." Jewell knew how stubborn Doss could be, so instead of wasting time in a losing debate, he told his men to grab the head wound and put him on the stretcher. Then they raced off.

Once Doss was alone, he began to worry. He looked around and decided he didn't like being so exposed out in the open. He spotted a rock formation in the direction of the aid-station. It was less than 100 feet away and looked like a good place to hide until the litter team returned. He got to his feet and limped his way toward it.

Corporal Jewell had made the round trip to the aid-station and back as quickly as he could, but when he returned, Doss was nowhere to be found. After several minutes of searching, he concluded someone else must have found the injured medic and brought him in. He and his team had plenty of other wounded men to transport, and he knew they couldn't hang around any longer looking for Doss.

When Jewell got back to the front lines, he ran into Private Byran in a foxhole along with one of the replacements who had been injured the night before. "Is it true?" asked Tennessee. "This jerk says Doss got killed last night by a Jap grenade."

"No way. We saw him a little bit ago about a hundred yards back thataway, but now we can't find him. He was hurt pretty bad though." Without answering, Byran jumped up and ran off. When Tennessee reached the area where Doss had been, he began to call out and look around. There was no sign of his friend. *Where would I go if I was him? Where would I go? Where would I go?* Then Tennessee had an idea. He would ask for help. *Jesus, will you please show me where Doss is?* Tennessee looked around again. His eyes were drawn to a jagged rock formation about 50 feet away. *Doc might have gone there to get under cover,* thought Byran. When he searched the area, he found the medic. He had crawled into a crevice under several large rocks and then passed out.

"Wake up Doc. We gotta git you outta here." Tennessee lifted Doss to his feet. Just as he placed the medic's left arm around his shoulder, it felt like someone slammed it with a baseball bat. Instantly they both heard the crack of a rifle. The sniper had been aiming for Byran's head but hit the medic in the arm instead. The bullet passed down the length of his arm, breaking it in several places. Now it flopped at a crazy angle. The medic grabbed it with his other arm to prevent the fractures from becoming compounded. Both men ducked for cover back behind the rocks. "Medic! Medic!" yelled Byran.

"Be quiet or you'll get us both killed. Those Jap snipers hunt medics."

"What'll we do?"

"Take your gun apart. This rifle stock should do for a splint. Now rip some strips from my shirt…" Once the medic's arm was immobilized, they both started crawling toward the aid-station. When Doss figured they were out of sight of the sniper, he told Byran he couldn't go any further. The pain was too much. He passed out once again.

When Doss came to, he was in the aid-station, and one of the doctors was saying something about morphine. When he woke up again he was in the field hospital. "We've got to set that arm and put it in a cast while you're awake, Soldier. Sorry, but it's gonna hurt like hell."

"Already does."

As soon as the cast was in place, they put the medic to sleep and started to remove the grenade fragments. The sniper bullet would have to remain lodged in his arm.

The death rate for wounded soldiers had surprisingly gone up once air evacuation had become readily available. After an investigation by the surgeon general, it was found that some field hospitals had become careless and were not debriding the wounds. They made the mistake of relying too much on penicillin and a quick air evacuation, but the 77th Division's hospital had never fallen into that trap. By the time they finished with Doss, the doctors had removed 17 pieces of shrapnel and cut back all his wounds to healthy tissue. Now it was safe to move the medic to a hospital ship and start him on his way home.

When the medic woke up in the ambulance, as he was being driven to the landing beach, he reached under the blanket, out of habit, to take the little Bible out of his left shirt pocket. It was then he realized that he was nude under the cover. "My Bible. Where's my Bible?" cried Doss. The aid-man riding along in the ambulance tried to pacify him.

"Don't worry Soldier. They'll give you a new Bible as soon as you get on the ship. They got boxes full."

"You don't understand. My wife gave it to me. That Bible's special." The ambulance had pulled up to a landing ship and two waiting navy corpsmen picked up his stretcher to carry him onboard for the trip out to the hospital ship. "Hold up a second guys," said Doss. He turned to the aid-man. "Tell them back at the 307th, 1st Battalion aid-station, that Doss lost his Bible. They'll know what I'm talking about. They probably kept it when they took off my clothes.

"You're Doss? The medic everyone's talkin' about?"
"Just promise me you'll give them the message."
"Sure thing Doss. You got my word."

June 1945
Going Home

After a short ride on an LCT that took him out to the hospital ship, Doss found himself lying in a bunk aboard the USS *Solace* (AH-5) along with about 400 other serious casualties. The men were being evacuated back to the states because they had no reasonable chance of recovering enough to return to duty within 90 days. As Doss looked around to survey the other injured men in the room, he realized he was lucky, because in his opinion, he had received a Hollywood wound. His injuries were serious enough to get him out of the war but not enough to disable him for the rest of his life. Some of the other men around him were not so fortunate. They had lost legs, arms or eyes. One poor soul was missing both legs and both arms. Doss shuddered when he thought about what it would be like to go through the rest of his life like that poor man.

He tried to get comfortable in the bunk. Because of his cast, that was easier said than done. His left arm had been set in an awkward position. The cast held it out at a 90-degree angle to his body and his forearm was bent at a right angle to the rest of his arm. He figured out he would only be able to sleep on his back until the cast was removed. The other problem was that most of his shrapnel injuries were on the backside of his left leg and buttocks. Doss soon realized he would be in for a very uncomfortable ride.

The *Solace* pulled out and got underway for Guam, after which the men were told that since the ship had a top speed of 18 knots, the trip would take at least four days. Doss didn't remain upset with the news once he got a taste of the navy food. He figured the trip would give him a chance to eat 16 good meals. Doss hadn't realized there were women serving on ships in the combat zone, especially after his recent run-in with Kamikazes, but during the trip, the men were cared for by female nurses.

When the *Solace* docked in Guam, the men were unloaded and moved to a holding hospital where they waited their turn to be air-evacuated back to the states. It was there Doss learned two things which disturbed him greatly. When he was talking to a fellow soldier from the 77th, he found out Captain Vernon had been killed. Apparently, the captain had never gone back to the aid-station, as he had promised Doss. Three days later, Captain Vernon was at a command post along with several non-coms when one of the Japanese "flying ashcan" mortars scored a direct hit. The explosion was so intense, the only thing it left was a crater 8 feet deep and 15 feet wide. Everyone inside had been killed instantly.

The second upsetting thing Doss learned was that he had been erroneously reported as killed in action. A clerk broke the news to him in the hospital. He said several of the replacements had reported seeing him killed in a grenade blast, and that information had mistakenly been forwarded to the war department. This meant his mom would be getting a telegram informing her that her son was dead. He was told it was too late to do anything to prevent the telegram from going out, but if he sent a letter, there was a possibility it would arrive first. Lt. Jeanette Morgan, one of the nurses, helped Doss write his mom a quick note. She was on friendly terms with some of the pilots and promised to arrange for them to hand carry it all the way to the mainland. They kept the letter short, so they could get it on the next plane out.

Dear Mom,
There was a paperwork foul-up. No matter what you hear otherwise from the war department, I am alive. I have been injured but am on my way home. Please tell Dorothy I am okay, and I will see you all soon. Love, Desmond.

Doss was held at the evacuation hospital on Guam for over a week until it was his turn to be loaded onto a four-engine C54 Skymaster for the 4,000 mile, 20 hour, flight back to Hawaii. Onboard were a female flight nurse and male medic to care for the 28 men as they made the flight. Doss had never been on an airplane before, and he was enthusiastic when they placed him in his litter because there was a window just to the right of his head. He found the takeoff and landing exciting, but the rest of the time, all he saw were ocean and clouds.

Once Doss reached Hawaii, he recuperated at the army hospital for several weeks before being loaded aboard another C54 and flown back to Seattle, Washington. While he was in Hawaii, he had written several letters home but had not received any in reply. He did not even know where his own wife was staying, and it had been two years since he had heard her voice. The first thing he did when he reached the mainland was to call home. "Hi Mom, it's me, Desmond."

"Oh Desmond it's so good to hear your voice. I've been praying and waiting to hear from you since I got that first letter."

"I'm in Seattle Mom, and the Army says they'll transfer me to a hospital in Virginia in a few days. Mom, where's Dorothy?" Desmond's mom said that his wife was teaching summer school and told Desmond how to get in touch with her. When Desmond talked with his wife, she wanted to rush out to Seattle to see him, but he finally convinced her they could wait a few more days, until he was moved to Virginia, to see each other. Desmond didn't know it, but Dorothy had a surprise she was eager to show him. She had received a package in the mail. When she opened it, inside was the little Bible she had given Desmond before he went off to war. There was also a letter.

Dear Mrs. Doss,
When we received word that your husband lost his prized Bible, when he was wounded during combat on Okinawa, all the men got together and searched the battlefield until we

found it. The men said they couldn't imagine seeing Doc without his Bible. It was waterlogged, and the cover was pretty much ruined, but we dried it out as carefully as we could. The men chipped in, and you will find enclosed enough money to have it rebound along with a little extra. None of us thought it was right that we got combat pay and the medics didn't, so tell Doc this is our small way of telling him thanks. We knew he couldn't wear his Red Cross armband around the Japs, but he must have had it with him when he was injured because we found it too. The men wanted him to have it back. Your husband is a hero Mrs. Doss. We are also working on another surprise for you both. We just don't want to say what it is because it would spoil the surprise.
With deepest appreciation, the men of the 1st Battalion.

After the bones in his arm had healed and the cast came off, Doss underwent another surgery to remove the sniper bullet that was lodged in his upper arm. The army doctors told him that he would never regain the use of his left arm, but he did not accept their conclusion. He continued to exercise it, and after several months, he could move it through almost its full range of motion although it didn't have much strength. Several times while at the hospital, Dorothy asked her husband what the letter meant when it said he was a hero. Desmond would always evade the question. Most times his answer was, "I don't want to talk about the war." Other times it was, "I didn't do anything more than the other men. Besides, I want God to have the credit."

One Tuesday, the colonel in charge of the hospital and his aide came in to see Desmond and his wife. "Corporal Doss, do you feel well enough to travel to Washington, D.C.?"

"Corporal? Washington?"

"That's right. Corporal. You have to go to Washington because the President of the United States is giving you the Medal of Honor this Friday." Desmond's mouth dropped open. "Let me be the first to salute you." The colonel took a step back and gave him a brisk salute. Doss didn't move. He was still in a state of shock. After a few seconds the colonel said, "Well, are you going to return my salute or not?"

"I'm sorry Sir. I've never been saluted before."

"Better get used to it Corporal. As soon as they hang that Medal of Honor around your neck, you'll be getting all kinds of salutes, even from Generals. Now we have to get busy. First thing is to get you decked out in a brand new uniform. My aide will take care of that. The Army will put you and Dorothy, and of course your parents, up in the best hotel in Washington. My aide will work out the itinerary and assign someone to drive you in my staff car. That should take care of all the details. Any questions?"

Desmond and Dorothy were speechless.

On 12 October 1945, Corporal Desmond Thomas Doss was seated, along with 14 other members of the armed forces, on the south lawn of the White

House. In front of them was a table with 15 highly polished cherrywood boxes each containing a Congressional Medal of Honor. The men were called to attention and Harry Truman, President of the United States of America, stepped up to the microphone.

> *"Well, once again I have a very great privilege. I would rather do what I am doing this morning than any other one of my arduous duties. This one is a pleasure.*
>
> *"When you look at these young men, you see the United States of America, the greatest republic on earth, the country that can meet any situation when it becomes necessary.*
>
> *"These young men were doing their duty. They didn't think they were being heroes. They didn't think they were doing anything unusual. They were just doing what the situation called for.*
>
> *"Now that the war is over, these young men will go back and become citizens of this great country, and they will make good citizens; and you won't find any of them bragging about what they have done or what they propose to do. They are just going to be good citizens of the United States, and they are going to help us take this Republic to its leadership in the world, where it belongs, and where it has belonged for the past 25 years.*
>
> *"Thank you very much for giving me this pleasure and this privilege."*

The men saluted the president and sat back down.

That morning, the men had rehearsed the procedure they were to follow next. Each man would be called, one at a time, in alphabetical order, to come forward and receive the Medal of Honor from President Truman. When called, each man would march forward to a line painted on the grass, stop, and salute the president. The man's citation would be read. The president would place the Medal of Honor around his neck and then shake his hand. The man would then take one step back, salute the president, do an about face, march back to his seat and then sit down. Doss would be called sixth, right after Cpl. C. B. Craft.

Corporal Doss was extremely nervous by the time his name was called, but he did remember to stop at the line and salute the president. Then something unexpected happened. President Truman stepped over the line, shook the medic's hand and held on to it the entire time the Medal of Honor Citation was being read over the loudspeaker.

> "The President of the United States of America, authorized by Act of Congress, March 3, 1863 has awarded, in the name of The Congress, the Medal of Honor to Private First Class Desmond T. Doss, United States Army for service as set forth in the following citation:
>
> Private First Class Desmond T. Doss, United States Army, Medical Detachment, 307th Infantry, 77th Infantry Division, Near Urasoe-Mura Okinawa, Ryukyu Islands 29 April – 21 May 1945. He was a company aid-man when the 1st Battalion assaulted a jagged escarpment 400 feet

high. As our troops gained the summit, a heavy concentration of artillery, mortar and machine gun fire crashed into them, inflicting approximately 75 casualties and driving the others back. Pfc. Doss refused to seek cover and remained in the fire-swept area with the many stricken, carrying all 75 casualties one by one to the edge of the escarpment and there lowering them on a rope down the face of a cliff to friendly hands. On May 2, he exposed himself to heavy rifle and mortar fire in rescuing a wounded man 200 yards forward of the lines on the same escarpment and two days later he treated four men who had been cut down while assaulting a strongly defended cave, advancing through a shower of grenades to within eight yards of enemy forces in a cave's mouth, where he dressed his comrades' wounds before making four separate trips under heavy fire to evacuate them to safety. On May 1, he unhesitatingly braved enemy shelling and small arms fire to assist an artillery officer. He applied bandages, moved his patient to a spot that offered protection from small arms fire and, while artillery and mortar shells fell close by, painstakingly administered plasma. Later that day, when an American was severely wounded by fire from a cave, Pfc. Doss crawled to him where he had fallen 25 feet from the enemy position, rendered aid, and carried him 100 yards to safety while continually exposed to enemy fire. On May 21, in a night attack on high ground near Shuri, he remained in exposed territory while the rest of his company took cover, fearlessly risking the chance that he would be mistaken for an infiltrating Japanese and giving aid to the injured until he was himself seriously wounded in the legs by the explosion of a grenade. Rather than call another aid-man from cover, he cared for his own injuries and waited five hours before litter bearers reached him and started carrying him to cover. The group was caught in an enemy tank attack and Pfc. Doss, seeing a more critically wounded man nearby, crawled off the litter and directed the bearers to give their first attention to the other man. Awaiting the litter bearers return, he was again struck, by a sniper bullet while being carried off the field by a comrade, this time suffering a compound fracture of his left arm. With magnificent fortitude, he bound a rifle stock to his shattered arm as a splint and then crawled 300 yards over rough terrain to the aid-station.

Through his outstanding bravery and unflinching determination in the face of desperately dangerous conditions, Pfc. Doss saved the lives of many soldiers. This is even more noteworthy as, on being inducted into the military service, he was and still is a conscientious objector. He refused to carry arms or even touch a weapon. His name became a symbol throughout the 77th Infantry Division for outstanding gallantry far above and beyond the call of duty."

The president turned back to the table, took the medal out of its box and placed it over the medics head. Then he took a step back, came to attention and saluted the medic. "Corporal Doss, I would much rather have done what you did and have that medal hung around my neck, than to be President of the United States of America."

Dear reader,

It is with heartfelt gratitude that I say, "Thank you for reading *The Medic*."

For new authors, reviews and word of mouth are vitally important. If you have enjoyed reading this book, or even if you haven't, please consider leaving a review on Amazon.

The wonderful thing about print on demand and Kindle books is that it is very easy to make corrections once they have been published. If you were to talk to my dad, who was also my sixth grade teacher, he would tell you that my spelling was, and still is, atrocious. Even though I went through *The Medic* fifteen times searching for mistakes and inconsistencies, it is quite possible there are still some to be found. If you find one and would like to let me know about it, or even if you just want to comment or say hello, you can e-mail me at **DJPress81@yahoo.com**.

Thank you for your time and input.

Adam

Made in the USA
San Bernardino, CA
07 September 2016